# There are Reasons Noah Packed No Clothes

a novel

Robert Jacoby

The characters and events in this book are fictitious. Any similarity to real persons, living or dead, is coincidental and not intended by the author.

ROBERT-JACOBY.COM

ISBN: 978-0-9839697-0-9
Library of Congress Control Number: 2012914772

Book design by Kimberly Leonard and Robert Jacoby
Printed in the United States of America

For my father, Raymond P. Jacoby, for showing me discipline.

And for my mother, Helen M. Jacoby, for showing me love.

"There is but one truly serious philosophical problem,
and that is suicide."

--Albert Camus, *The Myth of Sisyphus*


"What's never known is safest in this life."

--Dylan Thomas

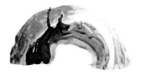

# Once

Void, and he in its midst, rising, consciousness materializing, blank black blanketing him, warm, so he understood he was alive, failed to kill himself. And he in its midst, rising still, a lazy whale rolling, an island of flesh bone blood and nerve, shimmering naked, simmering under the water's skin, heaving over, one eye blinking, incredulous, knowing. He would have to begin again.

He thought through depths of black viscous liquid: So I am alive, still here, not dead, not swallowed enough pills, not done with it, once and for all. They would find his Dear Mom and Dad, By the time you read this I'll be dead, I'm sorry, I'm so sorry but I don't see any other way. He had to stop them from reading what he'd written for them but could not move, his body was separated from his mind, sealed in a tank in a separate room. He blinked, deliberately, resignation and frustration collapsing under the crushing vacuum of his failure. Dear Mom and Dad, By the time you read this... He wanted to weep but had no strength for it. The room compressed the burning embers of his eyes, extinguished. Once. Blinked again. Once. Dark again. Longing for an everlasting sleep that he knew would never come, he surrendered himself to the blessed and enveloping void.

Billowing up through numb surfaces of sleep, his mind blossoming.

Hi smind *click click click.* Life's needle skipping. This must be the Quaaludes, he thought. He thought, he thought. Hi sbody wasd is dis connect ed connect ed from hi smind. Hi smind stuttered stepped *click click clicked.* He opened deep in his being he sighed; some relief in not dead.

But to live.

Anesthetized, sitting in a chair next to a desk in an office crowded with bodies, pen slotted in hand, positioned over sheet of paper on desk, head weighted, volcanic, a boulder between his shoulders, swaying over paper crawling with typed words, wriggling black maggots.

A woman's voice soothed, "Sign your name here," smooth cool hands teaching his fingers to grip the pen.

His head was an oscillating needle over the paper, his eyes and mouth baffling, spittle dribbling from his lip, couldn't feel his lips. The maggots on the page writhed. He was going to throw up.

The voice insisted his hand. "Sign, your, name."

He let go the pen and rattled his head. He didn't know what this was, who these people were. His mother and father had always warned him: Don't sign your name to anything unless you know what it is!

"He won't sign," she announced, fading.

Nearby, a deeper tone murmured majestically. Signature required. His parents' voices squeaked, hushed and intense. Then the deeper voice: No one admitted without a signature. He is of age. Insurance purposes.

Familiar bickering followed.

"You're his father," his mother's voice pleaded and accused. "*Do something.*"

His father's bitterness: "*Look* at him."

Don't leave, Dad. Don't leave me to drown.

But no words would come. They never did, with his father.

An awful pillar loomed. Oh God. His mother screwed the pen into his palm and wrapped his fingers around the barrel and targeted it over the paper and pointed to the line, spitting, "Sign it, sign it," gagging on the words as though they were fish bones in her throat. It was his mother. She must know what was happening to him. He relented, followed her indicating finger, wagged his head obediently. The straight line dissolved. He focused, forcing it clear. The tiny black maggots danced the date underneath: May 1, 1982. With care and deliberation he set the point of the pen above the line to trace the familiar stroke: *Richard Issych.*


Bodies and hands worked him into bed. Shoes unlaced, socks peeled. Female fingers buzzed around his belt buckle. No. No. No. No, his body was incompetently interpreting his protests. What are you doing to me? He had always wished for a girl's hands to free him, but not here, not like this. At every tug his body jerked, and he enjoyed the vague, prickling excitements she was causing. The buckle undone, she pulled in a single smooth motion until it caught and hung ghastly from his belly, a thin black twisted cord, a limp snake, silver tongue tinkling. A final clip and he was free.

Another time, another chair, another office, stooping old man groping to prop himself up, keep himself from falling to the floor. Mouth hanging open, hunk of cut flesh flapping fresh after a deep wet wound. Teeth throbbed blood. Body numb, mind on fire. He swayed, his fingertips clawing at the icy edge of the desk, saving him. Was this the pond where his father would leave him?

Sitting behind the desk, a man in white, creaking, the chair creaked, slivers of noise slit his ears, alternating questions and answers.

Screeeee?

Seeeee.

Screeeee?

Seeeee.

Richard spoke. Words splintered against teeth backs. His mind said, Can't you give me something? but on his cracking lips the words crumbled into a foreign tongue, "Ca u gi mi sofin." He chomped for air, lifted his head to see the man; neck muscles revolted, spasmed, a hot hand clenched his spine at the base of his skull and throttled him, told him not to do that. Two points of eyes glared from over the man's shoulder. His head crashed down. Let me die, he wanted to say, just let me sleep. "Le mi die," he heard himself drawl. A dot of spittle drew a line down to his thigh.

"I can't do that," the man offered generically, "I'm a doctor."

Richard's head lolled. I know what you are. You can do it for me. What good are you if you can't help me? This was absurd. He wanted to shout, laugh, cry. Enormous forces pushed up and bore down, readying to shear him. Sounds fragmented. He could hold nothing together and so burst into tears.

Screeeee?

Seeeee.

What new hell had he created for himself?

A nurse was shaking him, waking him, coaxing him to sit up. Figures in his room. His mind teetered. From nowhere his mother fell upon him, engulfing him, bolting him to her chest, sobbing hysterically, rocking them both, "O Richie. What did we do? What did we ever do to you? How could you do this to us?"

Her tears crucified him, transported him, and he heard her calling giddily, "O Richie, O Richie," while he shut his eyes tight to make everything and himself disappear and she would spout surprises and happiness, "Where did Richie go? Where did my little Richie go?" He believed her, that he had vanished, but he could stand to be gone from her for only so long, not very long, so when he was ready to return he shot open his eyes and his mother would shriek, "*There's* Richie! *There's* my little Richie!" and they would squeal their secret together and she would rush down on him, enveloping him, dancing with him, swinging him round and round, then cradle him, surrounding him with her scent—Ivory soap, menthol cigarettes, and the red and white peppermint candies she uncrinkled and sucked after each smoke— and he glowed being back, back in her arms, home.

Now her tears frightened him, unnerved him, unshackled him from the short chain of her existence, and who would be with him in that infinite unknown, that desolation? How could he convey his despair over her birthing him, over ushering him into this mewling bloody life? He was stained with blood, *her* blood. *How* could he face her again? undo time? Of all things he did not want to disappoint her. He could not bear up under that, the suffocating weight of her judgment. He was unable to communicate his pain, but he ached for her to know, longed for her to guess his sorrows. O God how he loathed himself and his life. He could only burrow his face into her shoulder and heave 19 years of tears.

His mother clung to him and wept, her sobbing resounding through him. "It's going to be alright, baby, it's going to be alright." She rocked him, shushing him, her breasts pressed his chest, and he hugged, hard, cringing as the shots of electricity through his cells let him know he was alive.

He wanted to say he was sorry, sorry for this whole rotten mess he had caused for both of them, that he only wanted to go away, to not be, but he was incapable of speech.

They propped each other up, and another form, liminal, hovered in the doorway before it detached itself, and that figure from which he required some ungiveable gift, some saving act, drifted away.

Don't leave, Dad.

He was on the floor of a frozen pond viewing the world through unending layers of water.

# On the Third Day

He lay prostrate on the floor of a dead dark ocean listening to the gentle waves lapping, lapping, lapping; light slaps graced his face. His eyes fluttered and he tugged away from the white figure above slapping his face.

"Wake up," the cheerful angel voice insisted, "wake up." The angel landed. "Come on. Get up." The nurse grabbed him, all of him, at his shoulders with the bedcovers and pulled him up to slump, kept him balanced while he steadied himself in his mind and body, then settled next to him, a mixed scent of strawberries and antiseptic soap. Her arm wrapped across his back, pressing them together, side by side. They were together, and he pleasured in the warmth of her body. No girl had ever touched him this way. She wasn't like the girls in the shiny magazines he collected under his bed in the crinkly brown grocery bags. So he thought maybe they would be married someday and sit on a park bench at dusk some summer evening watching the sun set in its calming fury as bare-footed children squealed and chased lightning bugs. They would hold hands: the surest sign of their intimacy. He would enjoy that very much, he thought. But he'd never really spoken to a girl before. He didn't know how. He was afraid to. What would she think of him if he started talking stupidly? No, he killed it, she could never be with him. He had tried to commit suicide! What had he been thinking? So the comfortable, sweet self-pity and despair returned for him to nurse and despise.

"Do you feel sick?"

No, he said and realized he had spoken nothing, his lips never moved. In his mind he had said it, but his body had done nothing. Two different worlds existed, foreign to each other, split by an impenetrable boundary: his flesh. He tried to speak again but nothing happened again. His lips were glued shut.

She removed herself from him, warmth gone, and set her face to his, speaking loud and slow, too loud and too slow, as if she were addressing a baby or an idiot. "Do you feel sick?"

His head was an enormous boulder drooping. His body slumped, warm and tightly wrapped in the blanket.

No, he said. His mouth did not open. He was broken. It must be the overdose. His insides were disengaged from his outsides. Again, this time deliberately, concentrating, heaving the orders from his mind, he pushed, pushed, pushed them through his flesh to his throat and mouth and head. Speak, dammit, *move*. All he heard come out was a spluttering growl.

"OK," she said in her idiot-baby voice. "Do you think you can stand?"

Yes. Yes, of course he could stand. Did she think he was an idiot? His body, his skin, was a mold filled with freshly poured molten metals. Jolts raked the lengths of his arms and legs. His spine stretched its way out of his body through the base of his skull. His brain was fermenting in its own hot juice.

When she pulled him and all of the bedcovers up to stand, lights and sirens ricocheted in his head. She encouraged him, a mother to her unsure toddler, "I'm going to walk down the hall with you." They started shuffling together, her arms tethering at his shoulders to lead him like a deep-sea diver across the bottom of a dead dark ocean.

In the hall the brilliancy of the fluorescent lights attacked. He protested, groaning and shutting his eyes; she hushed him, urged him on. The light still penetrated his mind. As she guided him down the hallway he gradually became aware of himself in his skin. He was getting cold. He felt himself in clothes. He was wearing clothes. Soaked swaths of fabric stuck in large patches to skin. He wore the same clothes the day Dear Mom and Dad, By the time you read this. Frosted razor blades scraped the nerve bundles wrapping his spine. He fisted the blanket to his chest. Through closed eyelids lights knifed his brain. Shudders rippled his body. He was shivering, cold and sick.

She led him out of the tunnel of the hallway into an open space with tables and chairs and couches and people. Somewhere a television blabbed. People moved in the room. He felt their eyes on him, the room's eyes, eyes large from dwelling deep in underground caverns unaccustomed to man or light. She pulled a chair from a small heavy wooden table and lumped him into it. He could not hold himself upright so hunched over the tabletop, slick and shiny, shutting his eyes from his woozy reflection. She situated herself next to him and used her idiot-baby voice: "We have some questions to get through. This shouldn't take long. Do you think you can do that for me?"

Strawberries smelled like summer.

"OK, great." Her pretty perfume sweetened his face. "Do you know who you are?"

His name? Yes, of course he knew that. Did she think he was stupid? His name was Richard. He opened his mouth to speak the word but it wheezed out, stale air escaping a tired old tire. "Reeeeeee." He gasped. She placed her hand on his shoulder. He enjoyed her attention but didn't want to trouble her, really.

"It's OK. Take your time."

Time. Wasn't it Spring? The flowers would be out, shouting, but he could not speak; he panted for air, sucking it in for another try. "Reeeherrrr."

"That's right." She squeezed his shoulder. "Your name is Richard." She scribbled on a clipboard. Objects and colors spun and smeared: a child's finger painting. His brain was bulging out of its physical limits. Mind and stomach juice churned. This was like no earthly hangover. He shut his eyes.

"Do you know why you are here?"

He wanted to nod.

"Do you know what day it is?"

He could not feel his teeth.

"It's Monday morning. You were brought in on Saturday."

His eyes: liquefying, gelatinous.

"Have you tried this before?"

He nodded, clamped his eyelids tight to stop them from oozing out.

"How many times?"

That was easy. This last time was his fifth time. What he could push out of his mouth was "Fi ties."

"Five times?"

She understood his new tongue.

"How did you do it?"

Pills, a plastic bag for suffocation. It was too complicated, too long, to answer.

"Did you use pills every time?"

He could not answer.

She scribbled, patted his shoulder again. "You can rest now, we're done." And she added medicinally, "Let's get you to bed."

Yes.

Bed.

Good.

Her hands moved around him as he heaved himself into a standing position and grabbed at the sagging blanket.

"Can you walk with me?"

She steadied him at her side and shuffled down the hall to his room where she eased him into the beckoning cradle.

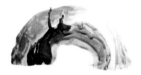

# The Keepers of the Dead

When he woke his bones told him it was evening. He opened his eyes to a misshapen world, without his glasses. He lowered his eyelids, slowly becoming accustomed to his body, stiff and sore, under the thin sheet and scratchy blanket. He lay motionless, afraid to stir, waiting, breathing. Was he awake? He didn't know what to do. Was he supposed to wait for someone again? He strained to hear from down the hallway the muffled noises of the television and the people that must be there, then listened for any sounds in his room.

Was anyone there? Where was he? He had told the nurse when she asked him if he knew why he was here, Dear Mom and Dad, By the time you read this I'll be I'm sorry, but I don't see any other way I tried, I tried work, I tried college, I tried I tried I tried, I'm too tired to try anymore.

I've failed at everything.

That was why he was here. He had failed at everything.

But where was here?

He opened his eyes. He was in a bed. In a room. Failed.

Shut his eyes.

Remembered: signing a form, crying, weeping, melting, Mom, Dad, before, the agony and the dread penetrating him, pinning him like some flailing winged insect,

hungering for a creator who would not show itself,

felt he had to do this, there was no other choice,

no other way

he was a sacrifice

for something he felt was there and feared knowing

that birthless and deathless and nameless *thing* pressing down upon him

the belt across the back of his legs

the tuck of his mother at night

of galloping screaming fantastic white wails crushing

counting like coins the pills the cost on the countertop in the bathroom at home, staring them into a cacophony of gleeful wicked screams into the abyss, praying and moaning and rocking and raging, clawing at his insides, howling and crying to God to forgive him because he didn't see any other way, there was no other way, asking for another way, he did not want this way, he did not ask for this life, this gift, no thank you, I did not ask for it, I do not want it, I do not deserve it, I do not know what to do with it so please

take it back,

take it back,

take it back,

I'm sorry o God I'm so sorry forgive me

when Michelangelo's finger of God touched him and a spear of purity pierced his mind and a wave of glory rushed through his body releasing him from every earthly contrivance of human understanding

so one by one at first serenely madly, swallowing the pills, placed on the tongue, sip of water, wash it down, pill on tongue, wash it down, pill on tongue, gulp it down with water, pill on tongue, force it down with water, pill on tongue, choke it down, two pills at a time, more water, two at a time, throat constricting, catching pills, tightening choke, chalking, more water, stomach bubbling, too much water, two more pills, three, four at a time, is it enough? will it be enough? nearly chewing their bitterness down at the last, he could taste their paste slickening the back of his throat now.

It had not been enough. He was alive, always alive, holy mother of God what would it take to be rid of this flesh, what *should* it take?

He despaired over the life in him that would not be extinguished. A wail rose up in his mind: What do you want from me? Why won't you leave me alone? Why won't you let me die? He only wanted to sleep, to go away. But what could he do now? Run out of the room screaming that it had been a horrible mistake, that he wanted to go home? No. He did not want that. He could not go there to face his parents. But—to get out. Escape. He could do that, couldn't he?

He rolled over to study the room, squinting for focus. Yellow imbued the air, dipped in a dull day's sun. His yellow wooden bed, dresser, desk, and chair filled one side, and the same yellow wooden bed, dresser, desk, and chair the other. Between them a nightstand with a white telephone on it divided the room, a mirror half. But in the wall next to the other bed a window, curtained, a black outline of night, and on his side of the room the two brown doors, one into a bathroom and the other into a hall. The walls were bare except for some drawings taped over the other dresser. The telephone threatened. He did not want to speak with anyone but reached to lift the receiver to his ear, to know.

Dead.

Relieved, he set it down and lay in bed, thinking about what to do next until his body could no longer stand the lack of movement. As a child he used to make a game for himself of lying motionless in bed until he was sore from lack of motion, but he couldn't play that game now. His body ached for him to move. And drink. The inside of his mouth was a parched sponge. Had he really slept for three days? It didn't seem possible. He forced himself to sit up. The floor was soothing cold tiles. His head was that boulder, difficult to hold up. If he lifted it the muscles in his neck started trembling, rebelling, so he lowered it chin to chest. He wanted to sit forever but knew he must do something. He needed to shower, shave. And get a drink of water. That was something. A start. He would do those things. Shower, shave, drink. He could do those things.

His glasses were on the desk. He did not want them yet. He was woozy, sluggish, and afraid he would not be able to stand without throwing up. He concentrated, pushing up off the edge of the mattress, then steadied himself upright. Everything was slow.

OK.

He could do this.

He grabbed the chair back and leaned on that for a while, gulping air. The bathroom was a few steps. He could do it, he was strong enough to do it, he let go of the chair and lurched, steadying himself by holding the heavy door, stepped inside and closed it. No lock. Great. Anyone could walk in on him. That was the idea, though, wasn't it.

The bathroom was as plain as the room: speckled white tile floor, a public toilet (tankless), sink stand, shower stall. No curtain.

Strange.

And no curtain rod. Only the stall, open, with a tiled lip about six inches high from the floor to keep the water from splashing out.

Strange.

Stranger was the object hung over, or, rather, embedded into, the wall above the sink: a stainless steel plate, the size of an overlarge notebook, highly polished with rounded edges, sunk into the wall so that a finger could run between the steel and the wall over the remaining gap. As his fingers grazed the cool metal he realized there was no glass mirror because glass could be broken into pieces and used to— He whirled, mortified at just understanding that everything in the room had been manufactured so that a person could do no harm to himself. No curtain rod in the shower stall because you could hang yourself, no plastic curtain because you could suffocate yourself. No loose item on the sink, no drawers to open, nothing on the floor. He returned to his reflected face, gray, rippling, and let his fingers slide over the cold, polished surface as over the lid of a coffin and the vague image he had longed to destroy.

The shower helped wake him. He drank from cupped hands, and he felt nearly himself—or what he had been—what he didn't want to be. He thought he should want to cry, but there was nothing inside for it, only numbness, an exhaustion towards peace he had never known, kept him from considering—deciding about—life things—he did not want to think about. Except what people were doing. Like his parents. Who by now must have read his note to them and other writings he had done in his notebook and left for them. Sent them careening in opposite directions, his mother to the television and her crossword puzzles and his father to his basement workshop where pieces of projects lay scattered in various states of quiet undoneness. And talking about him? Maybe. Maybe not. For his kid brother to hear? No. They wouldn't tell Alan. They would keep it secret. Would they tell Jim? He was stationed in West Germany and they hated making those long distance calls, bickering about the time differences and costs. No. They wouldn't want to bother his older brother with this, either. Best not to bring things up if nothing could be done about them anyway. He scrubbed his hair and scrolled through scenes of how he'd meet his parents in here. The thoughts sickened him. He pushed them down, squeezed it out of his mind. Nothing he could do about it now.

Now he had to meet new people. His roommate. Others. God, he hated meeting people. He felt so awkward, so stupid. How many were in this place? What were they like? Like him? Only one way to find out. He extended his hand to shake the shower handle.

"Hello." His voice was hoarse, unused. He coughed, cleared his throat, tried again, shaking hands with the handle. Shit. Hit the handle to cold, groped for it, adjusted, warm. This time he shook hands with the air.

"Hello, my name is Richard."

Stupid. First day in kindergarten. He tried again, pumping his hand.

"Hi, my name's Richard. What's yours?" He'd never gotten used to the sound of his own voice. It sounded foreign to him, but at least, one version after another, he felt better, waking up.

He finished showering. He wanted to shave but could not. No razor. They must not want anyone cutting flesh. He put on his glasses, opened a drawer to find clean folded clothes his mother must have left for him in the dresser—his dresser. He saw her hands carefully positioning all these things, his unconscious body behind her, and he pitied her and her nervous fingers, balling socks, smoothing shirts, stacking jeans. He put on pants and shirt and sneakers and, in the bathroom, watched his gray self shimmering in the steel plate. Stepping away made his reflection stretch, dissolve, as in a funhouse mirror. That amused him, stepping back, stepping forward, watching himself dissolve and appear, dissolve and appear. He tired of it and went to take account of the room.

It was a bland box, oatmeal colored, everything ordinary except for his roommate's dresser: the drawings on the wall above it and the gray figurines like tribal idols on it. They reminded him of when he was a kid and made model planes, cars, ships, tanks; kept some still on his dresser at home. He wanted to see what his roommate kept.

Taped to the wall were three drawings, detailed pencil renditions of a seashore, a man galloping on a horse, and children playing in a park under a lead-gray sun, a chiseled fist in the sky. In that one, one of the running children, dashing from the right edge of the page to the left, craned her neck impossibly backwards over her shoulder, laugh-notched mouth, marveling at the empty space chasing her. Tucked into a top corner of the drawing where you might find a spider web hung a rainbow with bands of gray bleeding off the paper's edge. That drawing he liked best. It made him want to live inside of it and run away with the children.

The barren plain of dresser top supported three clay figures, each the size of his hand, simple interpretations of the human structure, delicately formed. Finger impressions revealed where the maker pressed and pinched and pulled limbs tight to thin them out as strands of gray taffy. One sat, cross-legged and head bowed, flipper hands folded in his lap. Another knelt, but without arms this one appeared half-formed out of the womb, monstrous. Its blank head tilted to the sky, depressed oval eye sockets open and unblinking, mouth a fingernail indentation, a scream or a frown. The third, a female, the most detailed of the three, danced, frozen, with small square breasts, one leg supporting her, foot flattened to a thumb-print stand, one leg kicking to meet one thread of an arm and the other line of an arm raised high, reaching upward, the palm of her hand cupped daintily.

He witnessed the tip of his finger slow-approach her palm, at the point of touch she tipped, and he recognized every moment of her fall. She hit, her arm snapping at the shoulder, dry clay crumbs scattering like blood spurting from a wound.

"Shit." In her joy he had destroyed her. *Everything you touch turns to shit!* his mother screamed. He checked the door into the hallway. No one. He gazed down upon the crippled creature. "Shit!" he said louder. As if that could help.

He swore a string of obscenities and backed away from the dresser until his calves hit the bed, sitting himself down. How could he be so *stupid*? What could he do? Could he fix her? Up to the mess on the dresser. Impossible. Nothing could be done about it. Except—confess. Find whoever made her and tell him.

He went to the doorway and dared a step more. Counted sixteen rooms in the corridor, eight on both sides, all doors open. His was the third room on the left up from the lounge where people walked, talked, stood, sat. It all seemed normal. Out of his room he felt committed, so he began walking, and as he neared the lounge the people—the residents of the institution—in ones or twos or small groups began interrupting themselves to judge his arrival. Their eyeing froze him; he felt marked; he wanted to melt away.

The room was square, about 40 feet a side, with walls stretching up to a cathedral ceiling and two skylights staring into the blank black night, and off two sides to his left were smaller squares, one with a television set mumbling to a mute crowd, the other with a fish tank built flush into an inner wall. Surrounding the lounges stretched recessed areas of ceiling birthing illumination so that down each wall dripped a weeping, jaundiced light.

It was a giant child's playpen, filled with painted toy blocks and dolls. Squares and rectangles of cherry and yellow wood tables intermingled. Reds, yellows, blues, and greens upholstered the couches and chairs. And the shapes—he had never seen such shapes. Some of the chairs in the main lounge were nothing more than half circles or squares with a scoop for a seat; one red chair resembled an apple with a bite out of it. People read, played cards. Ghost images danced in the TV lounge at his left; the other lounge, cattycorner, glowed subterranean blue from the fish tank and conical yellows from reading lamps embedded high on the walls. Someone sat watching the colored specks of life darting through the luminous water. On his immediate right a room with half its wall made of glass, all around from waist level to the ceiling, jutted into the main lounge. Inside this see-through box white-uniformed women, nurses, he guessed, sat at their workstations, wrote on clipboards, scanned the lounge areas. A few of the white-clothed people dotted the lounge areas, too, sitting with residents, chatting. Back, purposefully, he retraced his eye path to the nurses in their glass room, locked a stare with one, who promptly mouthed sideways to another close by, and their seasoned eyes observed him with a zookeeper's devotion.

So: he was the same as the others. He stood there, waiting for someone or something, not knowing where to go or what to do. He was an idiot, and everyone knew. He avoided their stares and was on the verge of deciding to return to his room and crawl back into bed when there came strolling toward him a man, either 25 or 45, of slight build with light thin hair flattened across a tall sloping forehead, wearing shorts and sandals. As he moved he did not seem to be a man at all but rather a woman or an over-sized child, and Richard thought the first thought all boys think on first sight of another boy: could he take him in a fight?

"Hi," the boy-man said. "I'm Louis, your roommate."

He could take him. The sculptor's voice was soft and nervous and on the edge of breaking into a screech. Maybe he would tell him later about the statue. "Hi Lou. I'm Richard. Nice to meet you."

"Louis."

Hmm?

"My name is Louis. I prefer Louis. Not Lou. Or even worse—" he cooed—"*Louie*." He tipped his sloped forehead in introduction for the entire scene. "Welcome to your new home: Lakeview." He grinned as if he were too happy with himself.

Richard shuddered. "Lakeview."

"Psychiatric Hospital."

A psychiatric hospital. "Where is this?"

"This," Louis announced, "is on Lakeshore Avenue. Know where that is? Next to Lakeview General. In Willowview. We've got the grandest view of Lake Erie in all Northeast Ohio. How're you feeling?"

"Like I woke from the dead." Richard rubbed a shaky hand through damp hair. "I'm dying of thirst. Can I get a drink?" He smacked his lips.

"The snack room is right over there." He dabbed a finger at the far side of the lounge. "Let me show you." Louis guided. "There's chips and crackers and candy bars in the one machine and fruit drinks and ginger ale in the other. There's no caffeinated drinks. Everything here is decaf. That takes some getting used to. They don't want us being any more tense than we already are, you know. But you go ahead. Then we can sit and talk and you can wake yourself up, and I'll let you in on all the little rules they've made up for us in here. The first one is: Don't wander down that other hallway." He pointed in the direction of the snack room. "That's the ladies wing. You get in trouble if you go down there." He winked.

Richard said he would see him soon and wound his way by couches, tables, and chairs, avoiding eye contact, thinking about how he should approach telling Louis about the accident in their room, feeling a bit uneasy already over his roommate's puckering grin and overeager welcome. Torn and coverless *National Geographic* and *People* magazines were scattered about the couches and end tables. A brown plaque with white lettering marked the door: SNACK ROOM. He paused; down the ladies wing, identical, from what he could see, to the men's wing, a girl in jeans was walking away from him, and he eyed the precious molded ass arcs waggling until she ducked into a room, his mind connecting her to the flurry of photographs in the magazines under his bed at home, and he panicked: his mother would find them, destroy them, he knew, she couldn't help it, as though some maternal madness drove her, *drove* her to his life, *into* his life, to *be* his life. Every step here revealed some new disaster. Hopelessly he gawked at the girl's open door, then turned to the snack room but jerked to keep from bumping into a man, his hands working nervously into the pockets of a thin jacket, his hair cracked into short black pieces over his entire head, and his eyes—Richard had never seen such eyes—tiny shiny dead black marble eyes, like those pushed into the head of a stuffed bird. He looked embalmed.

"Have they numbered you?"

what

"Have they tagged you?"

"What?"

"Did they wake you from the dead?" The black marbles twittered, angry birds fighting over nesting ground. "Do you see them, too?"

Richard *click click clicked*

"They must have tagged you when you were sleeping. You can't get away now. They do it to all of us." The man stepped closer and lowered his voice. "They're everywhere—the keepers. The keepers of the dead. They take the living and make them dead. They keep the dead. They make us keep the dead." He leaned conspiratorially. "I keep the dead."

Who

"We all keep the dead, in here." He pressed his palm to his chest. "We keep what's dead inside of us. What are you keeping? Who brought you here?"

"My parents."

"I'm keeping my parents, too," the man rushed in. "And my dog. I had a dog once. His name was Buster. Buster liked to hump my leg. I liked Buster a lot. Buster was my friend. I miss Buster. I think Buster misses me, too. He'd say to me, 'Eugene, you're the only one who really understands what it's like to be me.' Or he'd say, 'Eugene,'..."

Richard's mind recoiled, stuttered through thoughts of how to stop the man, but nothing other than running away appeared.

"They'll tear you up, if you don't watch out, at night. They come at night to tear us up. That's when I see them, mostly. Trying to get out. Or in. Nights are the worst." The black marble eyes stopped twittering and scanned the walls, seemingly searching for answers, his voice quieting to near nothing. "Every night here I die." He spun and headed off.

Richard stared after him, then let his eyes roam across the people scattered about the lounges.

What kind of place *is* this? Who *are* these people?

It all seemed normal. People sat in chairs and on couches, talking, relaxing, watching television, reading books and newspapers and playing cards. He forgot why he was standing there or what he was supposed to do so that gradually he became aware of a rhythmic humming emanating near the nurses' station from another hallway, long and official looking, lined with so many doors and smaller openings to other hallways that, he supposed, it must stretch down to the main lobby of the building. In a nook against the wall a boy paced doggedly, moaning a monotone on each footfall. Five steps forward, the wall, turn, five steps back, the corner of another small hall, turn, five steps forward, the wall, turn, repeat. "Wah wah wah wah wah." Five steps, wall, turn. "Wah wah wah wah wah." Five steps, corner of small hall, turn. "Wah wah wah wah wah." His head a prow, his narrow face expressionless—a mule face—his whole being was bent on keeping pace with what was driving him, urging him to keep time. He had a day's growth of beard and a red stocking cap pulled down below his ears that matched the red suspenders someone dressed him in. Mucous coated his chin and shone in streaks on his shirt front.

Richard studied the nurses in their station, the lounge areas. Nobody noticed the boy. He could have been a plant.

Oh God, what is this place? Who are these people? He had to get out.

"That's Joey."

Richard's heart restarted.

Eugene indicated with raised eyebrows. "Did I scare you?"

Richard panted.

"That's Joey. He smells like vomit. You were watching him. You wanted to ask him. Why he does that. I could tell you, sometime, if you want to know, if you really want to know." His gaze crawled up to stare down the two cut rectangles of night. "It's supposed to rain tonight." A sigh and a thought slipped. "Joey doesn't like the rain; rain is bad." Suddenly sheepish, Eugene studied his shoes and screwed his fists into his jacket pockets. He apologized, "That's all," then turned and wove his way among the tables and couches, and Richard watched, making sure this time, and only then did he lumber on into the snack room.

Cramped and airless, sepulchral, the tiny room balanced one small table and two chairs along one wall and the snack food and drink vending machines along the opposite wall. Hunched over the table, a young man about his own age was writing, not bothering with who walked in. On the table spread a wire-bound notebook, rows bricked on rows of neat handwriting, and an open Bible, black and gold-edged, with red text splattered across its pages. Christ's words.

Richard scanned the boy and the machines and dug into his pocket for change but realized he probably did not have any money. He switched pockets and kept digging, then started checking his back pockets.

"First night here?" The boy smiled around a pimpled face, showing slight buck teeth, tiny white fangs that doubled his s's: *Firsst night here?*

Richard managed a nod.

"That'ss alright. There'ss a firsst time for everything, issn't there?"

"I guess so." The application of that cliché to his situation seemed ridiculous.

The boy bubbled, either ignoring his discomfort or trying to assuage it, "My name'ss Philip. What'ss yourss?"

"Richard."

"Why are you here, Richard?"

"Suicide." He had not thought to hide anything from anyone here and heard his own voice sounding ashamed, and he wanted to pick the word out of Philip's ears, dismantle it, change its power, but there it was, burrowing into his brain, he could tell, and Philip bristled, whiffed the air like a wolf snuffling weakness on a stranger, and Richard bowed his head, regretting he had shared his truth.

"Ssuicide," Philip puzzled, eyes crushing into gray points.

Don't you get it? "I tried to kill myself."

Philip huffed up a chuckle, chewing every syllable, "I know what the word meanss."

Yes. Of course. What was he thinking? Of course Philip knew. He was catching on and, hoping for an exchange, hazarded, "Why are you here?"

The grin ebbed from one corner of Philip's lips.

They looked at each other for as long as Richard could bear.

"Need ssome change?"

"Yeah." He felt his face go warm. "I do. I mean, I wanted a drink. I didn't bring money with me—when I came in I was..." He cleared his throat, finished limply, "I can pay you back."

"It'ss OK," Philip said, stretching in the chair, digging in his pocket, jumbling coins. "Pay me back when you can. I'll be around. Take what you need." In his cupped hand piled a lump of coins for Richard, who stepped forward but flinched, stumbling upon a secret too soon revealed. Three fingers of Philip's right hand were clipped off at the middle knuckles, the stubs rounded.

Richard avoided Philip's eyes and picked out the essential coins, and after he had the money he let himself meet Philip's expectant stare before breathing out in dread what he wanted to know but knew he should not ask: "What happened?"

Philip's nonchalance betrayed their mutilated witness. "I cut them off."

Richard choked on it.

"They touched ssomething they sshouldn't." The stumps wiggled playfully. "Sso I cut them off with my mom'ss garden sshearss and flusshed them down the toilet."

"Jesus Christ."

"*Blassphemer*," Philip spit the accusation. "Jusst do what you came to do."

Stricken at such physical self-hatred in another, Richard staggered back, bumbled a can of ginger ale from the machine, and wandered out, weariness cloaking him in a wet blanket, shuddering from what he knew were Philip's eyes arrowing into his back. He was shuffling along the bottom of the dead dark ocean again and needed to rest before he fell down. A small table was before him. A girl, a woman, either, both, with carrot-colored hair curlicuing to wisps of orange smoke about her shoulders had herself folded up in a heavy wooden chair, studying a stack of index cards, sipping from a Styrofoam cup with a tea bag string looped over its lip. A hardcover book the size of a shoebox rested on the table. He went to the chair opposite hers and collapsed.

"Do you mind if I sit here a minute?"

Tranquilly her eyes lifted: a cat waking from an afternoon nap, keeping a hundred secrets.

"I can't hardly stand anymore, I'm so tired."

"Glad to meet you, So Tired," she said. "My name's Red."

He thanked her and sat dumbly while the joke soaked in. "Yeah. Ha." His laugh was more a cough. "So Tired. That's funny. That's not my name, really. My name's Richard. I said I was tired because I—just woke up. I was sleeping. Do you know what day it is?"

"It's Monday," she said, amused, "evening," referring to the black windows in the lounges, and he followed her line of sight to the windows in the TV lounge, long vertical notches in pairs along the two outer walls.

"Monday. Evening." He counted. "I guess I did sleep three days." He couldn't stay dead.

"Why were you asleep for three days, Richard?"

He only half meant for her to hear; she seemed a little interested.

"I took an overdose."

"Why?"

The question and her tone stunned him because to him the answer glared apparent, persistently illuminated by an overhead sun casting no shadows of doubt in his mind.

But now.

Now he discovered that the constant furnace of self-loathing in his mind and heart had cooled—his horrible choice had burned it out— and left him with—what? For the first time in the longest time he felt he was thinking objectively, almost observing a different person with a different life. "Do you really want to know?"

"Sure." Her girl grin coaxed heat to his cheeks. "Tell me anything you want." In his entire life he had never heard those words from anyone, let alone a girl. She tapped her index cards into a neat stack on the tabletop and lifted the book cover, a lid, tucked them inside the trick box, drew up her legs into a lotus position, and cupped her tea to warm her hands.

"I didn't mean to interrupt."

"It's OK. It's nothing. Really. They're supposed to help. Famous quotes by famous people. You-can-do-it-if-you-believe-it stuff. Go on."

He was not sure but her look insisted. "The reason I'm here—" He checked for eavesdroppers. "The reason I'm here is that I tried to kill myself, and I didn't do that, obviously, I mean I'm *here*, right? It didn't work. And it wasn't the first time I tried to do it, either. I tried four times before. What's that say about me? I can't even kill myself right. Ha." He tested a laugh and waited for her reply, a lazy shuttering of the eyes and the slightest shrug of one of her small shoulders under the slope of red curls. "I haven't told anyone this. You sure you want to hear it?"

Permission graced her face, and that, and their anonymity, freed him.

He told her about his first time, using a plastic bag over his head to suffocate himself, the night before his 16th birthday, because he didn't want to grow up, he wanted to stay a kid, and he told her about being terrified of life, not wanting to grow up, because he didn't see anything to it, nothing his parents had would he ever want, they were two boards of wood clunking around the house, growling at each other, and he told her about writing letters to his parents and brothers, dressing in his Sunday-best shirt and pants, locking the door to his room. "I had one of those black garbage bags and some rubber bands my dad kept in a jar in the garage. I was closing the door to my room, and I could hear the TV set in the living room," and the light from the living room was transformed into rays he had watched as a kid, pretending another world was out there, pretending there were other people, pretending there was another me inside, "so I closed it and thought for a minute about my parents finding me the next day and how sad they'd be, then I thought how stupid they were for not knowing what was happening 20 feet from where they were watching TV, and I got kind of sad for them and started to feel sorry for myself, too, I guess. I stood there crying, but really wanted to get on with it. So I did."

"Why didn't you tell them?"

"Why didn't I tell them?"

She nodded.

"I can't tell my parents. You don't know my parents. Who talks to their parents?"

"I talk to my parents."

They looked at each other. He rattled his head. "Well I don't. They're idiots. They don't know what's going on."

"So why not tell them what's going on?"

She was interrupting his flow. "I can't tell my parents because I can't talk to my parents. Look, I'm not talking about them, I'm talking about me and how I was trying to kill myself. Do you know how hard it is to suffocate yourself?"

Red shook her head. "I could never do that."

"What?"

"Kill myself."

"You mean you never thought about it?"

She almost shrugged.

"About why you're here, I mean. Not *here*, here. I mean: here on this planet. Why you're *here*."

She looked at him.

"Well it's not easy, let me tell you. It must be like drowning. Have you ever seen someone drown?"

Red shook her head.

"I have. When I was a kid. I saw someone drown." He and the

others had watched the gentle surface of black water break with a solitary bubble. "Trying to suffocate yourself must be like drowning." He told her about grabbing the bag over his head and pulling the rubber bands down around his throat, and "I'm sweating the whole time and the bag's getting sucked into my mouth and I'm yanking on that trying to pull it out to keep from choking on it, the sweat's dripping down my face and it feels like I'm drowning in my own sweat and heat. *Drowning*." He shuddered. "Man, if that's what it is then that would be the worst way to go." Or by flames. Dad said that would be the worst way to go, burning. "I mean, I just wanted to die, go to sleep and not wake up. So I couldn't do that. I pulled the bag off and cried myself to sleep." He sipped his ginger ale, and the fizz stung good. "Jeez, I can't believe I'm telling you all this. I've never told this stuff to anyone in my life. You sure you want to hear all this?" Desperately he wanted someone to listen, the flood of words felt so good, and in their strangeness to each other he discovered a freedom that, as he talked and revealed things about his life he had never shared with another soul, he was jealous over. Where had this been all his life?

"Sure, but let me get a refill, OK?" She tipped her cup to show the soggy bag.

"Oh. Yeah. OK."

She sprung from her chair and moved to the machines in the snack room and braced her hip against the countertop to fix a fresh cup. Philip continued his scuttle-writing, his mouth wording at the same time his gaze tracked onto Richard's, then flicked away. Red's lips moved a syllable or two, and Philip winced as if he'd bitten a pebble.

Richard stopped watching.

At the edge of the opening of the TV lounge in a round red chair perched a woman, Sphinx-like, close in age to his mother, reading a bent-back paperback. Yellow hair spiraled about her head, and her berry-colored fingernails bit the book at its edges, splaying it before her. Over the top of the pages her eyes flashed, shimmering surface water eyes, and in that moment he felt known to her.

"Make a new friend?"

Oh! "Hi Louis." He hoped he hadn't seen him staring. "You mean Red?"

Louis puckered.

"She's a good listener."

From the snack room Philip's voice raised.

Louis tilted Red's chair back. "Is that what she's doing?"

Richard wished she'd hurry. He sensed himself shrinking from Louis and his broken dancer. "Yeah, pretty much. I got in the mood to talk, and she was—I mean, I don't talk much at all, this is the most I've talked in my whole *life* at once, I think, to one person, but I started, she was here, and..." All the words tumbling out of his mouth were passing mysteries to him, and he studied Louis' reaction to them and wondered at their power. Strange that another game he had challenged himself with in childhood was not speaking, once for so long that he almost convinced himself and his parents that he was mute.

"Well she must be a pretty good listener for such a long story."

Red re-emerged and Richard silently thanked her.

"Hello, Louis."

"Hello, Red. Richard was telling me about your excellent listening skills and how he's feeling so very talkative tonight, so I guess I'll be moving along and leave you two alone." With a thump Louis released her chair.

When he was gone Richard said, "Have you known him very long?"

She blew ripples across the amber skin of liquid. "Not very long."

"Everything OK with..." He'd forgotten already.

"Philip?"

He waited.

She cocked her head: a bird studying the ground for a stray seed. "Don't worry about Philip. He could only hurt himself. Did you want to tell me more?"

"Oh. Yes. Yes. Where was I?"

"You were telling me about tying a plastic bag over your head to suffocate yourself."

The words slapped his mind. Having the truth said so plainly made it somehow extra-alive and abominable, not his, now that it lived outside himself, now that it was someone else's truth, too. But she didn't have to be so blunt.

"Yes. Well. Later on I tried sleeping pills, a couple weeks after the plastic bag." He told her about buying a bottle from the store, swallowing half of them one night, waking up the next morning sick as a dog, oversleeping because of the pills, his mom coming into his room to wake him up around noon, and puking everything up. "I mean, it went everywhere. She sits me up in bed to wake me up and out it comes, all over me, her, the bed, the floor." What a stinking shitty mess! "And I was trying to tell her, 'It's alright, Mom, I'll clean it up, I'll clean it up,' but we both know I can't do that. I was so sick I could hardly even move. I was scared they'd find out, too, because I wore my Sunday shirt and pants again and wrote my note again and set it out on my desk. I was trying to sit up to help clean the mess, but my mom was pushing me down in bed saying 'You need to rest, you need to rest.' My dad was in the doorway yelling at me, 'Look at this mess you made! Look at this mess you made!' I'm completely out of it, couldn't even talk, and the guy is standing there screaming at me. 'Look at this mess your mother has to clean up!' He was completely disgusted. She stayed and got me into my pajamas, then changed the sheets and put me back in bed. She cleaned it all up, she let me sleep it off. That night when I woke up we both pretended I'd been sick, like it was some kind of 24-hour bug, and that was that. But she was looking at me weird, like she knew, maybe saw some undigested pills in my puke. I guess she did." He didn't tell Red about hoping she did. "I mean, she saw me in my clothes in bed. I don't think she saw the letter, though. If she did she didn't say anything."

"But then I didn't try again for a couple years." He told her about herding through his Catholic all-boys high school, not ever really trying but still getting As and Bs, never knowing what to do about any type of future, confiding in no one, listening to no one, steering clear of every thing and every one, never drinking, never smoking, never doing anything his parents would not approve of, graduating, crying at home alone in his bed that night, getting a job at a foundry a few months later, working the night shift, letting his hair grow long, drinking, trying drugs for the first time and finding some relief in that, letting his hair grow to a ponytail, wishing and wanting a good war to fight like his father and his whole generation had so that he could focus but there was nothing only always himself, finally coming to his senses 14 months later after one guy in the shop shot someone—

"Killed him?"

Yeah.

"You saw someone murdered?"

"No, no. I didn't *see* it. I went to the wake." He couldn't face going to the funeral. Melvin's body in the coffin wasn't how he remembered it, alive.

"You're pretty familiar with it."

"What?"

"Death."

He'd never thought of it that way. "It's never very far."

He told her about quitting work and starting school at the community college, feeling more isolated than ever, not lasting four months before dropping out of all his classes and starting to make plans, real plans this time, to die: *planning* to die. Trying an entire bottle of sleeping pills, this time only sleeping through the night, his body was so accustomed to real downers that it laughed off the baby ones.

"So I knew regular sleeping pills wouldn't do it. I had to use something stronger. I had this friend from the foundry, bought a bag of Quaaludes. Know what those are?"

She nodded.

He told her about buying the bag from one of his old friends at the foundry and asking how many he thought he could take without dying. "I wanted to know and there was no other way to put it, so I just asked. He looked at me weird, like, 'What the hell are you asking me *that* for?' and I joked and laughed, 'No, no, don't worry. I want to know how many I *shouldn't* take.' He didn't believe me, I could tell. He was looking at me weird, but people are funny, you know, they really don't care about you. So he told me about one of the guys in the shop who took three or four regularly, every night, to feed his habit, which is what I was up to anyway when I was working there, but he says he wouldn't take seven or eight in one night. He kept looking at me weird. I took three times what he thought was safe. I took nine one night, but the next day woke up feeling drunk, hung over. I couldn't think, could hardly breathe. It was pretty bad. But I didn't throw up. That was good."

"So by this time I was pretty upset. I couldn't figure it out. I mean, what did I have to do? Well I knew what I had to do. I had to take more. I figured, if nine didn't do it, I'd triple that, I'll take 27." His jersey number from little league football. "That should do it. How could it *not* do it? I was getting tired of playing around."

"So I do the same thing over again. I bought a notebook, I wrote some things in it. I wrote some notes and letters to my family, leaving some things to my brothers and two friends." He didn't tell her about the pages of words and drawings and maybe-poems he'd written about life and death and why he was leaving one for the other. "I did it on a Friday night, late afternoon. I wanted at least 12 hours before they'd find me. So I left a note in the kitchen that I was tired and went to bed early. No one was home. My older brother is stationed over in Germany, he's in the Army, and my kid brother, he was out with my mom. My dad was at the firehouse, where else. He's a fireman. Yeah. Big deal. So, anyway, I got everything ready. This time I wore jeans and a t-shirt, that's all I wanted them to find me in. I got the bag of pills and went into the bathroom and counted them out. And I sat there," and sat there and sat there and sat there, staring at those things and fiddling with them and sorting them out and playing with them and stacking them up like Halloween candies. "It was awful. I was going crazy. Pounding my head against a wall." He could not describe that exquisite mind pain: being turned inside out: eaten alive by the flames in his head and heart. "But I knew what I wanted to do. I knew. I couldn't stand it anymore. All the pain, all the shit, all the torture of getting up every day and nothing there. I couldn't stand it anymore. I just couldn't." He could not tell her about starting to cry, lifting a single pill, host-like, proclaiming, 'God, if you're there, forgive me for this, but I don't see any other way,' and immediately in the deep center of his brain that until then was to him unknown *snapped*, he felt it physically meltingly *snap* open like a flower blooming light speed and his being was awash in peace, completely filling him and completely calming him, God touching him, telling him: Do what you are about to do.

"So I started swallowing the pills. One at a time, one after the other. It was going slow, you know, I had counted them out into three piles of ten, so I started bunching them together in twos, taking them two at a time. They're kind of big, so I was taking huge gulps of water, and I was getting almost sick from drinking that much water, but I kept at it. I was taking three at a time by the end. I lost count after 25. I think I took maybe 27, 29. I was choking on them by then, almost chewing them down. They were bitter, really bitter. God I don't think I could swallow another pill as long as I live." Richard sipped his ginger ale. "I can't believe I'm telling you all this. You must think I'm nuts. But that's what happened. You sure you want to hear all this?" What a relief to unburden himself. He could go all night, the more he talked the more he found he had to say. Almost as though he was describing someone else's life, now that the horrible feelings of self-destruction had burned out of him. "This is the longest I've ever talked with anyone in my entire life, and I don't even know you."

Her grin caused him to wonder what she was in for, and the words were at his lips to ask when a faraway howl echoed down the men's hallway: "GODDAMMIT."

Heads periscoped, eyes searched eyes for clues.

Another howl, louder, closer, followed by raging feet. Richard scanned the lounges and not locating him knew immediately. He blazed out of the men's hallway, wild in his face and holding the broken clay dancer aloft.

"*Who did this?*" Louis shrieked. "Which one of you dumb bastards did this to my creation?" Seething, he pronged the crippled dancer and stirred the air. "You bastards keep away from my stuff. How many times do we have to go through this? Last time I was here you tore down my artwork from my walls. Can't have any drawings of the residents of the facility, you said." He mocked the conversation. "OK, I said, OK. But can I please have them back? They're mine. No, you said. No drawings of the facility or residents are allowed to leave the facility. So you took them. You *confiscated* my artwork. You *ruined* it. And did I say anything? No. Did I do anything? No. I did not. I did not say anything. But *this*." Here he shoved the dismembered figurine at the room. "*She* was *innocent.*" He stabbed the air with her. "You think you control me, but you *cannot*. And *that's* what drives you crazy about me, isn't it? *Isn't it?* That's what you can't stand about me." He whirled and stormed down the men's hallway.

There was a pause, then low, uneasy mutterings through the residents, and a voice from the TV lounge, "No, Louie, we just don't like you," and a few giggles followed. Two men in white pants and jackets made their way from different corners of the lounge areas down the hall after Louis, and that cued the residents to return to their worlds. Joey resumed pacing and moaning. The woman with yellow spiral hair erected her book.

"What'll they do to him?"

"The whitecoats? With Louis? Talk."

"Whitecoats?"

"Muscle."

Huh?

"Guys. Muscle. They need muscle in case things get out of hand. Nurses can't do it, you know, so they have the whitecoats."

"What'll they do?"

"Depends."

"On what?"

"On him. You don't push more than once. He won't end up in Isolation again."

Richard nodded just to agree. But he *didn't* know. He *was* stupid. Whitecoats. Isolation. He didn't know anything about anything or anyone in here. He wanted to ask about Isolation but really wanted to know: "So why are you here?"

Red shrugged.

They stared at each other until Richard had to turn away.

Jesus Christ. He was naked before her. What had he done? What had he just confessed? Red sipped her tea. He did not know what to do except go away.

"I'm going to watch TV or something, OK?"

A disinterested cat blink: "Suit yourself."

Deep in his heart a canyon of betrayal spread between them: he had given her everything and she had returned nothing. He wandered away thinking he could not be here with these people, he could not do this, he did not belong here, not at all, no, not at all, it was a big mistake, a terrible mistake. He ambled past residents standing or sitting around tables or in giant chairs or toy blocks, into the TV lounge. Louis was right, he thought. They didn't control him. They couldn't control anyone here. If he wanted to go, well, he could, couldn't he? The black windows attracted him. He brought himself outside the TV lounge. The windows shone in pairs, piercing the walls, unblinking eyes of some never-sleeping creature intent on seeing all. Few people there were reading, besides the woman with yellow hair. At the mouth of the room next to a bright green plastic tree he stood, watching the warped reflection of the interior life on the dark slots, pondering what lay beyond their edge, listening for the *shush shush shushing* of the waves washing ashore. He could hear nothing of the shoreline. He dropped into a blue chair, the last one open and closest to the main lounge. The neighboring chair was empty, but in the next one, in the half of a red apple chair, she sat reading, re-crossed her legs, long, smooth, curving out of whipped cream-colored shorts. The black windows winked; he knew what he could do to them with one of the heavy wooden chairs.

"This is a big mistake," he said loud enough for her to hear. He stared down the windows, convincing himself. "I really don't belong here."

The woman tented the book on her knee, folded her fingers in her lap, watched the windows with him. "Do you think any of us *really* belongs here? Don't you think it's a 'big mistake' for each of us?"

But I'm not like you. I'm not like any of you. "I don't belong here."

"But here you are. And shouldn't we try to make the best of it? Isn't that what it's all about? Making the best of it. Hmm? What do you think?"

"I think I have to get out of here. I think I can do it." He wrestled with the urge to shatter the black lens and escape through it into the blacker night. "I think I can throw one of these chairs right through one of those windows."

"Oh no, you don't want to do that. But I'd like to see you try." Her smooth voice matched her legs. "What I mean is: you'll need to do better than the obvious. The windows are unbreakable. I've seen a chair hit those things and bounce right off. They're not glass. Even the fish tank. They're bulletproof plastic or something. They're unbreakable." She motioned toward the nurses' station. "That, too. Do you think they'd sit inside their glass house with all of us out here if it weren't *safe*? With us tossing *chairs* around?"

He thought about it, disgusted at the apparent truth of the matter, how she talked about him being part of the "us out here." He wanted to bolt into the night. Where was the nearest exit?

"Don't be so *grouchy*," she said. "*Relax.*"

He didn't want to relax.

"You'll be OK."

He didn't want to be OK.

"You'll get used to it."

He didn't want to get used to it.

"Crappy lighting, no mirrors. Half the makeup is confiscated because of the chemicals. I have to use a metal *plate*, for gods sake, to get ready in the mornings. *Look* at me." She faced him and demonstrated by using him as her mirror. "See what I mean?"

He did not see what she meant.

Her face lightened. "When did you come in anyway? I know all the guys."

"Today. I mean, I *woke up* today. I got here... today."

She grinned: a schoolteacher to one of her boys. "So, 'today' is the answer. You sure about that?" She reached across the space between them and touched a fingertip on the back of his hand, pressing a button that he did not know was hard-wired to his groin. "Why are you here?" She snuggled herself, her perfume snuggled him, and a sliver of black bra teased out of her white sweater top.

He was gutted.

"I'm here—" he started but stopped to hold all of his truth closely, valuing it for what it represented to himself first and then to this stranger, surveyed the place he'd awoken to; Joey pacing, Red reading, the black impenetrable slots reflecting; and realized the possibility that he might be here for quite some time—"just because."

"What a coincidence." Her top lip curled, a crooked and beckoning finger. "Me too."

Richard had no spit to swallow.

"What's your name?"

"Richard," he heard his voice squeak.

Her eyes lit, lip curled. "It's so nice to meet you—Dick. I love that name—Dick. I think 'Dick' is such a... *strong* name."

He did not know what to say, think, or do. "My name is Richard." He heard the voice of an eight-year-old introducing himself to new classmates. "People call me Richard." Hello, my name is Richard.

People call me Richard. I'm here because I tried to kill myself.

"Oh. I'm sorry—Dick—Richard. My name is Sandra. People call me Sandy. After my sandy hair. But I suppose we're all named for something, don't you think?" She twisted, presenting her back, and red-tongued fingertips licked through her hair. She untwisted, her grin a tease, presented a slender hand in a queenly grip. "It's a pleasure to meet you," she breathed on him and in that breath he felt himself melt.

Timidly he took the offered treat, and whatever type of life coursed through those limbs sparked his flesh. Her hand felt too light and too heavy to hold. It almost hurt. He wanted to go away; he wanted her to go away; he wanted her to rescue him. He let go.

"Looking for someone?"

"My roommate. He said he needed to talk."

"Oh."

"I think I see him," he lied. "I'd better go."

"I'll see you later." And that top lip crooked deliciously, tasting the word: "Dick."



He did not find Louis in the lounge areas but decided to stay instead of returning to the room. That he did not want to do. But he did not want to meet any more people, either. So he wandered, stooped at the fish tank; the tiny eyes gaped fearfully, curiously, mouths puffing invisible smoke rings. The fish appeared distorted, enlarged, and with his fingertips and eyes he searched for and found the cause: the thickness of the glass. Sandy was right. There would be no going in or out of this aquarium. He pulled his fingertips off the surface. His mother had once scolded him in the dentist's office, "Don't touch it, you'll scare them. They see only their reflection in the glass, and if you touch your finger they'll think it's some kind of monster." So he pulled his fingertips away and remembered how one afternoon he had come home from school to find on the carpet in the middle of his room his goldfish, red-veined and terror-eyed, mouth clamping for air, body heaving against death. He went to it, tenderly lifted it to the bowl on his desk. Watched it float. He cried when it died and vowed in his heart never to care for anything that could leave him so easily, so quickly, so his mother bought a cat, she said, for him, to help him get over the loss, but every time he tried to play with the cat it hissed and strutted off with its tail high and showing off its asshole to him, and when his mother asked him how he liked his new pet he told her from what he could see the cat was a goldfish, with feet. That earned him a look and "Sit there and feel sorry for yourself." Now he backed away, discovering a corner seat deep in the fish tank lounge. He felt safe, back against a wall, watching what was viewable. The nurses in their glass room floated about. One, sitting at the workstation, merely a swiveling head, swept the lounge areas with lighthouse eyes. Two others' mouths moved, tapped at clipboards, and eyed the wall clock inside their room. Quarter to nine. And at the side Joey paced. "Wah wah wah wah wah." Waves washing up on the beach.

Some residents were gravitating to a closed door on the short wall opposite the nurses' station at the end of the men's hallway, a mirror of the same space in which Joey paced. A thin crack split the door in two above the waist, and a narrow ledge overhung the top of the lower portion of the door. More residents gathered, moving from the lounges and out of the mouths of the hallways, and Richard watched them, becoming frightened at not understanding what they were doing or what he should do while they organized themselves into a line trailing from the split door along the front of the nurses' station. Everyone was lining up. Philip, Sandy, Red, even Louis.

What should he do? Why wasn't anyone telling him what to do?

Three nurses, one older with silver-blue hair and a red line for a mouth, left the glass house and moved toward the split door, parting those before them like Christ Himself and two disciples walking through a crowd. The old nurse unlocked the door and ducked inside with an assistant, and the crowd shimmied back into line behind what appeared to be a thick red band taped or painted on the floor. The other nurses positioned themselves outside the door; the top half swayed in; the old nurse stood at the ledge.

Now Richard tasted understanding.

The old nurse summoned the first resident over the red demarcation, offered a brown cafeteria tray with a child-size paper cup of water and a thimble-sized white cup, the resident gulped the pills from the thimble and chased them with water, snapping his head back as if he were downing two shots of whiskey, and the nurse at the door guided him away and the next one in. So the communion line ratcheted down, person by person. To some residents a nurse outside the medicine door would speak, the resident would scoot to her and yawn and hold it, and she would squint, peer, angle for view and, satisfied, motion him away. Once she used a tongue depressor on some young kid who stood bored, mouth gaping, imbecilic.

In his room he did not know what to do. The bathroom door was shut, shower sounds inside. He kicked off his shoes and sat on the bed, listening to the rain press in gusts against the window. Curiosity got him. He went to the heavy curtain, touched it open at the side. Underneath was a black mirror. Somewhere outside above the parchment-paper moon. He shivered against the air conditioning, let the drape fall. Forms of residents appeared and disappeared across his doorway, nurses streaming among them. Intrigued by the quiet parade, he went to the door. Up and down the hall residents headed to their rooms. A nurse shuffled by with Joey. His head nestled on her shoulder as she mothered words. "The rain can't bother you here. You'll be nice and warm in your own bed. You'll have good dreams tonight of the park and zoo. Remember how much fun you had at the zoo? We're going back real soon." She frowned at Richard, and he regretted his intrusion.

On the dresser the two figures hovered over the felled one. Richard approached and tested various paths of telling Louis how the figurine broke, but on each path at some point he careened into a ditch of questions and accusations, none of which led him to being left alone. Indecisive, he gripped the bed sheets and slowly twisted them in his fists. The bathroom door swept open close to his feet.

"Oh. You startled me. I haven't had a roommate for a couple of days, one that's sitting upright, I mean." Louis, in crimson pajamas and slippers, padded around to his side of the room.

Richard tried to smile for the joke. His weariness burdened every muscle, every bone, pulling him to the center of the earth. He wanted nothing more than to shut his eyes and go to sleep. He would tell his roommate nothing. It would be easier that way, easier for them both. He struggled to his feet and went to the main door and started to close it, startled by the pattern appearing in the grain of the beautifully stained and polished wood: a winged creature standing.

"No-no," Louis chimed.

What now?

"The door. It stays open. Always."

"You're kidding."

"Hey, it's not my rule, it's their rule. It needs to be open all the time."

He stepped away and let the wooden angel observe him unbuttoning his shirt.

"That's what the bathroom is for."

Too weak to do anything but obey, he shuffled to the bathroom and swung the large wooden door closed, changed, emerged. The rain drummed harder against the window, the unbreakable window.

"Get the lights?" Louis said from bed.

Richard mumbled and stepped to flick the switch. Darkness *clicked*

42

but there remained the door of white into the hallway. He groped his way under the bedcovers, stretched out, set his glasses on the desk, fiddled fingers at his sides until determining to keep them quiet by interlacing them across his chest. He stilled himself. Tried to rest. Focused on a gray mist birthed out of the black in the room and the light from the hallway, diffused, hovering above him.

"How long will those lights be on?"

"Not much. Lights out is 10. Most go off then, but there's always some light all through the night."

A silence widened.

A clap of thunder sounded distantly, followed by heaven's rumbling.

"Angels are bowling." Richard offered the childish thought, he didn't know why, and he thought he heard Louis say, "Shall gods be said to thump the clouds?"

They let the silence return.

"Can I ask you a question, Louis?"

"Mmhmmm."

"How old are you?" Richard liked knowing ages of people: it gave perspective.

"Twenty-seven."

That was a world away. He could not imagine himself living to that age.

"And how old are you?"

"Nineteen." He was a kid who couldn't help asking more.

"Do you have brothers or sisters?"

"Two sisters. Both older. You?"

"Brothers. One older, Jim, he's in the Army. One younger, Alan, he's a little kid."

"My sisters are all grown and moved out and have families of their own. I'm the baby."

Some big baby. "Where do you live?"

"With my parents. Now. I had my own place for a while, but now I'm back home."

Richard thought that was odd, for a 27-year-old.

"Where do you live?"

"Home," Richard said, but that word did not describe it.

"Do you get along with your parents?"

"I guess, I don't know. My mom's OK. My dad's got his own problems. It's best to keep out of his way."

"What's he do?"

"He's a fireman."

"Oh, that's interesting."

"What's your dad do?"

"Nothing. He's dead."

Oh. "Sorry."

"Don't be. The nicest thing my father did for me was die. Basically, my mom and sisters raised me."

I couldn't tell, Richard didn't say. "Why are you here?"

"I checked myself in this time."

"*This time?*"

"Yes, *this time.*"

"How many times have you been here?"

"Three."

Jesus Christ. "Three times? *For what?*"

"Well sometimes things get to be too much on the outside, don't they? So I checked myself in. I've been here three weeks and should be leaving soon. I was here last year about this same time. I spent two months then. Things were getting to be a bit too much outside, that's all. My best friend died and I was back home with everyone, fighting all the time. I was crying nonstop. I lost it at the funeral. Tried to open his casket. I wanted to get him out, or climb in there with him. Isn't that nuts? I was drinking all the time, too. It was horrible. They found me one morning passed out on his grave."

Richard did not know what to say and so used the only word he thought appropriate: "Sorry."

"Sure."

Richard considered asking him if his best friend was also his boyfriend—but thought better of it—instead asked what he thought Louis wanted to hear: "Don't you want to know why I'm here?"

The answer surprised Richard not for its truth but for its presentation, cold and lifeless. "You've been asleep for three days, I *know* why you're here. *Everybody* knows why you're here. I mean, anybody who stopped to see your body."

The answer unnerved him. He'd been on display. The darkness around him was solidifying.

"Why's Red here?"

"In all that talk she didn't tell you?"

Well...

Louis explained the workings of the universe: "I think she should tell you herself, if she wants."

The lights in the hallway went out, graying everything, suffusing their room a few feet before being walled out by the darkness within. Nearly blind, Richard squinted to focus the clay figurines but saw only a fuzzy monolith. At the door a shadow leaned in.

When it was gone he whispered to the darkness, "What are they doing?" and the darkness answered, "Making sure we're in bed."

The gray mist over his bed dissolved into black. Car headlights shot past the drape and ran wild beams across the walls. From the other side of the room the darkness called his name.

He answered.

The darkness tested, "Do you like sex?"

Before he could reply the voice began to describe sexual acts in such detail and in such reality between men and women and men and men that Richard could do nothing but shut his eyes and cower under the bedcovers and pray to the formless mist above his bed to make it all go away. But not yet. He was curious and fascinated at such boldness, heard his father advising him before he went away for a weekend Boy Scout camping trip.

"Don't let anyone get queer on you," his father instructed.

Richard could only look, What do you mean?

"I mean," his father explained, "when you're alone, like when I was in the Army, watch out for guys who touch you like this."

His father reached to lay his fingers across Richard's arm, drew them back, and father and son looked into each other's eyes, not long but long enough.

The voice stopped making the images of sucking and fucking and asked if he wanted to try it.

It sounded so violent, so perverted. *You're a little pervert*, his mother had hissed at him, *just like your father*, shoving his porn magazines at him, as if she'd never seen them before, as if she didn't know his father kept some in his closet, too. *Where did you get this garbage?* One of the glossy magazines flopped open to reveal an extreme close-up of a woman's shiny red lips tensed around the man's flesh, bubbles of spittle ready to burst. His mother jiggled the magazines, the woman's head bobbed.

Richard shrank from his response to Louis, wincing at the dual pinpricks of his virginity and lust. Girls were foreign creatures, he was afraid of them, and when he watched them in real life too long they turned into something unreal, out of place, like a lion in a cage at the zoo. His porn magazines made it easier to deal with them in real life, keep them all at a healthy distance.

Silence stretched the room until somewhere far away out of the dim hallway came a howl. Richard shriveled.

"Louis?"

"Yes?"

Can I do that with you? "I don't think I can do this."

"What do you mean?"

You people are all nuts. I don't belong here. Mom and Dad will come. Dad will rescue me. "I mean: this place, these people, that kid who cut off his fingers—Jesus Christ—his own *fingers*! That retard who keeps pacing and humming, that—*freaky* guy with the talking dog and keeping dead people. I don't know—what kind of place is this? I just wanted to be *dead*—I didn't want to end up here. I don't think I can be here. I don't think I can do this." He did not want to cry, he knew he should not cry. His tears choked his throat.

"They won't let you leave, you know."

Richard did not know. He wanted to be held and hugged and rocked. Over squelched tears: "Why not?"

"You gave that up when you ate a bag of pills."

So.

"Think about it."

Richard did not want to think about it. He had done it. Alone. He had made up his mind to do it. Alone. Why couldn't they leave him alone now? He would not think about it. It would go away. He would make it go away. He shut his eyes. Mom and Dad would come get him in the morning, all he had to do was spend a night here, that's all. He rolled over to watch the white oblong leading out and letting in the night sounds. Joey continued howling, lower, slower, and down the hall floated a protracted, painful groan as from a stricken animal.

Richard felt his mind start to collapse in on itself, then expand that night's moments: his mind's accretions:

Rain is bad, night is bad. The nights are the worst. The dead black eyes spoke. Every night here I die. The keepers of the dead. We all keep the dead. In here. Richard clasped a palm over his chest, over his pumping heart, pumping, pumping. He was alive. He knew that much. That must count for something. He had some thoughts of sexual scenes, men's and women's bodies thumping, doing something with Louis—more moaning drifted in from the hallway—it all evaporated. He shivered and upped his knees to his chest and clenched the bedcovers under his chin and watched the space in front of his eyes; into the weak yellow light that drizzled in from the hallway he stretched out his arm and hand, suspended, a plank of wood. He was not in the grave but its icy tongue licked his heart. He had opened that door, welcomed death in, made it his heart's unavoidable roommate. Never very far. He wriggled his fingers. I cut them off. He curled and uncurled them into repetitive fists and listened to the rain and the thunder and the howling and wanted more than anything to be in his own bed in his own room in his own home. Mom and Dad would come for him. In the morning. He wanted to disappear, go away, go to some kind of void where he could—where he could—

Despair pushed up inside his heart against his flesh, threatening to burst out of his chest and throat. He quelled it, channeled it to tears he tried to bite back but could not.

Down the hallway a scream bulleted.

He tightened to steel under the covers, his heart shaking the bed. The grave licked his bones.

"It's only Joey." Louis' voice seeped out from the other side of the darkness. "It's the rain. Joey doesn't like the rain."

Fingernails scratched the window and crawled away.

"What the hell was that?" He couldn't quell his terror.

"Bushes," Louis replied.

Then, Richard thought, he heard a giggle so cruel yet so soft that he could not be sure of its presence. He felt his flesh absorbing the blackness and the howling and the cruel giggle—he could shut none of it out—edged into an emptiness that could not be called sleep.

They had to wake him the next morning. His first thought rising: so this is real, this isn't going away; his second thought: something smells good. A nurse had brought a breakfast tray and set it on his desk in a swirl of steam and urged him to eat so that he could get his body back on schedule. She pulled him up to sit in bed and said he had an appointment with the doctor.

"Doctor?" He yawned at her, felt his mind clearing, calm and under his control.

"Yes. Every resident has a doctor."

Resident. Doctor. She didn't get it. His parents were coming to take him home today. His next thought slipped out loud, "I thought I could go home today," and he was shamed to watch her face express the inanity of his statement. He might as well have suggested they fuck right there on the floor. He turned, unable to bear the sight of his own lunacy in her eyes—that *look*. Then she offered, but in an altered voice, with a soothing, condescending tone that he had heard before, the same idiot-baby voice the nurse had used during their interview, the same voice he had heard calming Joey last night as the nurse led him to bed with consoling thoughts of childhood dreams: "You can talk about anything you like with the doctor."

So that was it: she thought he was one of them.

"When do we meet?"

"This morning. Ten o'clock. A nurse will come get you. There's time to eat. And shower. You can wait here or in the main lounge. Later I can show you around and we can talk about linens and laundry and how we like the residents to keep their rooms."

He smiled up at her to tell her that he didn't want to be shown around and talk about linens and laundry and how they like to keep things around here, but the hot fist clenched his neck muscles, reminding him not to do that. "My neck is doing this spasming thing when I do this," he said and demonstrated.

She repeated in the idiot-baby voice: "You can talk about anything you like with the doctor."

"Can I shave?"

She fished in her coat pocket and produced a plastic disposable shaver.

"Can I have my own?" He hated those cheap blades chipping his skin.

"That's all you're allowed, I'm afraid," she said, not sounding afraid at all. "When you're done eating I'll be back so you can use it."

"You're going to watch me?"

She nodded.

"*Why?*"

She looked at him.

When he finished eating he went to the window in his room. Up close the glass appeared conventional, except for a small plug in its center and at its sides connecting to the walls where its thickness revealed at least half an inch. Dots of rainwater scattered across its surface. He stroked his fingertips over the transparent skin holding him in; there was no opening it. And Sandy was right: some kind of plastic, thick, with a plug like a bullet buried in its gut. A line of water teardropped. He pulled his fingers away, leaving three cloudy orbs dissolving. Flowing bushes of white-yellow taffeta sprouts towered up along both sides of the window and nearly to the top, blocking most of his view of the yard. This type of bush grew in the yard at home outside his bedroom window, and in the springtime their scent would be the earth's perfume as fat and drowsy bumblebees worked their way into flowers. Wavering tree shadows blanketed the grass. The drowned earth had spit up its worms. A short patch of ground ran to a tall chain-link fence slit with sky-blue plastic strips that in spots had been pulled away to flap loose in the wind, and on the other side the ends of cars sparkled in the morning sun. This was their job, he thought; they could come and go. Across the yard a rainbow struggled to coalesce and touch the earth, its colors unsure, its internal structure wavering. Richard shifted his weight; the fetal colors disappeared and reappeared inside the thousands of beads clinging to the window's surface.

He couldn't bear to be alone in the room any longer; he thought this must be how a caged animal feels; he wanted to see and hear and smell and touch the place in the light of day, to make sure it was real.

The residents all seemed new, none from last night. The nurses were enclosed in their station. Joey was not there. Slots of light crisscrossed the floor. He went to a TV lounge window, the same as in his room, put his fingers to that dividing line and gazed out; the world appeared the same as the last day he had spent in it: blue sky, green grass, bushes and trees, birds, the gray-green lake. Always the water. He had always enjoyed the water, watching it, floating in it, but at the same time there remained alive in him an unresolved fear; he was deathly afraid of it, its unknowableness, its permanence, its irresistibility. And the monsters it concealed. The shoreline was hidden, he could only see the white-flicked waves some distance from the beach as they started scrolling in preparation for destroying themselves at their destination. The building was set away from the cliff so that he imagined the main lounge as a torso and the two long arms of rooms for men and women stretching out to embrace the water. No sounds from outside penetrated. He dropped his fingers from the window. Buzzing and twittering on the windowsill was a fly in its death throes, and he watched it dance for a while before going into the main lounge and positioning himself at the end of one of the large couches closest to the nurses' station so that he could see through that window and all around the lounge area.

Not much was happening. He swiveled his head this way and that, taking things in. He wanted to know where he was, who these people were. The only difference from yesterday was the perception of color. Last night the light poured down from the ceiling and recesses above the walls, bathing the contents of the rooms in light amber. This morning sunshine beamed rectangles from the skylights and windows, sweeping the rooms clear from many views. Every corner overflowed with a tall green plastic plant in a brown container.

Gradually, people began to congregate, gel into a line outside the medicine room, fewer than last night. This time a different trio of nurses administered the drugs. He felt sorry for the residents; so helpless.

Out of the woman's hallway a nurse steered a wheelchair, its occupant slumped into a curve, a ripe old banana speckled brown. She had no teeth, he guessed, because her nose and chin shaped a crescent around two streaks of harvest moon orange that once were lips.

The nurse jockeyed the wheelchair back against the glass room and cattycorner to him, asking in the idiot-baby voice, "She won't bother you here, will she?"

Dumbly Richard shook his head. The nurse patted Banana Lady on the shoulder and walked down the women's wing.

Banana Lady grumbled. "Where's Joey?"

Richard gazed straight ahead at the people in the medicine line.

"Can you tell me where's Joey?"

He searched the fish tank lounge, the ceiling.

"Please."

Finally, he needed to see her.

Banana Lady met his gaze. He twitched. She stared off into the middle distance and sighed mightily and grunted, shuddering.

Oh my God, was she doing what he *thought* she was doing? Should he tell someone? Should he get up and walk away or *Jesus Christ*

Banana Lady was smiling, relieved.

Her rotten banana odor slickened the back of his throat, and he was thinking of leaving when a large middle-aged man with sad eyes in a green stained shirt approached. He had a stubby head and sunken chest, and above and below his belt great waves of flesh floundered. A giant overripe pear. "Did she do it yet?"

What?

Pear Man pulled out of his pants pocket a folded booklet, unfolded it, a book of puzzles. "Did she do it yet?" he asked again. He sat down on the couch opposite, unclipped a ball point pen from his shirt pocket and set it to a page, tracing straight lines, pausing, tracing, one, two, three—Richard followed the pen along the path on the page before it abruptly stopped. "She's pretty regular at messing herself. You like puzzles?"

"Sure." Richard folded his arms across his chest. His mother loved crossword puzzles.

"Oh?" Pear Man advanced. "What kind of puzzles?"

I don't know, I don't care, "Most any, really, it's not that important, I'm—" Richard searched the lounge for rescue—"waiting to see a doctor," so that I can get the hell out of here.

"They gave me this." He showed him. "Connect the Dots. It's some kind of therapy. How about Connect the Dots?"

There was no hope in sight. "Sure. Sure. I like Connect the Dots."

"Like this?" He flipped the puzzle book to display his handiwork.

Lines zigzagged across the page so that Richard could not tell what it should be.

"You can't see what it is, can you?" He flipped the puzzle over, musing. "This one should be a rabbit. It's not a rabbit. Yet."

"Should we tell them about her?" Richard asked.

Not stopping his dot connecting, Pear Man said to his puzzle, "They know. It's clockwork."

"Richard," a nurse said coming up to him, "it's time."

He didn't know what to do.

"Follow me. The doctor will meet you in his office. It's down the hall. Are you finding your way around alright?"

Finding my way around alright? Is that a fucking joke? He was afraid to move from the couch since they planted him. "Yes. I think so," he answered idiotically, shadowing her past the nurses' station and over a wide red band painted across the tiled floor.

Her pointing displaced his asking. "That's the furthest you're allowed to go."

Why?

"That's how far new patients are permitted to go. Unless you're with staff. We'll bring you your food until you're allowed to visit the cafeteria."

*New* patients? *Until* he was allowed to visit the cafeteria? She didn't understand. He wouldn't be here that long.

"His office is right ahead."

Good. He wanted to straighten this whole thing out.

Down the official-looking hall from around the final corner to what must be the main entrance walked Eugene. Richard focused his eyes above on the row of lights, the walls, the floor, anything else, but as they approached and readied to pass he was compelled.

Eugene's black stone eyes glistened. "Now I see."

Richard nearly stumbled staring after him.

He'd been in this room before.

The doctor wore a white lab coat. His head was the end of a loaf of bread with two raisins pinched in. A sweep of a hand to the chair was welcome, and he thanked the nurse and shut the door.

His door could *click* closed.

The windowless room was illuminated by one desk lamp, a tower shedding light among the mounds of folders and papers and magazines and casting the doctor's shadow monstrous and wavering against the wall behind him where shelves crammed with books to the ceiling. Spotting the other walls were a dozen or more black metal-framed photographs of birds, all sorts of birds, some in flight, some at rest on tree branches or fence posts. They made a disparate flock, flat and frozen. Over the doctor's chair an owl rotated its head, seemingly startled by some sudden sound in the room. The owl's two moon eyes welled surprise.

The doctor settled himself into his seat with a clipboard and pen and immediately began rocking, almost jerking, forcing questions and answers out of the chair.

Screee?

See.

It was bird cries, or a delicate tearing of the sky.

Screeeee?

Seeeee.

The name embroidered above the pocket in a rich crimson-thread script read "Dr. Will" or "Hill" or "Wall" or "Hall," he could not tell. The red thread blurred the word.

The first thing the doctor said that Richard really didn't care about and was too tired to follow was who he was, what sort of institution this was, what they could do for patients, what was expected of patients, and he went on from there, explaining things to Richard as if he were going to be there for a very-very long time, and Richard didn't want to hear any of it, *any* of it. He didn't belong here. But he was beginning to feel the sabotage of unseen forces. The first thing the doctor said that interested him was "How are you feeling today?"

About time. "Pretty lousy," he told the owl, and then the doctor, "I think I'd rather be dead."

Scree?

"You nearly succeeded. But here we are. We couldn't pump your stomach because it'd been too long since you swallowed the pills. They dissolved by then. What did you take, by the way?" His pen poised.

He didn't know? "Quaaludes. Know what those are?"

The doctor seemed amused by the question. "How many?" His pen scribbled.

"I don't know."

Seeeee.

"You don't know?"

"I lost count after 25."

"I'm surprised you're not feeling worse than you are, then." The doctor's look prescribed. "How's your stomach? Feeling sick?"

Richard waved it off because he didn't care about these questions and because he didn't like this guy's attitude. "A little queasy; comes and goes. It's getting better."

The doctor tried the words himself, "A, little, queasy," jotting. "You've probably seen the worst of it. Anything else?"

Yeah, OK, smart guy. "My neck is doing this weird thing. I get the shakes when I do this." He demonstrated, placing his palms on his knees, tilting his head up slowly until the shaking started. He thought he must look rather silly, like a baby bird bobbing for food. "See? I can hardly lift my head without it shaking."

The doctor offered breezily: "A side effect of the overdose. It should lessen after a while. Let me know if it doesn't or if you experience other side effects."

At first Richard felt an enormous dissatisfaction with the doctor's disengagement toward his predicament, then a burst of fury at his attempt at pleasantries in the context of his failed suicide attempt. "I didn't ask to come here, you know. I don't *want* to be here."

The doctor considered. "I can understand that. For the time being, though, in light of what brought you here, this is where you'll stay."

*What?* "*Why?* These people are a bunch of fucking wackos, do you know that? Do you even *know* what kind of people you have in here? Don't look at me that way. I'm not like them. I don't belong here." He repeated for the owl's sake. "I don't belong here. I did what I did, by myself, I made a mistake, by myself, I should be allowed to go home."

"You think you made a mistake?"

"Sure." Did he have to spell it out? "I *failed* to kill myself." Idiot.

Screee.

"Depression can be a deadly disease," the doctor said.

Richard didn't want to hear this.

"There's much we don't understand about it."

Look at him: so concerned, so soft. *He doesn't care!*

"What we do understand are its effects."

Richard struggled to follow the words about how "some think it's primarily social in nature" because he wanted to leave but was trapped just like when he was 10 years old with his mother and when he was trapped he'd shut out but couldn't shut out the world and curl up inside because "there are outside forces working to cause the disease, like the person's surroundings, work, and home life. Others think it's primarily chemical in nature—

Years ago his mother had come to him one evening with a stack of her library books, turned off his TV show, and when she started with "I was reading" he shut down. "Everybody has a life picture, new every day, and everybody colors and draws the way they see themselves and their world."

—chemical imbalance in the depressed person's brain that causes the disease. In this case, the chemical imbalance causes the person to experience his surroundings in a completely biased manner—

She was so excited, couldn't wait to show him something she'd probably discovered just that afternoon, knelt in the middle of the living room to block his escape and on the carpet flattened open a workbook. "You look so unhappy, Richie, and this book says it's because your picture is gray."

—doesn't experience the world, or himself in it, as it actually is. A sunny day isn't a sunny day. A beautiful flower isn't a beautiful flower. Even what he thinks about himself might not be true. He tends to focus only on the negative, and everything negative is reinforced by—

A box of crayons from Alan's room. "Everybody has a life picture." She spun the workbook so that he could see on the page the shell of a human form, boy or girl, man or woman, it could be anything. "We color our pictures every day," she was reading. "Some days we're blue, some days we're green, some days we're painting with reds or yellows or oranges."

—feel that he's to blame for how he feels, that it's somehow his fault. But there's no fault to be had. It's just a way of being, of seeing. Like your glasses—

"You look so sad all the time, Richie. And the book says that's because you're using gray to color your picture." She emptied the box of crayons on the carpet. "You're supposed to draw how you feel."

I am an empty outline.

"How would you color yourself? Use any colors you'd like to."

But he wouldn't like to.

"Draw," she was getting desperate, "what you're feeling." She fumbled crayons.

He did not want to feel anything, closed himself off, or felt he would explode, and walked away, leaving her on her knees in the middle of the living room floor.

—glasses were made for you and you only. No other person could wear your glasses and see properly. Think of depression as wearing a different pair of glasses. The depressed person experiences the world differently because he's wearing these glasses all the time and can't take them off. It affects how he thinks, how he feels, but it's not the true image. What do you think about that?

What?

"What do you think about what I just said?"

He was gazing at the door; he couldn't get up and walk away from this.

The wrong pair of glasses? How could he know they were wrong? They were *his* glasses. He pushed them up by the nosepiece to observe what would be the blur of the world without them. He tried the words aloud to hear if they made sense to him: "I'm wearing the wrong pair of glasses."

"I didn't say 'wrong'," the doctor said. "I said 'different'. There is a difference."

Richard didn't think so. And what about everybody else? Then who's to say whose glasses are right or wrong?

"How long have you felt like this?"

"Like what?"

The doctor spread his hands.

"My whole life." It was as if he had snapped his fingers in the doctor's face.

"Most suicide attempts are an alarm, a cry for help."

"I wasn't crying for help," Richard said, indignant. "It wasn't an *attempt*. I *thought* I was taking enough pills to kill myself three times over. I *planned* this for 3 *months*. I *wanted* to die. I didn't want to live. I wasn't crying for help. I *chose* to do this. I thought I was going to sleep and not wake up." Don't you get it? "I don't want to be here."

The silent space between them built significance for the doctor's next words. "Do you feel loved?"

He didn't know what that meant.

"Your parents are very concerned about you."

Richard felt his face growing hot.

"How do you get along with your parents?"

Richard looked at him.

"Your father?"

He yells a lot.

"Your mother?"

She sleeps a lot.

"It may help to talk about these things. How is your home life?"

There was not much talking, the TV was on all the time, he did not know what his parents held together in common besides their misery and contempt for themselves, each other, and the world, and masturbation was his relief, an elixir, it made living tolerable, most times, and other times he felt it bring him to the end of his desolate self; he shrugged. "Normal."

"They want you to get better, and this is the best place for that. Do you understand what you did?"

"I know what I *didn't* do. I *didn't* kill myself. Next time I'll have to do it *right*."

The doctor raised an eyebrow.

Was the man stupid? "Get a gun," Richard said to the owl. "Do it *right*." Was the man stupid? Or was he? It was his glasses. He probably shouldn't be telling him this. Did he even mean it?

The doctor sighed, "We can help—"

"I don't *want* your help."

The doctor paused. "I didn't think you were like these people here, as you say. I think everyone here is unique, in their own way." He seemed to be grappling for another word to speak to add to his point, but finding none, trekked off in another direction. "Where would you go if you were not here right now?"

Richard stared down the owl. Inside he burned.

"Home?"

Richard squirmed. He was losing, he could feel it, he knew the doctor was feeling it. The owl did nothing. Don't talk to me like I'm an idiot, he wanted to say. "You can't keep me here if I don't want to be here."

Plain and obvious came the reply, "You did sign the papers."

Fuck you. "I'll run away. You can't stop me from getting out of here and killing myself."

The doctor winced, and Richard was glad for doing that much, having some power over *something* in this place, but immediately regretted causing this man pain because he had nothing to do with him, he was a complete stranger; and, too, in his heart, he knew it was a lie, he didn't really want to kill himself, not right now at least. Death, the unknown of death, did not frighten him; he felt neutral to that blankness; it was the agonies along the path to that hellish choice that he dreaded reliving. It was never very far.

"Do you want to talk about why you did it?"

"I did it to die."

"I mean: why."

Oh my God yes yes *yes* listen to me listen to my tears *NO*, you wouldn't understand you don't want to understand why can't you understand why can't I understand why can't I say I'm going to— He felt tongueless with worlds to tell.

"You'll have no outside privileges, yet." The doctor had given up and was talking rote. "No visitors, except your parents, with few exceptions. We'll allow phone calls. Your meals will be served in your room. The limits of your movement are marked at the station. After that." His shrug indicated the simple truth: "We're an open facility. Not all of the yard is fenced."

*Ha.* He *could* get out! But then he realized he didn't really *want* to get out, because then he'd have to go somewhere, have to have a goal, and he had nowhere he wanted to go, nothing he really wanted to do.

He was stuck.

The doctor tried amicably, "We have many activities here for you to become involved with. The counselors are ready to help in any way they can. You have appointments the next few days, for some tests, so that we know where we stand, and then we can go from there."

Tests?

"Neuropsychiatric. Written, verbal, spatial. Have you ever done IQ testing?"

No.

"They're quite involved. They'll give us a good picture of where you are. A psychologist administers them onsite. It will take the better part of two days, starting tomorrow, and we'll get the results in a week or so. How does that sound?"

How does that sound. How does that sound. He sounded so fucking normal. Was there a choice? Not really. But it seemed interesting. Testing meant that he should study, though. He'd enjoyed high school well enough but it was boring. As and Bs without even trying. How could he prepare for tests here? Last month he had cancelled out of all his community college courses. Part of tidying up before... IQ testing sounded interesting, though. But his mind was a bowl of soggy cereal. "I'm feeling kind of slow from the overdose. But OK."

"Good," the doctor snapped the conversation shut. "I want to start you on medication, too. It should help you feel better. It's" a complicated name and more explanation than Richard cared to know about how they didn't understand how they worked, only that they did work, for many. "These should help you feel better, think about things in a better light, give you those new pair of glasses to see the world, think about things—differently. Are you willing to try?"

Is that what he needed? To see things, think things, differently. He wanted to die, go to sleep forever, that was all. Would medicine work? Was the fly on the windowsill dead yet? He shrugged.

"We need your permission."

He shrugged again. "OK."

"Good."

"How long will it take?"

"For you to feel the effects?"

He nodded.

"Days. Weeks. It depends. People respond differently. We don't know exactly how or why. There may be side effects, too. Some people experience dry mouth, diarrhea, slight headaches. Those are most common. You can chew ice chips for the dry mouth. Many of the residents carry a cup of ice chips around with them for that. There's an ice machine in the snack room. If there are other side effects, let me know, and we can adjust the dose, or try another medication."

And beyond that? "What if it doesn't work?"

The doctor said "There are other medications" with more complicated names and even more complicated explanations. "There's also ECT."

Richard came to attention.

"Electroconvulsive therapy. I'm sure you've heard of it?"

"Isn't that where they strap you down and shoot electricity through your head, like Frankenstein?"

The doctor didn't like that. "It's all done in a controlled setting. If you're unresponsive to other forms of therapy, we do have that as an option. It's gotten a lot of bad press because of indiscriminate use, a long time ago, and because of the movies, like *One Flew Over the Cuckoo's Nest*, but it's not like that. We don't use it as punishment." The doctor grinned reassurance. "In the past some patients suffered injuries during the induced seizures: compression fractures of the spine, shattered teeth. Today we use more controlled settings and the electrical current is better regulated. Patients are fully informed, and we must have their consent."

*Sign it, sign it.*

"The patient is immobilized—"

Strapped down!

"—a mouth guard is used so that the teeth aren't damaged during treatment."

Like he wore in little league football?

"We don't understand how it works—"

Do you understand how *anything* works around here?

"—but we find that it can be extremely beneficial in some patients, even life-saving, when the patient is unresponsive to medications."

I'll respond!

"We can also use it if the patient is having uncontrollable thoughts of suicide. It can be very effective for that, too. You'll let us know if that happens, won't you?"

*Are you out of your fucking mind? You're never going to strap me down. I'm never going to tell you anything about me!* It's how he lived, anyway. Richard hoped his horror inside was a smile outside.

"There are side effects, of course, as with any treatment. The most common is memory loss, but usually this doesn't last. Usually it returns with time. It can be a wonderful, life-saving choice for some."

The doctor smiled, and the way the doctor smiled made Richard swear to himself that he would never never never let this man strap him down on a table and shoot bolts of electricity into his head.

From a folder on his desk he shuffled out a sheet of paper, photocopied to fuzziness, handed it to Richard. "This is your schedule of activities and sessions. You'll find a nice balance, I think, between scheduled time and free time. There's a gymnasium, crafts room, a music room."

Richard pinched the paper, preparing for it to burst into flames, and deadened his senses to his surroundings. He was hardening himself against everything the doctor was saying, everything he represented. He would do what they wanted him to do, say what they wanted him to say, as long as it helped him survive. He would make his time here as short as possible and get out, be done with it. Put it behind him. And he held on to that grain of life. It made him feel better, like he had some control over *some* thing. The doctor's voice softened and hollowed and then loudened again. In the distance he thought he could hear the rising sound of beating wings. It was the doctor's chair, calling.

Screeeee?

Seeeee.

". . . and I think you'll find your time here well spent."

Richard waited until he was sure the doctor had finished. "Can I go now?" He wanted to go to his room to be alone and cry. It was like an awful camp. He had never been away from home before. What would his mother be doing now, now that he was gone? Going through his room, probably hunting for what she needed to find. His collection of porn magazines stashed underneath his bed. It'd taken months for him to build this time. Then a mood would overcome her and she would "discover" it, purge it. Such great material, too. So many beautiful women, all his, any time. Now it would be garbage. And what would he do here for fun? Masturbate? Anything Louis said? He glanced at the doctor. Doubtful. Not here. That shitty grin of his took everything out of Richard. Dickhead. *All of them.* An agitated, murderous rage took hold of him against them for keeping him here, against his will. Why couldn't they let him die! *Let me die!* Resting in a coffin like Melvin. What a relief that would be, what a release that would finally, blessedly be.

"What are you thinking about?"

Sex. Murder. Death. "Nothing."

They observed one another from opposite ends of a great chasm until some sudden comprehension pricked the doctor's countenance, and he called for the nurse.

On the way back to his room she acted as tour guide, started by walking him down the long hallway, toward the main entrance, she explained, just so he could see. Double doors of steel opened up to a lobby, but she wouldn't let him pass.

"When can I go out?" he asked.

"That's up to the doctor," she said.

Fuck.

Back down the hall she led him, indicating the art therapy room (a bustle of patients and projects), the group therapy room (closed, in session), the music room (where you could listen to records or get games and cards to play in the lounge), the cafeteria (where all meals and the nighttime snack were served, but not for him because they would bring his food to his room), the gym (large and airy, but he wasn't allowed there yet, either).

"When can I use the gym?" he asked.

"That's up to the doctor," she said.

*Fuck!*

She led him through the lounge telling him about when the nurses liked the residents to get up in the morning, when the residents could go down to the cafeteria to eat, when the residents should line up for medications, when they liked the residents to piss shit shower fuck sleep.

"We like the residents to keep to a schedule," she said. "It helps everyone."

By the time they made it to his room he had no more ears to hear.

But she had more to say about how residents should keep their rooms, make their beds, keep their dirty clothes out of the way in a laundry bag or in the dresser drawers or even in a linen basket you could have your mom bring you from home.

Get out, he wanted to tell her and shove her out the door. My roommate's a fag and wants to do gay stuff with me, and I don't make my bed, I throw the covers over it. He held the door for her on the way out.

"Always open." She smiled.

Huh?

"The door always stays open. Don't close it. We can see from our station down the halls. If it's ever closed we'll be here right away."

It was prison, and he was on watch. He asked if he could make a phone call, or if someone could phone him, and the nurse explained that the phones were turned on every day from 11 a.m. to 2 p.m., then again from 6 p.m. to 8 p.m. She smiled, "Have a nice day," and abandoned him.

The room was empty, the tray of food gone. The tears he had in the doctor's office were no longer there. At his desk he sat staring at the phone, holder of some dark ancient mystery.

He had to leave his room to check the time. There was no clock in the room because there were no wall outlets in the room because you could stick your fingers in them, so he waited in the main lounge. He played with his glasses, flipping the lenses up to defocus the world, dropping them down to refocus. Up, blur. Down, clear. Up, down, up, down. Years ago, sometimes at night riding in the car with his parents, he would remove his glasses so he could see how other people saw the world. It was a dream-world then, all the night lights haloing, and when they stopped for a traffic light it was Christmas morning, red and green bulbs sparkling.

He thought about what the doctor had said.

Up, not depressed.

Down, depressed.

Up, not depressed, blind.

Down, depressed, clear.

Up, down, up, down.

He left them down.

Anyone watching me must think I'm nuts.

He didn't feel depressed.

But they were made for him.

As the clock in the nurses' station ticked to 11 he hurried to his room and grabbed the receiver and went to dial but the line was dead. He set it down and waited a breath and lifted it again. Dead again. He did this several times, almost in a panic to hear any sound that would tell him he could contact the outside world, until the line buzzed. He dialed, beseeching God to allow his mother and not his father to pick up the phone. She would know what to do. She would know how to help him.

"Hello?"

There was a God.

"Hi Mom." He almost cried her name.

"Oh Richie," she breathed out what sounded like a long dreary night.

"I'm here."

She sucked in her dreariness. He had meant, "I'm here, in this place," not "I'm here, I failed to kill myself," but he had birthed the monstrosity of his reality, and it towered between them, staring them into silence.

His mother approached the monster first, warily. "Oh Richie, how are you?"

"I'm OK." Wah, wah, wah, wah, wah. "It's a nice place." I cut them off. "I have a roommate." The darkness giggled. "I met the doctor this morning." Screeeee? They make us keep the dead. Regret for what he'd done and dread for what he might face alone tore him apart—oh how he would give anything to be in the sweet suffocating familiarity of his own room at home. Out poured his plea-cry-confession: "Can I come home?"

"No, Richie." Her reply eviscerated him. "It will be better if you stay." Her voice was a point moving along a predetermined path through space. "You've got some things to figure out there while your father and I figure some things out here."

*Figure out what?*

"It won't be good for anyone if you're home right now."

*You don't know what they'll do to me!*

"Why don't you get some rest."

*Rest?*

"We'll talk about things later when you're feeling better."

*I feel fine right now.*

"I'll come by this afternoon, how does that sound?"

How does that sound. How does that sound. He could not hear it. Couldn't she see him drowning? *Drowning. Alone.* So that was it.

He was alone. "Is Dad there?" He didn't know why he said that. The thought of speaking with his father sickened him, but part of him thought that if he could hear the sound of his voice, his *voice*, not yelling, it might

"I think it's better if you two don't talk right now, Richie."

better?

"Your father is very upset by all of this."

He's upset

"You know your father."

who

His mother said she had to go, she would stop by this afternoon, so they said their "I love you's" and after she hung up he coddled the receiver to his chest and curled up on the bed. Rest, she had said, get some rest. Yes, that would be good. On the nightstand he set his glasses. His depression. He felt better already. After talking with the doctor. He could take their medicine. That would help. There was no need for them to talk about strapping him down and shocking his brain until his spine fractured and his teeth broke. He was cooperating; he knew how to cooperate. He'd show them.

Oblivion, what he always hoped for from sleep, called to him from the remains of his overdose.


Someone entered the room and went to Louis' side. Richard rolled and slit an eyelid, watched him at his dresser, watched unmoving, unbreathing. Louis stood hunched. Then walked out. Richard shut his eye to avoid being seen. After waiting for what he thought would be long enough for Louis to not want to return to the room again, he propped himself up and got his glasses and squinted. On the dresser the dancer lived once more, fixed, celebrating what she had been at the beginning. He vowed never to touch her or even go near her, closed his eyes, prayed to be relieved of his impossible burden of consciousness, and gave himself up to the gravity of the bed.

He woke sick to another tray of food on his desk: lunch. Done eating, he sat waiting, waiting for his dread of meeting new people to subside, waiting for something to happen, waiting. Waiting. Until he could no longer endure the pressure of the nothingness. He would have to do the something himself. So he stood up. That was something. Wandered out of the room. That was something, too. He walked.

In the distance at the first large table opposite the nurses' station he recognized his roommate with two other people. Red, facing him at the head of the table and studying her index cards, Louis on her left, but the other guy opposite Louis and on Red's right he did not know—a boy about his own age, somewhat good looking and too aware of it, with stray hair over one eye so that every so often he had to twitch his head to throw the patch aside to give himself two eyes. On the table he propped a *Green Lantern* comic book.

Cool. He used to collect comics; maybe he could get to know this kid.

"Hi."

Louis smiled up from his table talk—"Nice nap?"—with just a hint of last night's sex talk.

"Yeah." He wanted him to stop.

Louis motioned for him to join society; he sat next to his roommate with his back to the nurses' station. "You know Red."

She grinned up from the stack of index cards with nothing in her eyes from his confession last night. "Hi, So Tired."

"And this is Victor. Victor: Richard. Richard: Victor."

Richard said, "Hi, Victor."

Victor lowered his *Green Lantern* to reveal a tan t-shirt printed with the words "Wally the finger". "It's Vic, Dick. Are you a Dick?"

"No." I am not a dick, he used to joke with his friends, but sometimes it wasn't funny. "People call me Richard." He didn't want any trouble.

"Oh. Well. People call me Vic." He twitched the eye hair patch aside and glared at Louis.

Richard had to ask: "What is 'Wally the finger'?"

Vic liked being asked. He gave Richard the finger and said, "The finger," let his hand hang there, then swiveled his wrist. "Wally. If you're with a chick."

"Stop," Red said.

"Thanks," Richard said, blinking, not liking this Vic already, unsure if he could take him.

Louis made a too-sweet aside to Richard. "You can ignore him when he gets this way."

"It's a fucking joke, Louie."

"A joke," Louis countered, "is something funny that makes people laugh." He raised an eyebrow. "I don't see anyone laughing."

Vic seemed ready to pounce across the table but Red slipped in: "Don't mind Vic, they're still adjusting his medication. Or did you stop taking it again?" Ignoring Vic's gawking she addressed Richard, "How was your meeting with your doctor?" Her eyes told him it was safe.

"Who's your doctor?" Vic asked.

Richard said.

"He'd make a good woman."

Huh?

"'He'd make a good woman,' I said. He's a pussy. Alls he does is talk."

A talking vagina.

"I think his dick's gonna fall off when he's yapping at me. And those fucking *birds*!"

Richard thought it would be best not to say how much he liked seeing the beautiful birds.

Red re-tried: "How was your meeting?"

"Fine, I guess. I mean, I met him, we talked, he told me how things go around here." How they'll strap me down and hook me up if I don't get better. He tried to smile. While he spoke the others didn't seem to be paying too much attention; he guessed they'd all been through it already and were not terribly interested in his version; he saw no advantage in revealing so much as he'd done last night. "He said I'd be here for a while, until I'm ready to go." He drummed his fingers on the slick, polished table with their muddied reflections. "That's about it."

She sighed. "That's about always it."

"They do what they can," Louis said, "I suppose."

"I suppose," Richard half-heartedly agreed and searched his face to see if he was thinking about doing those things he talked about last night, but he could see nothing.

Red asked, "They're going to start you on meds?"

Uh huh.

"What kind?"

"Antidepressants." That's enough, he thought.

Vic flipped a page in the *Green Lantern*, and Red and Louis exchanged inaudible words.

He didn't like them being in cahoots.

"And God said." Someone had the TV too loud.

Richard let his eyes wander the room. In the fish tank lounge a bunch of high school kids gathered around a table. Off in a corner by himself a boy curled in a chair, reading a *People* magazine. Slowly he wormed an index finger into one of his nostrils until his face squinched—he hit bottom—out wound the finger, slowly. He sniffed, wiped it on his pant leg. The Nosepicker repeated the process for his other cavity. Wormed, squinched, sniffed, wiped.

"And God said." A disembodied voice crawled out of the TV lounge. Philip sat staring intently at the space where the set would be; part of the wall blocked it from view so he appeared to be watching dead space.

"And I had a vision."

Richard recognized the voice of Jerry Falwell. Every sentence was a new proclamation that faded away from hearing right after it began.

Out of the women's hallway emerged a young woman about his own age in tight white shorts that were too tight and too short and a yellow t-shirt taut across two heaving water balloons. She did not wear these clothes as much as the clothes wore her, and it pained him to see her move. When she spotted their table her face brightened, and she headed to them. There were two empty chairs; one next to Vic and the end one next to him; into the one next to Richard she plopped, puffing a pink bubble gum fragrance.

He was afraid of her and wondered what it would be like to marry her.

"Hi," she said breathlessly, her clean face beaming around a cute duck mouth. "My name's Susie." Then, confirming herself in front of the entire table: "I'm Red's roommate." She extended her hand; two telephone numbers smudged; warm butter pressed and released. "You must be Richard, Louis' new roommate. That makes us kind of related, doesn't it?"

Vic sighed too loudly, and Richard hunted for a response. He tried to keep his eyes off her heaving water balloons.

"Why are you here?"

"Not even one minute." It was Vic, buried in his comic.

"You are just so chronic. I am making conversation *here*, with *this* guy. Do you mind, Mr. Jekyll? Or is it Mr. Hyde today?"

Vic slowly scratched his cheek with a lone upright middle finger and lifted the *Green Lantern*.

Red corrected, "*Doctor* Jekyll." Earnestly: "It's *Doctor* Jekyll and *Mister* Hyde."

Everyone looked at Red.

"It's a novel, by Robert Louis Stevenson."

Everyone stopped looking at Red.

"So." Susie returned to her quest. "Why are you here?"

How could she not know? "Suicide."

She blurted "Oh let me see!" and grab-flipped his wrist, he was too shocked to protest, her breasts sponged the edge of the table. Dropped it, disappointed at finding no traces of violence.

"I didn't try to cut myself," he heard himself apologizing. "I overdosed."

A catastrophe of questions dominoed, clockwise.

"Really? With what?"

"Can you be any more stupid?"

"Can *you* be a bigger asshole?"

"I'm a magnet for the insane," Louis finished.

It was Richard's turn—he tried the question everyone asked first—tentatively, to Susie. "Why are you here?"

"Oh." She giggled sorrily. "It's my parents." In the moment their eyes met Richard captured and translated her scattered and self-loathing thoughts. "Why don't you wear contacts? I think you'd look a lot nicer in contacts. Take off your glasses. Let me try them on. Come on. Show us who you really are. Come on. I bet you look great without them. How long have you worn them?"

"Forever. Fifth or sixth grade." He felt uneasy about giving his glasses up for someone to try on. So playgroundish. And he was weak and helpless without them. He'd gape stupidly at a blurry, monstrous world, but he removed them anyway, as much to keep the subject off his suicide as to shut her up.

"See? Doesn't he look better?"

What was I before?

"He looks darling," Vic said.

"Show everyone."

Richard blushed and dutifully displayed himself to everyone at the table so that they could see what he was without glasses. He perceived faces as a mass of flesh with bleeding edges, and in the blotched blank eye sockets comprehended no humanity, no reality, and so he offered them all that reflection: his own uncomprehending mask. "I can't see anything," he said to nobody.

"So the blind man," Louis offered, "sees best."

Richard didn't know if he believed that: it sounded good; he *wanted* to believe it; but he couldn't understand when he read about how blind people were OK with their blindness, or how their other senses made up for their lack of sight. After he'd read about it once in the newspaper years ago, he snuck into his room with a clean dish towel from the kitchen and, needing to feel what they were feeling, blindfolded himself and wandered his room, working hands and fingers as antennae. He felt compressed by himself and the wall of blackness before him, and he could not stand it; he tore off the towel and thought whoever wrote the newspaper story was stupid and didn't know anything about being blind.

"Hey, everyone, lookit *me*. I'm Richard. Whoa. How do you *see* with these things?" She tilted her head sideways and upways and allways until she steadied to peer down the length of her nose at everyone. "That's better. Wow. Everything's so weird. Red, you're all wavy. Louis, you're currrveeee." Her lips spurted giggles.

She wasn't depressed, *couldn't* be depressed, he figured. "Done?" He held out his hand, set them in place unceremoniously. Not very long could he bear his visionless world.

A thought appeared to be formulating in Susie's head but he stopped it from tumbling out of her mouth by throwing out to the table, "What is there to do around here?"

"Oh plenty." Susie didn't need to think.

"Sometimes."

"Not a whole lot."

Louis laughed, confiding with Richard. "They are too much, aren't they? Who's right?"

"Me."

"Me too."

"Me three."

Louis said to Richard, "They are too much."

"There *is* a lot to do around here," Susie said. "It depends on what you want to do with yourself and what your *goals* are. That is, if you *have* goals." Her eyes rolled at Vic. "If you want to kill time, you can do that. I guess it depends on what you did outside. What did you do outside, Richard?"

Outside. What did he do outside? He sensed everyone waiting. "I went to school—"

"Where did you go?"

"Lakeshore Community—"

"No, no, I mean *high* school."

"St. Joe's."

Vic said, "You went to St. Joe's? All boys? Catholic?"

Susie ignored him. "Never mind him. What did you study at college?"

"Mechanical engineering," he said, "but I dropped out," and with each statement gave a little more to stop her from asking more. "I don't know what I want to do now, outside. I guess there's time to think about it, inside." He stopped, satisfied with how he had answered her and protected himself. But he still didn't have an answer to *his* question.

"There's lots of time to read."

Everyone looked at Red.

Louis sighed, perhaps recalling a dearer time. "Some of the trips out are nice. You missed one last week, to a movie. There's a trip to the zoo in a couple weeks—if you're here."

Vic said, "There's a gym with a basketball court and a pool table, and a ping-pong table."

"There's plenty of time to watch TV." Louis observed the people gathered in the TV lounge. Philip was gone. "It's always on, and someone's always there. And eat. You can eat as much as you want." Then more to himself: "Like cows before the slaughter."

"The food sucks," said Vic.

"It is fatty," said Susie. "I think I've gained 10 pounds since I've been here. See?" She lifted a thigh for Richard to see, and he saw.

"The ice cream's delicious," grinned Vic.

"I wouldn't know about that," Louis said.

"You play checkers?"

"In a couple of weeks there's Spring Dance," said Red, "if you're into that sort of thing."

"Do you dance?" Susie just-touched his arm. "Oh I love to dance." She danced in her seat, making the extra 10 pounds jiggle so that Richard was torn between staring and averting his eyes. He never danced, he did not know how, he had no desire, he thought it was stupid, but he very much enjoyed watching girls do it because their gyrations fascinated him. "After the dance," she said, twirling a thread of hair around a finger, "you could go for a walk in the yard or by the lake."

He didn't believe her. "You can go down by the shore?"

She stopped twirling. "I didn't say 'down by the shore,' I said 'by the lake.'"

"You can't go down on the beach," Louis helped. "The yard is fenced all around and by the houses, except out front. Keeps us in." He smirked. "Or them out."

"We're next to houses?" So much he didn't know.

"Don't lie to the new guy," said Vic. "You could go down on the beach if you wanted. You could go out, if you really wanted. Swim in the lake, go to the video arcade down the street—"

That sounded fun. He loved video games.

"—play putt-putt—"

"That's enough." Louis shredded the proposition. "That's crazy talk." It was a little slap to everyone around the table.

But Vic smarted back. "Don't get hysterical, Lou. I'm only giving the new guy his options." He quick-winked at Richard.

"You can bring albums in and listen to them in the music room," said Vic.

"And ruin them on their crappy turntable," said Louis.

"What kind of music you like, Dick?"

Lots. "King Crimson. Brian Eno. The Sex Pistols. Neil Young." He could sit and listen over and over to "Expecting to Fly" and cry.

"Ohhh," said Susie, re-dancing, "do you like The Eagles? I love The Eagles."

Richard hated The Eagles.

She stopped dancing.

"There's art class." Red continued the list for Richard. "Tell him what you made in art class, Louis. Why you made it."

Louis fidgeted, whether out of discomfort or delight for the spotlight Richard could not tell until he opened his mouth: "Fearful, as if treading on thin ice, or looking into an abyss. I see what is not, yet, art." He elaborated solemnly, a curator about to explain a particularly complex piece, "There was a vision of movement and freedom... That was the piece destroyed. The others represented contemplation and despondency in the face of an inexorable death."

Around the table in unison heads went off axis one way or another—dogs confounded by unusual sounds—seemingly deliberating on what had gone before and in anticipation of what might come, but as moments passed and evidently nothing further would be required of them they relaxed to their former selves.

Susie stirred it. "The one didn't have any arms, Louis. What did that mean?"

The question hung, ripe, and shadows of responsive thoughts raced across Louis' brow but Vic beat him to it: "He ran out of clay?"

Everyone blinked.

Richard's spluttering laughter jarred everyone at the table and he curbed himself to a purposeful, coughing stop, feeling like the village idiot until Vic snorted; and Louis spoke to a space above the table in front of him, "Those who have no arms have cleanest hands."

Nobody knew what to do until Susie said, "You can have visitors, too."

Now Vic spluttered.

Susie rolled her eyes. "If you're *worth* visiting."

Vic twisted the tail off his laugh. "You see any flowers here? Any Get Well Soon cards?"

Susie popped her mouth open and closed.

"Wanna know why?"

Louis and Red concentrated on a point over the horizon.

"People are *embarrassed* by you. *That's* why there's no cards or flowers. They're *embarrassed* you're here. They're *embarrassed* to visit you. You don't even know why, do you? You don't even know what people say about you behind your back, do you? Wanna know? Wanna know what people *really* think about you?"

All through the tirade Richard expected someone else to do something, someone else to say something, but it only went on and on and on until he could no longer stand it and spurted "*Stop it!*" He searched their cloudy tabletop faces for any kind of sympathy. "Stop picking on her. It's enough."

Vic was struggling with what to say, and under the anger Richard thought he recognized a little regret and—understanding?

Vic pushed away from the table, chair screeching.

With his eyes Richard asked him not to leave.

"I'll see you around," said Vic.

Everyone at the table watched him leave down the hallway past the mumbling, pacing Joey.

Susie clenched her tears and dashed off to the woman's wing.

An enormous sadness for her took hold of Richard's heart because he pitied the falsities he knew she believed about herself and how those untruths revealed her in her fallen condition, like Louis' beautiful but damaged dancer. He wanted to weep over her, but not now, because he realized it was her ass he had stared at walking away from him down the women's wing last night.

"Lover's quarrel," Louis said.

Red flipped an index card.

"Trust me."

Richard let it go. Part of him didn't want to know, part of him didn't care, but a greater part wanted to learn more about getting out. "Did Vic mean what he said? Does he *really* go out?" A kid asking a parent about Santa Claus. Is it *really* true?

"What Vic means, I suppose," Louis said measuredly, "is that he leaves the hospital grounds."

"Where does he go?"

"Where he said he goes."

It didn't make sense. "Nobody misses him?"

"There's a lot of people here. It's hard to miss some body."

"Have you ever gone out?"

"No."

"Why not?"

"I don't want to get caught."

"What would happen if you got caught?"

"Isolation. Or worse. I don't want to find out. Neither should you."

"What's isolation?"

Louis sniffed. "You ask a lot of questions." He did a nod toward Joey. "That door, over there."

Richard squinted. Attached to the wall next to the door was a small brown plaque with one white word: PRIVATE. At chin level to a standing person was a window about the size of a sheet of paper.

"If you misbehave you'll wind up there for a couple days, more if you do worse. Like start seeing things that aren't there. Or get into fights." He described a scene barely visible in the distance. "They have straps to keep you in bed, drugs in long needles to keep you still. There's one tiny courtyard with brick walls reaching up to the clouds—if you're able to sit up straight they let you in—but they won't let you draw or write anything—and if you scrunch your eyes just right—" he scrunched his eyes just right "—they've thrown you in the bottom of a well, and you wait for the charcoal birds to streak the paper sky." He closed his eyes.

Richard didn't want to know anything else about it. Instead he wanted to know the people around him. "Do you know anyone here?"

Louis answered half-heartedly, "You get to know some, some you don't want to know."

"What about him?"

"Who?"

"Him. Black hair, looks like he cut it himself. Squirrel eyes."

"Oh." Louis chuckled. "Eugene. He's a nut. You don't want to know the nuts."

Richard wanted to know anyway. "Why's he here?"

"Some things are best not known."

With his eyes Richard pursued.

"I don't know."

Liar. "What about him, over there."

"Where?"

"Going into the snack room with all those books and notebooks."

"That's Philip."

"I know. I met him last night. What's he writing?"

Red flipped an index card.

Louis replied, obviously, "Ask him."

Richard ignored the tone. "I think he's a nut. Am I right?" Louis grinned. "Who else do you know?"

"Not many," he said. "On purpose. Look at her."

A young woman was sitting alone in the fish tank lounge, just staring.

"You should have seen her when she first got here last week. Showing off her engagement ring, so happy, so sad. Left her at the altar; now look at her." Louis spoke again to a space Richard could not see: "Her now-anonymous diamond bleeds."

Where did he get this stuff?

"Most of the moms and kids are alright," Louis said, "but they keep to their own groups."

"Moms and kids?"

"Pampered housewives having their 19th nervous breakdown." Louis gazed to the TV lounge where a couple of middle-aged women sat watching a soap opera and Richard heard a woman crying, pleading with a man to stay or go, he could not tell, and the woman with yellow hair and shining eyes—Sandy—curled up in a chair as last night, reading her book. "And the kids. They mostly stick together." Around the table in the fish tank lounge the teenagers drooped. The Nosepicker was off in a corner doing his thing. "Are we done for the day?"

Richard thought Louis was a smart-ass and wanted to slap him.

"It's nothing fancy here," Louis said, "just a suburban madhouse. It's really up to you, who you want to be with, who you don't want to be with. Who you want to be. You make your day. I'm with Red a lot." At the mention of her name Red lifted her face from her cards. Louis added, "It's not so bad, once you get used to it."

It's not so bad, once you get used to it. Once you get used to it. Joey paced out his wah wah wah wah wah. It's not so bad. We all keep the dead. They make us keep the dead. We keep what's dead inside of us. Not so bad. I cut them off. Once you get used to it. They touched something they shouldn't. Wah wah wah wah wah. Every night here I die a little more. "I'm tired," he told the table. "I think I'll go lie down." He had to rest; his parents were coming to visit.

Red said, "See you later, Tired."

"I thought you weren't allowed to draw the residents."

"If they don't see it, it didn't happen." Louis' intense gaze shifted from Richard to the pad, Richard to the pad. Their drape was thrown open to let in the light. "You have such nice bone structure, do you know that?—Such high cheekbones.—Deep olive skin.—Turn.—Regal, aloof attitude.—I mean it, don't look at me.—Face forward.—Smile? Can you *try* to smile?—You look so damn *serious* all the time.—Face *forward*?"

Richard tried. "How long you been drawing?"

"About 10 minutes."

Richard sighed.

"Years," Louis said, eyes flickering, Richard to the pad, Richard to the pad.

"Where'd you learn?"

"I taught myself, from books, then I took a few classes."

Richard adjusted his head to glimpse the three drawings taped to the wall. "Why do you do it?"

Louis hesitated as if he hadn't understood the question. "For fun." Then he chuckled as if he had understood the question. "Don't you ever do things for *fun*?" His smarmy smile was all about his sexual talk from last night.

Richard frowned to make him stop. He wanted to answer "Yes, I do things for fun, but not what you're thinking about," but had to think about what he had fun doing, but then the silence expanded beyond an appropriate time to respond, he feared, while he chewed up his mind with what would have been various responses to the question: driving around, listening to music in his room, masturbating, reading books, getting high, reading comics, drinking beer, masturbating, playing video games at the arcade, masturbating. He had fun watching people, especially women, like when they unzipped and zippered pouches all over their purses in search of a piece of hard candy and triumphantly and noisily untwisted the wrapper, or squatted to mother a baby in a stroller, or adjusted a bra strap digging into a shoulder, or teased a single cigarette from its snuggled slumber with two red nails. He liked listening to women talk, watching women walk.

Only.

He thought the saddest sight he had ever seen in his life was downtown last summer at a Friday night festival, he and his friends happening behind a businesswoman *click click clicking* along the sidewalk, a horrible run in her pantyhose out of her shiny black heel up the back of a meaty calf. He imagined her in some office that afternoon with that run, not knowing, others seeing, indifferent, untelling, knowing what she didn't know, smirking. She *click click clicked* along so briskly, so assuredly, and he was devastated by her innocence and ignorance.

In a few minutes Louis announced "Here" and flipped the drawing pad for Richard's view. "Don't look so stunned. Take a breath. Say something."

Richard didn't know what to say. Alive on the paper was a penciled face, *his* face, delicate, stone, shadowed, lightened. The short hair waved along the forehead and around the ears, large glasses sat on a large nose but did not hide the bright spot in each eye, and the smile—he didn't know if that was his smile or if Louis had crafted it for him. He, rather, that person on the paper, appeared—he didn't know the words. "Is that me?"

"Yes, that's you." Louis handed him the drawing pad.

It is me, Richard thought. But not. He puzzled, almost touched his paper face. Is that how I am?

A nurse poked her head into the room. "Visiting time."

Louis and Richard looked up at her and then at one another.

"Richard," she said, stepping in. "What have you done there, Louis?"

"It's Richard, this time," he invited her.

"Let's see." She took the pad from Richard's hands, mulling over it, him, then the drawing and back again. "Very nice. Uh huh. Yes. Yes. It's one of your better ones." With a single careful movement she pinched the bottom edge of the sheet and tenderly tore it from the pad's glue binding.

Richard was about to protest but Louis shook his head.

The nurse creased the face, quartered it, slipped it into her jacket pocket.

"Thanks," said Louis.

"Visiting time," she said to Richard.

Robotically he rose. He felt an icy tongue lick his bones. The time he dreaded had come, but it had to be done. Meeting his parents for the first time. What would they want to hear from him? What would he—what could he—say to them?

Nothing. Make it nothing. Shut your eyes.

He could think of nothing. Nothing that would help, nothing that would change what he had done, nothing that would make any difference. He shut his eyes. Everything was gone.

But he had to open them to follow the nurse. Her white blouse was too short, her white pants too tight, and he tried to stare anywhere but at that frowning arc. In the lounge his mother sat at the same table he had been at in the afternoon in the chair no one had occupied— he realized they had stuck her there deliberately—and when she recognized him she started out of her chair but remained rooted.

She seemed to him old, and tired. He thought she could have been a patient but for the plastic orange tag shouting VISITOR on her chest. He went to her to do or say something profound, like Louis might do, to calm her, comfort her, appease her, but by the time he reached her and stood in front of her he had nothing but "I'm sorry" and the verge of more tears.

"Oh Richie." She breathed despair.

They hugged. She was shaking, this was how she used to shake sometimes at the kitchen sink after the phone call came that would take away his father, and she would remain, and the hills of suds would shudder with her. He held her tight, smelling peppermint candies and a just-smoked menthol and beneath that her shower with Ivory soap. He shut his eyes; he knew everyone was watching, waiting.

"How are you doing?" she breathed into his ear. "How's my baby?"

He opened his eyes to let the world in. "I'm OK, it's OK," he said and broke away. "Where's Dad?"

"He's not here."

His gaze scattered.

"He's on, Richie. He's at the firehouse—you know your father."

You see any flowers here? Any Get Well Soon cards? Some sort of response started somewhere deep within but he quelled it, crushed it, because he knew nothing would work, nothing he could say would make any difference.

"Let's sit down and visit," she said.

"Can we sit somewhere else? It's like we're on display out here."

Her expression braced him for the reply but not for her use of the idiot-baby voice. "They said we should sit right here, Richie. I told them that would be just fine."

Stunned, he stood appraising her, seeing in her eyes her visitor's view of him, whirled round to the glass enclosure, but all the nurses were flitting about; no one would meet his gaze; and he did not want to turn again to see himself in the mirror of his mother.

She tugged his arm. "Can we sit down?"

"Everyone can see."

"No they can't."

"Everyone can see."

"No they can't. Let's not bicker, let's not fight. Sit down and relax." She was dragging him down. "Right here. Right here is fine."

He sat opposite her in his same chair from earlier in the day with his back to the glass house, to be hidden. So they sat across from each other and observed the excruciating moments withering between them.

"Are you sleeping well?"

He silently thanked her for the mundane. "Like a log, I'm still a little groggy from the—" He barely stopped the reality from slipping out, and their gazes careened to opposite parts of the room.

Shaken, she tried agan. "And your appetite? Are you eating?"

"Yeah. It's alright. Cafeteria food. They bring trays to my room. I'm not allowed—" He retraced his steps out of that minefield. "I eat in my room for now."

With his mother he searched the tabletop for something safe.

"I finished the puzzle," she offered, "without the dictionary. But. You know. Tuesday's aren't so bad."

He smiled for her and thought of how he used to sneak through her dictionary looking up words he did not understand and then thought of telling her about Pear Man and his puzzle but did not want to upset her with that.

She faked shivering. "It's cold in here. Is it cold in here?"

"I'm fine," he said. His fingers were icicles.

Their conversation tapered.

She rubbed her arms. "I should have brought a sweater," she said. "They always keep big buildings so cold. Do you need a sweater?"

"No, Mom. I'm not cold." He clasped and unclasped the icicles in his lap.

"I brought you a sweater, your blue one, just in case. And your jean jacket." She bent under the table, shuffling and grunting. "I brought more clothes, too," she told the underside of the table. "They said I should bring your clothes and extra toiletries." She reappeared dragging up the burgundy suitcase she had received as a wedding present and used on her honeymoon at Niagara Falls.

Richard wilted.

"I packed everything you'll need for a while." She addressed every item with care. "Plenty of clean underwear and socks, shirts, your pajamas, blue jeans, they took your belt, I forgot about that, I wasn't thinking—stupid—your hair brush, your toothbrush and toothpaste, shampoo and soap and two washcloths—they said you could have your own washcloth, you don't want to use *theirs*—shaving cream and a pack of disposable razors—I know you don't like those, Richie, but they said they had to be disposable."

Death would be a relief now. He felt his mouth moving. "I can't come home."

"They said I should bring you more clothes." Her fingers traced the rectangle of the suitcase. "They said you would be here a while." She clamped shut her mouth on some errant truth. Tears rimmed her eyes as she told a secret to the suitcase: "I had to pretend I was packing you for a trip." She broke, choking, stifling herself. Richard thought she would want him to do something and so started out of his seat, but she waved him back. "I'm alright," she sniffed, pulled up her purse, rifled through it, produced a tissue pack, teased one out, wiped her nose. "Did you talk to the doctor today?"

He nodded, wondering if she had talked with him.

"What did you talk about?"

I wear the wrong glasses. "Not much." He knew that look: when she wanted she could be as relentless as the water wearing away the shore. "I mean, he told me about the place, the rules, stuff like that." Was the fly on the windowsill dead yet?

His mother leveled her eyes upon him. "The doctor said it was like wearing a bad pair of glasses that you couldn't see right with, but you got used to the lenses, so you adjusted. When I was a little girl we were so poor my mother and father couldn't buy me glasses that I needed, I had to wear the same pair for years. I adjusted." She sniffed. "Is that how it is?"

He couldn't say, he didn't know, he'd worn the glasses his entire life. "It's the wrong pair of glasses in my brain—my head—the eyes inside my head—" He didn't know what he was trying to say, and neither did she.

"They're going to start you on medication?"

"Tonight." She waited, and he obeyed her silence. "He said it should make me feel better. I should give it a chance. It may take a few days. But that's OK because I'll be here a while." He drifted off, hardly noticing his own voice, because if medications didn't work they'd try different medications, and if those different medications didn't work they could strap me down and shoot electricity through my brain until I feel better, feel normal, like everyone else, with a fractured spine and broken teeth from clamping shut a lung full of screams

"Richie, what's wrong?"

WHAT'S WRONG WITH YOU?

"What did we do wrong, Richie?"

I watched you.

"Why would you want to do this? Why would you do this to us?" *Why would you* stabbed him over and over, and he struggled against it with what to tell her out of the storm of worlds inside of him, the nothing

"Nothing."

"It must have been something."

To get away, to hurt, to touch. "Nothing, nothing." He was sinking he could he tell her nothing true that would crush her that he wanted to escape from them forever that she was wrong his father was wrong

"What's wrong? What did we do wrong? Was it something we did? Something we didn't do? Didn't I love you enough?"

it's all your fault and your life and there's no me drowning, nothing, nothing, clawing up toward a safe place he could not see until he frantically broke the cold solid surface spitting *You didn't do anything, OK? You didn't do anything. It's not your fault. It's all my fault. It's all my fault. Are you happy now? Can we talk about something else?*

She stopped.

His hands were hot and trembling.

His absolutions seemed to satisfy.

"I thought Father Walker could come visit you."

Who?

"We've been going to church your whole life and you don't know him? The fat, thin-haired one. With glasses. Poor man is nearly blind."

A vague image presented from his youth.

"Well he says he'd visit you."

"You told him I was here?"

"Well I didn't think you'd *mind*. He's a *priest*. This is what they *do*." She swirled a hand at the filled lounges. "If you can't call him *now* when can you? Why don't you let him visit, Richie?" She shoveled more words into the void. "Don't see things so much in black and white. You see things too much in black and white. The world's not so simple. Just *once*. Talk about things with him. Let him know what's on your mind."

If he did that Father would explode.

"For me?"

His teeth ground a shout to bits.

"Would you let him visit for me?"

He was nothing, he was she, and he yielded to himself.

"Good. I'm sure you'll feel much better after he visits. I do already. I'll tell him to give you a call." She nudged the suitcase off her lap onto the floor. "Well I think I'd better be going. There's dinner to start. You know your father... Is there anything you want me to bring you next time?"

Huh?

"People have books and things. Is there anything you want from home?"

Home. Yes. Sleep. "A pillow. My pillow. We're allowed our own pillow."

"I'll do that then." She gathered her purse, "I'll bring your pillow so you can get some rest," talking to the table and floor, "same time tomorrow." She wobbled to a stand and he reached too late to be any help. "I'll tell your father you said 'hello', Richie."

They could bear to only briefly search each other's eyes to share her hopeful lie.

Then she was gone.

He watched her go.

He was by himself.

On the black metal windowsill the fly was spinning with death. He might have had the heart to kill it, squash its existence—he might have had the heart, before he woke up in this place.

Two whitecoats entered his room without a word and went to his dresser and Louis' dresser and started opening drawers.

Louis was not paying attention; afraid to direct a question at the whitecoats, Richard asked his roommate, with his eyes, What are they doing?

"Room searches."

Richard's blank expression prodded him.

"Room searches," Louis said again and explained purposefully as if they were alone. "Every day they do room searches. Sometimes it's morning, sometimes it's afternoon. They mix it up so you never know when they're coming."

"What are they looking for?"

"Anything they don't want you to have. Drugs, alcohol, weapons: anything you could use to hurt yourself or others," and, eyes rolling, "*drawings* of the facility or residents."

The whitecoats sifted through drawers, closed drawers, went on to the next.

He and Louis did not exist.

At medication time Richard fell in with the other patients herding toward the door to form the line. He hated standing in lines. He never knew what to do with himself, his legs, his arms, everything stuck out at odd angles and he did not know how to fit in. He found himself standing behind a group of kids, jostling, giggling, peeking over shoulders. Their childishness and the eyeing of the girls pained him. He swiveled into Sandy with her crooked finger grin.

"Hello."

Richard folded his arms across his chest. "Hello."

"You must be a busy boy. Where have you been all day?"

She made him grin, shy.

"Cat got your tongue?" Two pink fingernails snapped at his forearm, made him jump. She purred a laugh. "Step up."

Her command jolted him.

"Step up to the line," she prodded. "We're moving."

He closed the gap between himself and the kids. A nurse was cuddling Joey toward the men's hallway, and a voice from the back of the line did a fake babyish cry, "Can you tuck me in, too?"

The line sucked in a breath.

The nurse did not lift her head from mothering Joey and replied to an infant squawking for its diaper to be changed. "If you need me to, Victor."

Subdued laughter approved.

A boy voice mocked, "Oh, Vic, you're my hero."

Another round of giggles.

Richard admired Vic's bravado.

They stepped forward again. The kids were getting their medications. Through shifting legs he saw the red demarcation taped to the floor.

"I heard you were the big man today," Sandy said to his back; dramatically: "Rescuing the damsel in distress." Warm breath teased his ear, goosefleshing his neck. "I could use some rescuing myself. In my room."

Didn't Louis tell him no visiting the women's wing?

She rolled her eyes and motioned him forward.

The silver-blue haired nurse at the door smelled of antiseptic. She presented the brown cafeteria tray with a tiny paper cup nestling three small round blue pills and a larger paper cup of water. This was it.

He wanted to do this.

He wanted to die, go away.

But before that he wanted to have sex.

You must do this first.

This will make you feel better. Pills and water, water and pills, chunks of chalk days ago. He copied what he'd seen: head back water gulp.

"Here." The nurse motioned beside the door to a large metal garbage can filled with used-once cups.

Before he let them fly he stopped, crunched them both, then let them go among the rest.

Richard thought he could do this thing with a guy for his first time, just to get it done with and out of the way, because it would count, but not really, because it would be with a guy, and he wouldn't be a virgin anymore, but he would, with a girl.

All the time up to going to bed he tried to push it away from him. No use in agonizing over a done decision. Find something else to do.

Except it didn't work that way. Not here.

He tried to move around a lot, from chair to couch to TV lounge to fish tank lounge and back all over again. Nothing satisfied.

There was nothing to do.

The people were insane.

He could not make it here.

After lights out he heard his voice squeak out to the other side of the room, "You know what you said last night?"

"What?"

"About a guy doing that to a guy." He was ashamed to say the words, to give life and meaning to the images with words.

Louis wasn't.

"Yeah. That. Would you mind if I did that to you?" A ridiculous question, but he didn't know how else to say it. He was so tired, and he didn't care about anything, figured he'd be dead in a week anyway, somehow, someway, what did it matter what he did right now? He didn't want to die never having tried sex.

"No," Louis said. "I wouldn't mind." The voice trembled. "You sure?"

Richard nodded but realized they were in the dark. No. Yes. "I'm sure." Now that it was out he could not back away from it.

"Stay there." Louis got out of bed and in the dissipating light became a ghost floating.

Richard whispered, "You said they walk the hall. What if someone sees?"

Louis whispered back, "No one will see." He was on his side of the room already. The bathroom door swung out into place. "The open door blocks the view from the hallway." Louis steadied it with one hand. "See? I'll jump back if anyone comes." He stepped to demonstrate the cover of the shadow. "Kneel here."

So this is how it is. This is how it feels. This is how it is done.

In the morning he woke expecting the world had changed. He felt hideous, special, awful, new. He wished he hadn't done it and wondered why girls complained. He hoped Louis wouldn't take things too seriously between them, telling himself things would work out, they had to work out, he had to make them work out. How could he do that? He did not know.

That's why you're here.

All this percolated while he feigned sleep, listening to Louis rustle about the room. After his roommate left a nurse entered with a breakfast tray; he smelled pancakes and sausages; so there was that. Richard pretended with her, too, letting her believe she awakened him. He stretched, groggily, enjoying that small fun, fooling them. But when he sat up and thanked her for bringing the food he felt foolish and insignificant; he hadn't tricked anyone but himself; perhaps they could see right through his thin skin into his mind and heart and tell him his thoughts and feelings, or, worse, they would not tell him because they did not care. Like the woman who did not know she had a run in her stocking.

He ate methodically, trying to figure out how things would be different, but he could not conjure a clear picture of anything that satisfied, and he tired of trying. What he could manage was what needed doing that morning. Finish eating, shower, dress, take the tests. Those things he could think of. Those things were in front of him. Last night was already behind. The glasses of his mind were removed, and everything present grotesquely blurred, his future so distant it dizzied and sickened him. But he wasn't depressed.

He brushed his teeth until blood came on the bristles.

He went to the lounge to wait for a nurse to take him for his testing, but changed his mind and walked to the window in the TV lounge to see what sort of day it might be. A few clouds tacked to the sky over the line of water. Waves humped dots of sunlight. On the windowsill the fly slept, legs curled.

"It's going to be a pretty day, don't you think?" A wall of pink bubble gum scent floated over him and he melted aside to let Susie see. "Mmm hmm." Her breasts heaved. "Can you come out today?"

"No. Still grounded."

Her eyes widened. "Really? Wow."

He waited for her duck lips to *quack*.

"Are you dangerous?"

He laughed. "Only to myself."

"Well someone must think so. I mean, doing what you did. You know. I could never do that. I've thought about it, but I'm too afraid."

He didn't know what to say after that, but she did:

"Thanks for yesterday. You know, sticking up for me, telling Vic to stop picking on me, no one's ever done that before, I really appreciate it, he can be such a jerk, I just hope they can help him with his problem."

His problem?

"You know. I mean, it's why we broke up, why I broke up with him, I mean, what are you supposed to do after someone says 'I love you so much I want to kill you'? What do you say to something like that?"

He didn't know.

I don't know.

It hurt to listen to her. He wanted her to go away. He hoped she would stay with him forever. He was afraid she'd be able to tell what he had done to Louis last night. Would she think *What's wrong with you?*

She backed away, girl steps and bitten lip. "Well I guess I'll be seeing you around? I better get breakfast before they close down. You know."

Time stopped as he wondered after her undulations.

94

Vic made the corner from the men's hallway into the lounge, eyed her trajectory back to Richard, sneered agreeably. "Nice ass."

Richard blushed.

"Whatsa matter?"

"Nothing."

"You like pussy, don't you?"

Richard nodded, ashamed and alarmed and defensive. "*Yes*."

"She's alright. A little off." Richard could tell they both knew Vic wasn't going to tell him what she was in for. "You eat yet?"

"In my room."

"Oh, yeah… You're on watch."

Richard sensed his newness and his history weighing him down, disabling him. "Why are you here?"

Vic twitched his patch of hair aside. Grinned. "Why am I *not* here?"

Wah wah wah wah wah.

"So," Vic said, "you really OD'd?"

Yes.

"What'd you take?"

"Quaaludes."

A pause for the user's mind to calculate.

"Where'd you get them?"

"I got them. I worked in a foundry, straight out of high school, quit a few months ago. It was third shift, nobody cared, you could get anything you wanted. *Everybody* was on *something*. Guys shot up in the bathroom during their breaks." Not that he'd ever done it; but he saw his rating go higher in Vic's mind.

"Could you get more?"

He shrugged. "If I wanted."

"Well," Vic said, "if you ever need help." He patted his front jeans pocket.

What the fuck, what did Louis tell him?

"Just in case," Vic said and pulled out a jackknife and opened the blade.

"Just in case *what*?"

"Don't be so dramatic." Vic closed the blade and slipped the knife into his pocket. "Just in case anything."

Richard was afraid to guess what Vic was in for.

"Catch you later?"

"I have testing this morning," Richard started to explain, "and this afternoon my mom's probably visiting—"

Vic crinkled his nose.


"How was your testing?"

Richard looked up from lunch to watch his roommate go to his side of the room. "Alright." He talked around his food. "The word tests were fun; so were the picture ones."

Louis seemed not to hear. "I feel great today. You know?" He stretched out on his bed, clasped hands behind head, wiggled his elbows. "How're you feeling?"

"OK." Richard already didn't want this conversation.

"Last night was great. Really great."

Richard chewed every bit of pleasant food in his mouth, deliberating over what exactly he wanted to say and how exactly he wanted to say that he wanted to move on, leave it all behind. "OK."

Louis whisked himself up. "Did you like it, too?"

"I'm glad I tried it—" Louis grinned "—but I don't think I'd do it again." Louis frowned. Richard wanted to avoid hurt feelings. "It was fine, really, you know, but I'm not that—" He stumbled as he watched his words shape his roommate's expression "—I'm not that way or anything. I mean—I don't think—I don't want to do it again, that's all, it's got nothing to do with you, I mean, I like girls, can we forget it even happened?"

Louis raised a hand in a stop sign and said in serious explanation, "It did happen. And girls don't know how to suck cock."

96

What?

"You won't forget that now, will you?" He puckered his lips, gave a dismissive smirk, collapsed on the bed, and re-clasped his hands and flippered elbows.

Jesus. He's a nut. "You didn't tell anyone, did you?"

Louis clucked his tongue at the ceiling.

"Louis, you can't tell anyone about this."

He lifted himself onto an elbow. "Listen—"

The phone rang.

Their eyes challenged over who would get it.

It rang again.

Richard jumped out of his chair and Louis grabbed the receiver. "Hello?—Yes.—Why yes he is. Let me get him for you." Louis hoisted the receiver and turned an amusing now-who-would-I-tell? grin. "A *Father* Walker would like to speak with one *Richie—Issych.*" Louis mispronounced the last name as "eyes itch".

"It's Issych," he said. Same as the boy from a page in catechism who was perpetually being sacrificed to God by his own father but for the saving hand of an angel.

He took the receiver from Louis. "Yes, this is Richard Issych."

"Oh." The deep male voice was sorry. "Richard. Issych. Yes, yes, of course. This is Father Walker." He hesitated as though he were lifting the latch on the cage of an animal he hoped would be tame. "How are you feeling?"

Caged. No one except other patients spoke normally to him. Every word jerked out as he waved Louis away, "I'm, feeling, alright," and Louis mimed dumb all the way out the door. "How are you?"

"I'm fine, Richard. Fine. Thank you for asking. I'm calling because I hear you wanted to talk with me."

Richard fingered his plastic fork. "I guess." He'd never said he wanted to talk to anyone. "I mean, my mom called you, right? She's worried about me so I said I'd talk with someone." He scraped a tine under his nail until he got blood.

"It may help to talk, Richard. The confessional is based on that principle. But it's entirely up to you."

"Really?" Richard didn't intend to give voice to his disbelief.

"Really," the voice echoed gravely. "Hold on."

Hold on to what?

The line clunked, shuffling sounds, papers flipping. "I could come by Sunday afternoon, about two o'clock."

How did it come to this?

"Would you take communion? It would be private, of course, in your room."

Kneel here. "I haven't been to mass in a long time, Father."

"I see."

Now I see.

How could this end?

"I'll see you Sunday, Father."

"Yes, Richard. I'll see you then."

Richard hung up the phone, thinking of Father in the classroom.

"Hey, Issych, lookit *you*," one of his friends in class had laughed and pointed at the bound and helpless shepherd boy. "And lookit that *knife*."

The lesson of sacrifice was one of the first, and Father Walker drilled his faith and fear into the nun's surrendered classroom. "This boy," he had quietly roared, "was an immolation to God."

Not a child stirred. The room was an airless tomb.

"A sacrifice was required, and it could only be blood. Blood makes everything new. Blood washes everything clean, makes all things new again."

No one breathed.

"Will you be an immolation for God?" he asked around the room while stabbing the air with an invisible knife, and Richard imagined that boy's warm tissue receiving the thin unfeeling steel.

In every class thereafter they turned pages past that one, but Richard had to pause—transfixed on that picture, the father's arm raised in obedience to God, the son readying to be slain, and the awful, fearsome robed angel staying the downward thrust of the long, serpentine blade—and wonder about his own father and what Abraham would have accomplished without that angel.

"Thanks for the pillow, Mom."

She would know what he'd done. Dirty boy.

She couldn't know, she was an orange-tagged VISITOR. He expected her to know, to smell it on him, see it on him, in him. She was his mother and he was transparent. Did she put cock in her mouth, too? He thought himself clever for thinking something so perverse about his mother that she could not know and that she could not do anything about, then he thought he should be banished from the human race for such monstrous thoughts.

They pecked cheeks.

"You're welcome, Richie." She patted him and the pillow. "I hope it helps."

"Where's Dad?"

"He couldn't make it, Richie. He's on again. It's his schedule. You know that."

"It's OK." Lies were easy.

They both sat in yesterday's chairs.

"How did you sleep?"

"Alright," if like hell was alright. He hugged his pillow. He didn't expect it to help him sleep, just remind him of the familiar.

"Are you getting to know people?"

Kneel here. "Some. Some you don't want to know."

"What's wrong with them?" It was profane meddling, and he re-saw her storming at him across a playground. *What's wrong with you?*

I'm afraid.

Why aren't you playing with the other children?

They're laughing at me.

The other mothers think you're some kind of *retard* sitting over here by yourself. *Get over there with the other kids.*

Don't make me, Mommy. Don't laugh at me Dickie Dickie Dickie glasses don't look at me

Get over there with the other kids right now. If I have to come over here to tell you again so help me God—

She had kicked grass all the way back to the bench with the other smoking mothers.

"Everyone's in for something different."

"And your roommate? How are you getting along with him?"

Women don't know how to suck cock and slowly, slowly, Richard ground the pillow in his fists. He thought she could read his mind. Maybe she wore x-ray glasses, seeing right through everything. He thought of last night and looked a moment directly into her eyes. No. No. It was not true. She could not see inside his head. "Fine."

"You got a letter from the college."

Really?

"To confirm that you withdrew from your classes this semester."

Oh that.

"Richie."

Why did you open my mail?

"Why did you withdraw from classes?"

His new home was his answer. "I didn't go to school the last month or two."

Her eyes bugged. "Didn't go to school? What did you do all day when you left the house? Where did you go?"

"Around. I went to the park, the beach, played video games at the mall, drove around in my car." Anything to remove my mind from my impending death.

She didn't want to hear about how she knew nothing of his real life: "What did you do today?"

"I had testing all morning."

"Oh, how did that go? What did they do?"

"A bunch of word tests, questions, pictures to match up, that sort of thing. There's more tomorrow."

"That sounds interesting." His mother addressed a certain space beyond his left ear. "And you started medication?"

"Last night."

"Well they certainly seem to know what they're doing around here." His mother looked like she expected the walls to sprout hands. "Has Father Walker called you yet? He did? Well, good. What did he say?"

"He said he could visit Sunday after mass."

"Not until Sunday?" His mother started one of her monologues, this time about how come Father had to wait until Sunday to visit, this wasn't a broken leg, she thought in this case he should make a special visit to Richard,

who floated,

detached,

miles below the peaceful surface above, watching her mouth move, missing his kid brother and their night talks in their rooms and thinking about what he was doing right now, what they had told him, if they had told him anything. "How's Alan?"

"Oh." His mother stopped, changed directions. "You know Alan. Can't wait for the end of school. He starts Little League next week already. He wants to be first baseman this year. Like you were."

"What did you tell him?" Richard didn't want him to know. Of anyone in the world he didn't want to know what he'd done—

"What did I tell him?"

"About this. About where I am. Didn't he ask about where I went, where I've been all week?"

"Well yes, Richie, of course he asked about you... but he's just a child."

"You didn't tell him I was here, did you?"

"Oh no, oh no, we didn't tell him *this*. Thank God he was over a friend's house when the ambulance came." She did not look at him as she said, "We told him you went away to a camp."

"A camp?" I cut them off.

"A camp, Richie. Yes. We told him you were tired and needed to rest, you'd be here for a while, and he couldn't visit because it's very far away."

The same lie about their dog going to a farm. "A camp."

"Yes, a *camp*, Richie." Anger and frustration pinched her voice. "We told him you needed to get a rest. That's all. This isn't easy for us, you know. Nobody is helping *us*. We didn't know *what* we should tell him. We didn't know how long you'd be here; he looks up to you, Richie." The corners of her mouth twisted down.

"Did you tell Jim? What did he say?" Richard did and did not want to know. Though he didn't agree with his older brother on so many areas of life, he respected him because, well, because he was his older brother and he'd been alive three years longer.

"He wants to talk with you. He says he'll call you tomorrow. At 11, our time."

Richard dreaded talking to his brother more than his father, because the one would engage him and the other would ignore him. "Who else did you tell? You didn't tell Grandma and Grandpa?"

"Oh heavens no, this would kill my parents. They don't need to know this. *Death* they could understand. But *this*." She waved a hand in definition.

So that was his shame: being alive. Dead, he would have been a memory, explainable and malleable; alive, he was their unsolvable problem. "Who else did you tell? Did you tell the neighbors?"

She shook her head.

"You didn't tell any of my friends, did you?"

"Like who?" She said it like he didn't have any friends. "Richie, you've got to understand. This is hard on everybody."

"Who did you tell?"

"Keep your voice down. Do you want everyone to hear?" Her eyes darted. "I told my family: my sisters and brother, that's all. And the girls in my book club—"

*Hyenas!*

"*Richie*, you've got to understand. I need support through this, too. You're getting the help you need here—"

In his head a scream bulleted and in its wake he screamed NO I'M NOT.

"Can you think about someone else for a change?"

There's no one in here but me!

"How do you think I feel, your father feels—"

I don't know, I'm not you.

"Do you think you're the only one who's hurting?"

I think I'm the only one who's in this hospital, and the doctor smiled compression fractures of the spine, shattered teeth, his teeth hurt now, like chewing chocolate cement ice cream.

"How do you think I felt," she said tearfully, "when I found you lying there—"

Awful.

"And now you're here."

Her tears obliged him to penance.

He had never intended to do this to her. He pitied her, now that he saw what she said he'd done to her.

After she left he stayed in his chair, mind wandering around why he was here, how he got from "there" to "here", he wanted to go away so they wouldn't be embarrassed by him, they're yelling, his glasses, depression, the lights during the ambulance ride poking into his eye, and before that

the time he enjoyed most was at the lake, sitting under a tree staring out at the horizon and letting his thoughts drift across all that water, all his life, what he'd done, how he'd lived, and what people would do once he was gone. It took him several months to break through a wall of sadness and self-pity to a sense of grand wonderment for life and a peaceful acceptance that he could not be part of it, had to end it. He thought of it as a gift he was not worthy to receive. Like communion. I am not worthy, make me worthy, Father, father, say a word, show me you are real, make me real. But there was nothing. So he had to give it back. In the final weeks before his suicide attempt all of his senses sharpened. Water tasted different, looked different, felt different on his skin. When had it been so silvery and shiny? He would linger in the shower, at the sink, touching, taking it all in. On the beach he'd sit and watch the surf burble up to his toes. Every grain of sand was a planet, and he was a god. He stood in the middle of a vast sense of relief and pride that he had made the most momentous decision of his life—*not* to live—on his own, and he'd settled on everything—where, when, how—

He did not want to arouse suspicion in anyone so he carried on with everything because he believed it was the right thing to do, to keep anyone from being upset with him and his decision. When he would think of each person in his family and how his death would affect that one—his mom, dad, Alan, Jim—he would grieve over that person and he would weep and rock uncontrollably—

In the fish tank lounge he found Louis, who'd dragged one of the heavy wooden chairs next to a window to prop up knees as support for his sketch pad. Richard thought he'd be funny. "Are you supposed to be doing that?"

With his pencil Louis continued flicking birds to life above his lake. "What are they going to do? Kick me out?" He hesitated. "I'm leaving in two days."

The floor of Richard's world dropped. "But I just got here!"

Louis smirked and hovered his pencil over the water.

"When did you find out?"

"This afternoon." He motioned for Richard to pull up a chair, but he couldn't sit. "This is what happens. People come, people go. You'll be OK. Don't let them push you around." He patted Richard's knee and giggled, and Richard was certain he'd heard that giggle before, certain he never wanted to be touched like that again. His father was right.

"When do you leave?"

"Friday morning."

*"Friday morning?"*

"Don't worry. You'll do fine." Louis seemed pleased that he could offer comfort to someone in distress over his departure.

"Two days," Richard muttered.

"That reminds me: I need to call my sister to let her know she has to pick me up. She hates it when I drop things in her lap at the last minute, but what are little brothers for?" He giggled again, and Richard wanted him to leave.

The pencil sped life onto the paper.

"I think," Richard said, "I'll go for a walk." For a while, though, he stood intrigued, watching Louis touch up jaws of waves readying to bite the beach and tracked his gaze out the window across the lawn stretching to the chain link fence marking the boundary at the cliff and beyond that the cut of blue-gray water.

"Pretty view, isn't it?"

Yes.

"Do you want to try? You seem interested."

"No, no." He didn't think he could ever make lines on a page come to life.

"Here," Louis said, tearing out a blank sheet of paper at the back of the pad, "take this," handed Richard the empty page over his shoulder, "and this," thrust a pencil at him, "and go over there." Richard followed the pointing finger, traipsed into the TV lounge where two high school kids played cards and Pear Man did a puzzle. He chose a half apple chair and smoothed the thick paper over his lap, used one leg to form a surface on which to apply the pencil, then without any plan drew the outline of a man. If he had a box of crayons, a million crayons, he wouldn't know which one to use. He X'd out the man and turned the sheet over and drew lines. Four lines. A small box. Four more lines beside it, an identical box. Inside the boxes he drew circles into tight balls, curved a nose bridge, fitted the earpieces onto the frames, around the ears, added a nose, he wanted a nose, to hold everything up. His new glasses. His new glasses inside his head.

He stopped to view what he'd done. He'd seen his kid brother do better in school projects. Underneath the face he wrote:

*See Dick.*

That was him, there was no denying it.

*See Dick in his box.*

He kept going.

*See Dick not see in his box.*

Richard X'd out the eyepieces.

*See Dick not see.*

He ruminated.

*See Dick die.*

He was tired of it, and no drawings of the facility or residents were allowed. He was folding the paper when Vic approached.

"You play checkers?"

Checkers?

"Checkers. Checkers. The game." He twitched the eye hair patch away. "C'mon. It kills time." Vic spread his arms and laughed. "What else you doing?"

"Sure."

"What's that? You make something?"

"No, no." He quartered the paper and pocketed it. "Get the game. I can't go down the hall."

As they set the game between them Richard wanted to know where he stood. "So how old are you?"

"Seventeen," Vic declared with charm and challenge.

Huh. He could be his younger brother; he'd always wanted a younger brother closer to his own age. Someone to do stuff with, talk life over, figure things out with together.

Vic addressed the pieces as he slid them into place. "You?"

"Nineteen. Twenty in two months." He let that sink in. It might or might not count for anything with Vic. Richard wasn't sure if he could take him, he hadn't been in a real fight since sixth grade, but sometimes age counted. "How long you been here?"

"Two weeks. More or less. In," his eyes flashed, "out."

"Why are you here?"

"Everything. Remember?"

Oh yeah. Smart-ass. "What did you do outside?"

"You ask a lot of questions."

How else would he find out? "Can you really go out?"

"Can you really get more stuff?"

Stuff?

Out? Vic returned.

So.

Richard noticed, "There's not enough pieces." He was short three reds.

Vic wasn't even listening.

"There's not enough pieces."

"So what? Use coins."

He was helpless, coinless. "It doesn't look right."

Vic sighed, stretched back, hand in pocket, and Richard half expected to see the knife come out. What Vic produced was a handful of change, picked three pennies and tapped them into place, used two quarters for his own missing pieces.

"Where do you keep it?"

"My change? In my pocket, Dummy."

"You know what I mean."

Vic looked at him, seriously. "In my pocket. All the time." He started setting up the coins.

"How come you get quarters?"

"Pennies are red. You're red."

Oh.

Vic asked, "Do you know how long you'll be in?"

Richard did not know.

"Suicides are usually the longest. Could be a month or more, depending."

A month, or more. Depending. Jesus.

"That's a long time in this place."

Richard couldn't think about it.

"You'll be climbing the walls, probably want to leave some afternoon."

Richard didn't want to think about it.

A nurse led Joey out of the hallway by the nurses' station, positioned him at one end of the wall, and shuffled him round to face the other open end of the wall. He hunched forward, a runner for his mark.

"What's his story?"

Vic roused himself. "Hmm?"

"Joey."

"Wah wah wah wah wah." Corner of small hall, turn. "Wah wah wah wah wah." Five steps, wall, turn. Satisfied that what she had set in motion would continue, she left.

"I heard he's some retard they dumped here. Or he's had too much ECT. Fried his brain."

"They wouldn't do that to him."

Vic twitched his eye hair patch. "Man, you have got to wise up. Elec-tro-con-vul-sive therapy. Shock treatment. If they run out of meds to try on you, they zap you." He illustrated, gripping a finger between clenched teeth, stiffening the length of his body in the chair, convulsing.

"That's funny. Yeah. That's real funny."

Vic kept at it.

"That's real good."

Vic stopped. "You should try it sometime. It clears your head."

"They're never going to do that to me."

Vic didn't respond.

"I won't let them." He was speaking to no one.

Vic started to say something, stopped, glanced around and outside at the trees and grass and lake horizon, spoke gentle agreement, "OK."

Close to dinnertime Susie scurried to their table.

"Lookit what Louis gave me." She beamed, holding an artist's pad of drawing pages. "And these." A few colored pencils clutched in her fist, clunking bones, an unbending rainbow. "Aren't they cool? He said he's leaving and wanted me to have these. Isn't that cool? Don't you think Louis is so neat? I think I'll miss him most of all. Aren't you going to miss him?"

Richard fought a grimace and dampened a plea to Vic to say or do something to this hovering girl, but Vic remained concentrating on the board between them, twitching his eye hair patch away and digging his knuckles into his pocket, when suddenly his response came mechanically, irritably, as of a weary father to an over-energized child at the end of a too long day: "Go color."

Susie opened and closed her mouth silently, trying to draw Richard's gaze, but he would not take his eye away from the game board, he hated moments like these, when circumstances colluded to force him to make a decision, and when he did nothing he saw her head snapping from Vic to him and from him to Vic, she was fumbling with what to say and who to say it to, until finally she let out a squeak and stomped off.

Richard let her round the hallway before asking. "Why are you so mean to her?"

Vic lifted his showing eye from the board. His fingers were stroking his pocket, and at the end of a long, low whistle said, "It's a long story."

"I think I have time."

Before five o'clock a nurse bent over their game, her white jacket forming a V like praying hands opening, displaying a brilliantly white t-shirt stretching across two captured globes. "I hate to break up your marathon session guys, but it's time to eat." With Richard she used the idiot-baby voice: "There's meatloaf and mashed potatoes and gravy with green beans, and cherry pie."

He loved cherries, tearing tight skin to the sweet red-black juicy meat. He considered himself a cherry connoisseur, once sitting with a new-bought box of cherries he got for break time from his stock job at the grocery store during high school and eating until his fingers were stained bloody, and for all that indulgence suffered the shits that entire night.

"And ice cream with dessert. Chocolate or vanilla?"

He struggled to maintain eye contact. Did she enjoy teasing him? "Vanilla."

"Great. Where did you want to eat? You could eat out here."

"Yes," Vic said, "you could eat out her."

Something buzzed around her ear.

"My room," Richard said. "I'll finish this up and have dinner in my room."

"Great," she said to him and was off.

They watched her all the way before exchanging leers.

"Don't even say it."

"Pie."

"Didn't I say, 'Don't even say it'?"

"She's one of the nicer ones."

"What is wrong with you?"

They set about dismantling the game, and Vic mimicked, "But really, what do you want for dessert?"

Richard held his pieces, waited for another line to drop.

"Not her, Dummy. I mean the ice cream."

What now?

"Don't eat the ice cream."

"Why not? It's the only thing that's really good here."

"You think they don't do that on purpose? It's the only thing that tastes good because they want you to eat it."

"So?"

"They put saltpeter in the ice cream."

"What?"

"Saltpeter. You never heard of saltpeter?"

His brother had told him about it.

"It's what the Army uses to control your sex drive."

"I know that. My brother's in the Army."

"So you know. So why sit there like a dummy? They use it here, in the ice cream. C'mon, we're locked up together, men and women, they don't want us going around screwing our brains out, knocking everyone up. Why do you think they let you have second helpings of ice cream but nothing else?"

"I hadn't thought about it."

"Well think about it."

His brother used to joke about it. "How could they do that here? They wouldn't be allowed to do that here."

To the checkers Vic restated the unbelievable claim: "They wouldn't, be allowed, to do that, here." He clunked the checkers in stacked place.

The nurse adjusted the tray on his desk. "I had them give you two servings of ice cream, same as last night. Extra special."

Richard sat eyeing the two rounds of vanilla ice cream with new wonder and comprehension, as if they were bare breasts, full of mysteies and invitations. He thanked the nurse and after she left went about methodically eating every bite of the plain meal while staring at the two lumps dissolving. His plate clean, he picked up the plastic spoon and dug in. The pie was good. The ice cream was very creamy, very vanilla, better than anything he'd tasted yet, morning, noon, or night. Two scoops and not one was a treat, not a threat. He savored spoonfuls, gobbled spoonfuls, played with the melting flavor on his tongue. If Vic were right, if this killed his sex drive, so what. *Good,* even. Outside, he had to masturbate once or twice or three times a day just to calm himself down and be able to get on with things. He could do without that torture for a while.

The nurse came for the tray; he stayed in his room and doodled on the page he'd already started. Around the crude face he dashed off words, phrases, anything that came to mind, not the type of writing he'd done in his notebook—to leave proof he'd been here. This was more mind doodling. Time passed. He was content. A nurse came for him at medication time.

In line someone rushed up behind, perfume fogging.

"Have you been hiding from me?"

Richard folded his arms across his chest and turned.

"You're so tall." A shiny red silk scarf pulled her yellow spirals tight from her face, all eagerness and awe.

"That's me." So tired and so tall.

"Do you like red?"

Red was his favorite color.

One hand with slender fingers and red tips lighted on his shoulder as she breathed up a whisper of chocolate breath, "I'm wearing red panties."

His spine shuddered.

"Want to see?"

She was serious.

He did not know what to do with what she said. Was she coming on to him? was she out of her mind? did it matter?

"How about tomorrow during lunch? Everyone'll be in the cafeteria. Sit by that table by the snack room." She dabbed a painted nail at the table where he'd confessed everything to Red his first night in, ages ago. "I'll give you a signal."

A signal?

"A signal. Use your imagination. A *signal.* I don't know. You'll know it when you hear it." She tickled his ribs.

He wrenched away. She tried again but he grabbed her wrist.

"Mmm. Strong, too."

He let go and stepped closer to the medicine door.

"Let me guess." She was rubbing her wrist. "I'm too short? You're too tall? You're too young? I'm too old?"

I'm too ugly.

"Would it make you feel better if you knew?"

Why not?

She said a number that might make her his mom.

He straightened himself, surprised and not surprised.

She pointed him forward. "You're up."

He shuffled to the wide red band painted across the floor. Red was his favorite color.

The nurse bid him forward. Same as last night: three blue pills and a cup of water. Immediately after the nurse outside the half door chirped, "Open up."

He did not understand and searched the other nurses' faces for meaning.

"Say Ahhhh," the one outside the half door twittered. "Let me see inside."

He understood—and was outraged—hesitated, exposed in front of the remaining line, in an instant saw one or two whitecoats around the lounges, recognized there would be no *not* doing this thing for them, and so relinquished, opening his mouth and tipping his head for her to peer inside his cavity.

"Squat down a little, please, you're too tall. Lift your tongue. Hiiiiigheeeeer." She was a bird, angling its head this way and that. "Ahhhh."

"Ahhhh," he repeated.

"Other side."

Jesus. He stretched his tongue.

"Hiiiiigheeeeer. Let me see."

Screeee?

"Alright." She wasn't singing anymore. "You can go."

He shut his mouth. Fucking humiliating. Inspecting him like cattle. That's what they did with their dog at home to make sure it swallowed its pills when it was sick. And stroked its throat. Good boy.

Sandy swallowed with no problems. Away from the crowd she tried to cheer him. "Don't sulk. They do it to everybody, sooner or later."

Right. Like the room searches. "It's fucking humiliating." He wanted to vomit his pills onto the floor at the feet of the nurses and triumph at them: There, there, *there's* your proof!

She rolled her eyes. "It's their job." Tipped a glance at the snack room. "Buy me a drink?"

She was frightening him. "I think I'll go lie down. I'm kind of tired."

"Right," she said, meaning "not right."

At least he got to watch her wiggle away.

"Checkers?"

What?

"Man, is there anybody in there?! Just nod if you can hear me. I said: wanna play checkers?"

No.

"Whatsa matter?"

What's the matter? What's the matter? "See what they're doing to The Nosepicker?" They were checking his mouth.

"Yeah. So?"

"So they just did that to me. It's fucking humiliating." Richard wanted to punch something. But he was pleased with his phrasing: fucking humiliating.

"Don't be so dramatic. You're in a mental hospital."

Really?

"Don't take what they give you."

Really.

"Jesus Christ, are you that dumb? Put the pills between your cheek and gum and spit them out in your room. If they catch you, swallow them, then go to your room and put your fingers down your throat in the toilet. Just be quiet about it." Richard wasn't sure he did not want to take his pills that bad and felt he glimpsed one of the everythings that Vic was in for.

"You can get away with murder, if you're quiet about it."

"I thought you were different."

Susie rose above his doodling.

"I thought we could be friends, you know?"

She plopped in the chair next to his.

"But friends stick up for each other."

Who are you?

"They don't sit there if someone's in trouble," and after that he tried shutting out about how upset she was all afternoon because she thought she was over Vic already and ready to move on, but when he says things that hurt her she gets so upset still, I know I shouldn't, I know I should ignore him, but sometimes all these old feelings come back and it makes it even harder to ignore him, that's what my therapist tells me I should do, but it's not so easy to do all the time and are you even listening to me, are you, are you listening?

The black windows created a starred altar.

"Checkers?"

Richard shook his head.

Vic sat anyway. "So. You saw someone get shot?"

Jesus that got around fast. "No. I saw someone *drown*. I knew a guy who shot another guy. That foundry I told you about? I worked with them there."

"A drug deal?" It was too eager and too innocent.

Richard shook his head. "No. They were fighting over a girl. Now one's dead and the other's in jail."

"Oh," Vic said. "You saw someone *drown*?"

Getting ready for bed, Richard and Louis exchanged few words, and what they tried was clumsy and tired, so that Richard imagined this was how his parents and other married people behaved in their bedroom at night with so many years between them: an exclusive indifference nurtured by man and woman together too long, passing phrases, eyes bowed, followed by stillness in the growing dark as each hoped for sleep to ease their descent into a dreamless void.

"How have you been?"

"OK."

"Have you thought about what we talked about?"

You mean what *you* talked about?

"Seeing things differently, thinking about things differently."

Oh that.

The doctor waited.

Too long.

"Yeah."

The doctor said, "Yeah?"

Fuck. "Yeah. I can see your point, but these glasses aren't on my face, they're in my brain." How are you going to fix that when you don't even know what you're doing?

The doctor said, "Yes, that's where the medication should start to help." He crossed his legs, one dangling over the other.

Like a girl.

"You had a visit from your mother."

You know this already.

"And how is she doing?"

"OK."

"And your father?"

Richard knew he knew that, too. "He didn't come. He was busy."

"Oh, what does he do?"

You know this already. "He's a fireman."

"Ohh. He must have some stories to tell about that."

If you say so. "Everyone thinks they're so great. They're not superheroes; they're just people."

"They do good work," the doctor measured out. "They help save people's lives and property."

"And rescue cats in trees?"

The doctor looked sardonic.

"I'm being facetious. Sorry."

"They do important work."

"In children's books?" Sorry.

"What do you mean by that?"

What did he mean by that. "Sometimes, it doesn't matter who you are, you can't save someone."

The doctor's expression challenged him.

OK, OK, if you really want to know, he hadn't told this story to anyone in years, about the kid drowning, watching him drown, watching one bubble break the black surface in the cracked ice hole. He told the doctor about the sledding trip, one of the only times he remembered his father taking them anywhere without their mother. "We went to a golf course, the one in Wickliffe, on Ridge Road. You know that one? It has this *huge* hill off the first tee and a pond at the bottom of it. It's great for sledding. So anyway, he takes me and Jim, Alan was too little to go so he stayed home, and we're sledding, having a great time, it's 20 degrees out, there's a foot of packed snow on the ground, when I hear this kid screaming—screaming at us from the bottom of the hill next to the pond." Screaming and sitting down crying in the snow. "I told my brother and some of the other kids, and dad—he was the only adult there—so we go over to this kid, about our age, 10 or 12, and he's bawling, he's soaking wet, completely *drenched* in winter clothes, and cries how he and his friend tried to cross the frozen pond and his friend fell through the ice and couldn't get out but he did. All of us look over at the pond and the hole in the ice. Two sets of foot prints went onto the ice from the other side, one set of prints came out on our side"; the snow documented a struggle out of the hole and to the bank. His eyes found his brother's, and they read each other's thoughts: Dad's a fireman, he'll know what to do, he'll save him.

"What did you do?"

What did they do?

What *could* they do?

"We watched him drown." He told about his father ordering some of the older boys around, go to a house, tell them what happened, get the cops, get an ambulance, bring some blankets. He was the only adult there. "I think partly it was for show. All we did was watch, just watch. And that's all he did, too. I was waiting" —expecting— "hoping he'd dive in, I wanted him to jump in, rescue this kid," because that's what my dad did. That's what he did. "I thought he could do it, should do it. He told us to stay back, though, don't fall in, our wet clothes would drag us down, too, and we couldn't fight the cold." Then would he save any of us?

Would he save my brother?

Me?

He kept secret about watching his father surveying the situation, reading the calculation and anguish in his face, his eyes.

Jump in, Dad! Save him!

*NO! You'll drown!*

"My father wasn't going in to save him, I could see that. I despised him for it. I wanted to jump in to save that kid myself, but I was afraid of drowning, too," being down there with that dead boy.

He kept secret about wanting to hold his father's hand, *Don't leave me, Dad*, but all the boys crowded him. "So I stood along the edge, watching with everyone else," unbelieving what the unmoving surface of the black hole in the punctured ice hid beneath. Breathing clouds. Waiting. Expecting the kid to come screaming up from the hole howling for air. But as time stretched in the stillness, feeling the numbing creep of the cold in his toes and of the group knowledge that the boy was dying at the bottom of the black pond, wondering what he was feeling, what was going through his mind at the bottom of the pond, if he could see them on the other side looking down at him and the fish—were they woken from sleep by the boy's sinking body? "For the longest time we stood there, watching. Nothing happened. Then." My God. "This big bubble, one bubble, broke the surface—*blooorp*," and ever since that time the scene was a splinter in his psyche, how he died, was it close to falling asleep, did he know he was dying? Nobody tried to save him. He must have known that, down there in the cold dark water.

"What happened?"

He told the doctor about the ambulance, the cops, how they said his father, all of them, did the right thing by not jumping in to try to rescue the boy, any of them would've drowned, trying to save him. But part of him thought that was bullshit; the pond was only 20 feet deep; his father could have done it; should have done it. But, what if he couldn't, what if his father was *unable* to save him? "The divers—" in their wet suits like oily seals "—pulled him out," gray and stiff, and his face—my God, they had us stay far back but not far back enough—between the rescuers there flashed a vision of the boy's face, what you see in nightmares, a wild- and wide-eyed frozen scream, full of fury and questions. His arms were lifted up expecting help from the surface. "They had to push his arms down to get the blanket around him."

"That must have been upsetting."

"*Upsetting?*" Idiot. Even at eight he had realized that he had seen what should never be seen: the look of a child's face understanding death coming. In that boy's face he saw what it was, and he didn't want it for him. He wanted to control death, his own death, when, how, where. He vowed pondside it would never take him like that, by such surprise and horror, he'd make sure of it. He wanted to be like God, God for himself.

"Do you know what my father said?" One clipped laugh was all that was in him now. "This is how goofy he is: He said to the cop, 'It's no way to go, but he got to sleep, at least. Fire would be worse. You're awake the whole time, feeling it eat you.' That's what he said to the cop. And the cop looked at him like, yeah, just like that."

His eyes lazied along the photographs on the wall over the doctor's head as he caught phrases—I'm sure your father—under the conditions—tragic accident. In one of the frames opposite he was able to line up his eyes' reflection with the birds'. At home his father had a framed newspaper clipping: "Frozen Hero. Unidentified fireman carries Jessica Stezelwalski, 8, from her burning home, background." The girl had been his age at the time. His father, fixed, dark, and hulking in the fireman's suit and hugging to his chest a girl in her pajamas, filled the picture. His helmet dripped tiny ice spikes, head tilted to the winter sky, mouth opened slightly, water trickled down his face, and his eyes in the picture weren't eyes at all but two burnt holes below a helmet. Beyond his shoulders the house burned black and white flames, stationary.

Richard remembered touching his fingers to the cool glass and tracing his fingertips down the motionless streams on his father's face, how scared he was of his father after he had first seen the picture in the newspaper, so that all he could do was point to it and say, "Daddy, why are you crying?" His father, lifting the paper out of his hands, said, "I wasn't crying," slowly, "that's snow melting on my face from the heat of the fire." He watched his father clip the picture with care, glue it smooth onto cardboard, stick it in an old frame, hang it on the wall by the front door, and for a few weeks it stayed there, and every day before leaving for school Richard would pass by and think of his father, busy at the fire station, "on" as his parents would say, frozen in the picture, "unidentified"—he had to ask his mother what that meant. She said anonymous, and he had to go look those words up in the family dictionary. He was so taken by the picture that once he took his glasses off and pressed his nose to the glass, just to see how the picture dissolved, leaving dots, innumerable white and black dots, spread over white and black splotches. He pulled away, the dots disappeared, and all the grays shaded into objects between the white and black spaces. In the entire picture his father's eyes where the tiniest, blackest holes, empty and distant. One day when his father was on he watched his mother take the picture down and put it away in their bedroom closet. She moved with all the care and deliberation of Father Walker at his alter. In the kitchen, at the counter staring out into the backyard, she spoke: "Your father saved that little girl's life." Richard never saw the picture again, and his father never talked about it, but whenever he thought of his father he had that terrible image in his mind, something he liked.

"See something you like?" The doctor was speaking to him. "It's one of my hobbies. Shooting birds. *Photography*. Do you have any hobbies?"

Richard wasn't listening, only noticing the different birds and thinking how his cat had pawed at bird shadows on the white window shade, expecting them to be the real thing. "Penguins don't fly."

"What?"

"The penguin. On your wall there. Penguins don't fly. All the other birds on your wall can fly, except that one. Penguins don't fly."

The doctor appraised his photographs. "That particular photograph I shot at the Cleveland Zoo, on one of our field trips. I never meant this to be a collection of birds that could *fly*. It's a collection of photographs." Irritated: "A *hobby*."

Richard must have thought too long.

"Things you enjoy doing in your free time."

# There are reasons

"I know what the word means."

The doctor ignored him. "What sort of things do you enjoy?"

Nothing. Masturbating. That soothed most every day and night. Getting high. Watching people. Writing. "Reading, listening to music, puzzles. I forgot how much I liked doing puzzles until I did some as part of the test this morning."

"Yes, how did that go for you?"

Richard couldn't think of anything to say in response but "Fine" and suspected that it would not be enough.

Screeeee?

He added: "Some parts I liked more than others. That match test, the time puzzle. That was pretty cool. Where you match the pictures up in the order they're supposed to happen? It was like a jigsaw puzzle. I liked that one."

"You like jigsaw puzzles?"

He had to think. "My mom said I loved them when I was a kid, would do the same ones over and over, faster and faster. Tear them up then do them right over. My kindergarten teacher said she'd never seen anyone do one so fast."

"Your teacher told you that?"

"My mom told me that. I don't remember." He didn't remember most of his childhood, just scattered scenes. One thing he could recall was when he'd gone nuts tearing through the house in search of the last missing piece to a 500-piece puzzle only to have his mother produce it from the green goo in his baby brother's diaper. She rinsed it off and told him, "Here, take it, it's fine," but he gagged, refused to touch it, and that was it for him and jigsaw puzzles.

"What else?"

What else what? "I got bored near the end, today. I mean, all those complete-the-end-of-the-sentence questions. You know, 'Jane went to the store so Dick could stay home to *blank*.' I was getting kind of goofy at the end. Filling them in with weird things. I mean: the words. Don't take them too seriously."

122

The doctor looked like he was taking everything too seriously.

"You mentioned you enjoy reading. Who are your favorite authors?"

More testing? He could play along. He sort of enjoyed the interviewing. In school he preferred a few above all. "D.H. Lawrence, Flannery O'Connor, Conrad, some Joyce, a little Camus."

The doctor grinned camaraderie. "Camus is best taken a little at a time."

Richard blinked.

The doctor cleared his throat. "You're allowed to bring your books in, if you want. There's also a stereo system in one of the common rooms. Patients listen to their albums there."

"I know. Vic told me about it."

"Vic?"

"Vic. The kid with the eye hair patch." Richard imitated.

"Yes—So—Victor told you about that? What else did he tell you about?"

Don't eat the ice cream. People are embarrassed by you. You could go out, if you really wanted to. You can get away with "Not much." Not enough. "You know, this and that." Richard looked at the owl.

"How are you sleeping?"

It didn't rain last night, so there was no screaming. His roommate understood the meaning of the word no. He shrugged.

"I'll take that as a 'Fine'?"

"Fine enough." He was feeling noncommittal, to himself and everything around him. As the doctor scribbled a note Richard started bouncing his legs. He wanted to move, to run.

"Feeling alright?"

"I've been sitting a lot lately, that's all. I'm not used to sitting so much."

The doctor returned to writing.

Richard stopped bouncing his legs. "Can I go now?"

The pen paused.

Screeeee?

"My brother's calling me as soon as the phones come on. He's stationed in West Germany. My mom told him about me being here—she said he wanted to call me. He said he'd call at 11, our time. He's pretty punctual. He's in the Army." He started bouncing his legs again, observing his reflection in the birds' eyes.

Seeeee.

The doctor jerked his wrist to expose his watch. "You have two new sessions beginning tomorrow: Group therapy and art."

"I know." He'd seen it on his schedule.

"The rooms are down the main hallway. I hope," he said solemnly, "that you'll help us help you."

So many birds.

"Is that alright with you?" The doctor seemed irritated again.

"Sure. Fine."

The doctor expelled air loudly through his nose as he wrote. "Our next meeting won't be until Monday."

Richard thought he should be more responsive to this man who thought he was trying to help him and so tried to offer up a sincere "OK."

When the phone rang he jumped. He hadn't talked to his brother since Christmas.

"Hello?" The line crackled, and Richard heard his name being called out of a storm.

"Hi, Jim," Richard answered softly. He didn't want anyone in the hallway to hear.

"Richie?" The line crackled clear.

"Hi, Jim. I'm here."

Through the storm he heard his brother, "Good, Christ, you, a, scare, Mom, Dad, there, the, going, what, hell, you."

"Jim, I can hardly hear you. I think I'm getting every other word, I don't know. I don't know what I was doing. I guess I wasn't thinking. I was really upset." These answers weren't convincing him, how could they convince his brother? So he started making things up. "School wasn't going well, you know. I was bored. I didn't like it. I didn't know what I wanted to do with life. You know—Mom and Dad." He gave up.

The line crackled.

"*Richie.* Am I hearing you?"

"Hello? I'm—"

A laugh exploded from the phone and cleared the line. "*You don't know what you wanted to do?* Jesus Christ, Richie, *nobody* knows what to do. You figure it out as you go along. You think I know what the hell I'm doing over here half the time? Or any of these jerkweeds I'm with?" The line crackled angrily. "And *Mom* and *Dad*—why do you think I'm 4,000 miles away?" He emphasized their titles in that older brother way to be interpreted as all the explanation he should need. "They are who they are, what do you expect?"

The question floored him. What *did* he expect?

"Listen, little bro, I gotta move out over here."

OK.

"You take care of yourself, Richie." He thought he heard another, milder *Jesus Christ.*

OK.

"Watch what you do with yourself. You never know what you'll do until you're away from home."

"OK."

"I'll be back this summer, Richie. Stick around, baby bro."

Richard breathed deeply to control himself and push everything down, but he was splitting at the seams. Now he remembered: It was his brother's hand he had found to hold at the side of the drowning pond.

"I love you, Richie."

No man had ever said that to him, and it left him without words.
The line went dead before he could think to say I love you, too.

He couldn't eat, suddenly wasn't hungry, hearing the sounds of
people walking and talking their way to the cafeteria for lunch.

Should he really be doing this? What was "this," anyway? She didn't
say they'd *do* anything.

No, Dummy, she told you she was wearing red panties. She wants
to play checkers.

Well, what if I don't go to her room?

Then you'd be passing up your best and first chance to get laid.

I don't know if I should do that *here*.

You had better plans?

No.

Right. Listen: she was practically throwing herself at you last night.

You think?

Sigh.

Silence.

What's wrong with you?

Shut up.

Did you like it with Louis a little too much?

What's that supposed to mean?

You know what it means.

Silence.

You did like it.

That's not the point. The point is: what do I do about Sandy?

Go see her.

To do what? Have sex?

He'd seen it and read it, of course, hundreds, *thousands*, of times in
pictures and words, seared to permanent monuments in his mind, but
as far as observing its effects—from what he had witnessed growing

up he supposed his mother considered sex as his father considered taking out the trash: a chore that demanded to be done with some regularity regardless of how one felt about it.

What the hell do you think?

Silence.

You're scared.

Silence.

You don't want to, do you?

I do. I think I do. I mean

It's alright to be scared. Let's go.

What if I get caught?

Come on. You told her you'd be there.

I did?

Sort of. Come on. See what happens.

What if...

What if what?

What if she laughs at me?

Silence.

What if she laughs at me Dickie Dickie Dickie don't look at me

It would be worse than death. It would be worse than drowning or burning.

Richard waited for a reply from another part of his head but there was only emptiness, and as that emptiness unfolded into more emptiness he found himself rising from bed and moving down the hallway to the table where he'd confessed all to Red his first night in. He sat in the same chair. Philip was at the snack room table writing again. Loathe to be the only thing in Philip's view, Richard inched his chair toward the women's wing. Two nurses were in the glass box. Joey was gone.

He waited.

Not long.

*Kunk kunk kunk*, knuckles on a door down the women's wing.

She must have been watching for him.

*Kunk kunk kunk*, more persistent.

Richard acknowledged that he had heard by waving a hand below the table.

*Kunk kunk kunk*, demanding a stronger reply.

He pretended to yawn, stretching, gripped the back of his chair and twisted to see.

Her head poked out of her doorway several rooms down on the right. A body towel tightened, but her hair wasn't wet, and that crooked finger of a grin signaled before she disappeared into her room.

His heart withered.

This was it.

He untwisted himself and strategized about how to get from here to there without being seen. He stretched again, studying the entrance to the women's wing: two large metal doors propped open *into* the hallway. That was good; there was some cover against those walls. If he could make it there he could press himself against that space, make his way down the hall against the left wall, out of sight of most of the nurses' station, then dash across the hall to her room. He could do it. Maybe.

He observed the nurses, sitting at either end of the glass box, heads bowed. Before he could make his move the one nearest him needed to move, to the other end, closer to the medicine room, away from the women's wing. He waited. Watched. Waited some more. They shuffled around in there all the time, filing things, why weren't they moving *now*?

*Kunk, kunk, kunk*, more insistent, irritated.

Richard waved under the table to stop it.

The nurses weren't moving, they just sat there, heads bowed, doing paperwork. It was driving him mad. They were waiting for him to move first.

So he would.

Keeping his eyes on them, quietly and quickly he scooted out of his chair and back-stepped to the metal doors, then flattened himself in the space made by the left door where he was hidden from most of the view of the main lounge, and out of the first patient room came two girls working fingers to keep nervous giggles in their mouths. They walked on, one of them flashing a warning smile and tra-la-la-ing, "Be careful."

He had an overwhelming urge to urinate. His heart was failing. He was weak and frightened, far from any type of sexual being that Sandy or anybody would desire. What the fuck was he doing? This was nuts. He had to get back to his chair in the lounge before the nurses discovered him missing or anyone else saw him. He wanted to see her naked.

He shimmied along the wall: a prisoner making a break for it. Across the first pair of doorways, the girls' doorway, he did a long step and went on to the next pair, listening. Someone inside was crying. The paired doorways—the furthest one to Sandy's room—was cattycorner; he could make it in a concentrated dash. The crying from inside the room continued, pitifully, almost a dying breath, and the miserable girlish whimper finished in a wheezing moan, "Nobody loves me."

Whatever excitement he carried to his rendezvous deflated there. His only goal now was to get out of the hallway without being caught. Besides, her room was closer than the lounge. He checked once at his empty table, the empty hallway, and, satisfied, pushed off the wall and found himself standing in her doorway, trembling.

The moment consumed him.

Her room was perfumed with the sweetness of the yellow-petaled flowers that bloomed in Spring outside his bedroom window at home; drapes muted the noon sun; a lace coverlet with fish net mesh adorned her dresser. On the pillows of her crisp bed propped two stuffed white rabbits with red lace ribbons tied for necklaces. Her books stacked tidily on her desk. The bathroom door eased open.

"Hello, Dick."

My name is Richard

mind unmooring

as the door swung open to reveal Sandy in only red panties

this close and alive on

hallowed ground

Her tan soaked all seven layers of skin, breasts rested like caramel apples tipped with penny-colored gum drops, and her exquisite belly curved in all soft directions to tight borders about the breadth of her precious hips surrounding the most delicately formed upside-down triangle. This hard architecture of her flesh sparked in him what men would live and fight and die for.

"Didn't I tell you they were red?"

She did. They were. Blood red. Shiny wrapping-paper-under-a-Christmas-tree red, tight like another skin red. It stopped his blood.

She purred, "Why don't you come here?"

Yes. Go there.

That's what he should do. But someone might see from the hallway and get him in trouble.

She grabbed him and pulled him in to her, all of her, so that their bodies pressed from shoulder to belly, belly to thigh. Her fingers scoured.

"Mmmmmmm."

Her hands burrowed their way into his pants.

"Mmmmmmmmmmmmm. Depression never felt so good."

He did not know.

"Let's go into the bathroom."

The phone rang—out whipped her hand—and rang and rang and rang and rang until it turned her ugly and she pounced. Stooped. Gravity scooped full cups of breast in the warm air, the same air that was so difficult to breathe.

"Hello?—Oh it's you." She responded vaguely, sat on the other side of the bed, held the receiver out to him, and for one sickening instant Richard wondered how his mother knew where to find him. "Say hello to my husband."

Richard's heart dropped out of his pants.

She retracted the receiver. "Oh yeah?—Yeah?—Who says?—I'll fuck whoever I want.—Why not?—What are *you* gonna do about it?—You're all talk, talk, talk." Her voice twisted down cruel. "You're not *man* enough.—Yeah, why don't you try.—Oh yeah? *Well fuck you, too, you rotten bastard.—Don't you hang up on me!*—Hello?—*Hello?*" She held the receiver aloft: an announcer at some great championship boxing match. "*You rotten bastard. Didn't I tell you never to hang up on me? Didn't I tell you never to hang up on me?*" What followed were screaming curses, or cursing screams, the likes of which Richard had never heard from a woman, or a man, in his life; a tirade of obscenities into what he assumed was a dead phone. Still she went on, exhausting herself, then turned to using the receiver as a hammer and the nightstand as its anvil. She would beat the rotten bastard out of the phone. At some point Richard thought this would merit the attention of the nurses. Finally she wearied of hammering the nightstand, the receiver slipped from her grip and clunked on the floor, and he viewed her anew, naked and weak, sated, her shoulder quivering and a hand shielding her face from him. Her hair drooped at her shoulders, her bronze torso curved sweetly out of the red band rimming her waist, a lip of fat protruding like out of a cupcake.

He considered taking one step toward the door when she squeaked, "Go."

Nothing he could think of to speak to her would make any sense: he left noiselessly. Out of the women's wing he darted, landing in the chair, sucking air, trying to act normal, trying to nonchalantly scan the glass box and the lounges for anyone who witnessed his return, relieved to find no one took notice, until an uneasy feeling of being watched tingled under his nerves, and in the snack room Philip wrote, head bowed.

Had he seen anything? Heard anything? Richard couldn't tell.

On cue they met eyes.

When the phone rang he jumped.

"Hello?"

"Hello, Richie. I've been calling and calling—where have you been? I was ready to phone somebody to find you—don't *do* that to me!"

"I'm right here, Mom."

"What's wrong, Richie? You sound all out of breath."

"Nothing's wrong." How did she know? "I ran to get the phone from the hallway. I heard it ringing."

She gave a flat, "Oh," which meant that even though she did not believe him she chose to pretend to so that their conversation would continue. "Well I was calling to ask if it would be alright if I didn't come in today. Alan had something come up at school, and I need to go there to straighten some things out."

"What happened? Is everything OK?"

"Oh yes, yes, everything is fine, fine. It's school. Don't you worry about it. So you're alright if I don't stop by this afternoon?"

"Yeah."

"You're sure?"

"It's OK, Mom."

"Did you want me to bring you anything else from home?"

Nothing—nothing from home—but there was so much time. "Could you bring a notebook? A new notebook?"

"A notebook?"

"I want to write."

"You want to write." His mother was his blank echo. "Write what?"

"Just words," he assured. Not another note. "Nothing fancy. Just get some thoughts out." He felt that he could let himself become enamored with the thought of keeping a journal. Not a diary. Diaries were for girls. But a journal—where he jotted random thoughts, ideas, scribbled drawings. That, he thought, he could do. Like a hobby.

"Like what you wrote in that notebook you left on your desk?"

"You *read* that?"

"Well of course I read that," his mother said. "How could I not?"

How could she not—of course—he wrote it for them to read. But after he had killed himself, not while he was alive. Death would have made it proper; his living made it rape. Words from his mind had been taken against his will. Didn't she understand that? He didn't want anyone reading his poems, his ramblings, his will. "What did you do with it?"

"Your father threw it away."

"*Threw it away?*"

"Yes, threw it away. Why would I keep that around?"

"But it was mine."

"I'll bring you another one."

That's not the point.

"So you can do it all over again."

*What?!*

She caught a breath, "Write whatever you want, I mean," and plowed ahead: "Tomorrow. Alright, Richie? Tomorrow. I'll get the same kind, one of those spiral bound ones you used in school. What color? On the cover. What color would you like?"

"Red," he heard his voice say. "I like red."




He stayed in his room for as long as he could stand it, then ventured down the hallway to the lounges, bracing himself for the sight of Sandy dashing around in her red underwear. But she wasn't there.

"Checkers?"

There was nothing better to do.

He was becoming jealous of the fish in their tank.

With the others Richard formed the line for medication and anticipated her presence maneuvering behind him. Her fingers spidered between his shoulder blades. "Miss me?"

He wiggled away.

Her hair was tightly and completely wrapped up in her red silk scarf so that the trapped spirals dangled helplessly behind. It was as if she'd stuck a gun in her mouth and pulled the trigger and all this hair blew out the back of her head.

He whispered, "Who was on the phone?"

"Oh." Her grin crooked in mock sadness, shushing him. "Nobody important."

Whispered fiercely, "Was that your *husband*?"

"Move up."

What?

"Move up."

He shuffled his feet. "You're *married*?"

She teased him with her ringless finger. "Would it matter?"

Her now-anonymous diamond bleeds.

"Anyway," she declared, "I don't wear a ring. It's so," her eyes traced a lazy circle, "*confining*."

He needed to ask. "What did he say?"

Her eyes puzzled.

"He sounded really mad."

She wouldn't look at him.

"What did he say? Was he threatening you?"

Her face strained against a response as she shook her head, and the dawning realization of who her husband had threatened crept into his chest and scraped the blood from the inside walls of his heart. Catatonically he did an about-face.

"Oh, don't worry." The voice was breathing under his ear at the base of his skull. "He's all talk, talk, talk, talk, talk."

Sometime during the night Richard woke eyes wide to see Joey, his mule face clay-like, standing in the doorway, and behind him the angel, ascending. Terrified, Richard clamped his eyes shut and huddled under the covers.

It can't be, it can't be, it can't be real.

But he's there. He's right there.

It can't be.

You'll look and he'll be gone. He'll be gone. Look now. Look. Look.

Fearfully he tunneled up from the bed covers.

Joey stood there, expressionless, raised his hand slowly in a signal to

Richard shut his eyes and buried himself under the covers.

What's he doing there?

Why weren't the nurses coming for him?

Maybe he would go away on his own.

That's it. Joey would see him asleep and lose interest and go away on his own.

Richard tried to keep absolutely still, control his breathing, deep and slow and measured. He thought he heard Joey shuffle into the room. His heart quickened. He wanted to look but his terror was immobilizing.

Go away, he screamed inside his head. Go away! Go away! *Go away!*

Joey started humming, low, at first, and faltering, perhaps unsure of his rhythm because he was in an unfamiliar space or afraid of being caught, then increasing, gradually, louder and louder—

*Jesus Christ!* He's *pacing* in here!

Wah wah wah wah wah. Pause to turn. WAH WAH WAH WAH WAH.

Why aren't they coming for him?

135

*Why aren't they making him stop?*

Beneath the covers Richard shrank into his mattress and ached to dissolve, praying for Joey to stop, *stop*, *STOP*, and that is how he must have fallen asleep because he woke the next morning to a roomful of light and Louis packing his suitcase.

The angel had returned and was watching, fixed, on the door.

Richard sat up angry that it could have happened, reached for his glasses, his depression, fucking stupid metaphor.

Louis froze with a pair of socks in his hands. "What?"

"Last night. You didn't see that? Hear that?"

The suitcase yawned; Louis arranged the socks. "Hear what?"

"*Joey.*"

Louis shrugged. "He was OK last night. No rain: no screaming." Lifted a stack of clothes out of his drawer.

No one could sleep through that. "I'm not talking about that. I'm talking about last night—when he was in *here.*"

Louis stopped again, irritated. "*Who?*"

"*Joey.*"

"Joey?"

"Yes. *Joey. Joey,*" Richard said, "was here, in our room, last night, pacing and howling," and recognized his reflected madness, finished hopelessly-idiotically-quietly, "I can't believe you slept through that" o god

"You sure about that?" He patted down his clothes. "I mean, how could he get out of his room and wander down to our room and pace around here without anyone seeing him or hearing him. I mean, come on. He can't even dress himself. You know that's crazy talk." The term patients used on each other to keep each other in line, because if someone in a mental hospital was calling your talk crazy talk...

"Oh." Richard watched his roommate pack. Oh. In Richard's skull a switch flicked: despair flooded. Louis' tone was the same as the nurse explaining Richard's own madness to him. He mumbled about not sleeping very well and managed his way to the bathroom and the comfort of a warm shower.

He was losing his mind. That was the only explanation.

Dear God, dear God, he cried in the shower, it's finally, really happening.

I'm losing my fucking mind, and this is how it feels.

Normal.

It feels normal.

Joey was there.

He wasn't there.

Then what did I see?

Maybe it's the medication.

Yes.

Maybe it's a side effect.

Yes!

Maybe they could try something different, if you're unresponsive to other forms of therapy—

Yes!

They can strap you down, Vic mocking convulsions, his finger a rubber stick to stop shattering teeth

He dropped to his knees, sobbing, warm water raining over him.

He got dressed, alone, and reviewed the day's scheduled activities: his first therapy sessions, group in the morning and art in the afternoon. The nurse brought him breakfast and asked him how he'd slept, and he probably replied too quickly, "Fine, fine," stifling the urge to scream at her, "*What the fuck is wrong with me?*" He ate, staring at the gaping mouth of Louis' suitcase. His dresser was empty but for the reconstructed dancer; the wall was clear. He ate quickly and pushed the tray away and wished he had a notebook so he could write.

When Louis ran in—"She's here!"—Richard nearly jumped out of the chair. He slammed his suitcase and snapped the locks. "Before I go I want you to have these." Sidestepped to his dresser to showcase the reconstructed dancer. "First *this*. My dancer." Correction: "My *broken* dancer." Did he suspect? "I'm not even going to lift her up. I'm afraid she'd *crumble*. But I think you'll appreciate her even in this state, and—" The more Louis talked the more Richard wanted him to leave. "*This.*" Louis switched to his suitcase and extracted from underneath—a shirt? It looked like a bowling shirt. With two hands Louis flipped it open to display. "Now this is yours." It was a bowling shirt, huge and baggy.

"What is it?"

"What does it look like?"

"It looks like a bowling shirt that could fit a whale."

"Almost." Louis checked the tag. "It's triple XL. Don't see these too often, huh? It's yours now."

He tossed it and Richard caught it. Pulled it open to see over the left breast pocket the name *Noah* stitched in red script. "Noah?"

"Noah was a large man. Had to be. All those animals to control. And bowling night, too."

"Why?"

Louis shut his suitcase and snapped the latches. "Why what?"

"Why are you giving me this?"

"What am I going to do with it? I wouldn't wear that thing to a Halloween costume party."

Richard could never tell when he was being serious or not.

"Story goes," Louis said on his way to the door, "there was a man who was a patient here a while back. Story goes he wouldn't take what they gave him. One day, Mr. Noah couldn't take it anymore. It was the food, the ice cream, the no-drawings-of-any-residents, the room searches, whatever it was, he'd had enough. From that day on, he never changed clothes. Didn't bring any more in. That shirt was the only thing he wore. And pants, we hope. Before he left he wanted his roommate to have the shirt, to pass it along, so he wouldn't give in, either. So he gave it to him. But when that roommate was getting ready to leave, he wanted *his* roommate to have it, to pass it along. So he gave it to *him*. And it's gone on like that for a few months, a year, who knows. Nobody wanted it to leave the hospital. Pass it along. Keep it going."

"Keep what going?"

"They bring her out yet?"

Pear Man did not raise an eye from his work. "She's not here." He continued connecting dots. "They took her out last night."

"They took her out last night?"

"Yes," Pear Man said, drawing his line. "Sometimes they do that."

Sometimes they do that. Sometimes they do that. If you're unresponsive. Richard switched gears: "How's the puzzle coming?"

"Good, good. See?" Pear Man shifted the book.

Richard could see a rabbit, or a dog, or a cat. "Uh huh." Added an unenthusiastic, "Keep going," but didn't know why, because he was already watching Joey at the wall, humming and pacing, humming and pacing

in his room last night

and in his peripheral vision he saw Pear Man staring.

"That's kind of big on you."

Group therapy was like a sauna: no windows, two carpeted sitting steps built into the walls around three sides, so you could sit on the bottom step and lean against the top step, or sit on the top step and lean against the wall, carpeted halfway to the ceiling, he supposed, in anticipation of someone's urge to take a stroll sideways across the walls.

The nurse let him go in the room on his own, and he identified immediately, upon crossing the threshold, the therapist. She had too-big eyes for a too-big head, and she was overpleased with her surroundings. The patients, cagey, bored, doped, sat, slumped across the steps.

Philip was alone on the lower seat near the therapist. A few of the kids and housewives lounged along the length of a step in one corner. In another corner propped against the carpeted wall on the top step stretched a man, about 30, in jeans and a black t-shirt tight across defined muscles. Richard had seen him around the lounges, was curious for why he was here, so went and sat next to him.

One thing he discovered inside was that meeting people was easy. Before, outside, the thought of introducing himself to new people strangled him; now, inside, he'd learned how introductions should be casual, even perfunctory. You said hello, you said your name, you asked, Why are you here? as easily as asking, What's your favorite color? "Hi, I'm Richard."

The man pained through a smile and extended a hand. "Hello, Richard. I'm Mike. Nice to meet you."

"Nice to meet you, too, Mike. Why are you here?"

Mike looked away.

"It's OK," Richard said. "You don't have to tell me."

A moment passed, then Mike asked: "Why are you here?"

"Suicide."

He winced.

"It's alright." It was hardly his own anymore. "I mean, I'm feeling better now. They started me on meds. You know. They're making me feel better already. Really. Like I don't even belong here." Except for seeing things.

Mike nodded and mumbled things about not sleeping and fighting with his wife and waking up with nightmares and being in Vietnam.

Cool—a vet, like his dad. Richard smiled and nodded back. He loved war games, movies, and books with lots of maps and pictures.

The door closed with a definitive *click*. "Welcome back everyone," the therapist said to the door and turning round announced to the room, "and welcome to our new members."

Mike said to him, "You bowl?"

"Nah," Richard said. "My roommate gave it to me."

The art room was the closest room to the main entrance. As he and his nurse escort approached he thought he heard from around the corner the sound of the front doors of the institution opening and closing, and he had a fleeting image of himself dashing into the sunshine; but dismissed it immediately, because that would not be the right thing to do, and he would not get away anyway. The room couldn't be missed, even without the brown plaque on the wall by the door: ART THERAPY. Inside was an explosion of materials, colors, and projects, gobs and streaks of paint—red, blue, black, yellow, orange, green, white. Wood and clay and paper projects littered the countertops. Drawings in color and pencil and poster boards with shiny sparkles and dripping yarn covered the walls.

No one was there. The nurse reminded him to report to the main lounge when the session ended. He paused, fearful that she had led him to the room too early. He didn't want to be the first one, the only one, there. He poked his head in.

"Hello!"

Shit.

"Come in!" The therapist left her paperwork at the countertop and came at him super-enthusiastically, nodding to the nurse escort that the hand off was complete. "Welcome to Art Therapy. You're the first one here today, so we can get you started before the others arrive. You're Richard?"

"Yeah." Wary of her sparkliness, he stepped in and scanned the room for who else might be there because she said "we" can get you started, but as she talked he realized she included herself in the "we" to mean more than one of her existed.

"How was group?"

Therapy? How did she know? "OK."

"Great, great," she didn't care. "Do you prefer 'Rich,' 'Richard,' or 'Dick'?"

I am not a dick: "Richard."

"OK. Richard. First, we'll get you a jacket." She and her other selves went to a cabinet and brought a stiff splotched work jacket. "Wouldn't want to get that messy. Do you bowl?"

"No." He slipped on the multi-colored jacket and zipped it up.

She was waiting for more but nothing came. "Well. Richard. Let me give you our tour." As she spoke in minimalist sentences her fingertips dabbed diverse pieces of wood, clay, and paper projects of art-in-progress. He imagined her as a storybook fairy lighting upon sleeping flowers in a magical meadow at dawn, touching them to awaken their silly hearts to a brand new day's song. "Have you ever done art therapy before? No? OK. Well. Here we use different media to" go on and on and on about feelings and touching and *groundedness* (is that even a word?), "wood, clay, leather, paints," every word surged with meaning for her; fingertips butterflied. "Have you ever worked with these materials?"

In another world, another time. "Some. In high school. Pottery. Wood. I made a box in high school wood shop." It was a nice little box, now that he thought of it, and he brightened remembering what he'd made. "It had a hinged lid, I lined it with green felt, I keep it at home on my dresser." He described it with his hands.

"OK."

He was an idiot.

She led him along the length of a waist-high bench squatting in the middle of the room with racks of tools and clumped dirty rags and holders for myriad sets of brushes. "We're not allowed certain tools, of course." She tipped her head, apologizing. Her explanation continued about how the residents worked at stations, the types of tools available, all the while her fingers flitting, unwilling to settle on any one thing, and Richard had a vision of how the room came to be awash in colors: a room full of patients unleashed in their madness, spurting tubes of paints and brushes dripping, fists mashing potter's clay, and safe instruments swiping; shouting and laughing bestial ejaculations of newly discovered and unfettered emotions. In that environment, observing the remains of the orgy realized by patients past and present all over the floors, walls, cabinets, ceiling, he understood his disconnectedness.

"Did you have an idea of what you wanted to do?"

Get out of this nuthouse.

"Did you have an idea of what you wanted to work with? You don't need to know right away, but if you have an idea... Oh here's more." She faded away to greet the patients coming in but before completely leaving him offered, "You can stay right here or pick another station," and he mustered for her a thank-you smile for taking the time to explain everything to him while he half-listened. Patients dribbled in and wandered to various parts of the room to retrieve their projects-in-progress, which they took to a station—an open place at the bench, a table, a small portion of countertop—and set to with brushes or paints or glues or—

Susie entered the room and maneuvered to him. He hoped she still wasn't angry with him for not sticking up for her when Vic told her "Go color." Thinking about it made his head ache, for her, for him, for them both.

"Hello, Richard." Her body exuded the aroma of fresh pink bubble gum. "I didn't know we had art together."

"Me neither."

"Do you know what you're going to work on?" She play-sorted through a box of colored markers. Another phone number was penned on her palm. "You don't need to know *right away*, but it helps."

"I don't know, maybe leather, maybe clay. Clay sounds good."

"Like Louis?"

No, like *me*.

"I'm drawing," she said.

He was afraid to ask.

"Want to see?" She was off to retrieve her work before he could say yes or no and was back again. On the table she spread two large drawing sheets. In one a herd of horses dashed, the pencil-stroked torsos of the animals careening turbulently across the page, right to left, from darkness to light; no earth, no sky; the animals were suspended in an indeterminate space of gray-white, thrashing a path through it. The other sheet, in contrast, was stark, white, static. A penguin stood lonely, half a man, upon the desolate edge of an enormous cliff of ice and snow, facing the distant clean ruled horizon with the sun peeking up, or going down.

He wanted to ask what she was in for.

"I've always loved horses. And penguins. They're so cute, their tuxedos, ready for a dance. My mom says I've always loved animals. She thinks I should be a vet. But I say, just because you love animals doesn't mean you want to be around them if they're sick. Well. What do you think?"

"I think they're good." He touched the edge of the penguin one. "They're very nice. I think you really have something there." He shut up, afraid he was sounding the same as his father doing a bad job of lying about what he thought wasn't very good but kept saying that he did.

"Do you think so? You're not just saying that?"

Richard shook his head. He did think so. He wasn't just saying that.

"Then why didn't you stick up for me when Vic was picking on me again?"

Huh?

"You two were playing checkers and I came up to you to show you the drawing pad and pencils Louis gave to me, I was only trying to be nice, and Vic made one of his smart-ass remarks again, and you just sat there and wouldn't even *look* at me."

"What did you want me to do?"

"You could've said *something*."

Why?

"How do you think that made me feel?"

"I don't know," he said. "I'm not you."

She reminded him of a kitten surmising a dangling bit of yarn. "Anyway—Louis said he gave you something, too."

144

No!

"I think it's cool of him to give it to you. I mean, you're his new roommate, I get that. But why aren't you wearing it?"

Oh. Relieved, he touched open the art jacket.

"Oh. OK. He said he might give it to me before he left. That's all. Before you came along."

The therapist-fairy lighted nearby. "Are we finding everything alright here?" Before either of them could answer she suggested brightly, "Susie, why don't you help Richard settle in today?"

"Sure." She knew where everything was, what everything did, what everyone was working on. She took him in tow. Through the tour he tried to keep out of the way in the crowded room. Some patients he recognized from the lounges or from his group therapy session. Eugene hunched over a piece of white cardboard studded with hundreds of shiny beads like eyes of gold and silver, blue and red. As they passed by he was gliding a bead into place in its drop of white glue.

He looked up: I keep the dead.

Susie kept on and Richard followed, unnerved.

At the table where they had started Susie asked, "So you think you know what you want to do?"

No, he did not know what he wanted to do, but he did know what he wanted to work with: clay. Of all the materials he'd watched people work with, clay seemed to him the most immediate, the most permanent. Your fingers pushed and groped and gouged the shapeless mass into *something*. Of course, there was Louis' shattered dancer. But Richard thought he could craft something sturdier, not so delicate, something that might last.

"Clay," he said with a strength that surprised himself as he heard it.

"You've got the fingers for it. Long and lean." She grabbed a wrist and held it up for examination, running her fingers along the length of his.

No girl had ever touched him like this.

She dropped his hand. "Ever work with clay?"

Could he breathe?

"OK."

He delighted in her sharp march to and then back from a cabinet with a handful of plastic-wrapped packs of gray squared logs.

"Then you know what to do?" She heaped them on the table.

He picked up one of the smooth bricks and turned it in his hand. Once, years ago, with his family at a fair, he had sat in the potter's chair during a craft show. The old potter picked him out of the crowd to demonstrate the simplicity of the craft, even a child could do it. The wheel whirling, the lump of clay blurred, glistening from the water the potter drizzled. Hands huge and firm and caked with mud confidently guided his tiny fingers, suddenly let go; he was on his own, the spinning wet earth gliding under his skin; and in those moments, knowing the gathered crowd was anticipating with him with the true potter, Richard wanted to go on forever, to find himself there, re-shape himself with the old man's help. His mother had boasted over his misshapen cup all the way to the parking lot until his father determined, "You really have something there." Here, there was no potter's wheel, no crowd encouraging him, no hands to guide him. Any creation would be his alone. So he could create, alone. He would find something to create. He nearly destroyed himself, so he might start there. With himself.

There was no one else.

There was no one else to do it.

He did not know what to do.

"There's not much to it," she said. "Let me get you started." One of her warm palms spread too gently across his shoulder.

"Is that a boat?" Eugene poked.

Richard finished placing the moist paper towel and growled, "No," tucked the towel to the clay.

"It looks like a boat. Or a coffin. Did you make a coffin? Except there's no lid. And it's kind of small. There should be a lid."

"It's not a boat." He used his own idiot-baby voice. "It's not a coffin. It's a *box.*"

"A box. For what?"

"To put things in."

"A marble collection?" His eyes jittered. "I got a marble collection. Want to see it?" His enthusiasm would not be ignored.

Richard sensed in those eyes a creature trying to reach out to another of its kind and could not deny it. "Sure, Eugene, sure. I guess. Sometime."

He met his mother at their usual place. She went up to him but stopped short, openmouthed.

"*What* are you *wearing*?"

"My roommate gave it to me."

"It's a *bowling* shirt."

"I know that, Mom."

"It's an old bowling shirt five sizes too big with—what is that? Is that what I think it is? *Noah* stitched over the pocket? Is that supposed to be *funny*? Where did that come from? Turn around."

He acquiesced.

She read: "'Forestside Lanes.' What is that?"

He swiveled. "It's a bowling alley, somewhere, I guess."

"A bowling shirt." She spoke, discovering the words: "Noah had a bowling shirt." She spurt one laugh and clipped it. "Of all the things I gave you to wear you pick a bowling shirt that could fit a bear."

He rebelled. "I like it. It makes me feel like I belong."

"To *what*? A *bowling* team?"

He winced. "I think it's cool."

"Who would name their son Noah?"

"It's from the Bible."

"I know where it's from. I mean, who *today* would name their son that? The name died with the man."

"It's a bowling shirt, Mom. It's a joke."

"Well I don't think it's anything to joke about. What's to joke about? You're not going to wear that when Father visits, are you?"

He imagined Noah drinking too much beer on bowling nights...

"Anyway—"

Noah could piss a flood, he nearly giggled.

She tinkered with the clasp on her purse. "You say he gave you the shirt? Your roommate?"

"Yes. Well, he's gone. He left this morning. There's a story that goes with it. He told me. Do you want to hear? Let's sit down." He led her to the fish tank lounge.

"Oh, look! A fish tank, like in our dentist's office. Do you remember?" She changed course, he tramped after. "Do you remember when we got you your goldfish?"

No.

"When I asked the man at the store how big goldfish get?"

No.

"He said, 'They'll grow as big as they're allowed to grow. The bigger the tank, the bigger the fish.' Isn't that something? And you said, 'Is that where whales come from?'"

He left her in her retrospection, went to a small table by a window and pulled out two chairs. She came along and whispered, "What happened to that young man?"

"Who?"

She was trying to point without being seen.

"Don't do that, Mom. Sit down."

She rolled her eyes. "That boy," she said. "What's wrong with him?"

*What's wrong with you?*

She leaned to conspire loud enough so that heads turned at tables. "Is he retarded?"

"Can you hold it down? Everyone can hear you."

"Oh no they can't." She looked around to convince herself.

It was useless. "That's Joey. I don't know what happened to him. They put him there by the wall and he does that."

"All day long?"

"Not all day." Only most of the day.

"Poor thing."

"They watch him. He's not hurting anyone. Look, I don't want to talk about him. Can I tell you about my shirt?"

"Oh, yes. That. Go on."

Defeated already, he told his story, and she attended in her way, waiting to speak when he was done, deliberately pressing mortar between rows of bricks: "Isn't that the most ridiculous thing you ever heard."

That was her trump, the inevitable invocation of the biologic fluke that crowned her into motherhood, like all mothers, he supposed, an accident that willed into being a self-assumed natural maternal infallibility, which he interpreted as foolishness, and so he didn't hold it against her. "I didn't make it up, that's what he told me."

"Well I didn't say you made it up, I just said it was ridiculous. Who would pack no clothes to stay in a place like this?"

He knew she let it go before its meaning touched her mind, and their eyes met in an instant of shame, veered off to their own far sides of the conversation.

"That's what he told me this guy did."

"Well I hope you're not going to wear that thing every day. I packed you plenty of clean clothes. *Your* clothes."

He toyed with a loose string on his pants cuff. "You did, Mom, you did." He felt like dying by any imaginable death. He let his gaze wander off to the gleaming fish tank and became jealous for their life.

"That's some story." She fiddled with the clasp of her purse, locking and unlocking her mouth in false starts. Finally, "So, you're not going to keep it?"

He flicked the string decidedly. "I don't know. I just got it."

"Well if you keep it that would break the cycle. It's sort of a chain letter, isn't it? You pass it on or it's bad luck."

"Who believes in that?"

She waved at the shirt. "Maybe Noah did."

She was funny. "Maybe Noah did." He paced a finger along the hem of the shirt and thought aloud. "He had faith."

"What?"

He felt trapped and compelled to follow his thought. "Noah. He had some kind of faith." To do what he did. He smoothed the embroidered name above the shirt pocket. "I wonder how he bowled."

His mother rolled her eyes. "Maybe Noah bowled a perfect game."

"Maybe Noah bowled a perfect game," he said.


In his room, alone, he got out the new notebook and the fresh pen pack. The notebook cover was blue.

"They were out of red," his mother had told him. "And I thought: Well, it's only a color. Is that OK? It's only a color." She was so painfully hopeful that he did not want to disappoint her.

"It's OK," he lied. To him, it was not a color. To him, rather, somehow, it was what he could do, what he could get out of himself. Red was bright, bold, bloody—it hummed. Blood made everything new. Blue was cold and static. Dead. He tore open the pen pack, picked one from the many, flipped open the notebook cover to find the first clean page, and plunged to dirty it.

*I have a shirt.*

He pulled back, considered, plunged again.

*It is a Noah shirt.*

He paused to think about what to say, then down went the pen with his mind flowing from it.

*Louis told me what happened, when Noah was a patient, how he*

*(Noah) went nuts one day over (Louis couldn't remember what, maybe a room search) and from then on refused to change his clothes, didn't pack anything else. He wore the same shirt every day the rest of his stay. Louis said it was weeks. That's hard to believe. I think they'd force you to change. —Before he left he gave the shirt to his roommate. The roommate kept the shirt, but before he left, weeks later, he gave it to his new roommate. He wanted to pass it along, too. So that new roommate kept the shirt, but when he left, he didn't want it either. So he gave it to his new roommate. The shirt passed along like that, Louis said, for over a year, because nobody wanted to take it out of the hospital, until it came to him. —And now it's mine. And I'm supposed to pass it along to someone before I leave, to keep it going.*

"Keep what going?" I asked Louis.

"Depends on what you believe," he said.

"Will I ever see you again?" I asked.

"Let's hope not," Louis said.

*I wanted to strangle him or burst into tears and didn't know why because I didn't even like him. I think he saw all that.*

*He said, "You're a blank slate here. Be anything you want to be. What do you want to be?"*

*Wanted.*

*I think he saw all that, too.*

He disengaged his mind and stared the characters into wriggling black maggots, closed the cover, wanted a place to keep the notebook safe from room searches. There were only a few drawers, and under the mattress. He thought neither would do, but where else? He decided on the mattress, lifted it as high as he could, and slid the notebook to the center.

He watched the clock in the nurses' station tick to seven: one week since he'd played with the pills, stacked them up on the bathroom countertop.

"Whose move is it?"

Vic sighed, "Mine."

Tonight they played chess. Neither played very well, and time stretched so long between moves that each had to ask the other whose turn it was, and still Richard wasn't sure Vic wasn't cheating, sneaking extra moves.

"I went to my first group and art today," said Richard, careful to use the patients' slang, calling it "group" and "art" and not "group therapy" and "art therapy," pleased with himself that he could fit in so quickly, in this regard, at least, not drawing any extra attention to himself from someone like Vic.

"Yeah?"

He began to detail his group session, the people he'd met, the adults, the kids, the stories he'd heard about failed suicides and failing marriages, affairs, deaths, manias, depressions; then the touch of fun he'd had in art playing with the clay, but he didn't mention Susie helping.

"That sounds great." Vic reached out and slid a pawn forward a space. "Who're you giving that shirt to when you leave?"

Alone in his room at night for the first time since being inside, Richard reveled in his newly acquired privacy and hoped he would be able to keep the room to himself. Over the game Vic assured him he would not. "If there's a bed to fill," he said, "they'll fill it." Richard supposed so and immediately began fretting about who might be his new roommate, gazing around the lounges and wondering to himself and then aloud until Vic told him: "It's all chance, so stop worrying about it. C'mon, move." Richard supposed he was right about that, too, and tried to convince himself that he missed having a roommate, not Louis, a roommate, another, someone whose presence would reassure him of his belonging to a whole outside himself.

Richard undressed for bed. He folded the Noah shirt carefully and placed it alone in a dresser drawer, smoothed it flat. Reading the embroidered name he imagined Noah, a huge man, bellowing about some perceived slight and standing his ground for what he believed in and hoping—

What?

That someone would listen?

That someone would come?

That someone would save him?

What?

What was he thinking about?

The shirt.

Noah hope faith and "Who're you giving that shirt to when you leave?"

"You mean the Noah shirt?"

"Yeah, the Noah shirt."

"I hadn't thought about it. I just got it."

He couldn't conceive himself bellowing about anything or standing up for anything—it seemed so violent, so demanding. Most of the time, before, he wanted to lie down and die. But that was fading, being replaced by new feelings of wanting to live, like when he was with Susie, or when he was playing checkers with Vic, or when he was eating. Maybe this was the medicine working. Maybe he was getting new glasses. He closed the drawer and his thought on that.

In bed he waited for lights out, hoping, praying even, that Joey would stay in his own room. He resolved that, if Joey *did* visit tonight, in his head, he would tell the nursing staff.

Maybe.

Probably.

Probably not.

That would be crazy talk.

He started from what he thought was sleep to what he thought was wakefulness, night enveloping him and the black pillar standing at the end of his bed oh my God.

Richard shuddered and shut his eyes and pulled the covers tight.

What's he doing? What's he want? Why doesn't someone get him? The questions leapfrogged until he wearied himself and determined to settle himself down. He told himself this was stupid, he was being stupid, there's nothing to be afraid of: Joey wasn't there to *do* anything, he probably wandered out of his room again and got lost and now was searching for someone to help him back to bed, that's all.

That's all. He's probably more afraid of you than you are of him: what they say about cornered animals.

That was it.

Richard had convinced himself so completely that he fully intended to ask Joey what he wanted after opening his eyes but instead found Eugene and

no air to scream.

The night light shone sallow on Eugene's face, cut clay illumined from within, and two black unblinking bits of glass eyes.

Richard slammed the covers over his head.

This can't be real, this isn't happening, he's not really there.

It's the medicine, the overdose. He's not real. No one's there.

But if I'm thinking this clearly about him not being there, I must be awake, and it must be real. He must be there.

No, no, he can't be there. He couldn't get out of his room.

Why is he standing there? What does he want?

Find out.

No.

Look, see if it's real.

No.

Under the covers the air turned hot and moist, another bag tied around his neck. Fathoms of water stretched all around dark and paralyzing, and he wrestled with himself and with what to do until he opened his eyes to light and morning in his room, alone.

The apparition of the unearthly Eugene, a silent sentinel, was terrible, haunting. Even under the hot water of the shower Richard shuddered. He had to find out what was real, what was not, what was happening to him. But he knew he could not tell the doctor or nurses. No. There would be no help there, only idiot-baby questions and reflections of his madness. And worse. More medicine. Isolation. ECT. What Louis and Vic said. First he tries to kill himself, they would say, then he starts seeing things.

No, he thought it through, he would have to figure this out himself.

He found Vic in the fish tank lounge and challenged him to a game of checkers. He thought he might ask Vic, somehow, someway, during the game. After they'd set up at their table Richard began noticing the near-empty lounges.

"Where is everyone?"

"It's Saturday. A lot of people get to leave for the weekends."

"Don't you get to go home?"

Vic twitched the eye hair patch.

Oh. OK. Richard scanned the lounge, too. "It's dead."

"Yeah. That's how it is. If you're good and they're thinking of releasing you soon, you get a weekend home. It's a test run. Don't get too excited. You ain't been inside long enough. Plus you're a suicide, so I figure they won't let you out for at least another week. C'mon, you tried to kill yourself. That's the way it works."

"I'm going *nuts* in here, man, I can't even *breathe* anymore, I think I'm starting to see things. When do you think they'll let me go outside?"

"Who knows? Ask your doc. C'mon, it's your move. Try not to think about it."

Right. Locked in a suburban madhouse with a nymphomaniacal middle-aged housewife, a kid who cut off his fingers to teach himself a moral lesson, and a guy who talks with his dog. Right.

Vic was so calm, relaxing in his chair, making his nice suggestions, Richard wanted to lean over the board and slap him. But he had things to figure out.

"Do you ever go out at night?"

Vic shook his head without taking his eyes off the board.

"Too dangerous?"

"And—" he stretched to move a piece—"why do it? You go out during the day so you can do things, have some fun. Right? Plus it's a morgue in here at night. They lock it down. You'd get caught."

"So you think anyone walking around at night would get caught?"

"Didn't I just say that?"

Richard winced.

"What?"

He checked for eavesdroppers. "I think I saw someone in my room last night."

"A patient? In the hallway?"

"In my room."

"Doubt it."

"But could it happen?"

"I doubt it. Who'd you see?"

"I think—" Richard started to tell but inside of him the truth about himself and his predicament and what was real and what was not real blended, congealed, to form a new mass, a new world, that played along all the possibilities a picture might be, as you connected your own dots, as you were seeing it with whatever glasses you had to wear, as you were seeing what you thought you made. He couldn't tell; he couldn't tell anyone. "It was too dark."

They played the game over and over until they tired of it, and Vic announced he was off to the gym to see if anyone was playing basketball or pool. He disappeared around the corner by the glass room where Joey should have been, and Richard wondered if Joey was home, too, and where he might be pacing (in his room? in a hallway?) and how his parents managed their lives with a son like that.

Red emerged from the snack room with her fake book and steaming cup of tea in hand and went to her small table, settled into the chair, opened the lid, shuffled the index cards out, and hunched, unmoving, reading her famous quotes by famous people. He was regretting terribly how much he had told her his first night in, a world ago, and

What does she think of me?

Does she think of me?

She's cute, in a plain sort of way.

He got up and went to her table, not with anything specific in mind to ask her or to tell her. Maybe he wanted to know how old she was, why she was here, and maybe he would ask her. Maybe he only wanted to be near her; perhaps, he told himself, because he felt a connection with her that he did not feel with anyone else, because he thought she knew him better than anyone else who had ever existed—how crazy was that?

he had shared with her things about himself

deep things

vital things

he'd never told anyone

and he thought that must count, that must mean something to her, he must mean something to her.

She was older, Louis had said, but maybe that wouldn't matter to her. Maybe they could be friends, secret friends, like the sister he never had. Maybe she would even

what?

Have sex with you?

*NO!*

He was at her table.

*What's wrong with you?*

"Hi."

Her feline indifference always offered the same faraway satisfaction that she was guarding some secret ingredient to life. "Hello, So Tired."

Ha. "Can I sit down?"

He caught a hesitancy and a bewilderment in her face trying to cover the reflection of his madness, and instantly-utterly-shamefully he comprehended the devastating nature of their relationship. How could he have been so wrong?

"Sure."

He sat down wanting to bolt from her. "What're you reading now?"

"Inspirational ones. But I haven't figured out what they're supposed to inspire. Want to hear one?"

No. "Sure."

She flipped a few cards and fake cleared her throat and read semi-dramatically: "The first thing you need to understand is that you do not understand." She smiled up.

He did not understand, her, this place, his place here, anything.

"Isn't that nuts?"

Thanks, Red.

"It's by Sore... Sore—*N*, I can't even *pronounce* his fucking name."

It was destroyed. Her image, their façade they had together built up, he couldn't pinpoint what, but whatever it was was gone. The mask that was her face protected and projected, and he was afraid to ask "Why are you here?" He wanted to disappear. He spied Eugene coming out of the main hall, his heart leapt, and he blurted, "There's someone I need to see," then scrambled away.

Eugene was heading to the fish tank lounge, and Richard followed, slowly, tracking his late-night visitor. In the lounge Eugene sat at the large table, opened his fist to dump its contents in a gentle clatter on the tabletop, and proceeded to alternate cupping his hands around and over it as though it were a living thing with a mind to escape. Richard needed this to go well. If he scared Eugene away now he might never know the truth.

"Hi, Eugene." Cautiously, cautiously.

Eugene hand-domed his treasure. "Good morning." Didn't that grin want to give it away?

Richard sat next to him.

"Want to see?" Eugene flapped open his finger-tent to reveal a pile of multi-colored bits of stone and glass, none larger than a lunule, all washed out by the pounding of water and time.

He knew but asked, "Where did you get those?"

"On the beach. There's *millions* of them lying around. I picked each one for my collection. Did I show you my marble collection?" He fingered the pile so that the glass and stone pieces chatted pleasantly.

"No, no, not yet, maybe some other time." Could this guy make it to his room last night? Richard studied him toying with the bits of stone and glass, smashed pieces of bottles washed soft by years of roiling in the surf. Could people really leave the hospital whenever they wanted? for whatever they wanted? He watched this man-child tinkling his collection. The face was an enlivened replica of the apparition in his room last night, and the weight of the question pressed him unbearably, squeezed his voice out, "Eugene, were you in my room last night?"

Eugene's finger stopped the chattering. The lounge was empty but for them, yet he searched around to make sure. Their eyes met, and in them the dead-blankness colored with weariness and fear and— "You see them, too?"

What?

"They talk to me do they talk to you?"

what

"The keepers of the dead. If you talk to them they'll talk to you. It's the angels; you see them on the doors, don't you? They're here to help. Do they talk to you?"

Jesus Christ. Yes. No. No. "*No.* I'm not *talking* about that." It's not like that. "I'm not seeing things." I'm not the crazy one here.

But in Eugene's eyes Richard became aware of the unborn idea he kept secret from himself, that they were more alike than not alike, and in that recognition Richard's disposition toward Eugene transformed close to kinship.

"Sso there you are!" At the mouth of the lounge appeared Philip, exasperated and excited, cradling his notebooks and books. "Are you ready?" he said to Eugene and frowned at Richard. "You ssaid thiss morning." Back and forth he eyed them, settling on Richard with some suspicion and curiosity.

Eugene erupted: a hopelessly cluttered table in his mind suddenly swept clear of a dozen different thoughts. "Yes. No. It's fine. I'm here. This morning. Now is good."

To Richard: "Isn't it?"

To himself: "Yes it is."

To Philip: "Come on, come on."

To the bits of colored glass and stone as he palmed them clinking off the table: "Let's go. Can Richard listen, too? I think he'd want to hear what you have to say."

To Richard: "Wouldn't you?"

To Philip: "Is that OK?"

Philip adjusted the weight of his cargo and said seriously, "Thiss iss for thosse who have earss to hear," and with a fever in his eyes asked Richard, "Do you have earss to hear? Eyess to ssee?"

Seeeeee?

Eugene nodded enthusiastically and elbowed Richard.

Philip waited.

Richard stopped himself from touching his ears, his eyes, to show himself and everyone that they were functioning, and wanting to know what Philip wrote in those notebooks, wanting to know what he was in for, wanting to know what kind of person chopped off his own fingers because they touched something they shouldn't, said yes.

A smile pushed into Philip's face. "Let'ss do thiss over here." He led them to the rear of the fish tank lounge to a small table for two, pulled it away from the wall, arranged his materials, jostled one of the chairs between the table and the wall, sat, and motioned his audience to gather seats close.

Philip picked one of his notebooks and located the precise page and splayed it open before them—crammed pages of inked drawings, taped illustrations, and text written over, under, and curving around the pictures, a revelation of what Philip was in for.

Forlornly Richard gazed out of the lounge.

Philip made a show of pausing elegantly before he spoke: a preacher's authority on the verge of a sermon. "Haven't you been dogged by ssomething your whole life? Thiss feeling that ssomething out there iss waiting on you, watching you, lisstening to you. Haven't you felt dogged?"

Eugene wagged his head.

"I knew you did; I could tell when I firsst sspotted you and I can tell right now. It'ss in your eyess, in your blood. I can ssee it, *ssmell* it. You know what I'm talking about. You have earss to hear and eyess to ssee, and if your hand or eye causssess you to ssin—but let me sshow you." He picked his black Bible off the pile and began flipping gold-edged rice pages, and Richard peeked at the open notebook with its drawings of a cross, a mountain, and, above that... a cradle? "Let me sshow you. Here. Here it ssayss how our faith ass a musstard sseed will move mountainss. Move mountainss! Do you want to be a mountain mover?" With stub fingers Philip stabbed the notebooked mountain. "Of coursse you do! And here. *Here.*" His eyes ricocheted across the pages. "Ssee how He choossess uss from the foundationss of the earth. That'ss called predesstination. From before He laid the *foundationss* of the earth He knew what we would do."

The *foundationss* of the earth.

"Have you ever read the Bible?"

"Yes," Richard said. "Once. I mean, I tried. When I was a kid." He was eight and studying for his First Communion and wanted to be prepared and asked his mother if he could read the Bible, so she got him the family Bible, as big as a phone book, and he took it into his room. "I got a few pages into it." He had to get his mother's dictionary and keep it with him as he read to look up words he had never seen before, like *firmament, yielding,* and *fruitful.* "After the flood when the guys were living to be 900 years old, I couldn't believe it so I gave up."

"You gave up?" Philip re-stabbed his notebook over the cradle. "*That'ss* the sstory of Noah."

Richard wondered how he did it. At what point did he finally say to himself, Thiss iss it, I've had it with thesse fingerss, they're coming off. And worse—Jesus Christ, even *worse*—that moment the wedded blades snugged the digit and snapped together home through flesh and bone.

"Can you find a better sstory of faith?"

*Ker-runch.*

"Do you know why he did what he did?"

There must have been so much screaming and blood.

"Look how they live"—the mutilated hand flicked at the finger-size fish—"without worry for food or drink or clothess."

I'd rather be dead than mutilated, Richard thought.

Eugene was contemplating the fish.

"They neither ssow nor reap yet look with what ssplendor they are clothed."

Eugene said, "Fish don't wear clothes."

Philip flinched. "Why do you think He flooded the earth?" At Richard, "Why do you think Noah packed no clothess?"

The horror of it stretched Eugene's face. "Because he was a fish?"

One of Philip's stubs leveled at Eugene. "I'm going to ignore that blassphemy becausse of your ignorance of the holy word of God and becausse you're a fucking nut." His eyes challenged Richard as the stub backed down, and his countenance metamorphosed into composed friendliness.

Richard took the opening. "Look—"

"Yess, look and ssee how you ssee. Thiss Laodicean attitude of yourss will get you sspit out. Don't you think Noah wass dogged by ssomething hiss whole life, ssomething he jusst couldn't get rid of, out of hiss control, couldn't esscape?"

Noah was a fat man on a bowling team.

"But who wass righteouss in thosse dayss? Who believed? Did anyone find favor in Hiss eyess? Everything He ssaw grieved Him. And it goess right back, ssee? It goess right back to that. To what? *Faith.* In *Hiss* eyess. *Hope.*"

Faith, hope, love. And a bowling shirt.

"And if your *own* right eye causess you to ssin, pluck it out. Ssame ass the apple off that tree." Philip smacked his lips, *pop, pop.*

Richard gazed jealously at the people in the main lounge and berated himself for letting himself get trapped. He wanted to know about God and how He saw him, but not from this nut.

"Ssometimess I ssee everything sso clearly, it'ss all glassss, the wordss on the page, the ideass in my head, what people ssay, how they act. It'ss like I ssee what'ss not really there. Do you?"

yes

Eugene nodded solemnly.

"And it'ss all in focuss, thiss terrible focuss, all at once, becausse I ssee everything, hear everything, for what it really iss. I know you know what I mean," he said to Richard. "I ssaw you writing. You know what I'm talking about. It'ss having new earss to hear and new eyess to ssee." He described his visions to the space behind them. "I can ssee thingss the way they're ssuppossed to be sseen and hear thingss the way they're ssuppossed to be heard. Like the angelss all around uss, messssengerss, and Joey'ss hymnss. But then it goess away. It alwayss goess away. It never sstayss. I can never keep it." His face worked pre-cry contortions, and Richard was afraid to speak because he was afraid he would say he agreed with everything Philip was saying and cry with him and hug him and call him brother—a *sick* brother—but brother. "Thingss get out of focuss and thick again. It alwayss getss thick again, out of focuss, I can never keep it."

Richard and Eugene crowded around Philip's pause as pedestrians drawn to a car wreck.

"Maybe," tried Richard, "you aren't meant to keep it."

Philip called from his own world. "He goess around looking for ssomeone to devour. But we have to risse up, every morning, like a lion for the sservice of the Lord. That'ss what I think every morning. Risse up. Risse up like a lion."

How is this happening.

"Becausse the dead will come back."

Eugene pricked.

"The dead will risse again to vissit the living and judge the living. The empty tomb iss a sseed, don't you know that? Do you want to live forever?"

Not here.

"If a man asskss you for hiss coat, give it unto him. You could give that sshirt away, you could jusst give that sshirt to me, it sshouldn't be anything to you at all."

It's mine.

"What would you ssay? What would you ssay to Jessuss if you ssaw Him today? Would you be prepared to sspeak?"

Richard was thinking that he would like to say I'm sorry to Jesus for causing Him and his family all this pain and trouble when Eugene said, "I did last night. I told Him thanks for telling me about Buster. Buster was my dog. He was my friend."

Philip looked like he was swallowing two handfuls of Eugene's bits of glass and stone.

"He was in my room. Not Buster. Jesus. I asked Him what He was doing there and He said He wanted me to not worry because He was going to

"*Sstop!*" Furious eyes accused from Eugene to Richard and back; but instantly he contained it; and with precision and resolution methodically gathered his notebooks and Bible and himself, scooted from the table, and abandoned them there.

They watched him leave, and not until Philip was out of sight did Eugene try, "Do you think he was mad?"

Richard hardly heard him because he was thinking about what Jesus would want to say to Eugene, or to him.

*Time goes by so slow. There's not much to do. I can't leave the lounge, and I think I've watched as much TV as I can stand. The windows have a view of the lake. It's beautiful, as much as I can see past the cliff and the far horizon. At night the dark edges of the trees fade to black against the silent water. It's weird watching without sound. I've played checkers until I hate the game. Listened to Philip go on today about—everything he was trying to say. I hope God would understand him. I think God would understand him. And forgive him. Love him. Like me.—Eugene smarted off and I had to stop from laughing. "Noah was a fish." That upset Philip.—Mom's coming to visit later. I called this morning. Dad answered by mistake. He didn't think it would be me, I could tell. He sounded almost afraid.*

*Dad: Hello?*

*Richard (not expecting his father to be home): Hi. Dad.*

*Dad (seeing a ghost): Hello.*

*Richard (wondering what to say to a stranger): How's it going?*

*Dad (wondering what to say to a ghost): Pretty good, pretty good. (picking at the telephone cord) How you doing?*

*Richard (stunned his father would care to know): OK. You know. (but he doesn't)*

*Dad: That's good. Good. (Pause) Your mother's not here right now. She went to the store to get a few things. You know your mother.*

*Richard (not knowing how to speak): —*

*Dad: I'll tell her you called. Okey doke?*

*Richard (dying, thinking, I wanted to tell her something, Dad, that I think I understand, I feel sorry for you, I love you, but you won't remember. You won't remember.)*

*Dad: Okey doke?*

*Richard (thinking, Remember)*

*(Mumbled goodbyes.)*

It'll be OK.
It'll be OK.
There won't be anymore visitors at night.
There won't be anymore visitors at night.
The medication's going to make things better.
The medication's going to make things better.


*Monstrosity.*
*Monsters.*
*Monsters under my bed.*
*There is no "under my bed", they're in my head.*
*Better there than dead.*


Richard was falling under the thin surface of sleep but snapped awake to see his father, instantly shut his eyes and lowered himself beneath the covers because this isn't real

but I'm awake, I'm seeing it, Dad's standing in the doorway, the angel is there with him.

If you talk to them, they'll talk to you.

You're seeing things again.

But he looks so real.

Nothing is there. Nothing was ever there. Joey wasn't there, Eugene wasn't there, your father isn't there. There is no angel.

But I'm awake.

You're not.

I can pinch myself. They say if you can pinch yourself you're awake.

You're asleep.

I'm pinching myself. See?

You're asleep.

I'm pinching myself. I can't be asleep.

It's the medicine, a side effect, you're unresponsive, need to be strapped down, don't look.

It's not the medicine, he's come to visit, I need to look.

Don't.

It's Dad.

Richard:

eased the covers down and

opened his eyes to see his father sitting on the bed peering at him and

flew the covers over his head and

O God O Jesus his face, his eyes, gray like

alive

yet

out of the pond

dead.

If you talk to them, they'll talk to you.

He did not want ears to hear. He did not want eyes to see.

He curled fetally and cupped his hands over his ears and shut his eyes and rocked himself and prayed to God to make it stop.



The morning was bright and hurt.

So.

It wasn't real. His father was never there.

Couldn't be there.

Impossible.

He addressed the static outline of the angel on the door: You held back that knife forever. Where were you when I needed you?

Once, his father had brought a fireman suit home to his children for them to try on, and Richard drowned in it. Later, his father modeled the suit, chuckling, combing strong fingers through his little boy hair. How he towered over everything and everyone. The ax was as big as the boys, its head a silver tooth for tearing.

*Bored. Boring. Boredom.*
*Bored.*
*I'm bored.*

"What're you doing today?"

"Going nuts." Richard slid a checker.

"Going?"

Ha. Ha.

"Any visitors?"

*What?*

"Mom?"

Oh that. "A priest." Why

"You his mercy call today?"

Richard was getting used to ignoring his comments. "Yeah." Right.

"You must rate."

Richard wasn't going to bite.

"I'm surprised they let him come."

But curiosity got him. "Oh?"

"They screen visitors, especially for suicides. I mean, they don't want you going off again and slitting your wrists this time."

"Thanks for your concern, asshole." He couldn't stop the mental dots connecting. "He's coming to talk."

"About what?"

"I don't know. Things."

"Things. OK." Vic twitched the eye hair patch away. "What's his job?"

"His job?"

"His job."

"His *job*—king me—his *job* is being a priest. That's what he *does*. King me."

"Don't be a spaz. That's what he *does*. But what's he *trying* to *do*? You don't get it, do you, Dummy? You don't know why he's coming here."

"I told you. To talk. King me."

"About what?"

"What is with you, man? Do you wanna play or not? If you wanna play, king me. If you don't wanna play." He couldn't even think of words. "Can you just shut the fuck up?"

Vic stacked a black checker and touched a red one over a square. Both let a silence develop.

"Your mom visits."

This was getting weird.

"You got a dad?"

Richard pretended to study the board, sensed the pull of Vic's gaze, knew he didn't need to say it but felt compelled to fill the void. "He's busy."

"Brothers or sisters?"

"Look, are we playing a game, or do you want to know all about my social life, because if it's all the same to you I'd rather play the game and not talk about who's coming to visit me or *not* visit me. Or let's talk about *you*, Vic. Let's talk about *you*. No one visits you. Why don't we talk about *that* for a while? Why don't you tell me about that for a while, Vic the Dick? Why isn't anyone visiting you? Who's embarrassed *you're* here? Where's *your* mom and dad?"

Richard had never seen a loaded checkerboard fly, triangling in a summersault, gunshot red and black kaleidoscoping midair, dots disconnecting a picture, wheeling across the floor in every direction and past departing feet.

The nurse came to his room to tell him he had a visitor, and he thought he was ready. He thought he was ready because he had spent the better part of the day in his room on his bed—he could not write, he was too nervous to write—ruminating. About what he should say to the priest, what he would want to say to him, what he even *looked* like. Although his mother had kept telling him, "Father *Walker.*" She seemed so desperate for him to recollect that he thought she worried he had forgotten God Himself and not the parish priest. He told her what he thought she would want to hear, not exactly as he remembered. Because what he remembered was loneliness and confusion and boredom, every Sunday morning at Mass, trying to listen, trying to sing, trying to pray, but the altar of God was a world away, beyond a forest of adults, unseeable, untouchable, unknowable, and after awhile it felt like he was genuflecting on glass kneecaps. When he was old enough to approach for communion the larger-than-life carved Christ in agony spread and hanging on the cross pierced his heart with dread and awe. He was weak and worthless, and this Christ, suffering eternally on that cross above that altar, had died for him. *Him!* Couldn't he show a little gratitude, some respect? His mother had cruel retorts for boyish missteps. Years later, as an altar boy, he would spy Father stiffly performing the ritual of communion, red cheeks puffing, irritated at the winding line of bodies. The hand that fed the host was a wand of flesh, withered and trembling. In the sacristy Father would call for help removing the vestments. Stuck in an overhead whirlwind of purple and gold brushing cloth, he bent at the waist, and Richard positioned himself at the opposite end of the tunnel looking up at Father's splotchy nose, smelling the sour wine breath. All those years later Richard had held back, waiting, because he thought there had to be some truth, some truth for him to latch onto. No opinions, no choices, only a truth that was always there, constantly unchangeably there. But it never came. Maybe his mother was right. Maybe he saw things too black and white. Now he wanted to know if this priest could see into his heart, test what special God-connection he was supposed to possess.

He followed the nurse into the lounge, scanning for a man in— there, on the far side of the nurses' station near Joey.

The priest stood holding a small wooden box. As they approached the nurse faded aside; his black garb was clean and punctuated with the white square throat dot and a distinctive plastic purple tag with a bold white cross and CLERGY; and Richard, needing to know if the priest could see through him, mustered all the fury and sex and death he could, and all the man had for him in return was a quiet, "Hello, Richard," and a soothing handshake.

So nothing he thought mattered.

"It's nice to meet you."

Re-meet? "Hello, Father." The man was older than his father.

"Wah wah wah wah wah."

They met eyes and a memory *clicked* of this priest demonstrating before the entire class the restrained wrath of God upon Isaac. How those eyes had raged behind the thick black glasses slipping to shiny tip of nose. "Only the hand of God, through the angel, stayed the knife from thrusting"—here his hand stabbed an imaginary blade into the heart of the room— "thrusting through the heart of the innocent lad." The priest agonized: God made human to try the faith of children. Who would want to be an immolation to God? That evening while she was preparing dinner Richard asked his mother if he should want to be an immolation, and she quick back-handed him to his lips and threatened to wash his dirty little mouth out with soap if he ever talked liked that to her again. So in secrecy he stole the family dictionary, searching for its meaning, but he only got lost, hopelessly gloriously lost in the thicket of words on pages after pages after bible-thin pages until he did not know what he was looking for or why he had entered that sacred realm.

"Are we allowed to meet in a more... private setting?"

"Over here."

The priest stooped to retrieve a brown shopping bag with corded handles—the same sort of bag his mother stockpiled in a kitchen drawer, for all occasions, just in case. The priest righted himself, huffing breaths and pushing the black glasses back in place. "Go on."

Leaden footfalls moved the priest, nostrils gaped for air. The pacing sounds of Joey faded as they made their way into the fish tank lounge, empty but for Philip at a small corner table with his materials. Surprised at the sight of the priest, he made a show of leaving, scooping up his papers and notebook and books.

Richard was glad they would be alone. He didn't feel up to asking Philip to leave. "Thanks."

"It'ss not for you."

Richard wanted to smack the back of his head but instead went to the farthest corner of the lounge to a pair of soft blue chairs.

"These look comfortable," the priest said.

Each sank into his own.

"They are." What a stupid thing to say. They are. God, why did he let himself get talked into this?

They both made their personal settling-in noises, appropriate slight gasps and moans. Father picked at an invisible piece of lint on the arm of his chair.

Did he really want to be here? How could he, really? Richard looked out at the collection of people. What *is* his job?

The priest flapped open the paper bag and announced, "I brought you this," and a hand disappeared into its depths and reappeared with a heavy red-jacketed volume, tight plastic-wrapped like a pound of hamburger from the grocery store. "A gift, from Mr. Webster. It's the latest edition. Your mother mentioned that you enjoy reading and writing, and so I thought—well, I thought you might need one. Every writer needs a good dictionary. I'm a writer myself, of sorts." Benevolence shone on his face as he served Richard the book and made plain: "My sermons."

How embarrassing. He didn't need it spelled out. Or maybe he did. Regardless, Richard didn't enjoy receiving gifts, drawing attention to himself, getting things he didn't do anything to deserve. He tried to say thanks but all that came out, he feared, was a pitifully weak attempt at a smile. He cradled the book in his lap, talking to it: "I'll open it later, Father Walker." Did he just say that? About a dictionary?

The priest seemed unsure whether he had heard correctly; his reply was an obligatory yes or well, and he began fingering the small wooden box in his lap, tracing its outline. Richard did not know why but suffered an enjoyable onrush of jealousy over all this man's accouterments, the garb, the necklace, the ring, the box, that mysterious box he bet wasn't lined with green felt, oh no, not for Christ's body and blood encapsulated.

"Richie," the priest said, "why don't you call me Father?" He sounded the name deeply as a pebble gulp in the cold water at the bottom of some dark well.

"OK." Richard wrestled with it. "Father." Why don't you call me Richard?

"Richie—"

Richard.

The finger tracings found their rhythm, back and forth, back and forth, wah wah wah wah wah.

"Is there anything in particular you wanted to talk about?" The fingers planed monotonously, mimicking the voice. Richard wondered at the box, Christ's body and blood, miniaturely interred. The fingers fluttered lovingly, caressing the gouged lid engravings. Window light became material across Father's legs: a polygonal tray of sunshine in his lap. The intruding daylight diluted the blue glow of the fish tank. A nurse whoaed Joey to a stop.

"Do you want to tell me why you're here?"

Father was speaking. The tray of sunshine lit his lap.

"Do you want to tell me why you're here, Richie?"

Didn't he know? Didn't anyone tell him? Forgive me, Father, for

I have sinned, forgive me father, for I have sinned against you, dear father and mother, Dear Mom and Dad, "I tried to kill myself," the more he said his truth out loud the weaker its hold on him became, "I swallowed a lot of pills," not enough, he should correct himself, "and I woke up here." He lifted a hand in resignation. The self-murderous agonies that had culminated in him devouring the hill of pills had dissipated, through medication or time or the chemical and emotional avalanche of the overdose, and speaking about it now was akin to speaking about historical events of vague significance juxtaposed on present-day realities. He tightened his grip on the dictionary, a brick of hope in his hand.

"I meant," said Father, "do you want to tell me what brought you here?"

The truth: "An ambulance brought me here."


"Honestly, Richie, what were you *thinking*, saying that to Father?"

Lucky for him she had telephoned and not visited, or she would be getting even more upset at his sneaky grin. "I don't know, Mom, I guess I wasn't thinking. Maybe I was thinking only about myself."

"No, I don't suppose you were thinking, were you, with your snide remarks. Maybe you *were* thinking only about yourself, your selfish self. Now I have to clean up this mess again, don't I, apologize to Father—"

"It was a joke, Mom."

"Some joke, some joke, Mister Facetious. Did you wear that silly shirt, too?"

"No, Mom."

"Good. Because I don't know *what* Father would think about that. Noah on a bowling team, for heavens' sakes, can you imagine?"

"No, Mom."

"Don't get smart. Did he take your confession?"

"Yes."

"Did he bless you?"

No, he cursed me. "Yes."

"Did you take communion?"

Kneel here.

Richie, Father had said, I asked the nurse at the front desk if you could partake of communion in your room. If you wish.

Jesus Christ forgive me, forgive me for who I am but You made me, didn't You? *didn't You?* in the name of the Father, in the name of the Son, in the name of the Holy so on and so forth, Richard received the white meal with weary supplication and a common grace. There was still holiness left in it for him. Would the priest, like the nurse, check his mouth? No. God was chewed and swallowed.

"Did you take communion?"

"Yes, Mom, I did all that."

"Well I'm only asking. Don't be so sensitive. Was he there very long? What else did you talk about?"

I can't help you if you won't tell me what's troubling you, Richie.

I know that, Father, he didn't say. There's nothing troubling me, he wanted to lie. Really. I don't know why you're here. I don't know why I'm here.

What a *magnificent* lie, he laughed at himself.

You know the thousand reasons why you're here.

I just don't have the words to tell.

Which is why he brought you the dictionary, whispered the still, small voice. Find your words.

"Are you there, Richie? Did you want me to come down today?"

*Why won't you come, Mom?* "No, Mom, I'm OK." *Why won't Dad come?* His guts churned with his good despair and started to burn with self-loathing and self-pity. "I'm OK." He fought the hot tears. He was so adept at lying, his lies blurred with his truth, the dots disassembled. He held the phone at arm's length and buried his face in his pillow to take the explosion of emotion. When he could he lifted the receiver.

"Richie? Richie? Are you alright?"

"I'm OK, Mom. It's OK. I'll see you next time."

"Next time, Richie."

He and his mother someway said their goodbyes.

He and Father had said their goodbyes at the red line on the floor.

"It's as far as they'll let me go."

"Sometimes limits are set for our own good."

Sometimes Father had a ridiculously axiomatic way of speaking. Richard didn't know how he should respond, and Father filled in the blank. "Perhaps next Sunday we might go for a walk outside."

I'm not allowed outside. I'm a suicide. The church's view on suicide is clear. What's your view? Next Sunday? That was a world away. I might be dead by then.

"I've enjoyed meeting you, Richie."

Richard. "Me, too. Father." Jesus.

"I hope you put the dictionary to good use."

The gift. "Yes, yes. I think I will. Thank you." He clutched it.

"Would you want me to come by next Sunday?"

Yes. No.

"You know, Richie—"

Richard.

"—you won't hurt my feelings by saying 'no.' But I'll tell you what: let's say that we meet again, same time, next Sunday, for a walk, unless I hear from you sooner."

Sooner.

"You're a bright young man."

No.

Did you experience anything?

No. These things he wanted to keep in his heart.

"I'd like to get to know you better."

why

Did you administer last rites?

No, they said you weren't going to die.

Every night.

Abruptly Father swaddled hands, warm and pressing and tender, the fingers of a writer, urged, "Be well, my son," and jerked their bodies together to minister Latin quickly, reverently, eyes clenched, and Richard had to shut his eyes, too, he could not witness this, then abruptly again they were released from each other to mumble uninspired goodbyes in an overused tongue.

*Father Walker visited today. He brought a dictionary because Mom told him I wanted to write. He visited once in catechism and we were studying how Abraham tied Isaac to the altar because God told him to ("because God demands a sacrifice")—Father was raving. I was scared shitless, watching him stab the air, thinking: this guy would do it, no angel could hold him back.*

*Listening to him breathe made me think of dad.*

He closed the notebook, not flipping through past pages. He didn't want to look at words he'd written before because he thought it somehow unfair, cheating himself in the present, like peering into a coffin at what once lived, only it wasn't ever how you remembered it alive and you went away discouraged with yourself and disillusioned and blaming the dead.

Like Melvin.

He slid the notebook under his mattress toward the center.

The rest of the afternoon he gave over to investigating—he felt safer, emboldened with few patients around—trying to sit in all the different places he could sit—chair hopping, he told himself—feeling the place out for various views inside and out. He was a spy. The main lounge was of course most exposed to the nurses' station, and the chairs were the least comfortable. All straight backs and heavy wooden things married to their matching tables, big or small. They offered no great view outside, and anywhere you sat a nursing eye was picking at you. These he surrendered first. Next he tried the different couches, which, while cushiony enough, had the same problem: no unobstructed view of the yard, full exposure to the nurses' lair, and, worse than the chairs at the tables, an open seat next to you on a couch was an invitation to many passing residents to cozy up and start a conversation. Fortunately, the belligerent indifference he had lived outside served him well inside. The windows in the TV lounge provided a clear view of the yard to the fence overlooking the lake, but no chair was close enough to enjoy it. He dragged one from the wall and was settling in when a nurse arrived and told him he wasn't allowed to do that, all furniture had to remain in place, please put it back.

He contemplated her request. "I was going to read."

She looked at the dictionary in his hand and worked through peculiar shades of a peculiar smile. "You don't want to do this."

He saw the sense in it, maneuvered the chair to its original position, didn't resist giving her back a dirty look; and returned to chair hopping while the TV played an old mystery movie. The fruit chairs—red, orange, blue ovals—were pleasing to behold, but once ensconced in them he had difficulty moving, breathing, and he knew why a baby wiggled in the womb. Most of the chairs against the inside wall and some of the chairs against the outside wall were out of sight from the nurses' station. Privacy. But the blare of the TV. He settled into a chair against the inside wall with a view outside and tried to drown the TV with his empty thoughts.

So he felt before he saw the two boys outside at the window. They were doing it on a dare, he could tell, neighborhood kids about his brother's age, jostling each other to look, which they eventually did, together.

At Richard.

Who could not did not want to look away from what they were seeing, a gray lifeless body being pulled from a pond. Splintered. He caused and witnessed a fading of childhood from their eyes. The boys scrambled away: a moment later a nurse flustered by the window outside, checked the scene, shook her head and grinned at their impish deed. Repeated their stance.

Her expression one of the practicalities of madness. Flooded him and left him dumb and dazed, searching through the wreckage of the moment.

When he found the strength to stand he went to the fish tank lounge, cooled and shadowed because of the angle of the building under the sun. In the same corner at the same table Philip wrote, intense and unyielding. Resting in front of the fish tank was a single padded chair, perfect for slouching. He had noticed this before; perhaps the nurses could allow this one item out of place, for meditation. The fish tank was the length of a body and adequately deep and wide, a glass coffin, an ark bearing its inhabitants nowhere. Marbles of air gurgled up the tubes. Slivers of greens and yellows and blues scattered about in leaderless masses while the larger, lonely triangles of fish drifted purposelessly, mouthing private monologues and staring wide-eyed terror.

"That sshirt," a voice raised from the back of the room, "mockss God."

He bristled.

"I ssaw you with that, *priesst*, today. I think you want to know what'ss right. I think you want to do what'ss right. If you give me that sshirt—"

"Look. Philip." He was trembling.

"Pride and vanity—"

He launched himself out of the chair and nearly ran to the asylum of his room, shut the door, huddled under the covers, gasping for breath. In a minute he heard the door swing in and a nurse ask if he was alright.

He nodded, probably a wiggling lump to her.

She took a step in and asked if he was sure.

If he spoke he would bawl.

She asked if he would like to talk.

That's all they wanted to do around here. He checked his tears and prepared himself for a clear response. "Please leave."

She admitted the real danger: "Keep the door open." Then he was alone, weeping horribly for all the misery he'd left and for what he felt was sure to come.

From their weekends home trickled in the Sunday night people, lugging suitcases, pillows, and bags, campers arriving. Alone Richard sat, watching them, from a couch in the main lounge. Everyone looked normal. As normal could be. Two weeks ago if he'd met any of them outside this place he would not know that they needed to be inside this place. With a mix of negative attitudes and behaviors he had already repelled The Nosepicker, a terribly fat girl with terrible acne, and Pear Man, who was patting a stack of new puzzle books. Only Pear Man had noticed his shirt.

"Have we met?"

Richard wasn't sure he was speaking to him. But no one else was nearby.

"I've been here before," Pear Man said as if he'd just discovered one of his own life facts.

Was there no one sane in this entire place, someone like him? "Every morning you sit here and do your puzzles. My first day in I sat over there and you showed me one you were doing." He was speaking a foreign language. "You showed me the puzzle you were working on, last week." Richard eased himself away from trying to explain what seemed to have no hold in the man's mind.

Pear Man had been staring at the shirt the entire time and tested new words: "I used to bowl."

Richard offered no encouragement.

"I had a shirt like that."

"Really?" He pinched the fabric to a tent. "Just like this?"

Pear Man lowered his eyes.

Richard regretted his tone.

"I can't remember."

"Why?"

"It's this ECT," he confessed to the floor. "I can't remember things so good. If something reminds me of my life before, it helps... sometimes... Sometimes I get it wrong. My wife helps with that." He flipped through the corner of the puzzle book. "I saw your shirt, it reminded me, I thought. I had a memory: bowling. Things flash by and I don't know if they're real or not. The doctor said that would happen. Things return in a flash, but I don't know if they're real, if they happened to me, or if I've just made them up to fit something I need to fit. It's like I'm seeing someone else's life in my head."

Me, too, Richard wanted to say but had to ask, "Why are you here?"

His shining eyes worked inward and he swallowed hard. No ice chips. "Depression—my wife—she told me what I lost—" He gathered up his puzzle books and trundled off.

Poor Bastard. Vic's right. They fried his mind. They'll never do that to me.

More people straggled in. Richard waited for her. Throughout the weekend he remembered how she had touched him in art, first his hand, then his shoulder, and he argued with himself about what she meant by it, what it meant to her. No girl had ever touched him that way. Did she like him? No. That couldn't be it. She knew what he was in for. What could she like about *that*? Or *him*? He was ugly. The mirror—even the funhouse mirror in his room—told him that.

But she didn't have to hold my shoulder.

She did not *hold* you.

Her hand was on my shoulder.

Not *that* way.

Why not—*that* way?

Look at you.

What.

Look at yourself.

*What?*

You're ugly and dumb.

I see her.

Remember how those boys looked at you Dickie Dickie Dickie glasses.

There she is.

*What's wrong with you?*

I think she's pretty.

Retard.

She might even want to talk with me.

He knew how a conversation might go.

"Hi, Richard." She was so bright and beautiful. "Hi, Susie." She would hug him and say "It's good to see you," and mean it, he would be able to tell. "It's good to see you, too," he would say, and they would let go of each other but she would linger gentle fingers along the sensitive inside of one of his arms the way he'd seen a women do with a man. "Tell me anything you want." In his self-pity he would hesitate, but she would insist, because she was sincere: Tell me anything you want, Richie.

She sees me. She had a fun weekend. All that stuff: suitcase, shopping bag, purse, pillow. I'll bet her pillow smells of bubble gum, too.

"Hi, Richard." She sparkled, leaning over the back of the couch opposite.

"Hi," Richard marveled. Why are you here?

"I had such a great weekend." She bounced away toward the women's wing.

See. She didn't miss you.

At the entrance to the women's wing she spun and, lifting her arm with the shopping bag, waved, mouthed, Be right back.

Everything shut up inside of him.

*immolator: to offer in sacrifice; esp: to kill as a sacrificial victim. to kill (oneself) by fire.*

If he burned himself all away he was afraid of what would remain.

The doctor made his monochromatic observation before Richard sat. "That's an interesting shirt."

"Thanks."

"Where did you get it?"

It sounded more knowing than threatening, so he told the truth. "Louis gave it to me."

"Louis gave it to you."

"Before he left."

"Before he left."

Richard tried once more. "On Friday."

The doctor didn't play along, merely sat, blank faced.

Richard locked onto the pitying owl eyes.

Screeee?

The doctor jerked forward from his reverie and flipped open a chart on the desk. "How are you feeling?"

"Fine. Great." Which was true. The past two mornings he woke up with no feelings of wishing for death, and he had no explanation for it, and if this was how people woke up every day, he knew he could do it; live; and it made him wonder what the hell normal people complained about when they said they were having a bad day, because if you woke up feeling like *this, not* wanting to kill yourself, you couldn't honestly say you were having a bad day. "I mean, I feel really good—" except for seeing things and scaring children—"but I don't even know why, you know? I wake up feeling good and happy, and I'm not thinking about killing myself. It's really the furthest thing from my mind, it really is. I feel great. Can I go home now?"

Madness reflected, "Oh no—no." Idiot-baby, "You just got here."

"But I just told you: I feel fine. I don't feel like killing myself. I want to leave. Why can't I go?"

"The medication is beginning to do its job. Now you need to do yours."

He didn't understand.

"You have *work* to do."

He still didn't understand. Hadn't he told this guy he wasn't like these nuts? "Work? What work?"

"On what *brought* you here."

As the words left him he knew he should not say, "An ambulance brought me here," so besides madness he saw reflected his own helplessness and naiveté. The doctor could order anything, couldn't he—Isolation, pills, ECT—pushing his mind to some in-between state of death and life. Pear Man's mind. Or keep him inside for how long? How stupid could he be? All he wanted was to breathe fresh air. "I'm sorry. I'm sorry. That was dumb."

He tried to re-do everything: "Can I go outside at least? Please. I haven't been outside since I got here. I haven't seen the sun in more than a week. I'm going *crazy* cooped up in here. You *know* what I mean. Not like that. C'mon." Richard calmed himself so that he could speak so that the doctor could hear what he wanted to hear, what they both wanted. "I won't run away. I promise. All I want to do is breathe fresh air again, feel the wind and see the sun. I promise. I won't try to kill myself." It was weird and good to give life and meaning to those words. He lowered his eyes or knew he would cry. Please. He was a dog on its back. "I haven't seen the sun in more than a week."

Screeee?

Seeee.

"I'll let you step out the front door—"

Giddiness erupted

"—immediately after our meeting." The doctor scribbled. "With a nurse. Starting *tomorrow*, you'll have yard privileges. Cafeteria and gym privileges, too, starting tomorrow." He stopped scribbling and leveled a serious face: "Can I trust you with this?"

What did he want to hear? "Yes! Yes! I won't go anywhere. I'll stay right here. I won't try to kill myself."

*Madness!*

He didn't care.

The doctor continued his scribbling, stopped, rippled the paper from its pad and set it on the desk corner, crossed his legs, pulled the open folder onto his lap.

Seeee.

"I should have talked with you earlier about our fraternization policies."

What?

"Last night. With Susie."

She talked about everything except why she was there.

"No contact of any sort is allowed between residents."

Kneel here.

"You may talk all you want, of course, we encourage that."

They talk to me do they talk to you?

"But no contact is allowed—"

Didn't I tell you they were red?

"—such as hand holding—"

We didn't do that.

"—hugging—"

We didn't do that.

"—or kissing."

He'd never kissed a girl.

"It may disturb the other patients. Do you understand?"

Richard did not want to disturb the other patients. He did not want to understand.

"And you have an interest in writing."

Alarms went off. Of course they'd seen him writing. It's their job. Stupid! He pictured them right now going through his notebook in his room.

"Writing can be a very helpful tool, get what's inside out"—

He was going to say he didn't want what was inside out. He imagined one of the doctor's birds in flight spontaneously exploding inside out, continuing its voyage. How freakish it would seem to all the other birds. Nobody would want to *really* see what was inside, out.

—musing up and down the page before announcing, ticking off another check box, "And you had a visitor yesterday."

Nothing was his own.

"How was that?"

Richard shrugged.

The doctor's expression told him to try again.

"Alright. A priest came from church." Richard didn't think it would be enough.

"And he stopped in your room."

"Yes! Yes! He stopped in my room, I took communion in my room, what is the big deal?" He caught himself, nearly too late. The slip of paper allowing him passage outside lay on the desk between them.

The doctor's lips pursed. "No 'big deal'. I'm interested in how the visit went for you, if he'll visit again, that's all. If you found it helpful."

Helpful? Richard hadn't thought of it that way. "He brought me a dictionary."

"Are you having any troubles with your medication?"

"No, no." Images of his night visitors appeared to him with the PRIVATE ward door and Vic's convulsions and Pear Man's ECT-erased face.

The doctor's eyes doubted.

"Dry mouth," Richard gave him, "like you said. I'm chewing ice chips for that, like you said." A scripted ending, he knew, and he went back to the owl eyes over the doctor's shoulder.

"Let me know if you experience any side effects, anxiety, suicidal thoughts, hallucinations. We can always adjust the dosage or try something different."

*Never!*

"You'll be getting a new roommate."

Though he knew that was coming he still tried: "Is there any way I could have the room alone?"

"Oh no, no. Two in a room. We keep everyone paired."

"Who is it?"

"I'm not sure."

"It's not one of these nuts you have here, is it?"

The doctor looked at him.

"When will I get him?"

*Screeee?*

"I'm not sure. The order's already been filled. It could be today."

Clutching his day pass, Richard stood at the heavy double doors, pulled one open, and stepped into the carpeted lobby. A wall of glass (real glass?) separated him from everything outside: grass, plants, cars, asphalt, trees, all glowing, all soaked in sunshine. The waiting area was a nook of couches and plastic plants and end tables with lamps with cords that tailed off to walls. One enormous frenetic painting took up most of the inside wall: a rainbow striped of its bands haphazardly slapped back across the canvas and bleeding colors. Out of the wall on his immediate left a sleek reception booth the color of his room's gold wood wrapped around a woman, head resting chin in palm, reading a magazine.

Richard thought she was asleep, but at the sight of him she turned guarded and irritated. He displayed the paper as his excuse. "Pass. I have a pass."

She took it to study and ignored him. "I need to check." Lifted the receiver.

They waited together, together uncomfortable with his presence.

"Hi Judy, this is Ann. I have a Richard—" she squinted at the pass—"Eyes, Itch—"

*God!*

"—with a day pass.—He's standing in front of me.—Yes.—Alright." She hung up. "A nurse will be here to escort you."

He stepped forward to look.

"Not yet."

He spun, "I *know*," idiot, "I'm just *looking*."

Well!

He sort of apologized in a blink and went to see the glass-enclosed entranceway with automatic sliding doors at both ends; between, a ten-foot chamber separating the two worlds. Outside, sunlight coated everything. A line of tall fat evergreens ringed the parking lot and trailed off to the left to the fence of the hospital yard and the backs of houses. How far did the fence go, how far could he go today, where was that nurse?

On cue a lobby door opened and she appeared, full of grace.

He needed to know.

"Where I can watch you," she said with what he felt was some pity.

He didn't care, Jesus Christ, he didn't care, he was on the abyss, hadn't been outside, seen the sun, in 10 days. What did air smell like? what was wind?

When he stepped onto the black mat the inside doors *wooshed* aside, the chamber air was unbreathably hot, pierced by thousands of darts of shining sun rayed from glass and cars and sky euphoria sickening him as he rushed the second black mat to charge into an orgasm of color

sky of suns, exquisite pain

face to the tarpaulin blue mural

braced against the orange fire exploding stars across lidded eyes

carnage

no shutting it out.

The freshness and grandeur intoxicating.

It hurt to witness the clouds in their glory, frozen explosions of liquid-luminous white, foamy tendrils twirling away in slow-motion movements to the lake breeze. He stopped breathing to feel the lake breath brush his skin, then re-breathed, gulping great chunks of thick warm air. He removed his glasses and shut his eyes and faced the wind rushing in off the lake and swallowed air—delicate precious delicious air.

This was Adam his first day—where the universe breathes and ends.

He wanted to shout, laugh, run, cry.

He opened his eyes to the sun-punched blue, a blue so deep so tight so ripe it was ready to burst.

Now he saw the world how he was supposed to see the world.

How could he

why would he

how could anyone

want to leave?

Forgive me Father for I have sinned, I did not know, I did not know, I did not know.

How could anyone?

He set his glasses back in place.

Behind the window-wall the nurse watched. He had to fight to control himself, keep from crying or laughing. He could not let her report that.

A gust from the north tinged with clean, clear smell of lake water air and the vinegary odor of decaying wet wood. Fresh, damp mulch, the rotting flesh of trees, heaped new in the flowerbeds

the soft breeze

his fingertips rubbed

braille air

God's word

In the hospital yard trees split up the sky undulating newborn leaves under the breezes, millions of leaves whispering the secrets of their being, a gigantic, invisible finger caressing limb tips swaying, plastic plant branches in the fish tank; black bulbs, birds, in budding arms; up the trees steepled and down into the ground—how far did the roots of things go?

White gulls lamented, wavering aloft on currents of air sweeping up from the lake.

Screeee?

Seeee. Seeee. Seeee.

Was this the same sun, these the trees, of 10 days ago? Had air ever smelled this sweet?

He could run away. The road was right there. But then what?

The doors accordioned.

He spoke with her their mutual secret at their last opportunity that could be uttered in public only through the knowing expression of their names.

"Richard."

"Sandy."

"Mom!" Down the sidewalk called a boy, all 6 feet and 200 pounds. "Dad's waiting in the car."

So they were the non-lovers interrupted once more.

"Be a dear and tell your father I'll be right there."

"He said I should come back with you, Mom." The boy scowled at Richard.

"Oh alright," Sandy gave up and with her eyes apologized to Richard and told him to wait right there, don't move, I'll be right back. "Let's go then." She off-loaded the suitcase and pillow and purse and bag on the dutiful son and marched him only a few steps before halting and miming, I almost forgot.

Neat trick.

She pranced the last few steps to Richard and hummed, "I have a present for you. To remember us. Hug. So nobody sees." She groped a hand in her jacket pocket. "Hug."

He did not want to but did.

The boy was staring. Richard shut his eyes.

She hugged too tight and teased in his ear. "Think about me when you use them." A soft bundle cushioned into his rear pocket; he realized what it was and let go.

That grin crooked devilish play.

"C'mon, Mom." Impatient, the boy threatened with what he could: "Dad's waiting."

"Are you coming back for the dance?"

Her giggle scorned and forgave his silly question. "Dancing is for girls who don't know how."

One last time she tweaked his arm, she who was his best chance of losing his virginity, and then was gone. In the rear pocket of her tight jeans was the distinctive outline of a condom. He would have to console himself with her gift, her red silk panties.

All the way to his room the smell of the hospital filled his head, and trying to name it. It didn't smell like a regular hospital, antiseptic, medicinal, what he remembered when he would visit a grandparent. No. This smelled like nothing, nothing he had ever smelled before, outside. He imagined that in a vacuum, this is what remained: the smell of nothing.

He returned to the disconcerting scene of Eugene in his room, laying out on the empty dresser his collection of colored glass and stone pieces.

"They told me I should pack my things. They showed me where to go. They didn't tell me who was here. Is that yours?"

Richard stepped to the restored dancer to display ownership. "Yes, it's mine, Eugene. Louis gave it to me." He protected her with his hand. "Don't touch her. She's mine, alright?"

On Louis' bed a suitcase and a pillow testified to the truth of the matter. On Louis' dresser a Styrofoam cup labeled MINE in thick black magic marker was the sole witness.

"Who told you..."

Eugene's eyes twittered. "They did. And..." Those eyes—tugging against some pull.

o god

"Stop."

what

Eugene settled his gaze over Richard's shoulder at the angel on the door. "Yes," he said. "Yes."

Richard retreated one step, didn't think he could ever take Eugene, not because of physical strength but because of madness.

"Don't leave!"

Those eyes.

"The keepers."

Where.

Black marbles. "There."

Now?

He shook his head. "They're gone."

The room was empty.

"Everyone has them." He diddled the bits of glass and stone, *clitter clack*. "Most people can't see them, can't see what's right in front of their eyes. I can. I see the things nobody wants to see. They say they're not real. So I take this medicine. That's what they tell me. They're not real."

He heard his voice ask, "What do you think?"

The black marbles dulled the shine of life. "I've seen enough to know the difference."

Richard *click click clicked*. He did not want to see, did not want to know. The bulge in his pocket was a bowling ball. "Do you mind?" He stared sideways until Eugene backed to his side of the room, shouldered privacy for himself, yanked a drawer open—the red of her panties became a stain of blood against his white socks and underwear.

How to hide it, how to hide it—

He flipped one pair of socks apart and stuffed the red swath down a throat. Some silk tongued out and he poked it neatly back in.

There.

Normal.

He slid the drawer shut, pleased with his thinking in this one small thing, grabbed his notebook. "I have to go."

*the trees breathe*
*sighs echoing*
*God's fragile thoughts.*
How did the trees imagine their creation?

At lunch, at dinner, in the lounges, everyone knew about his new roommate. They had seen him unpacking, bumping around in the room. Some smiled sympathies. Others:

"Fucking psycho, that's what he is," Vic sneered at the dinner table. "Seeing things, talking to his dead dog." He grinned at Richard. "Ain't that right?"

The diners laughed deferentially, and Richard tried, too.

Talking to what's dead.

Ha ha.

We keep what's dead inside.

Ha ha, ha ha.

Seeing things.

He could not look at Vic.

When Richard returned to his room Eugene was in the bathroom gazing into the steel plate mirror, touching his face, then the mirror, then his face again, and, startled out of his horrible perturbations, pushed Richard away with a helpless and hopeless gaze. Like his cat puzzling and pawing at its reflection in the water bowl, poking the surface expecting another cat, another world, on the other side. Later, alone in the room, Richard approached the steel plate and his mirrored self, longing to see himself as others saw him, not as a reflection in their eyes. His poor sight of himself was, he feared, colorless and murky, unanswerable in the steel plate. He longed to be viewed as part of the people around him, not at the bottom of a pond, not as a body in a coffin.

*Today I went outside for the first time in*
he counted fingers backwards
*10 days. I*
It took many minutes for a tear to drop, a dot for his *I.*

Minutes before lights out he turned aside to their room out of the river of homing patients. In bed under the covers Eugene muffled, "Did you have any visitors?"

Richard didn't know how to respond, didn't know what he meant, if he were serious or talking about visions, but thought it might be best to speak what was known. "No."

"That's right. Your parents are dead."

Dead? Oh shit. His first night in.

"Siblings?"

Shit. "No."

Why are you saying these things?

Because he's a nut.

Maybe he'll get the hint.

Richard sat on his bed to kick off his sneakers and put his back to the lump of covers.

"Why are you here?"

"Suicide, Eugene." How could he not know? "I tried to kill myself."

"I know what you mean. I was just wondering." The voice was clear. "Where did you go?"

"Nowhere, Eugene. I was in my bed."

"What did you see?"

Nothing. Except…

"Why did you do it?"

No one had ever asked him so plainly, so madly. Unsure how to respond, Richard went to brush his teeth. His shimmering self had to answer for him but he made it to be nothing. Any responses felt flaccid now that the pills they fed him every night calmed his mind, the ice cream they fed him every day numbed the fire in his cock, and every "because" that answered some part of the "why?" as he could articulate it before seemed here and now utterly vain and reasonless. He was a different person trying to imagine someone else's life. He was trying to make there only be the now. And the *reason* why he was here—no one ever explained to him his purpose. He was afraid to look on his own, and he had given up trying to explain to himself why he had done it. It hurt his head. He wanted it to be behind him and get on with whatever was in front of him. He went to bed praying for a quick lights out.

"How did it feel?"

"What?"

"Trying to kill yourself."

Oh God, "I don't remember, Eugene," but he did remember and did not want to remember. It was still close enough to taste.

The hall lights went off.

The darkness on the other side of the room said he should write it down in his notebook so that he would not forget.

# There are reasons

*I thought I was ending my life, I will never forget. I know what it is—what did I read about some Russian writer—Chekhov?—when he was a boy he hid under the bed from his father when the father came home drunk at night because he was afraid of his father because his father used to beat all the children in the family, whichever one he could get his hands on first, and Chekhov wrote that he would ask himself every morning as he opened his eyes: Is this the day I will be beaten? Is this the day? And I wanted to laugh so hard when I read that, I wanted to scream laughing shouting in the class.* THAT'S *what you're afraid of? You're afraid of* THAT? HA! You COWARD, you WEAKLING, you PUSSY. *When I wake up every morning I ask myself: Is* THIS *the day I will kill myself? Is* THIS *the day I will choose to die by my own hand?—and one day*

"You have a pretty one here. The angel on the door. Do you see her?"

There's nothing there, Eugene. It's a fucking door. "I see her, too." Under the bedcovers and with the dark giving distance he felt safe enough to ask, "Why are you here?"

The delay in response was warning enough.

Jesus.

"I see things wrong."

Out of the darkness on the other side of the room came sucking, slurping sounds.

Richard restrained himself for as long as he could before whispering fiercely, "What the hell are you doing, Eugene?"

The noise stopped.

"Are you playing with yourself?"

No response.

"Eugene."

Nothing.

"I know you're awake."

Still nothing.

"Eugene?"

A loud fart ripped.

The bathroom was the only place to be alone, but even there you could not be sure because the door had no lock. Richard enjoyed his bathroom time, especially in the mornings, in the shower: the day was new, naked and unspoiled, and he felt kindred with it. If he were taking a test and had to fill in the blank he might want to write "happy." He was even getting used to shaving in the wall plate. Under the shower he let drops of water form nodules on his forearm—swelling tears—bending the room's reflection. He lowered his head to make the reflections blink. Raised his head: reflections opened. He played with making the room open and close, open and close, slowed it to a disinterested blink, a cat's eye, self-absorbed, then shut his own eyes, relaxed under the warmth of the water and steam...

A breeze

He wouldn't

"What the fuck!" Richard groped for the water handle.

Eugene didn't move.

Richard grabbed his towel and started drying off. "Do you know how crazy you are?"

"No." Eugene blinked and asked, "Do you?"

Richard stopped toweling and tried to backtrack over Eugene's response to his question to determine the real meaning of his next question, but it all fizzled. "No. Yes! *That's not the point!* The point *is*, Eugene, you *don't* barge in on someone when they're in the shower. You don't stand there gawking at someone when they're in the fucking shower." He tightened the towel at his waist. "Will you get out of here?"

"I only wanted..." He was apologizing to the floor.

Richard would have to push him out of the way.

"I see things others don't see," he explained to the floor. "And I tell them. That's what I do wrong. I know they laugh at me, call me names. I'm not stupid. I'm not deaf." He wiped his hand across his eyes. "I'm not telling any of them what I see anymore. I didn't want you to leave without me. I want to go to breakfast with you. I don't want to eat alone anymore."

"You're not stupid, Eugene. You're..." Like looking into a mirror. "... just like everybody else. Everybody's different."

Eugene smiled. Ear to ear, Richard thought. He's going to split his head in half from his smiling and I'll be able to see what's going on inside.

They went together to breakfast.

There was a new kid, in a wheelchair, rolling himself up to the food line. One leg encased in a white cast and raised level with his hip so that, when he swiveled the chair, he looked like a human compass seeking true north. Another kid was helping the wheelchair kid with a tray.

"Who's that?" Richard asked the whole table. "The new guy in the wheelchair?"

"Don't know his name," Vic said. "But I heard he jumped." He smirked around a mouthful of food. "Not high enough!" Two high school kids sitting with them grinned, and Vic snorted, "Hey, Eugene. Psycho. That's a joke. You know what that is?" He winked at the kids.

"Shut up," Richard said.

"A joke is something funny that makes people laugh," Eugene said. "But no one's laughing at what you said. So it must not be a joke."

Red rushed up Vic's face, the kids braced themselves, and the plastic plate bounced off Eugene's head, trailing scrambled eggs and toast in his hair and down his shirt.

"That funny?" Vic said. "That funny now, you fucking Psycho? You see people laughing? You see people laughing at you?" He scooted his chair from the table and walked out of the cafeteria.

*Rage, fury, madness.*
His mind consumed
word to word to word
dot to dot to dot
points on reality
*Frenzy, fixation, burning.*
The thesaurus at the back of the dictionary was slim but fun.
He could only guess at what Vic was in for.


Think about me when you use it. He tried to use it. Behind the unlocked bathroom door. He kept trying. Until it wore him out.

Fucking ice cream.

Just as well, he thought. At least he could think now, because for the first time in his life his cock was numb and disinterested in any scenarios his mind could conjure, and he felt his mind becoming his own, under his control.

For the first time in his life, he feared, he was going to have to face everything as it really was.


The doctor said, "You worked full-time before you went to college."

His mother had been talking again. "Yeah. In a foundry."

"What happened there?"

"I worked there."

"How long?"

"Fourteen months, right out of high school."

"What did you do?"

"Lots of drugs," he laughed.

The doctor didn't think it was funny.

"I was a parts processor."

The doctor stared.

"We made aluminum casts. Transmission parts for cars, natural gas units for homes and commercial buildings. The machinist had a little pail, like a kid's sand pail you see at the beach, on the end of a long pole, poured the molten aluminum into the mold. In the side of a machine as big as a bus. After a minute the part was cooked, he pulled it out, launched it down a chute to a table. I processed it: filed it down, did a quality check, marked it with a red wax crayon; if it was a good piece; stacked it on a palette. We did that all night long."

"What was it like?"

He could recall: his boyishness revealed and shamed in naïve flubs and trampled among the rough men, the bearded, tattooed, drugged, drunken, pony-tailed motorcycle men,

working 11 at night to 7 in the morning,

watching them ignite their cigarettes by dipping the tip to the surface of the vat of fiery orange liquid aluminum, heat their frozen tinfoiled TV dinners at the end of long tongs in the roaring jet flames shooting from the bottom of the vats,

crying himself to sleep every morning his first month there, his first week his father at the dinner table telling how he had to listen to the other guys at the station brag about their kids going off to college, but "I gotta tell them what my kid does," his mother protesting

it's honest work,

learning how Father was wrong, there *could* be a sacrifice without bloodshed, from only words and a simple gesture,

it took everything from him,

learning the power of assorted pills carried like candy in pockets all night long, and crank, the joy of speed,

learning how to complete an income tax form when his father decided he should, last month, together discovering he'd made about $12,000 last year but his savings account showed $300, and

his father's look, the *look*, and the slow question, "Where did it all go?"

He had no answer because $700 a month was what it took to numb himself.

He learned how to keep the dead.

Richard shrugged. "It was a job."

"You had friends there."

"I knew people there."

"What made you quit?"

I didn't want to die, like they were, every day, rotting above ground. He told them before he quit. I can't live like you. "I was bored, I didn't want to work there for the rest of my life. And," he gave him what he wanted, "there was a murder."

Without speaking the doctor said, Please continue.

There was nothing to tell, really. "Two work buddies were high one night," as usual, "a fight started over a girl, one got his shotgun." At the wake—at the wake—he told him about how the other guys said that Melvin's chest had to be wired and propped up from the inside because the shotgun blast had torn him to pieces, sent him flying 10 feet against a living room wall, and his face—Melvin's face— the face on the body in the hard, smooth box—Richard thought: he doesn't look young, like me, he looks old. It was no monstrous clay indentation. It was real life, gone. What he didn't tell the doctor was that in the bathroom of the funeral home in one of the stalls someone from work was shooting up. As soon as Richard walked in he knew it. Felt it. Jesus Christ, in the funeral home. No fucking respect. Soon after he quit to enroll full-time at the community college. Some kind of escape...

A long, terrible silence followed, filled with the doctor's stare. "Have you thought about goals? What you want to accomplish here?" A monotone ensued about finding interests, discovering what you enjoy so that what you enjoy could become a part of you, that went on for so long Richard got lost wandering in his responses, and without provocation an image of a talking vagina popped into his head and he had to stop himself from giggling

—damn Vic—

circled back around to staying alive,

not killing myself or my new roommate—

He had to stop it, but as soon as he said "I like writing" he realized his mistake: the doctor followed too agreeably too quickly. "Yes. About what?"

"Anything."

"Anything."

Not this again. "Anything, anything." Was every sentence a fucking test? "I just like to write."

"I understand. But what we're trying to help you determine is what your likes and dislikes are so that you might better know how to develop your skills, focus your abilities, set goals. Goals can be hopes. To figure out what you want."

I want to be left alone.

"There are any number of things you might do."

"Really?"

The doctor prepared to re-load.

"I know," Richard said. "It's an exaggeration. To make your point."

The doctor breathed, "Yes."

"We all exaggerate, to make our points."

Screeee?

"Take my hobby; for instance." When he waved his hand a shadow stormed the walls. "I very much enjoy shooting birds—I mean, *photography*, of course—to the point that I've had several shows of my work at local galleries, and I'm preparing for another next month. Some of these you see here will be displayed." He tapped the air. "That one. The owl. And the cardinal on the fence." A streak of blood on a white railing. While the doctor continued discerning his treasures Richard's eyes roamed over all the animals captured in one frame of life. He enjoyed most the birds caught in flight. How they tipped on the sky! The doctor's voice droned to background until his name was used again.

"What do you think you'd want to write about?"

I don't know. "Things." Speaking could be such a chore. How about: "I want to write what I see."

"What you see?"

"Things I see, things I see people do, things I hear people say. You know: life."

"You talk about it as if you're not a part of it."

That's stupid. Of course he was a part of it. He just didn't *like* it.

"How do you feel about that?"

"About what?"

"About what I just said."

"About how I feel about what you said or about how I feel about not being a part of it?"

The doctor waved his hand, "Either one," shooing away a fly. "Whichever's most important to you."

Nothing's important to me. Can I go now? He was struggling for what to offer, to get him through this, while his eyes wandered the walls, but in his peripheral vision the doctor remained, embalmed. "What was the question?"

*How shall I describe madness? It comes creeping through a door that's never closed, the fevered drumming of an idiot's song, the voices down the hall, the people who are not there, my angel, frozen.*

He gazed at the words that had come from his pen in hand. His new elixir. The ink in the tube was blue, the color of blood in the vessel in his wrist. He pressed the tip there, where Christ's nail would have been, pressed hard, traced, to make it his own. Ink flowed and blotted and bled over the vein. It hurt so it had to be real.

On his way out Richard passed a nurse sitting on a couch with the fat girl, sobbing, the nurse at a loss to console her. The fat girl was blubbering: "Nobody loves me! I'm fat! I'm fat and I'm ugly! I'm so fat people think I'm pregnant! They ask me when's my baby due, but I'm not even pregnant, I'm just faaaaat!"

And Richard said to himself, you are right, you are grotesquely fat, you are painfully ugly, you are so fat I do think you're pregnant, but you are so ugly I don't know how anyone would want to fuck you to make you pregnant. He felt bad for what he thought about her and sorry for her in that wretchedness, but didn't know what to do about any of it. The cute nurse was in a fidget to stretch her slender arm halfway across the fat girl's back, he guessed what lies she was using as salve, and as he passed by he was not able to turn away from this accident; their silent exchange of truth was quick and excruciating.

He quickened away, hearing the fat, not-pregnant girl's tears until Joey's refrain ascended and floated hollowly with him down the hall to the side double doors out into the open yard to the edge of the near empty parking lot, and years ago how he'd asked his mother, "What's it feel like?"

His mother patted her stomach that looked like she'd swallowed a basketball.

"Do you want to feel?"

He nodded, all grace and wonderment. Placed his palm flat. Felt. "Can I see it?"

She smiled.

He wanted to see what was inside, what made it, in its holy place.

"You can listen."

He set an ear upon the curvature of her engorgement. A seashell on the beach. Nothing. Set his palm back in place. Snuggled. Felt pulled from the womb too soon, even now.

"Will it hurt when he comes out?"

"He?" His mother had patted her round belly and smiled. "We don't know if it's a he *or* a she."

"Will it hurt when he comes out?"

She grinned.

"Or she."

"Yes," his mother said. "It hurts. A lot. But not how you're thinking."

How else was there to think about hurt?

She looked down on him with the most beautiful face, he couldn't ever recall her looking more happy before or since.

"What's it feel like?"

She was still smiling her beautiful smile when she said, "It's the most wonderful hurt in the world."

No, he wanted to say, no, you can't be happy about that; I mean: "What's it feel like being born?"

She laughed. "Oh, honey, I don't think anyone remembers."

But he wanted to, felt he *needed* to, remember where he'd come from, for some reason, but never could, never could force it, easily, like the delicate melody seeping into his head, "Puff, the Magic Dragon," the song he didn't know any of the words to; did anyone? He hummed along, over and over, the song he'd played on his portable record player in his room as a little boy, sitting mesmerized by the sad tune. He hummed along and along until his mother barged in one day, puffing, "Can you play something else, *please*?" When she slammed the door behind her he only turned the volume very low and wriggled on his belly closer to the record player's speaker. Days later when he came home from school pieces of the record vinyl were arranged on his desk like a broken pie jigsaw puzzle, and when he took them to his mother in tears she admonished him, not turning from her dinner preparations: "What do you expect when I sweep your room and you don't put your things away?"

Now Richard detoured down the hall to the music room and poked his head in to see a nurse and Joey, sitting next to the record player with his eyes shut.

Few patients were outside. He didn't understand that, on such a beautiful day. Gulls winged up and down the coast. The chain link fence, interwoven with blue plastic privacy strips yanked out here and there to flap derisive tongues, ran, left to right, from the edge of the cliff at the lake along the backyards of four or five homes to the evergreens bordering the parking lot and blocking the view but not the noise of the city street beyond. He swung to face the yard, tall oaks, one willow, a beat up picnic table carved with names and dates, and a dirt path winding from the side entrance toward the parking lot where it fizzled out before meeting the sidewalk at the parking lot.

How simple to escape. Or leave for a day. He judged for himself: no staff, few patients, only a thick line of trees at the sides of the front lot. Walking away would be easy. But it wouldn't be right. The fence, the trees, framed his world now. Here he would stay until—what?

He strolled the fence and from one of the backyards ahead an opaque ribbon of blue-white smoke connected earth to sky. The acrid smell of wet leaves smoldering: burning incense offered in a clinking censer.

*Tink tink, tunk tink.*

The sensual sound of thin tines scraping burnt brick: a doting lover's nails at the back of a neck.

*Tunk tink.*

Stooping over a rake, an old man overdressed in a long-sleeve flannel shirt tended the struggling fire, tendrils smoking lazily skyward. In the yard with the old man a few of the same flannel shirts danced, bodiless, clipped to a line, sleeves flapping hello in gusts off the lake. Seeing the old man saddened Richard because he reminded him of his grandfather and how his mother said she could never tell him *this, this* he would never understand. Death he could understand, but not this. The old man glanced and Richard stared a moment too long to find in the old man's expression a warning and a fact: I've been alive and here for many many years, my friend, and I know you, I know all about you and your kind, so you keep moving, you just keep moving along. Richard did, head bent, and only when he was down toward the lake did he dare peek back at the old man, leaning on the rake, watching.

Then the old man did the unexpected: lifted a hand in greeting.

Richard mirrored, and the old man returned to raking.

Richard faced the breeze blowing up the smell of decaying fish and rotten wood from the cliff and walked faster along the fence to the lake and the corner of the hospital yard. No blue plastic strips wove through the fence lining the cliff; a full view was allowed up and down the coast for miles and below to the crashing water and out to the rolling waves and beyond to the water's smoothness where some sails glittered, white-silver pin tips poking the upper border of water. To his right the shoreline curved out for half a mile or more and disappeared behind a high outcropping where the lake had chewed its way beneath the earth before being halted with concrete boulders the size of small cars scattered along the shore and up part of the remaining slope. At the peak of the dangerous overhang a clump of trees clung to life; one leaned precariously, the others beseeched or hid from its threatened dive. Underneath, where earth once was, twisted roots dangled in daylight: life underground. Below him the concrete boulders formed the slope.

To his left the shore continued west some 20 miles to Cleveland, a blur of gray-blue buildings lumped in the distance, stone markers on the edge of the long stretch of water. In front of him the two fences did not corner but gapped. Jerked pencil strokes of bird shadows terrorized the boulders and maniacally shot the slope, yard, and trees.

Screeeeeee?

Seeeeee. Seeeeee. Seeeeee.

He followed them to the lone picnic table under the willow tree's weeping limbs. The roughness of the bark sent him back to their own willow knocked over in a night thunderstorm years ago.

The next morning his father had surveyed the horizontal tree and steadied himself in his work boots at the rim of the awful hole created by roots torn out of their home. "It's a helluva thing." Broken limbs stabbed the earth, and the spared ones praised the unblemished blue sky. "A helluva thing." Arms akimbo, motionless, his father observed the fallen tree so long that Richard became afraid. Silence from his father was normal; a long silence was to be feared like that mysterious twilight before a late afternoon Spring storm. His mother had already gone back inside after talking about what types of trees she might want to plant now that this one was dead. She kept changing her mind, out loud, until Richard asked "Which one?" to make his head stop spinning as he tried to follow her words. She looked at him as if he had popped out of nowhere, and she proclaimed that changing her mind was a woman's prerogative. Alan mis-echoed, "A wimmin's perogi." His parents bugged eyes at each other and laughed, he couldn't remember when his parents had laughed that hard together, and he tried to laugh with them, to join them, though he didn't know what they were laughing at, but it was too soon over, the spark of magic gone, his mother heading back inside, his father steadying himself at the edge of the hole. "A helluva thing," he kept saying. No one was there to hear him but Richard and his toddling brother, and they were playing hide-n-go-seek in the unimaginable branches that yesterday evening silhouetted the storming sky.

"Richard."

He straightened.

"That's enough monkeyshines."

"Yes, sir."

"C'mere."

"Yes, sir."

His father motioned at the mess and blamed. "This won't take care of itself, will it?"

Richard shook his head.

"Here."

The bush clippers' lopsided distribution of weight nearly flipped them out of his grip.

"Know how to use these?"

He did not but did not wish to appear weak to his father. Besides, he had seen him use them.

"Show me." His father's arm swept. "Along the big limbs here. I need clean spots to cut." The chainsaw waited on the lawn.

Richard lifted the heavy clippers, a hand for each handle, steady, steady, scissoring the blades open, a fingering branch, clipping them closed, steadily, steadily. The sun and his father's eyes judged.

"Not like *that. Here.*" His father shoved the blades down the thin branch to its base. "Get it all. Don't leave anything."

His boy hands could not do it.

"Jesus Christ." His father's hands engulfed his own at the handles and forced their strength to become his own, and it hurt. "Now do you see?"

They were bundling branches to burn. But there was no altar. In the end his father used the chainsaw, lowering it screaming into the fallen wood.

Richard slid his hand down the skin of the tree.

The side doors of the hospital burst open.

Philip.

Scissoring finger branches.

Richard tried casually to make for the lake fence. Philip followed, notebook in hand.

"Ssince when can you go out?"

"Since yesterday."

"Eugene'ss been looking for you. Insside."

"OK." So what.

That cued Philip, who shuffled open his notebook and produced a sheaf of papers. "I made you thiss." The papers, stiffening in the wind under pressure of his good left hand, were littered with drawings and tiny lettering cocooning objects: crosses, mountains, black caves or coffins. "Maybe thiss will help you ssee—what I mean to ssay. The other day—I get sso excited ssometimess I can't think sstraight."

As much as Philip creeped him out, Richard felt sorry for him, too. He tried to give a good show over the pages, *hmmm*ing, but then got irritated. He didn't want any of this. "Thanks." Philip observed his fumbling with the pages: he started to fold them, stopped, scrolled them.

"You're not going insside?"

"I'm walking." Richard swooped his hand toward the homes.

"That old man. He'ss a pagan, won't lissten to reasson. Yessterday I talked with him."

Richard edged away.

"Sshould I tell Eugene you'll be in ssoon?"

"Sure." He shuddered, not against the lake breeze. The fence guided him, drawing him back to the old man's fire burning low and unattended in the circle of charred bricks, the rake propped against the fence. The scroll of Philip's papers weighed in his hand. He stopped, checked. The hospital yard was empty.

Quickly and without thinking he balled the papers and spun, did his best jump shot. The ball bounced off the brick rim and settled against the bed of glistening, glowing leaves, unburning.

"*Goddammit.*"

He rechecked the hospital yard. Still empty. The old man's yard was the same, except for the scarecrow shirts, and the rake. He grabbed that and poked with the metal fingers, teasing the ball to the flames. It tipped. Once more. A tongue of flame tasted a wing of paper. The fire consumed the dryness, rejoicing, blackening and twisting the words and drawings into hypnotizing incomprehensibilities. Richard, relieved there'd soon be no evidence of their encounter, set the rake in place and turned to see Philip standing by the side doors.

Philip came at him across the yard. Within hearing distance he said, "I thought you were different."

"I get that a lot."

Philip balked. "Don't you want to be ssaved?"

"From what?" The hospital was emboldening him.

"From your ssinss. I'm trying to help you. Don't you know why you're here?"

"That seems to be the question."

"Don't you ssee the blood on your handss?"

Richard looked at his palm. I like red.

"Don't you want to be ssaved?"

Yes, from the foundations of the earth, he believed he was already, from something, at least from himself, for now, but he could not tell Philip about God's finger touching at the point of swallowing all those pills because that was crazy talk.

"Thesse people are goatss here. Only the ssheep will be ssaved."

*Baaaaa.*

"Ssome clay jarss were made for ssmasshing. Only the potter'ss handss can make or break what He doess."

It came out as he thought it: "Do you think this is crazy talk?"

That stopped everything.

They were shooting baskets in the gym, Vic leaning over the foul line, taking aim, lofting the ball, Eugene scrambling for the rebound, Philip sitting off to the side. The gymnasium was twice the size of the main lounge, one corner of its square legged out in a low-ceilinged cubby hole for a treadmill and a bumper pool table, and another corner glassed in, the nurses' sanctuary. The gray-painted cinder block walls were bare except for several health and motivational posters. One series portrayed a human body progressively de-layered from flesh to muscle to organs to nerves and vessels to bone; instructional, he thought, to know how the insides work, but they really didn't explain anything at all, only pointed to objects in place. Vic shot again and missed again, and Eugene loped idiotically, chasing the ball past a series of small posters of words step-stacked: Level, Direction, Speed, Pathway, Force, Concepts. This was about teamwork, or athleticism, or attitude, he was guessing.

Richard went to Vic, getting the ball toss from Eugene. "Now you're pals?"

Vic smirked. "Me and Psycho? We came to an understanding." Shot again. "I won't throw food at him." Missed again. "He won't kill me in my sleep."

Richard laughed.

"It's not funny," Vic said.

Eugene smiled at Richard and waved and scrambled.

"What about him?"

"Who? Bucky?"

Bucky?

"Look." Vic did not move from his stance of waiting for the ball. "Don't be a dick, Dick."

Richard could have punched him.

"How was your walk?"

Fuck you.

The ball bounced back.

Vic aimed quickly. "See how easy it is?" Shot an arc into Eugene's waiting hands.

"Missing a basket? Yeah, you make that look very easy."

Vic twitched the hair patch out of his eye. "I meant going out."

Eugene dribbled the ball to the foul line, and Vic and Richard stepped aside.

"Well?"

The question required some response. Richard did not want to appear afraid, but his hesitancy probably already revealed that. Eugene was doing a ridiculous pose of practicing before shooting, and he tried to make that and not his response the focal point between them because he could not tell Vic how afraid he was of breaking the rules, of getting caught, of doing anything he wasn't supposed to do and later paying the price for it; he longed for invisibility, any way out, any miracle to rescue him; and Vic waited with his well-how-about-it? face until Richard's miracle happened: the gym door opened and in bounced Susie, spied them instantly, moved with a mission.

"Here we go," Vic said.

Richard felt mocked by his own jealousy.

"I've been looking for you *everywhere.*"

He couldn't bear to watch, to listen. In his whole miserable life would he never hear a girl say those words to him?

"Have you been hiding from me?" she teased.

Richard hated Vic, hated them both, for their lightheartedness and easy way with one another. He had to leave, run away, he could not be in this place.

"I *was* going to ask you to the dance next Saturday. Where are you going?" She sprinted to Richard's side and let her fingers linger down his shoulder blade, pressing electricity. "Shoot some pool? Come on, it'll be fun." Her gaze was convincing. She nearly skipped away, treating him to the sight. He needed to make sure he wasn't hallucinating. Vic, Philip, Eugene each reflected a unique madness and reassurance.

"I smell bubble gum," said Eugene.

"Shut up, Psycho," growled Vic.

"Who has bubble gum?"

"I said, 'Shut up.'"

She had come for him, and he went to her. At the bumper pool table she chalked her stick, blew off dusty excess. "Would you do me a big huge favor?"



"Can I borrow that marker?"

"Sure," said Eugene.

Richard got the black magic marker from the dresser, shifted for privacy, held up his Styrofoam cup he had marked MINE 2. "So we know whose is whose."

He handed it to Eugene, who looked ready to clap he was so happy.

Richard smiled. It was silly, he knew, but making a simple connection like this with Eugene, someone like Eugene: it made Richard feel more human.

He was walking past the music room when he heard the tinkling of a piano. He looked in. The room was empty but for the wheelchair kid, who was pulled up parallel to the instrument.

"Hi," he said, stepping in.

The kid turned in his chair. "Hi."

"You play piano?" His mother used to play piano. He loved when she used to play.

"Yeah." The kid tapped the keys.

"My name's Richard." They shook hands.

"David."

"Why are you here, David?"

"Accident." He smiled and slapped his leg cast. "I'll be out in a day or two."

"Oh." An accident. Out in a day or two. Richard wanted to be kind and not give him the look. "Can you play?"

"This is really out of tune." His fingers played.

Richard couldn't tell.

David adjusted himself before the keyboard, paused, one breath, then pounced.

The two-hand attack on the keyboard produced an intense loud-lush wall of music—the most beautiful Richard had experienced this close in his life—a push of glorious notes, fingers raced and danced and nailed cries of joy home in his heart tore open his soul forced him physically from the piano—and he was glad, so that David would not see his tears, his insides bursting out.

He was running out of ways to entertain his mother. "I can go out now. Yesterday was my first day. Or we could go anywhere inside. We don't need to sit here. Do you want to see my room?"

"Are we allowed?"

Eugene scrambled out from under the bedcovers.

Jesus Christ, you fucking nut, can you pull yourself together for two minutes, and as he said the words, Eugene, this is my mom, Mom, this is Eugene, what are you keeping? my parents, and how the dead will rise to judge the living.

Eugene's eyes went wide. "Philip was right!"

His mother made Louis' dancer the object of her exaggerated attention.

*I played bumper pool with Susie today. That was fun. Vic was getting pretty upset, watching us play. Eventually he left. Eventually. eventually—"at an unspecified later time," "in the end." Eventually. In the end. Eventually, in the end, I should find*

"You shouldn't keep your notebook in the room," Eugene said. "They snoop, search for hidden things."

Oh. And who else snoops? "Where would you hide it?"

"Not under the mattress, that's the first place they try. If you're not in your room. And not in the drawers, or behind the drawers."

"Where then?"

"Keep it with you."

What?

"Keep it with you all the time, wherever you go, whenever you go. That way they'll never get it from you. If you keep it with you, all the time, they won't find it, whatever it is. It's just who you are." He reached into his pocket and pulled out a clump of brown hair.

What the fuck?

Eugene was surprised any explanation was needed. "It's Buster's."

Richard enjoyed his time out in the yard among the silent green sentinels. A row of hedges along the building draped bunches of branches heavy with thousands of petals glowing yellow-white-pink. Bees poked in and out of flowers; a butterfly made a frozen yellow-black V on the edge of a leaf. At a corner foundation a toothless grin cracked, trailing through the dust a strip of tongue of tiny red ants, serpentine, a crawling artery. As a child he would sit so long, just like this, in the dirt, spellbound by the ripe-bellied dots loose-linking lines undulating to and from a pinhole in the earth. The ants followed antennae to ass.

"What the fuck are you doing?" Vic was jiggling a bent cigarette out of its crimpled pack. The *Green Lantern* was folded beneath his armpit.

"Watching ants." He scrambled up and dusted off. "I didn't know you smoke."

He tamped the cigarette on the fat pad at the back of his thumb and forefinger, slung it between his lips, match snapped, hands cupped.

Richard loved the smell of a new-struck match mixing with the smell of the first puff of a cigarette. It was powerful and sexual and of the earth, and he wished he could smoke, but it didn't do anything for him. "You like comics?" Vic ignored it, strolled to the fence of flapping loose plastic blue tongues wagging in the breeze, and Richard trailed. "I used to collect comics. Used to sell them, too. Me and a friend, we'd buy a table at these mall shows, or in a hotel, sell a whole bunch."

Vic didn't seem to be listening.

"I always thought I'd make a good superhero."

That got him.

"Captain America. You know, solving crimes, kicking ass."

Vic puffed. "Captain America's a fag." He stared defiance. "Wanna know why she's here? Why she dumped me?"

Because you're a nut?

"I told her: You know, it's not always about your pussy."

It came down to this? This is what guys did to each other because of pussy? Is this why Melvin died? For nothing? Richard saw himself in a coffin. No one else was in the yard. "We were just talking." He tried to laugh it off.

Vic approached, smoking.

Richard could not move because he could not comprehend, and the speed of the gut punch stunned like stars and buckled his knees

whooping for air, his mind opened wide

—god

—*damn*

From here they all looked like ants.

*godly, godlike*
*I could have killed you.*
*Well thanks for not, then.*
*Don't ever do that again.*
*What?*
*Sucker punch me.*
*Don't steal my girl, then.*
*I think that's already done.*
*Well. Vic smoked. I hope we're not done.*
*No. We're not. You owe me one.*
*For what?*
*For not killing you. Remember?*
*Vic grimaced.*

"What are you writing?"

Thoughts. Feelings. You. "Nothing."

"Let me see?"

I don't think so. Gently: "No."

"Why not? I would let you see what I write." She giggled. "If I wrote."

"I wouldn't ask to see what you write, if you wrote." I would leave it unruined.

*Holding her hand is like holding hands with a summer day.*
Like I want to live.
He wrote that down, too.
She had told him, if you want to write me, write me here, easing open his palm and touching the hollow of his hand. "So it lasts. And you can keep it secret, all the time, to remember." She folded his fingers to shut his palm-page.

"I've been thinking about what I want to do when I get out."
"Oh?"
"I've been thinking about going back to school."
"Oh? For what?"
"Writing."
"Oh?" His mother took that and chewed it around a moment. "What would you write?"
"Stories," he struggled. "Books."
"About what?"
"I don't know." He tried what was true: "Maybe this."
"*This*? What's to write about *this*? Oh my God, Richie, what are you thinking? Don't put your name on anything about this. What would people think?"
Miserable, defeated, push. They're all dead. "I'd dedicate it to you and dad."
A light beamed out of her and her hand motioned out the marquee while she declared: "And you can write it: I owe it all to my Mom and Dad!"

# Isolation

The familiar siren sound started when he was leaving his room, alone. It cut through the undernoise of the hospital clear and clean. His first childish thought was: Dad's coming, Dad changed his mind and he's really coming. But that was destroyed by the siren screaming in the hallway, shrill-crescendo-heartbeat in his head, a razor slice inside left ear, took him to one knee, he cupped-clawed-beat the ear to stop it.

*Stop! Stop! Stop!*

It stopped.

He lowered his hand, surveyed the hall, up and down. Silence. The lounge had people. He made his way.

Everyone was normal

daylight cascading from the skylights

*Words are blocks brightly painted and shiny to sit in.*

The one thing that was his, he could call his own, was his words, his journal. At night it was peaceful in the lounges and the TV flickered in the dark. Richard sat in the comfortable chair in front of the fish tank, basked in the glowing blue water light, kneed up writing surface, feet on a straight back chair, contemplated his reflection, somber, scooped eye sockets, and joyed at the liquid world in which every living thing floated, glided, effortlessly. The world glowed, free from pain. Only warm enveloping water and soothing movement. He doodled words. He felt safe on the outside, looking in, shut his eyes and, inside, floated away. Most of the residents were already background to his life in the hospital.

He felt a presence materialize beside him, closed his notebook.

"How'ss it going?"

Richard fluttered his eyes—shut them again, listened to him walk away, strained one eyelid up: Philip sat at the far end of the lounge by himself in the dark. Jesus. Richard lowered the lid. Jesus Christ. He decided to ignore him and continue his empty meditations, but it felt like napping under a noon sun.

A howl ricocheted from the main hallway.

Heads craned.

The howl edged to violent shrieks, mixed with scufflings, wall bangings, and muscular grunts, struggling closer. "*Get offa me!*" the desperate howler shrieked. "GET THE FUCK OFFA ME!"

With the other residents Richard anticipated, and out of the main hallway the scene erupted. Four whitecoats stumbling together, each clutching a limb of a man in their midst, each urging one another to hold on, mates on a ship tossed by a violent storm. With a quick twist one whipped away and smashed face first into the clear wall of the nurses' station. With one leg free the man became possessed. He tornadoed in the three holding him, and the whitecoats braced but another leg tore loose, then both arms, and sudden freedom lit his face, he jumped away and gargled a hideous wet laugh. He was a stalk of a bearded man, a crazed giraffe, and the residents scattered screaming in every direction, screeching chairs and couches.

The whitecoats scrambled all legs and arms.

The man rushed pell-mell, eyes wild for escape.

Richard jerked up, legs locked, their bodies tumbled together. His glasses scuttled crab legs across the tiles, the world blurred, the man's jacket billowed out a tracer of small-silver—striking tiles—metal—clattering into a fast slide to Philip, who snatched it up and set it between his legs and clamped them closed so that Richard was not sure he had really seen a gun.

The whitecoats swooped.

The man spun frantically for what he'd lost, bicycled his legs into Richard, and pushed up screaming, "Get offa me!" Charged headlong into the black window reflecting the fish tank. A dull thud as from a coconut dropping on sand, a group gasp, a breath-hold as the man righted himself. His body tottered, stilt-stepping, then crumpled.

The whitecoats descended, silently, dragged him up and hurried him away, silently, toward the small hallway to the PRIVATE door with the one small square window. It opened from the inside, closed and *clicked* after them.

Richard got his glasses and notebook and with the other residents stood blinking in the vacuum.

A wail—protracted, protesting—lifted higher and higher from behind that door, and Richard sensed the other patients lifting with it, with the man, perhaps in hope, or defiance, or brotherhood, but before their apex it was cut off as with a knife. The empty air built a boundary between them and him, and Richard imagined stabbing injections and leather straps pulling taut. Eyes locked on the closed door with the one small square window, then braved glances at grave faces nearby, and they all knew together, shared the same dread, the same unspoken understanding, which is the deepest understanding, the deepest companionship, that that could be any one of them in there.

For the first time Richard thought Louis was wrong: this was no plain suburban madhouse.

He looked among the others to see if she was safe, but did not find her.

He turned to ask Philip what he scooped up but the chair was empty.


It was a gun.
It was not a gun.
It was a gun.
It was *not a gun.*
It *looked* like a gun.
You're seeing things.
It looked like a gun.
They'd search him.
Then why did he have a gun?
You lost your glasses.
It looked like a gun.
But it wouldn't be a gun.
Because they would search him?

They would search him.

Still...

It looked like a gun.

Richard waited, watched the snack room from across the way in the TV lounge, waited for the right time. Pear Man rounded the corner and sat in a chair by the window at the edge of the lounge, opened a small photo album in his lap and began flipping through its pages. Richard forgot about him as Philip walked out of the men's hallway toward the snack room.

"Waiting for someone?" Pear Man asked.

"No."

"Want to see some pictures?"

No. "Sure." He could make this quick.

"These are me. And my family." Pear Man displayed the book.

"Nice." Richard eyed the snack room.

Pear Man was flipping through the pages, narrating the photographs with a word or two: "fishing", "backyard cookout", "fixing the car", "Christmas". In each one Pear Man overwhelmed the picture with his size.

"They're all of you."

His sad smile complemented his vacant eyes. "My wife picked them. She said they might help me. Sometimes they help. Sometimes... I'm looking at a stranger. Here she is, my wife. Isn't she beautiful?"

In the photograph Richard saw another Pear Man. Only female.

One of them needed new eyes, or a dictionary.

Philip was sitting down, spreading out his notebook and papers. "I need to get a drink. Dry mouth."

"I'm sorry." Pear Man continued muttering.

He got his drink from the machine. "That was some excitement last night."

Philip grunted.

So this is it.

It was a gun or it wasn't a gun.

It was or it wasn't.

Was or wasn't.

Was wasn't.

"What did you grab off the floor last night?"

"What?"

"Off the floor. Last night."

"Lasst night? What do you mean?"

"You didn't see anything fly out of that guy's jacket? It hit the floor and slid across to you and you picked it up."

Philip chewed his lip.

"I'll tell them what I saw."

"What—" Philip false-started a response and then measured it out. "What would you tell them?"

"What I saw."

"What do you think you ssaw?"

"It's not what I think I saw. It's what happened."

"Your glassssess fell off."

Bucky and his goddamn double s's. "That guy *tripped* over my legs and fell, and *something*—"

"—ssomething?"

"*something—popped* out of his jacket"—

"—*popped* out of hiss jacket?"

*Goddammit.* "—*slid* across the floor, *landed* at your feet, and *you* picked it up and sat on it."

They stared at each other until Richard felt it forced from him: "It was a gun."

Philip was unmoved.

"I'll tell them."

"Sso?"

"They'll search your room. They'll find it."

Philip didn't think so. "I think they'll adjusst your medication. Or worsse. You're sseeing thingss. That happenss, you know. People hear and ssee all ssortss of thingss in here that aren't true. And if you really get worked up about it they might jusst put you in there with him. Think about that, why don't you? Think about what you do. All for what didn't even happen. There wass no gun. That'ss crazy talk." Philip sighed so that Richard thought he saw a light bulb *blink* behind his eyes. "It wass a ssunglasssss casse."

"A sunglass case?"

"A ssunglassss casse."

Goddamn Bucky.

Their staredown forced Richard out of the snack room.

"Checkers?"

Huh?

"Checkers. Wanna play checkers?"

Richard nodded, refused to look him in the eyes.

As they set up at their usual table, Richard felt the weight of their view from the Isolation door window. "That guy gives me the creeps." The bearded face was scowling.

"Who?" Vic said. "That dick?"

"Right. You're brave with a steel door and a bulletproof window between you and him. Every time I go by he's staring at me like he wants to kill me."

"I would too if you tripped me."

"Did you see that?"

"What?"

"He pointed his finger at me."

"I heard he shot somebody. But then, I heard your roommate talks to God."

"That's funny. That's real funny. Can we play over here?"

"Hmm?"

"Change tables."

Vic scoped the area.

"Over here." Richard led the way to a table around the corner in the fish tank lounge, out of the line of sight of the Isolation door window.

Vic stepped over. "Why?"

Richard sat and unfolded the game board and dumped the plastic checkers. "Look, do you want to play or not?"

Vic sat. "Can't see shit in here."

"Then get your hair cut." Richard plunked his pieces into place. "A haircut, a haircut, to get that damn hunk of hair out of your fucking eye so you'll stop twitching every five seconds. Or wear a bandana, that's what I did, when my hair was long."

"You had long hair?"

"Yeah, I had long hair. So what? When I worked in the foundry. Longer than yours. Longer than Susie's. Down to here." He put his finger two inches under his shoulder. "What's the big deal? I kept it in a ponytail to keep it out of the way."

"Try not to worry about him."

"Who?"

"The creep."

"He keeps staring at me." Reminding him of the violent ones from the foundry, the ones who liked guns.

"How's it going with the doc?"

"My test results came in. How'd you do?"

"Alright," Vic said. "Closest to a hundred I ever got in my life, I think. How'd you do?"

When the doctor had said his score was 132 Richard started to make excuses because he felt so blunted by the effects of the overdose. The doctor told him the therapist wrote a note that he had never seen anyone complete the picture matching exercise so quickly so perfectly. "132."

Vic's mocking was leavened with respect. "I'll call you Genius from now on."

Richard grinned, embarrassed but secretly hoping others would view him differently, too. He felt some shift of power between them. "How long will he stay in there?"

Vic shrugged. "A day or two, or three."

There wasn't much time.

What should I do?

Tell your doctor.

He won't believe me. That's crazy talk.

Philip's right about that.

I'd be locked up in there *with* that nut. And get more medications. Or worse.

But they could prove it, prove that Philip had the gun.

How about Vic? Tell Vic.

Vic would know what to do.

If he believes you.

He'd know what to do.

"How would I sneak into someone's room?"

"Why would you do that?"

Richard checked for eavesdroppers, out of habit, for show. "I think I saw something last night, when that guy came in, yelling and screaming, when he tripped over me."

Vic's body vibrated an interested *yeah?*

"When he tripped, knocked into me, something popped out of his jacket—silver—heavy—slid across the floor to Philip. He picked it up and hid it."

Vic was listening.

"Nobody saw it but me. Philip didn't tell anyone about it. I asked him about it right now, before you came in, and first he said it wasn't anything, then he said it was a sunglass case—a ssunglassss casse."

Vic was unimpressed.

"I think it was a gun. I *know* it was a gun. Help me get it out of his room."

"Why would you want a gun?"

Jesus Christ, "I'm not going to kill myself, if that's what you mean. Look, I don't want *him* to have it, that's all. I see the way that guy's been staring at me. He thinks I stopped him from getting away. Every time I go by Isolation he's there, in that window. If you don't want to help me, just say so. I asked because I thought you'd want to help me out here. Pal. Buddy."

Vic's gears were working, he could see.

There always had to be that. "When I'm out for a weekend, I'll see what I can bring back in."

It was a simple plan. At dinner time, with the patients and most staff gathering in the cafeteria, the two of them would sneak down to Philip's room, Vic positioning himself inside the doorway, as a lookout, allowing Richard to search the room. Vic told him there weren't many places to hide things. Desk and dresser drawers, inside folded clothes, under the mattress, inside a pillow—these were the obvious places. Check those first and fast. The more difficult spots— under the bed, under the dresser, *behind* a drawer—would need two people: one to lift, another to search.

"That's where he's probably keeping it. If he has it."

"*If* he has it?"

"I mean, if he's not carrying it around with him. That's what I would do. If I had a gun. Not in here, though. So what could you do with it?" He patted his pocket. "I wouldn't trust it alone in my room. If I had a gun. Or outside," Vic mused. "I might even hide it in the yard, or on the beach."

"How do we check his room?—the bed, the dresser?"

"I come into the room with you. We do it together."

"You said we needed someone watching the hallway the whole time."

"We should, Genius." His eyes played. "Got any ideas?"

No. "What if we get caught?"

Vic studied the walls. "Don't fight them. That only makes it worse. If you fight—you saw what happened. If we're lucky, they'll just tell us to get out."

Philip's room was identical to every other room, so in a panic Richard thought that they had broken into the wrong room, but Vic, irritated and waving him in, was his assurance, and Richard moved in.

The neatness was surprising. He didn't know what to expect: volumes of books, yellowed scrolls and maps of the Holy Land, a gargoyle or two perched high in the corners. But the room was tidy.

Now where would he hide a gun?

The first dresser was empty but for a small clay pig, hollowed and painted pink. An art project. Marbles stacked in the pig's back. The knobs on the drawers were the same as his own. Of course. Everyone's the same. He slid open the top drawer. Empty. He hadn't expected that. Of anything being empty in this room. He slid it shut and tried the next one. Up fluffed mounds of white underwear and socks, pyramided. Flinching from thoughts of where these items snugly fit, he reached underneath, and there, there—touched the metal spiral spine of a notebook.

This he had to see. Just for a minute. It was red, blood red. Gently he lifted it, as if it were some ancient manuscript, spiraled it open over the clothes, flipped pages from the back to the most recent entry at the very top of a page on one line:

*something in*

Two words alone on a page.

Who writes two words alone on a page?

Such small hard handwriting.

The opposite page was blank.

He had to flip a page back.

*There are reasons*

Noah packed no clothes

Opposite page blank, flip back.

Found? Found what?

*I think I found*

231

There are reasons

every one of them

*Noah packed no clothes*

*puzzles amuse them*

There are reasons

*We are being devoured all day long.*

"Are you a *retard*?"

*RETARD!*

Vic marched. "What the *hell* are you doing? Reading his fucking *notebook*? Is that what you came in here to do?" He squeezed Richard's arm, hard. "You're supposed to be *looking* for something."

Richard closed the notebook and shook free.

"Get to it."

Back at the doorway Vic surveyed the wing, did a nod that all was well.

Richard scooted the notebook under the white pyramids and closed the drawer. The others he opened and searched efficiently, found nothing, finally examined the dresser in its entirety. It fit the floor all around, same as his, though this one... He squatted, ran his fingers along the line between the dresser and the tiles to the middle where the wood gapped. He got on his knees and smushed his head against the cool tiled floor. Along the other side a cut of light lay, interrupted. "I think I see it." His eyes weren't adjusted to the shadows, he could not be sure. "Maybe." A small lump? He tightened his face to the gap. Reflected dots of light glowed faintly off metal. He pressed closer still and couldn't contain a sudden horrific sneeze.

Vic glared.

"I—think I—"

"Well go ahead."

Well go ahead what? Tilt it himself? He tried, but it squeaked angrily. "Help."

Vic evaluated.

Richard waved him in.

They did not need words to understand or communicate the risk of what they were about to do or how each needed the other, and Richard thought he was feeling a little of what his father must feel with men at his side fighting for a common goal. They grabbed the dresser, together, Vic crouching and lifting at one end, Richard sitting and bracing the bottom at the other end, concentrating, to reveal the secret buried underneath, intent on any sounds in the hall, so that he first heard but did not see the clay pig legging its way over the edge. Years ago, he had read about how people, during unnaturally high stress events, might experience hallucinatory states, how actions, even time itself, smudged into unreal motion: staccato moments: the pig dove, freefalling, leered devilishly, in telepathic cahoots with Philip, tilting loose its insides of glass marbles, marble eyes accusing swirls of red, blue, green, his hand shot up to greet them, Vic sucked air, the marbles separated, tugged on individual strings before the pig landed in his lap, clinking and nestling grinding glass and clay sounds, the rest of the eyes pinballing around the room.

They were late for dinner and had to take the last empty seats on opposite sides of the circle. Philip was there, and some of the high school kids, and Eugene.

"You guys are late," said one of the high school kids.

"It's a sign from God," said Eugene.

"Out shopping?" said another.

"What iss, Eugene?"

"Him," said Eugene, and activity slowed under the realization of who he had named and as he searched the faces around the table for some sort of recognition. "That new guy in Isolation. He's watching all of us. Waiting. Like he's been here before. Like he's been sent back for something. I heard he *shot* someone."

If it were anyone but Eugene the reaction might have been different.

"Chocolate ice cream tonight," said one of the high school kids.

"Chocolate was *last* night," said another.

"I like vanilla."

"Me, too. Chocolate makes my ass itch."

The table talk continued but Eugene wouldn't be ignored. Conspicuously he stretched straight in his chair to dig in a pants pocket, and when he retrieved what he'd sought his face lit up in defiance. "It's a sign from God," he demanded and displayed his treasure pinned between his thumb and forefinger, "like this marble that rolled to me."

Of all the faces Philip's stared the keenest.

*Red left. I didn't see her go. Susie told me. It dawned on me that I hadn't seen her for a while, so I asked, and she said, "She's gone, she left yesterday." I must have looked surprised. "Why so surprised?" she said. "Did you want to say goodbye? Were you friends?" Not exactly friends, I didn't say. More like I told her more stuff about me than anyone on the planet. "What will you do when we leave?" Susie wanted to know. "How will we say goodbye?" I told her it didn't really have to be goodbye.*

"No."

"Come on."

"No."

*"Come on."*

"Fuck you. Move."

"Vic, c'mon."

"Genius, are you listening? I said *no*. I can't believe I let you talk me into that bullshit. We're even. If I ever get caught again..."

Richard pushed a coin. "We'll know what to do this time. We'll know where to look. It'll be easier this time."

"No, *we* won't, because *I'm* not doing it. Don't you get it? It's gone. If anything was ever there. *If* he ever had it. He's not gonna keep it after last night, not after that. Not after that." He mocked Eugene's pose of show and tell: "'It's a sign from God, like this marble I found.' Jesus Christ, did you *see* the look on Philip's face? He knew we were there like he saw us go in. And it's gone, man. If it was ever there in the first place. It's gone. Leave it alone. C'mon. Move."

But Richard could not leave it alone because it would not leave him alone. Walking by Isolation compelled him to look, to see who he had put in there, and there was the man's face, staring out of the window; or his hand might be shaped to a gun, thumb cocking off a round. So Richard wandered, anywhere, the hallways, up, down, back, forth, anywhere to get away from his empty room to the lounge past pacing Joey, out he went into the sunshine and fresh air and green yard and screaming gulls over the cliff where Eugene stood hurling slices of bread.

Seeeee. Seeeee. Seeeee.

Screeeeeeee?

In answer a white slice arced, a mad flapping of wings powered to the apex, trumpeting screeches, and Eugene would watch after them, turning his head this way and that, looking at what Richard could not tell.

Before he was close Eugene asked without turning his head, "What's the strongest animal?" And answered without waiting: "Snails are the strongest animal."

Clouds covered and uncovered the sun, shuttering the sky light on earth; light strobed Eugene.

"Snails are the strongest animal," he said again.

Richard wandered nearby. Overhead, gulls were buffeted, feathers sheeting, steadying themselves in the updraft. "What are you talking about, Eugene?"

"Snails are the strongest animal because they carry their home on their back." He turned and grinned, and Richard couldn't help but share it.

"Where'd you get the bread?"

"Cooks gave it to me. Tossed it over the fence by the kitchen. The door's always open. Nurses don't go back there." He frisbeed another slice, the gulls angled and dove, and Eugene looked after the air where the birds were.

Richard needed to know, afraid of the answer, "What do you see?"

He smiled, watching. Pointed. "I can see their sound, trailing."

"You see sound?"

"Not all the time. It's pretty. They leave traces when they cry. It's like they're paint brushes, stroking when they cry across the air. Or sparklers at night on the Fourth of July, writing your name in the air. You won't tell them?"

"I won't tell them, Eugene."

That made him happy, and he was off running, like a little kid, through the yard under the birds, winging bread slices high, chasing their shadows. "C'mon!" he was shouting and laughing, waving Richard in. "C'mon!"

In a yard next door to the hospital an old woman was hanging clothes to dry. Shirt arms flapped maniacally in strong gusts.

Richard considered his roommate and any normal qualities he could espouse, or fake.

It might work.

It could work.

He would make it work.

It was a simple plan.

"Let's go over it one more time," Richard said, and as he listened to his roommate he watched for any patients or staff drifting too near. It's simple, Eugene said: "At lunch I watch for any people coming by Philip's room. You need to go in because he took something of yours. Like he did before. That's why he cut his fingers off. What was it? Was it the shirt? The Noah shirt? Buster took my socks once. I had to chase him around the house from room to room, he was so funny, he'd go like this:" Eugene pawed his arms.

"No."

"Because I'd like to have that. Aren't you supposed to give it to your roommate when you leave? How come you're not wearing it? Is that what he took?"

"No. Eugene. It's not the shirt. Look, I need to get this—all you need to do is watch and tell me if anyone's coming, OK?"

"That marble sure was nice. Sure would be nice to have more of those."

*Is there anything more degrading than walking into a conversation that stops because of you?*

The room was the same. Even the pig was in its place and grinning. Richard knew he should take less time than the first time and so worked swiftly. The dresser, the nightstand, the desk, the bathroom, the mattress. He tried to lift the bed but could not and figured if he couldn't then neither could Philip. When it was time to tilt the dresser he motioned Eugene into the room and placed the pig on the bed. The dresser creaked up heavily, and Richard crouched to check the darkness and the undisturbed dust underneath.

"Is it there?" Eugene called.

No.

Now what?

Richard was confused, and afraid. He motioned for Eugene to lower the dresser.

"Did you find it?" Eugene crept back to his post.

Richard scanned the room. It couldn't be anywhere else.

Jesus Christ. It *had* to be. I *did* see it.

"My marbles," Eugene reminded. "Don't forget my marbles."

Marbles. Yes. Eugene's fucking marbles. *That's* why I'm here:

*Marbles!* Richard scooped the pig off the bed and poked a finger into its back.

"Blue and green," hissed Eugene. "Blue and green."

Yes, yes. Jesus fucking Christ, blue and green, blue and fucking green. The top layer pleasingly clunked glass balls of yellow and red and white. Deeper he fingered, coaxing methodically. He didn't care if anyone saw him. Nurses could come in, Philip could come in, he didn't care. His fingertip rooted to the bottom and struck a cool, metal surface. He stopped, peered down into the pig through the colored glass balls to a small gold cylinder, submerged. Into his palm Richard tumbled the pig guts, marbles of assorted colors and one bronze cartridge.

"You don't need to do that." The *Green Lantern* didn't lower.

The gulls' secret screams arched overhead.

"Put it in your pocket and keep it there. Don't take it out. Don't show it to anyone. Better yet, throw it in the lake. Did Eugene see it?" The *Green Lantern* hadn't moved.

Richard shook his head. He'd been saving it for Vic. "He was happy with his marbles." He rolled the cartridge between his fingers in the sunshine before slipping it into his pants pocket and keeping it tight in his fist there. "What should we do?"

The comic lowered. "'Do'? 'We'?" His one free eye squinted against the sun.

"What'll they do to him?"

"If they think there's a gun in there? What do you think, Genius? Cops'll be here in a minute, hauling him away. Turn this place inside out for anything else. Talk to people, hear what they have to say. You better hope he doesn't get away then, *ever*."

"So you're saying I should pretend I never found *this*?" Richard bulged out the hand fisting the cartridge.

"Your balls? C'mon. Look. Genius. Alls I'm saying is—*look*, calm down. Alls I'm saying is you should *pretend* to be sane, so you can get the hell out of here as soon as you can and forget this ever happened." The *Green Lantern* flipped open and raised.

"You don't care that this guy has a gun in here? That he probably killed somebody? That I'm next?"

The *Green Lantern* edged down. "Know why you're here?"

Fuck you.

"Got any idea how long you're *gonna* be here?"

He could not answer, he had given up asking.

"How long you *think* you're gonna be here?"

Screeeee?

"That's because," Vic said, "nobody knows. Your doctor won't tell you because he *can't* tell you because he doesn't know. Louie had one thing right: you act up: you get a stay in Isolation. You start seeing things: maybe you get more meds, or different meds, and another week in Isolation, or worse. Jesus Christ, Richard, before you came Eugene was in there for days because he threatened someone. How much crazy talk do you think they'll listen to before they do something to you? You wanna end up same as fatso in there, playing puzzles and flipping through family photos to remember who the fuck you are? or Joey? You show up with a *bullet*—to a *gun*—you say you saw someone come in here with—but you couldn't find it even after you snuck into someone else's room with your *schizophrenic* roommate who talks to his *fucking* dead dog and *Jesus fucking Christ, Richard*—" Vic stopped, sniffed, upped the *Green Lantern*. "You haven't been strapped down."

Richard could barely give voice to his despair: "You don't believe me."

Behind the comic a sigh mollified. "Do you know who you are."

Jesus. "You sound like my shrink." He took the cartridge out and weighed it in his palm.

This isn't a toy.

Are you afraid to look? Afraid to see?

The people in the room, they come at night.

I was dreaming.

The siren in the hall was during the day.

I was wide awake.

Hallucinating.

The *Green Lantern* was implacable. Do you know who you are?

Richard understood: he was alone.

It would be alright.

You don't need anyone.

This isn't anything new.

Except now even the nuts are rejecting you.

Even the nuts are rejecting you.

It unhinged him, and he fled from it, back to his room, where he wanted to slam the door but couldn't because he wasn't allowed, because someone would come for him, so he paced the room, end to end, clenching and unclenching his fist around the hard cartridge. It was real, wasn't it? It wasn't a toy. He stopped to study it. It was real. It had to be. But it was so small. He marveled at what damage it might do. Then without thinking at all he set the tip of the bullet against his temple and pressed, hard, pressed hard until it hurt and stopped after a good long time of pain. It made sense to him now—the pain. It woke him up. It should hurt so that you wouldn't do it, wouldn't *want* to do it. Like suffocating yourself. Which was like drowning? But not burning. Not burning alive. That's what his father said. He rolled the cartridge around in his palm, playing with it. Bright, brass, and warm. He could not throw it away, ignore it. It was real. He knew what to do.

His mother answered, "Hello?"

"Hi, Mom, how's it going?"

"Hello?" she repeated.

"Hi, Mom?" he said louder, "It's me, Ri—"

"Hello? Is anyone there?"

"Mom, the line must be—"

"This isn't very funny. *Hello?*"

"*Mom!*"

"Asshole." The line went dead.

In his entire life Richard had never heard his mother use that word.

"You seem preoccupied."

Me? No. With what?

Screeeeeeeeeeeeeeeeeeee went the doctor's birds.

"How are you feeling today?"

How do you want me to feel today?

Silence eventually forced the doctor to give up.

The note paper he tore from the bottom of a sheet in his notebook. The handwriting he made block and wrote with his left hand. He'd seen that on a TV show. Sneaking it down to Philip's room was easy. One foot of the pig he left holding the folded note. The pig could keep a secret for him, too.

The therapist beamed, "How is everyone this afternoon?" She seemed genuinely interested in how each one of them in the group was feeling, and Richard wondered why anyone would, how anyone could, care about that, why a decent-looking woman would want to work with a roomful of nuts. She never did get much response, except from the housewives and high school girls, unnaturally eager, as if they'd found a real friend, a true confidant, in their lonely, epic struggles. The guys were mainly leery. Mike propped against the wall with his arms folded. Philip leaned against the opposite wall, digging his heels into the carpet.

"This afternoon," the therapist glowed, "we're going to talk about secrets, when secrets hurt, getting what's inside out." She was quite excited and serious about this matter of secrets, and why people keep them, and why some are good and necessary, and why some are bad and debilitating.

De–bil–i–tat–ing.

What a beautiful word. What did it fully mean? He would have to look it up later.

She used it two or three more times, and each time he admired her syllabling. But suddenly she was talking about breaking off into pairs and motioning for them to move, and everyone except Richard knew what to do. His slow response left him searching for a partner. Mike was already paired with another older guy. One of the high school girls was available—no, one of the housewives latched onto her.

Philip was examining one of his heels.

"Why don't you two pair up?" She was so pleased with her conducting, waving him over. "Philip needs a partner."

In his pocket the cartridge was a brick. Richard didn't know how Vic could do it, he thought everyone would see his guilt. Glumly he tramped across the room, and they sat next to each other, adjusting themselves to avoid eye contact, listening to the therapist explain her exercise, "How Secrets Hurt," how each of us has good secrets and bad secrets and how some secrets have power over us because we give them that power because we keep them hidden so deep inside of us and how we might break their hold on us if we share…

We all keep the dead. We keep what's dead inside of us.

Immediately after she stopped speaking Philip piped, "Why don't you go firsst? Tell me a ssecret you've been keeping."

They both knew.

"It could be a ssecret from yearss ago… or jusst thiss morning."

Richard twisted his heel into the step, and up from nowhere gelled an image of Eugene and "My dog. I had a dog once." His name was Buster. I liked Buster a lot. "I killed him."

The stubs scraped chapped lips.

Why did he lie? To scare Philip? He hung his head. Why was Philip here? The cartridge outlined in his pocket.

He did not want to know, but it was his turn to ask. "So what's your secret?"


Richard had to make his lid. The lid had to be made. He wanted to make the lid. He wanted to make it as straight and as even and as smooth as possible so that it would fit perfectly onto the box he built last week, to hold whatever he put in, to keep everything in. He didn't know what he would put in. Maybe the cartridge. Maybe his stick-faced self-portrait. Maybe other secrets. Maybe his own secrets. He wandered among patients and projects, got the new clay, the box. He needed a lid. He had to make the lid. Jesus Christ. The fingers had to come off.

His hands were shaking so hard that he could not unpeel the plastic wrapping from the clay.

The room filled with faces he recognized from the lounges, the cafeteria, the yard.

Who are these people?

The fingers had to come off.

Why am I here?

Because the fingers had to come off.

For a *reason*.

Screee?

Seee.

Secrets.

Everybody has secrets.

Some are good secrets.

Some are bad secrets.

Jesus God some are bad secrets.

Philip's words kept describing the severed fingers falling through the air, how they had to be cut off, because I was bad and needed to be punished, to learn, like Jacob learned after wrestling with the angel, the angel asked him his name, he was touched forever, marked forever with a limp, and people knew by looking at him that he'd been marked, they could see, he could see, I could see me doing it but it wasn't me, I took my mom's garden shears, I could see me doing that, too, but it wasn't me doing it, and it wasn't hard, I mean it didn't hurt, and when I saw them fall it was like watching a pretty waterfall over and over, you just sit there and see it over and over in your head, the water's all the same but it's all new, every time, you know it's all new, and that's how I felt after I'd done it, all new, so I took my fingers and put them in the toilet bowl like we did with our dead fish and flushed them down to the sea, out with everything that's dead and dirty, the blood made trails in the water, circles and circles lower and lower, little fishies back to the sea, little fishies back to the sea, like a baptism, that's what it was, my time of testing, my bloody baptism.

"You always eat with Vic or Eugene." It was near a complaint or whine. "I don't mind." He inferred differently, and he had nothing other to say than he's my friend or he's my roommate, but she beat him to both with "Anyway it doesn't matter I'm going home this weekend. I think that's a good thing, don't you?" and he was thinking to say yes he did but she beat him to it with "My doctor thinks so, so do my parents, they think I might get to go home soon, for good, but I have to go get ready now bye." Her hands squeezed his hand. Her hands were clean, without numbers.

Richard was one of the first in line for medicine. He got what was his and went to his room to be alone. Before sleep he reached down and smoothly inserted the cartridge between the mattress and box spring. The tightness made it safe there, at night. Keep it with you, all the time. He rolled onto his side and watched his gray plank of an arm in the limp light and listened to the rhythm of Eugene breathing, fearing how he lived and dreamed.

In the morning he told himself he must be doing better. They let him keep his plastic disposable razors. So he told himself he must be doing better. "Doing better." That's what he heard people say a lot. "I'm doing better." Or, "It'll be OK. The doctor said I'll be doing better, in a while." But what if, in a while, it didn't get better? No one ever talked about that.

Shaving to your reflection in a metal plate was not easy. He thought he must be a funny sight anyway, angling for a clear enough picture to use as a guide. It had been an uneventful night. No hallucinations. No devils, no angels, revealing themselves. He dressed, feeling fresh in what light crept into his room. He put on Louis' shirt, the Noah shirt, his shirt, and patted his pants pocket to convince himself of the reality of the cartridge. He was late for breakfast but didn't care. He enjoyed the quiet of Saturdays. He ate leisurely, alone, relishing any attention from new people about his shirt. After, he wandered to the gym to see who was in for the weekend.

Vic and Eugene were shooting baskets, Vic at the free throw line, Eugene under the basket, waiting for the ball to drop. And Mike. Wordlessly they acknowledged him.

Few others played in the gym. Too early. Saturday. A nurse sat in her room with a whitecoat. A couple of high school kids shot bumper pool. One of the gym door windows in the hospital hallway was blocked with the face of the man from Isolation.

Richard shut his eyes.

It's not real.

He's not there.

His face won't be there when you open your eyes.

He opened his eyes and the man was swinging open the doors and strutting in, stutter-stepping, he wasn't put together quite right, like some small but vital part was missing or damaged.

"Hey, Four Eyes! Nice shirt!"

Richard's bowels collapsed.

Vic giggled but shut up with one look from the man.

"Yeah, you, smart guy." The man swaggered to Richard. "I'll bet you're a *smart* guy." Richard was tall but the man had to look down, *down*, on him. Tagged to his lower lip a tired cigarette, unlit. "What's your name?" The cigarette danced, his eyes widened at the stitched name. "*Noah*?" A wet throat laugh gargled, and he asked the others preposterously, "Is that the most dipshit name you ever heard?"

The face from behind the window was breathing on him with the smell of dirty fish tank, stray hairs from the beard and moustache vining into the mouth where one tooth turned sideways, an opening door.

"Wanna know my name?" the man teased. "It's *Bug*." He jerked up his sleeve to show off his left shoulder. "See?" Tattooed, a bright winged insect buzzed, its fat round striped belly curled up to showcase a quivering stinger. The bug leered devilishly, and Bug, the man, mimicked. "Like that?" He rolled the sleeve down. "Thought I'd say hello to the guy who tripped me the other night, that's all. Cuz when I sting, you stay stung. Got that? *Lookit me when I'm talkin to you.* What's your name, Four Eyes?"

Those who postulated two responses to danger—fight or flight— should have considered an appropriate third response: on-the-spot internal decomposition. The scrambled eggs in Richard's stomach screamed for evacuation.

"His name's not really Noah." Eugene sounded so helpful. "That's the shirt he got from his roommate Louis."

o god

"He has to give the shirt away before he leaves, for good luck, and I'm his roommate so I think I should get it. His real name's not Noah. It's Richard. I'm Eugene. That's a nice tattoo. Is that a wasp or a bee?"

Bug twitched as if a fly had landed on his nose, then a shitty smile spread his beard and his eyes slit at Eugene. "Who's the fuckin retard?"

"I'm not crazy," Eugene said.

"Leave him alone," said Mike. "He's a schizophrenic."

"*I'm* not crazy. *You're* crazy."

jesus, jesus.

Vic was eyeballing for help from the whitecoat.

"What did you say?"

"I said, 'Leave him alone.'"

The whitecoat charged out, time enough for Bug to assess, murmur to Richard, "I know who you are, I know what you got."

The whitecoat neared. "Is everything alright here?"

Quieter, "I'll kill you."

"I'm not crazy. You're crazy."

"What's going on?" The whitecoat wanted an answer from someone.

"Now see what you did," Bug said loud. "Broke up the game, made the nurseman come out."

The whitecoat ordered, "This is a no-smoking facility."

"Don't worry," Bug said, toying the cigarette at the lip of his grin. "It ain't lit." He winked at Richard. "Yet." Bug whirled and everyone watched him stutter-step back into the hospital.


After lunch Richard wanted to be alone. This he told to Vic and Eugene while everyone asked everyone what they were going to do the rest of the day. He left the table not telling them what Bug had whispered partly because he wasn't sure he had heard correctly, partly because he wasn't sure he had heard at all, partly because he did not want to hear. Still, he didn't want to do anything with Bug loose in the hospital. He wanted to get away from him. Get out. Think. He headed out to the yard with the sunshine and blue sky and lake breeze and gull cries. What was driving him now? He felt nothing in his pocket. He had to keep touching the cartridge through his pants, to make sure, make sure it was there, make sure it was real. Then seconds later he would do it again. To make sure. And then again. To make sure again.

I know who you are, Bug had told him. I know what you got.

In the grooved path near the fence strolled a high school girl and a housewife. Under the willow tree a nurse, middle-aged and with no discernible female features, coddled Joey, who nuzzled in pre-breastfeeding motions. She guided him into position next to the table.

As he approached he realized but did not want to believe what she was about to do. The space from the picnic table to the willow tree was approximate.

Of course.

The nurse nudged Joey. The mumbling, the pacing, the turning, all were the same. But the fresh air and sunshine.

Richard felt brave and funny. "Nice day for a pace."

The nurse glowered.

Why do you keep doing this to yourself?

She stared him into turning away, and he slunk to the worn path by the fence, slowed down to try to enjoy the freedom of outside. As the girl and housewife finished their walk by the gymnasium doors, Bug and Philip came out, together.

Philip saw him and waved.

Richard returned the gesture.

Bug talked.

Philip laughed. Shook his head.

Everything was clear to Richard. He kept on.

Bug pointed in his direction and talked.

Philip shrugged.

Richard kept going, nearing the cliff, where charcoal bird shadows cut the new boundary of his life.

*Susie's gone for the weekend again—I miss her. She said she might be going home for good in about a week. I couldn't tell her when I'll get out. She said if she was out and I was in, she'd come back for the Spring Dance. I told her I don't dance. "That's OK," she said, "we can sit and talk or go for a walk or something." I think she wants to dance anyway—or something.*

He paused.

*Bug is out of Isolation.*

If anyone sees this.

All afternoon he stared at the TV and thought about what his mom was doing, and his dad, and his little brother, and his older brother, and his grandparents, Louis and Red and Sandy, one by one he went through everyone he knew trying to picture exactly what they would be doing outside with their freedom, through the windows, light and unblinking, and he reached to touch the plastic—a high school boy came up to him all eager eyed.

"Food fight tonight. At dinner. In the cafeteria. Spread the word."

Richard didn't want to spread the word.

The boy dashed off, proselytizing.

Richard didn't want a food fight. He enjoyed dinnertime, especially on the weekends, because with half the patients gone life inside was calmer. He didn't want any trouble.

As dinnertime approached the high school kids became more restless. He watched them colluding, then going forth to giggle their impending mischief, and he smiled politely when they continued to approach him, one after another, but finally he held up his hand to preempt the announcement. "I know. I know. Food fight tonight."

He slipped into the cafeteria already knowing what he needed to do: find a nut to sit with, the strongest, the craziest, the most dangerous patient, someone *nobody* would dare start a food fight with. He stepped away from the line making a scan of tables for refuge. Luck! Three at one table: Mike, Bug, Eugene. He didn't care how or why they would sit together; he was only looking for shelter among them. Plus, he had a sudden absurd notion that he could maybe smooth things over with Bug, until he caught the tail end of Bug's comment to Eugene: "Sure, he's a nice guy. For an asshole."

Richard didn't want to know who he was talking about. "Mind if I join you?"

Mike motioned him to sit. Bug stared holes into him. Eugene chewed with all the affect of a cow.

They ate while the teenage storm brewed. Boys at different tables made daring faces at one another, pantomiming their opening volleys.

Bug was slurping his soup as if he hadn't eaten in days. "Goddamn soup is *hot*! Got cat tongue. But it's good! Alls we needs a bigger spoon."

Richard couldn't stop his response, "Or a funnel."

Eugene giggled, Mike grinned.

Bug said, "You think you're funny?"

Not especially.

They tried silence.

The boys continued their fake starts.

Richard couldn't stand it any longer and said to his tablemates, "Better watch out, huh? It might get messy."

Mike declared to the air around him, "Boys better think twice about what they're gonna do. I *know* nobody wants to get hurt." The words were a sedative to the high schoolers.

"Any food hits me," Bug chomped a mouthful and waved his plastic knife in one-upmanship, "I'll take this knife and carve his heart outta his fuckin chest." His laugh dared anyone to challenge the veracity of his statement.

Mike paused his fork midway to mouth, Eugene gazed straight ahead and chewed. When Bug laughed Richard felt the laughing directly at him, right in his face.

"What the fuck are you lookin at?" Bug's eyes flashed and Richard flinched.

A french fry plopped on his plate in a pile of ketchup, a dismembered finger in a pool of blood. "Wanna fight? Huh?" Bug bent greasy fries into his greedy hole. "Huh? Food fight? Right now?" He giggled idiotically.

Mike sighed, pained but noncommittal.

Bug flicked half a fry, hit Richard in the chest, and Richard wilted. A moment of rage flashed within him to take his tray of food and smash it into Bug's shitty face, but he knew he could never do that because he knew what would happen.

So he did what was safe.

"Where you going? Huh? Guess he don't wanna food fight. Guess he don't wanna."


Richard realized his glasses were stolen when his hand brushed through the space at the corner of his desk where he had placed them last night—every night. In their place was a note, the feel of it immediately and eerily familiar. Held it to his nose to read in the morning light his own scrawled block letters:

I KNOW WHAT YOU HAVE

He checked under the mattress. Thank God. Left the cartridge, decided against that, it would be better with him, dressed quickly, pocketed it. Then he flipped through his notebook, only a few pages' worth, nothing special. It looked untouched. He checked his dresser drawers. The Noah shirt was where he had put it. So it wasn't about that.

He thought of waking Eugene, but for what he didn't know. He thought of going to the nurses, telling them he lost his glasses, lost them

Where? they would ask. How?

He knew they wouldn't believe anything he said.

They'd think it was crazy talk.

Maybe he'd get more meds, or different meds.

Maybe Vic can help.

Maybe Vic would know what to do.

The long hall to the lounge was a wash of toneless morning color, without movement. Going to a friend's room to get him for breakfast was nothing unusual. He bumbled into Vic's room, relieved to find him there, and explained.

"See now? *See* what I *told* you?" He kept twitching the hair patch. "You can't go to them *now*. Not now. They'll turn you inside out. Did he take anything else?"

Richard patted the cartridge in his pocket.

"Good. At least that's good."

He tried reading Vic's face for thoughts, but everything fuzzed. "Any ideas?"

"Eat breakfast? Genius, they watch everyone come out for breakfast. You gotta go down there, do that first, or they'll come down for you. Think you can do it? Can you see anything? How blind are you? How many fingers am I holding up?"

"You think they'll give me an eye exam?"

"How many fingers?"

"Three."

"Funny. Really, how many?"

"Two?"

"You kidding me? How many now?"

Richard raised his middle finger, too.

"Walk."

Richard steadied himself, practiced a stroll to the window, returned.

Vic groaned. "What the hell was *that*? You move like *Joey* for godssakes. Can you *pretend* you can see, OK? The floor's still there. It's not moving. Follow me, OK? Right behind me. Jesus Christ, you take the fucking cake."

Richard was afraid to ask because he suspected the answer. "What if somebody stops me? Asks me where my glasses are?"

"No one's gonna stop you."

"What do we do after breakfast? I mean, Father Walker's coming today. So's my mom." She would know. She always knew what she wanted to know. "How will I get them back?" And the childhood terror of telling your parents you lost your glasses to the playground bully seized him.

Vic, already out the door, paused: "Maybe Bucky wants to trade."

Alone, they ate breakfast quickly, and if anyone was noticing anything unusual, Vic did not say. Richard saw nothing to tell him anything. The plate of food before him might as well have been vomited there. He could not focus on anything; it was making him sick. All the bodies were trees walking, and he stared through them, beyond them. He sat eating, visionless and alone.

In his room he waited.

Near the time for Father Walker to arrive he went to the main lounge to sit. He didn't want a nurse coming down to his room to get him; he counted on seeing Father well enough as a black pylon near the nurses' station. And it happened that way. In his myopia he saw the black stump appear at the end of the hallway on the other side of the red line, and Richard went to it. They said their hellos and waved at the nurses, and Richard followed Father out the side hall to the yard.

"What happened to your glasses?"

Richard hadn't thought through a completely believable lie because he couldn't believe it himself. "I stepped on them," he experimented. "They fell off my desk. This morning. When I woke up."

"That's unfortunate."

He'll tell a nurse! They'll catch you!

Father did not believe him, adjusted his own glasses with the care of someone who has depended on them for life. "You're having them repaired?"

"Oh yes, yes," he lied some more. "Blind as a bat without them."

"Well, you know, Richard," Father said, "certain creatures have certain proclivities. Bats may not have eyesight as we think of it, but they've been created to make up for that, many times over. They have other fine perceptions, without sight. For them, they're normal. To us, they're beyond normal."

Richard didn't know why Father was talking so much about bats because he could care less about bats right now and so remained mute.

"It's a beautiful day," Father observed, "isn't it?"

Richard nodded. Green blotches blighted the landscape and black-brown streaks truncated at the earth to dissolving edges. The air felt cool but the sun goosefleshed his naked skin.

"Is that a path over there?"

"By the fence?"

"Are you game?"

What a strange man.

Father led the way to the blue tongues wagging.

"How have you been feeling?"

"OK. Fine." Fearing for his life and wanting to keep it were new feelings. "Good. Better." Best. Bestest. He flipped through words and emotions like keys, fumbling for one that would fit.

The priest stopped, searched his eyes from the end of that vestmental tunnel.

Hey, Issych, lookit you.

Richard had to turn away.

And lookit that *knife*.

"You know, Richard, none of us lives in a vacuum. You've heard the saying, 'No man is an island.'"

"Uh huh."

"Do you know what it means?"

"No one can do it alone." Except me.

"More than that, we need each other, we need each other's help. I think you have an opportunity here, if you *see* it this way—"

With *new* glasses!

"—to redeem the time. If you think your life was saved for a reason."

Screeeee?

The birds were naked, Richard sensed. The fish, too. But they were not ashamed.

Father continued on the path before them near the fence, and Richard followed blindly, the silence louder than the gulls. He felt himself floating, clothesless.

"Don't you want to know why?"

To stop from drowning, Father.

*What's wrong with you?*

"Who are you waving at?"

"The old man," Richard said, "there in the yard. We wave to each other." He felt Father look the look.

"There's no one there, Richard. It's a shirt on a laundry line."

Wah wah wah wah wah.

He squinted and saw nothing where he thought the old man should be.

"Salvation," the priest began anew, "has many meanings; it is not always a one-time process."

Prō-cess, Father said. Prō-cess.

"Some look out—back—on a life and see a field of selves. We get to an age where we don't even recognize who we were."

I'm there right now, Father.

"Putting on Christ means leaving an old life behind. Your old life should be foreign to you."

"*Every*thing is foreign to me, Father."

The priest stopped.

"Well we *are* pilgrims in the world, Richard. Many times you struggle with it—" his hands worked the air to mold it— "figure it out, see what you have a hold of—" stabbing a knife— "or what's got a hold of you. This is part of life. Even our Lord wrestled with this awful dread and mighty love, in the Garden of Gethsemane, against what He knew His life was for, His Father's will, to the point of sweating blood."

Inside out.

"Now," Father agreeably argued, "has any of us sweat blood for His sake?"

The pills were laughing at me, I had to eat them to shut them up.

"Does that make sense, Richard?"

He didn't know. He didn't think so. Jesus, after all, was God. How could He go wrong?

"If you've confessed your sins, you are absolved. Does your guilt remain? Confess again, be absolved again. This is a natural process— in the spiritual sense, of course—your soul is seeking reconciliation. To remove the power death has over you."

Richard gulped air and nerves.

"I only say this because I think you can hear it."

You have ears to hear.

"Sometimes we're called in the strongest way, and sometimes we're called by a delicate voice, a gentle voice."

If you talk to them they'll talk to you.

"What I'm trying to say is: Sometimes forces act upon our lives. We are all God's creation; some are meant for glory, some for the fire."

Why not both?

Then came a whisper from the dark confessional: "Don't miss the voice calling you to His peace."

Piece of the puzzle. The missing piece: God's peace. What he'd felt flowing into him before swallowing the pills he could never tell anyone, that's crazy talk. Richard sensed more than saw the hand alighting on his shoulder only to lift off, spark the ashes of his unworthiness to flames: throat constrict: gulp tears.

"Are you alright, Richard?"

Drunk on hot shame, he felt his head creak a nod. He was ancient and new.

"You don't need to say anything to *me*, Richard."

The priest would be there when he opened his eyes.

If he held a fistful of crayons he would draw draw *draw*

Across the yard his mother trundled, waving near hysterics, shouting his name.

Why aren't you playing with the other children?

Patients in the yard stared.

He jogged to meet her, to stop her. They met talking through one another.

"What happened to

I tried to

your glasses

call you yesterday."

Asshole.

"Was that you?" his mother asked coyly. "There was nobody there. I thought it was a prank."

"It was me."

"Well that's too bad." And she noticed. "What happened to your glasses?"

"What happened to your glasses? You listened to me, didn't you? Lookit you!" Susie stepped away from her spot in the medication line to take all of him in. "See?"

No, that's the problem. She was bringing him to a grin, he couldn't help himself. But he couldn't tell her his truth. It was easier with his mother.

"Lookit you," she hummed, sucking her tongue.

The line opened up to present him to the silver-blue haired nurse.

"Even she noticed," Susie said behind him. To the nurse, "Doesn't he look better without his glasses?"

Her red line split. "I knew there was something different about you."

Practically the only person all day who had not asked what happened to his glasses was Eugene. Richard found him hunched over his dresser, fiddling.

"What are you doing?"

"My collection."

Yes. The collection. Richard stretched out on his bed. The collection, bits of glass and stone. "Where you been all day?"

The bits tinkled under the guilty reply. "Around."

"Did you go out again?"

"It's pretty outside." Eugene's voice was a breath of caught air. "The trees. The sky. The sunshine. Down on the beach it's so loud." Richard listened intently to descriptions of the sand, the smell, the spray of water on skin, because he could not see the face illustrate the heavy words. "I can't be here."

"Nobody wants to be here, Eugene. You'll get out soon."

"They won't let me. I know. They're going to put me someplace I don't want to go. But I have a place to go. They think I don't, but I do. I have a place to go." He sounded detached, mechanical. "No."

Was he talking to his devils? Or angels? "Do you see them now?" Richard asked.

"Yes."

"Are they talking to you?"

"Yes."

"What are they saying?"

No response.

What are they saying?

A breathless struggle. "It's not time yet. Wait and watch. It will be your time."

All the while the angel on the door vibrated.

Upon awakening, out of habit, he reached for his glasses, and all thoughts collided that they should not be here because they were stolen but that they were here where they always are. The world was clear once more. And the slip of paper, a mat for the glasses, with block lettering.

YOU NEED YOUR EYES, DON'T YOU?

He was too tired to be intimidated, if that's what this was supposed to do. He rolled. Eugene was gone. Time to shower.

A creak of the door and a cool breeze signaled someone interrupting the water's comforting warmth.

"Eugene. Get out of here."

A footfall answered.

"You're letting all the cold air in," he sang over the shower.

"I thought we'd have us a talk, Four Eyes." A blur but Richard could make out his glasses dangling from Bug's outstretched hand. "Be a shame you lose these again."

Richard scrambled his hands for cover and whimpered come on, give them, pathetic and shower hollow.

His glasses dangled.

He reached.

Bug *tsk*ed. "Let's talk."

A flash and fingers clamped his left nipple to pain.

"Ah ah ah," Bug warned, "I wouldn't move if I were you," squeezed.

stars shot

"That hurt?"

jesus god

"I'll ease up. Tell me where it is."

The stars subsided.

"Tell me where you put it."

"I don't—"

Pinch.

"*know*"

Twist. "*Listen*, Four Eyes, you're gonna hand it over. *Today*. Got it? By the end of the day." The fingers snapped, bursting stars. "And don't even think about tellin anyone."

He was alone again under the warm water.

Out of the shower he was shivering, not from the air-conditioning. Asshole. He put on his glasses and grabbed for a towel, but all were gone. Not even a face towel. His pajamas, too. He went into the room dripping and pulled the bed sheet off, wrapped himself in that. Fucking asshole. His shoes, socks, pants—everything was gone. There was nothing on his side of the room except the dictionary and the dancer.

No.

Richard moved to his dresser. The shirt and pants drawer was empty. The sock and underwear drawer, empty.

His journal.

His clothes.

The Noah shirt.

Sandy's panties.

Fuck.

*FUCK!*

Richard rested his head on his arm on the empty dresser.

What to do.

What to do.

What to do.

He went to his bed, snaked his hand between the mattress and box spring. He left it.

He needed clothes.

Vic was leaving for breakfast. "Don't even ask," he told him. He couldn't explain, anything, to anyone. Vic had extra gym shorts and a t-shirt and a pair of sandals.


"Would you do me a big huge favor?"

Always.

"I have something to tell you and I don't think you should freak out about it. I mean—you *know* what I mean. Don't take it the wrong way. What I mean is, I better just say it, my doctor said I could leave—in a couple days—isn't that great news? Did you hear what I said? Isn't that great news? You aren't mad, are you?"

Mad.


"Ssorry about your clothess."

Huh?

"Vic told me what happened."

Well. Shit.

"Sorry about your clothes."

"Who told you?"

"Buster."

Oh god.

"I'm joking. I'm joking. It's a joke. I can joke, too, can't I? Andy told me."

Who are you seeing now?

"You know. The Nosepicker."

The Nosepicker. The whole world knows.


You need to get your clothes.

You need to get the shirt.

You need to get your journal.

You need to get Sandy's red panties.

You need to stick up for yourself.

You need to be a man.

Stop hiding in your room.

Go down there and take what's yours.

Give him the stupid bullet.

The stupid bullet.

Richard got the cartridge and marched down to the lounge with it in hand so he could find Bug and shove it in his stupid face so this whole stupid thing could be over when he saw

Bug standing in the main lounge wearing the Noah shirt, blue notebook open in hand, reading.

Bug mimed being caught off guard. "Oh." Red Christmas package tufted from the shirt pocket. He tugged Sandy's gift and fluffed it like a magician's handkerchief before an awed crowd for any takers: "Are these yours?" To one of the housewives, sillily: "Yours?" To Richard, daring: "Yours?"

Giggles tittered before they're laughing

laughing at me
looking at you
inside out


Later.
Returning from bright dots
pieces locking
waking unmoving
wrists side-strapped
stomach and ankles cuffed
remembered
the picture fracturing
racing to Bug and
flying at his throat and
screaming and screaming and screaming
and it was him screaming, lunging at Bug, clawing at his throat, patients squealing and scattering

He had witnessed the scene as an outsider, from above, his fingers digging into Bug's throat perfected disconnection exhilarating breathing new air seeing through sun-shut eyes beautiful beautiful it was so fucking beautiful he could dance on this motherfucker's head all day his mind screaming out of his lungs *I'LL KILL YOU I'LL KILL YOU I'LL KILL YOU*

They were tackled together with such force that everyone collapsed grunting and kicking and hitting, screeching couches and chairs and sending magazines airborne, birds shooting off the ground. He remembered how it hurt to be punched. They were dragging him, lifting him, he was off the floor, fighting, flailing, and he knew, he knew, he saw it in his hand-drawn eyes in his fluttering face, "*NO NO NO*

An oily hairy hand muffled his mouth, he snarled at it, and the hand grabbed his hair at the height of his skull and yanked his head back to violent silence.

He'd become the ancient sacrifice, uplifted. Prayed his father had prepared many bundled branches.

Hands and bodies wrestled him into a bed where leather straps dug into his flesh around his ankles and stomach and wrists. He struggled because they hurt, they hurt—*it hurts!* Bodies leveraged and deep into his arm a bug buried its stinger, burning venom raced up his shoulder and chest, pouring thickly into his skull and all its dark recesses, coating his screaming and his kicking.

The world was softening, the room darkening, only a sick light diffused the doorway. He thought he recognized the angel on the door, its wings fluted overhead, body ephemeral, arms side-straight, palms outward, signaling. It vibrated, ascending or descending, he could not tell.

Don't leave! Don't go!

Do you have a message for me?

The angel was motionless.

What should I do?

The angel was mute.

You talk to Eugene, *talk to me.*

Tell me what to do.

I don't know why I'm here.

The angel was mute.

What new hell had he created for himself?

Cockroach feet scurrying across the back of his hand startled him from what wasn't sleep. Both wrists were cuffed and strapped at his sides with a stomach strap, his ankles locked to the bed frame. The cockroach feet scampered up his wrist, his forearm, and instantly dozens of insects coated his arms, gnawing his flesh, screaming, and when he screamed with them he could watch the exhausted air leave his body like colors bleeding from a painting.

Far away a howl answered.

Bugs! There's bugs all over me! Help!

He recognized his voice, crying. That's when they came to watch him, standing in the doorway, and one by one they began pointing, taunting: Vic, Eugene, Sandy, even Joey. They were laughing, they were all laughing at him, and he could shut none of it out; his arms were strapped at his sides. Bug was there, too, holding his gun. And Susie, sad Susie. Behind them all his father, immobile and intent, in his fireman suit.

Where was the blade when he needed it?

Once, he was so furious with his parents over what he couldn't recall now, he ran away from home. Not really; he was afraid to leave; he did not know where to go outside; so he crawled underneath his bed and scrunched up against the wall in the warm, close, dark space and watched his mother's feet hurry about his room and listened to her yelling his name, angry, frantic, crying to his father, then quiet at the kitchen table on the other side of his bedroom wall, pressed his ear to the cool wall to hear what they were saying about him, but there was nothing to hear.

Then his mother's sobs, like he had never heard: lonely and wounded. He felt sick with the pain he'd caused her and wanted to walk out and show her: Here I am!

Now he was warm and close in that dark space again but could not move.

"How are you feeling?" asked the blotch in the doorway.

Richard could not twist his head far enough to watch it walk to sit down in the chair at the head of the bed.

"That was some excitement, I hear. Can you tell me what happened?"

"I guess I lost myself."

"Yes," he heard the doctor's voice from above, "I think you could say you lost yourself." You are here for a *reason*. "We'll need to keep your journal."

"You can't do that." He tried but could not move against the straps.

"I'll have the restraints removed. Soon. And visit when you're able to think more clearly."

But I'm thinking clearly *now*! Wait! he shouted. Don't go! Let me tell you! Let me tell you why I'm here!

The doctor was gone but the angel was listening.

They unbuckled him unceremoniously, sat him up, showed him where to shower, let him shave while they watched, brought him food, let him walk, not outside, not yet, maybe later they would let him out into the brick square courtyard, viewable through the tiny window in the door at the end of the hallway, as Louis described it. A table, some chairs, potted plants. Real plants. Locked in a small square of bricks running up, up, up so high you could not see the sky even by bending down and pressing your face against the door and peering up. He was free to move to the other end of the narrow hallway, past his new room, past the small nurses' station, scraping a fingernail on the unbreakable glass, past the shared shower and toilet, doorless, to the door with the window the size of his notebook paper where he could place his face to watch the world he'd left.

From the window-page he saw Susie sitting at the end of the closest couch, facing him, talking with the people around her, her high school friends, and he watched her, mesmerized by the heavy round of her breasts, their completeness, how they stretched her shirt to the edges of their arcs. She caught him, surrendered a girlish grin of awareness and allowance, then remained in her pose, even jutted more, he thought, for him. A brief refuge.

Disturbed only by the passing sight of Eugene.

Richard tapped the window-page and flip-flapped his hand, and when his roommate shuffled over mouthed, How did you get my shirt?

Eugene tilted his head quizzically: a dog pitched an odd sound.

Richard repeated, mouthing precisely: How, did, you get, my shirt.

Eugene shouted, "You have to speak up! I can barely hear you!"

Richard lunged to shut him up but found himself in the ridiculous position of flattening his palms against the window-page.

"Hey!" shouted Eugene. "Where'd you go?"

Richard tore his hands away. *"Are you a fucking retard, Eugene? I said 'HOW DID YOU GET MY SHIRT?'"*

That did it.

With dog-dejected eyes Eugene retreated.

In the station the nurses scrambled, and down the Isolation hallway a nurse called out his own name.

"I'm sorry, Eugene." He couldn't hear. I'm sorry for everything.

On the other side the nurses were out of their door and upon him, ushering him away.

"You better go." He knew he could not hear. "I'll see you later."

The nurse clamped to Richard's side, leading him to his room.

After a long while of sitting he felt he could chance another excursion. The hall was empty, both ways. He was the only patient. In the window-page bodies floated, left to right, unreadable. A meal was over. He went closer to watch, wait—*there*—he knuckled the window-page and every nearby head turned, including Vic's. The others swarmed past.

Richard flapped his hand and mouthed, Come here.

The unspoken words pulled him out of the stream of patients. What, his squinted eye said, are you really in for?

Did you get it?

Vic nodded once over his shoulder down the men's hallway, then walked off into the lounge area.

Wait! Wait! Where are Sandy's...

For lack of anything else to do, Richard paced, from one end of the hallway to the other end of the hallway. At each he would set his face in the window-page to glimpse what was happening on the other side. At one, nothing changed but the division line of sun and shade creeping up the red bricks. At the other people shifted in and out of the page: it was less consoling than watching fish. A woman sat on a couch reading a romance novel. An old Chinese woman sat on the couch opposite her, bouncing. She sat with her arms folded and she was bouncing in her seat. Bouncing, bouncing, bouncing, bouncing. The Nosepicker was in the TV lounge, doing his thing. Once he lingered too long at the lounge window and was startled by Joey, peeking in. Dumbly, they eyed each other, Richard fixed, Joey rocking slightly. Richard let his hand flatten against the glass, some small part of him hoping Joey might understand, and reach his hand, so they could touch, not be alone. What Joey did was moan and rock.

Richard started singing words he did not know to "Puff, the Magic Dragon" through the door, and that made Joey shut his eyes.

In the evening a tray was offered, a cup of water and a paper container with his usual three blue pills, plus a white capsule.

He asked the nurse what it was.

"It'll help you relax." Her smile was pinned to her face like a name tag.

"I don't need to relax," he stressed. "I feel fine."

Her smile unpinned. "It's up to you how to do this."

The cups waited: pieces on a game board.

He felt a twinge of old rage tempting him to slam the tray up, catapult the cups and pills and water into her face, roar triumphantly.

In the periphery the leather bed straps dangled. The angel observed. Richard took the cups and drank and swallowed while she stood there waiting to say "Open."

Later, in a dream or in the hall, he was pacing. Pausing at the lounge door only agitated him more. Vic talked with Bug where they used to play—*checkers*?

Wah wah wah wah wah. Wah wah wah wah wah.

And he couldn't even catch Vic's eye to ask him what the hell he was doing because his back was to the Isolation door. But Bug. He could see.

Jesus.

He could see.


In the morning Susie was waiting outside his window-page with her suitcase and pillow. They hadn't really discussed what they would do after they got out of the hospital, when, if, they would want to know each other outside. They were saving up for some sort of momentous goodbye, he supposed. Which was now.

He felt the weight of their ignorance and innocence pressuring them to this point.

She motioned she wanted to show him without anyone seeing, then squeezed fingers into her jeans pocket and puffed red silk panties. She tipped her head lounge-ward and stuffed the blood-red material out of sight and raised her eyes, urging him on to some sexual place unknown. It was tearing him apart, and he wished she would leave, be out of his sight.

She lifted a hand for goodbye and flashed her palm to reveal a black magic markered I ♡ U.

He felt his mouth working incomprehensible oaths; everything he could say to her would be wrong; he spun away to hide his outburst of tears.

They let him have his dictionary and some magazines. But no pen and paper. He alternated between reading and looking up words and writing pages in his head.

"Really, Richard. Over a shirt?"

His mother would not stop hugging.

"At least you found your glasses."

He had to pry himself away. "Let's go out to the garden."

"Oh? You have a garden? Let me bring this." She toted a worn, veined brown shopping bag with corded handles, the kind she warehoused. A white poster paper tube poked out of the bag. "Where can I put this? Here?" She unshouldered her purse; he pointed to the only chair in the room and thought she took too long noticing the leather straps dangling off the sides, middle, and end of his bed; she set her purse on the seat and returned, dreadfully cheerful. "Ready."

He led the way to the garden door, unlocked, now that he'd had two nights of good behavior, and he showed her in to his paradisiacal retreat.

"Well isn't this cozy?" She arranged and re-arranged her grip on the thin handles of the shopping bag as she sniffed out the four corners of the garden pit. "This place just goes on and on, one door after another." They wandered in the bottom of a well filled with sunshine, the sun-shade water line hovering three feet off the ground.

She stood, a tourist, and eye-lined the length of brick wall up to its square sky end. "It's like a chimney." She looked at him with her own owl eyes.

They sat in the two metal chairs at the small metal table; she brought out of the bag the long scroll and rolled the rubber band down one end.

273

"Alan says hello. He misses you, Richie, and hopes you're having fun." Her incongruencies were slowly disfiguring her. She unrolled a poster paper finger painting. "He made this for you. To cheer you up while you're away."

"What is it?"

"He painted you in camp." She offered interpretations. "You're swimming here. Here you're playing basketball. He had—has—so much fun playing basketball with you in the backyard." She was using the idiot-baby voice. "Here you're flying a kite together." A small figure gripped the hand of the Richard figure. "He said I should tell you that he misses you, Richie." She chewed her lip. "He said he hopes you're having fun at camp. He wishes... he could be here with you... having so much fun..." The painting drooped. "He wants you home... like things were before..." Her voice dried up and the child's rendition of life lowered.

Like things were before.

Kneel here, think about me when you use it, wah wah wah wah wah.

You see them, too? We keep what's dead inside devoured all day long.

Now I see.

Like things were before?

Before what? There was no before that he wanted to see.

Richard lifted the poster and let his fingertips trace the painted surface, track the child-size grooves of blue sky and green shocks of grass. Circles upon circles of yellow-orange sun swirled. He smiled at his happy figure of smeared reds swimming and playing and jumping, such a pretty and child-like lie.

"Everyone misses you, Richie. Even your father. *No.* Listen to me, *listen.* I know he doesn't say it—"

"He doesn't say *anything.*"

"He's not here to tell you—"

"He's *never* there!"

"I *know* he's not the easiest person to get along with, Richie. Don't you think I know that?"

"Then why did you marry him? Why do you stay married?"

She tightened and softened. "We love each other, Richie. That's why we got married, that's why we stay married."

"You don't act like it."

She snapped, "Watch your mouth, you, and keep your snide remarks to yourself. Learn to show some respect. And don't be so antagonistic. Now I mean it. You listen to me, you *listen to me now*. You think you know so much? Well you don't. You think too much but you don't know so much. Your father loves you, and he works hard to pay for everything you've got. He loves you in his *own* way, Richie. *Remember* how he played with you when you were a little boy and laughed with you? I know it's hard to remember those times, but we had those times. Let me show you something. Now *wait*, let me *show you something*. I brought a picture. You were a baby, one month old. See? It's so old it's in black and white. I wrote the date on the back. Take it. *Take it*. That's you and your father, when you were one month old. The date's on the back. See? That's in our old house. Look at your father. He was so proud of you, so happy to be your father. Listen. *Now you listen to me*. The world's not just black and white; there's more *to* it than that, Richie. Stop trying to see things one way or another. I know. I know it's not easy to get along with him. Don't you think I know that? But it's *who he is*. But that—that picture—that's who he is, too, and you need to remember that. It's the memory you get along with, Richie. The memory is what keeps you going. Sometimes it's all you have are memories. He's your father. And he'll be just like his father before him: a son of a bitch when he was alive and a saint after he's dead." She marveled at the damage around them. "There are so many disappointments in life you have to learn how to live with." She expelled a breath as if from a punctured lung. "You might as well start here." They looked at each other. "Sometimes I wish it was me in here getting a rest instead of you."

He remained in the courtyard, chair-slouched, square of sky overhead clean of any cloud. An azure slate. Through the coolness of coming twilight filtered the chortling of birds. Some sort of childhood lost overwhelming. Alan's painting was unfurled and wedged open in an opposite chair. On his chest the photograph of the proud young man cradling his infant boy. He had seen this photograph before, so long ago that at first his child mind had thought he could place that captured moment of being in his father's lap, exchanging adorations. But the more he looked at the photograph the more he realized that must not be true, he had made it up to confirm the scene in the picture. His own myth. He could not remember any photograph of his father showing his teeth in a smile. Years ago he had to have all his teeth extracted, Richard did not know why; he and his brothers guessed at some lingering war wound; he'd been wearing full dentures since his early forties and did not show his teeth for smiling. Over time his mother had picked up the habit, so any family photo recalled the days of the settlers with frozen glum faces. Over time the pose and attitude blanketed their children, seeped into bones.

How our choices stick to everything.

He marked the stunning setting sun's schedule rising up the brick wall. A fly buzzed above and about and out, spiraling up to freedom, and Richard removed his glasses and stretched in his chair and waited, waited, waited under the wind's softness for the charcoal birds to streak the paper sky at the lip of the well.

The lip of the well where he might write glass words, echoes of bright blood

*My skin does not fit*
*my tomb, my flesh*

He wanted to stay there forever, drawn.

## Your life is in your hands

At night he tried masturbating to Susie. He wanted to masturbate to Susie. All of him wanted to masturbate to Susie. But not that one part. Unfeeling, a floppy life-lost fish.

Fucking ice cream.

There are reasons

The Isolation ward door window-page framed a scene far down the men's hallway: Pear Man—strolling to the main lounge with a woman who could be nothing but his wife—wearing the Noah shirt.

The Noah shirt.

Dumbstruck, Richard watched them approach, angling his view to keep them framed.

The Noah shirt.

It fit the man as neatly as you could get anything around all that man.

His shirt.

To the nurses in their box they did goodbyes and smiles and waves. They were leaving. *With his shirt!*

How?

*Wait!* His breath tinted the window-page. They rounded the corner, the wife, the bitch, pretended he wasn't even there, but Pear Man stopped.

Recognitionless.

His wife at his side very sweetly and much like a widow tugs the leash of her errant poodle crawled her fingertips to the base of his fat neck to bring him back to her; Pear Man clasped and re-clasped the hand that had his, began swinging their arms. She led him on. Richard mashed his face against the window-page to watch the broad back in the bowling shirt disappear from frame.

Noah was gone.

There was no magic in it.

Not much later the doctor blocked the angel.

"How are you feeling this morning?"

Devoured. "Better."

The doctor sat in the chair, the angel rematerialized. "Ready to go?"

Was he *joking*?

"To your room. On the ward."

Oh that. Yes. Of course.

"The zoo trip is today," the doctor mentioned unremarkably, his words commingling sympathy and pleasure, "and I thought you might enjoy new scenery, if..."

Richard felt the weight of their gaze, the angel and the man, and lowered his head, nodding reverently.

"Reginald will be staying in today, so it's all the better that *you* go out for the day. Give you both some time to yourselves."

Reginald?

"The man who was involved with you in the altercation. You didn't even know his name?"

*Reginald?*

The doctor clicked his teeth.

"He stole my shirt." And my journal, my glasses, Sandy's panties, the shower, the fries, said he'd kill me. A miniature bell tinkled. Did the doctor hear that? No. He only fidgeted, but no gulls cried questions and answers in this room near the bottom of the well. He was mouthing about alternatives to fighting, the staff is here to help you, you can report that type of

*tinkle* the metal belt on the leather strap chimed. It was almost the type of belt you'd wear with pants, only wider, much wider, unlike the kind his father used to beat him with *under the bed* arm swinging down, down through the air *because he used to beat all the children in the family* and he made a promise to himself to hate his father forever and ever and look, look, do you see the look on your father's face, do you want to be an immolator for God?

The doctor's lips were moving: Reginald is not my patient, but I spoke with

*Reginald.* Who would name their kid *Reginald*? *Reggie.* No wonder he's screwed up, calls himself Bug.

I hope, the doctor was saying.

I hope

I hope

He hopes a lot, Richard thought.

I hope you realize your situation here, because we cannot abide

another episode and he would have to look up that word—abide—
and hope, and faith, and love, and we cannot help you if you will not
let us help you, if you will not help yourself, cooperate with the staff,
so he thumbed the sharp edge of the leather strap that bit his wrists
some nights ago while his arm remembered the stab of sunshine,
the bugs tearing, the angel leaving, them laughing, all laughing and
looking at him, wah wah wah wah wah, every night here I die a little
more: "I understand."

The doctor was justified. "I don't expect we'll have another episode
like that?"

Richard shook his head, resigned and resolved. Above everything
he felt for the doctor was pity, pity for his ignorance, pity for his
disconnectedness.

"Can I trust you?"

He checked a wild urge to burst out loud laughing. Instead,
nodded. With a sound of rustling paper and clothing the doctor rose,
and Richard followed. There was nothing to take with him except the
photograph in his pocket; he'd brought nothing in. He followed the
doctor out, secretly caressed the angel. A buzz signaled the unlatching
of the door.

A nurse came up behind. "Aren't you forgetting?" She held out the
scroll of his brother's painting.

The door swung in. Outside some patients interrupted their TV
or reading or themselves. That was his welcome. They let him go. The
door swung shut behind him, the latch *clicked*. Susie was gone. His
shirt was gone. Bug was inside, over in a dim corner of the fish tank
lounge.

Richard went to his room. Everything was as it should be, the
angel watching over. Except. On his dresser by the dancer, his clay
box, lidded, from art. He set the scroll on his bed, went to his dresser,
and carefully, expecting anything, lifted the lid. Inside, a folded note.
He picked it up knowing immediately who left it. The paper was fine
and smooth, the handwriting circular and peach.

Dear Richard,

I hope you don't mind I took your box out of class to bring it to your room. The therapist and nurses said I could, and I wanted to make sure nothing would happen to it while you were—away. I hope your feeling better real soon. Sorry I couldn't stay longer. See you at the dance.

Love—

Susie

He had never received a note from a girl with that word, she had never mentioned that word before, and he wondered what she meant by it. She had dotted eyes and curved a grin to make a little face of the "o" in *Love*, and that made him smile. He mused over the misuse of "your" for "you're," touched the page she had laid her hand across, traced with his fingertip the thin embossed line edging the paper. He put the paper to his nose and breathed her in.

"Man!" It was Vic, wonderstruck, in the doorway, "I never seen *anything* like that," with a double dose of the look and something else, something new. Respect? Fear? Beside him, Eugene, his usual, usual.

"Like what?" Richard said. He wasn't in any mood for Vic's bullshit.

"Like what? Like what," he joshed Eugene, then Richard, "are you fucking kidding me? Like you going completely *nuts* on Bug—"

that word

"—like you going *nuts* when they dragged you off—"

"Yeah. Well." Richard needed to score when he could. "Be glad I wasn't going nuts on you." It worked: Vic stopped. "She left me a note." He waggled it.

"They brought your clothes." Eugene wanted in, too. "They got everything."

"My shirt."

His friends froze.

"Why did you give him my shirt?"

Eugene explained, "I didn't. I didn't *give* it to him. He said it was his. But I *traded* him. Look. Look what I got." He brushed past to his own side of the room and his own desk where puzzle books stacked. "See?"

He flipped one open, a Connect the Dots one, and the pages showed ridiculous attempts to connect dots that had no right to be connected. He stopped on one page where all the lines were correctly laid, and more. It was a train. With extra everything drawn in: windows, smoke out the engine, trees and grass by the tracks, a sun in the sky.

"You got to be Noah for a long time."

So that was all. The three of them in a room, stuck in stares. The shirt, gone. Susie, gone.

But that wasn't all.

"Where's the bullet?" he asked Vic.

What bullet? Vic said without speaking, rolling his eyes at Eugene.

"I asked you, through the window, did you get the bullet."

"Through the window?"

"What the hell did you think I was signaling you to do, steal second?"

"I thought," Vic re-emphasized, "you were, talking about... you know. I gave them to Susie."

"The bullet," it's gone.

"We heard you one night," Eugene's marble eyes mesmerized, "screaming."

"I was strapped down," Richard said.


*What's inside comes out, sometimes, from something in*


Everyone going to the zoo seemed bent on staring the clock to 10. Vic waited with him but wasn't going. "Dumb animals in cages. Fuck that."

A nurse announced in the hallway that the bus had arrived, triggering a polite but determined stampede. Richard did his inner car-racing sounds, passing the slower ones, the fat girl, The Nosepicker, shifting into high gear, arriving nearly first in the lobby, skidding to a stop. A pleasant commotion bubbled as the nurses tried to settle everyone down before leading them out.

The patients rushed in a bunch, and of all the things Richard expected to find waiting to take them to the zoo it was not a retard bus.

But there it was.

A short yellow bus.

What he and his friends growing up had called "the retard bus." Whenever one of these had rumbled by they'd yell out to each other "Retards!" and point and laugh at the kids inside wearing helmets or sitting with empty staring eyes. As they grew older and became aware of the meaning of the retard bus nobody pointed and nobody laughed; but their play would pause in a ritual silence and a world of room for one's thoughts. Richard would shudder for the boys and girls riding, and for their parents he imagined at home. He felt terrible for the ways he had made fun of them without knowing who or what they really were, without knowing them at all. They were just people, after all. Like him. But now his horror was that he would be the retard, the one causing children playing in yards to stop and point and laugh.

This could not be their ride. They wouldn't do this to him.

On the sidewalk in front of the bus a nurse clutched Joey by the wrist. To her Richard marched, flabbergasted: "We're not riding in *that*?"

Joey moaned *Ohhhhhhhhhhhhhhhhhhhhhhhh.*

Her response was an idiot-baby "yes" cut from stone.

He guffawed. "But that's—" that's—he could not voice it because that would make it true.

"That's your ride to the zoo," retard.

I hope you realize your situation here.

*What's wrong with you?*

He backed away, numb with fresh understanding, waiting with the other retards to be told what to do to take their trip to visit the dumb animals in the zoo. Two whitecoats stood guard.

Half-heartedly he listened to a nurse explain the buddy system they would use that day. Anyone with their roommate should buddy up with their roommate, and those without a buddy would be a buddy for someone else without a buddy. Eugene appeared at his side, smiling buddy-like, and they lined up to board. The driver was not with the hospital but with the retard bus company. He thought she looked like a whale, with breasts and a moustache, and he imagined her sitting at home at night in front of her television, alone, and he regretted his cruel thought and to himself asked her and God to forgive him.

Eugene and Richard boarded the bus, together, sat down on a padded seat, together, waited for the other retards to sit, together. Richard snuggled into his window seat. He preferred the window seat, the window-page. Everything outside was viewable. Behind the wall of windows in the hospital entrance lounge stood Bug, a stone at the bottom of a pond. Just: there. The thought occurred to him to tap Eugene to ask him if it were real. He giggled at that. One madman to another.

The bus grumbled to life and eased away from the curb, and he did not look back because he knew Bug would be there. Instead, he let his excitement for the trip take hold. He had not been off hospital grounds since he got there, hadn't been to the zoo since he was a kid, and he got giddy thinking about it. At the end of the hospital driveway the bus lurched to a stop. A sign called out below the red octagon:

Buckle Up!
YOUR LIFE
IS IN
YOUR HANDS

No seat belts were on the bench, but he groped anyway.

"What're you doing?" Eugene asked.

The bus growled, jerked them forward. Now, he thought, he could use a waist belt strapping him down. Ha. He thought that might be funny for himself but found nothing funny in it. Nothing to save them now. "Nothing," he told Eugene.

The bus chugged an arc left onto the boulevard, bringing into view a familiar figure strolling down the sidewalk along the line of evergreens.

That mother. He *wouldn't*.

But he had.

The bus rolled past him in his "Wally the finger" shirt looking exactly where he belonged exactly where he was. Richard twisted in his seat to watch him as the bus picked up speed, leaving his friend and home.

On the freeway he stared out the window at everything and nothing, letting his view defocus and refocus. Bug was far away, barely remembered. Philip wasn't on the bus. The sun shone, the sky was blue, he felt good. This beautiful life was better than death, after all, wasn't it? Because death was unimaginable to him now. He let the buildings and trees and white lane markers blur. Tops of cars edged by below: leaves riding a fast stream. He could look down on the drivers. He wondered what they were doing, how they lived, if they were happy in their lives. He thought if he caught some glimpse of how they lived, what made them keep on wanting to live, he could use that for himself, make it his own. They must know something, he figured: they were on the outside, and he was on the inside. He searched their faces for any clues. The more cars that went by and the more people he saw—businessmen, old people (alone, together), mothers with children—he thought he'd be able to see something different in them, different than what he thought was in him. But he wasn't seeing anything special, nothing different. In fact, most of the people looked dull and tired, unimpressive. His frustration at finding nothing in them to tell him how to live was starting to piss him off. A station wagon pulled along, inside a young mother with two boys in the back seat scrambling and pointing excitedly at the bus and all the people and Richard. The boys poked and yelled at their mother and nosed their faces to the window, elbowing each other and pointing and giggling and making faces at the

*Retard!*

Is that what they wanted to see?

Richard screwed up his face into a hideous mask and silently barked and clawed at the window. The boys yelped, eyes bugging out, stabbing fingers at Richard and flapping arms at their mother's head; and she snarled over her shoulder at them and veered away, leaving Richard laughing at the boys' as they searched for what just happened.

"Are you alright?" Eugene asked.

Richard could not stop giggling.

Curbside at the zoo entrance congealed a minor chaos of school buses, children disembarking, teachers shouting orders through cupped hands, mother-chaperones forming small smoking groups. Wrought iron fences enclosed flowerbeds and two concrete, life-size lions, regal but bored sentries on either side of the boothed entrance. Some guy in a penguin suit flippered his arms in greeting, and Richard thought that might be fun to do. Excited children slapped the penguin high-fives; one or two ducked, trying to poke him before an adult found them out. One kid in particular, a tall boy, would dash and smack the penguin on its head then dart back into the crowd. Richard wanted to race up to the tall boy and collar him. Somewhere a baby bawled for air. Several buses down emerged a column of little children, clasping hands with the boy or girl behind or in front, color construction paper cut outs of animal silhouettes on yarn necklaces wind-dancing on their chests like fish flap-fighting at the end of a line. They halted next to the human penguin, and while teachers and mother-chaperones conferred, one woman ordered the children into groups. "I need lions over here, bears over here, wolves over here. Hippos!" She clapped for attention. "Where are my hippos?"

Their short bus remained at the curb while one of the nurses went ahead to the booth, leaving the other nurses and the two whitecoats. Richard wandered the edge of his group thinking the ugliest thing in the world must be a woman smoking. The mother-chaperones posed together. He wandered the edge, and from the pack of children closest to him voices squealed.

"They got pitchers. Pitchers tell what's in the cages. That's how you know."

"If you could be any animal what would you be?"

"I'd be a lion," a boy roared and grabbed the gold cut-out of his lion to show off.

That made Richard smile.

"I'd be a monkey."

"You *are* a monkey."

"I'd be a dog. Grrrr."

"You *smell* like a monkey," the tall boy said and shoved dog boy.

"I'd be a horse," said a bucktoothed girl who neighed a laugh.

"That's dumb," said tall boy.

"Yeah, that's dumb," dog boy affirmed.

"How *dumb*."

"You can't be a horse," said tall boy. "*Horses* aren't in *zoos*."

"Yeah," said dog boy, "*horses* aren't in *zoos*."

"Neither are *dogs*, dummy."

Dog boy blinked.

"Nobody said you had to pick an animal in a zoo," horse girl reasoned.

That stopped everyone.

"Do over," said one of the boys.

"What?"

"Do over."

"Yeah, do over."

"Do over!"

"Man, 'do overs' are for games," said tall boy. "This isn't a 'do over.'"

"Who says?"

Other whiney voices joined the argument, but eventually the group spiraled toward calm as one by one in a chain reaction each became aware of Richard, lost listening to their game of animal guessing, brought back suddenly to a quiet, noticing pond of curious child eyes.

Tall boy was a periscope rising to confirm the scene behind Richard, who imagined his view: the nurses and whitecoats, humming and rocking Joey, the fat girl, The Nosepicker, Eugene nearby, and beyond them all at the curb the short yellow bus. Tall boy germed the look and sprouted a sneer: "What are *you* looking at, *retard.*"

A burst of wind fluttered the silhouette animal pendants on the children's chests.

Eugene lurched forward and spoke so helpfully, "He's not a retard. Vic calls him 'Genius'. He was Noah. He had the shirt. He did. Then I got it. I got it from Bug. But I traded it because I'm not Noah. My name's Eugene."

There was a humiliating blank for the childish fulfillment of knowledge before their little mouths worked horrible laughter from lips peeling dryly away over gnashing rows of precious white marbles, and it went on and on and on, a feasting on the weakness of the flesh of their prey, until Richard snapped with derision and dread, "AHA HA HA HA," maniacal laughter ripping his throat, "AHA HA HA HA."

The pond of embryo eyes shivered, and Richard was unable to see deeper than this surface.

A mother-chaperone scurried over breathing smoke and clucking at the children to move along, get going, stop staring at the man, he can't help it, stop staring at the man. She herded the children away and in her own idiot-baby voice wrapped an order within a suggestion, "You'd better get back to your group."

My group?

Yes.

You think I might hurt them.

Yes.

My group.

Turned.

But they're not my group, he needed to tell her, have her understand.

The mother-chaperone was walking away.

I'm not like them! He could see himself striding to her and grabbing her by the wrist and forcing her to listen, you *listen* to me now. *See?* Can't you *see?* I'm *not* one of them. Don't you understand? I'm one of *you*, just like *you*. I want to be just like you.

But he knew in his heart he was not like her and he did not want to be just like her.

He felt lost and soulless.

Eugene was calling his name.

The patients were entering the zoo, buddy-by-buddy.

On the return trip he and Eugene talked, once.

"What's that?"

"What's it look like Eugene?"

"A penguin."

"Then that's what it is Eugene."

"I didn't know you liked penguins."

"I don't Eugene."

"Oh."

Already he'd let out too much.

"Then who's it for?"

Richard pinched the penguin by its flippers in an awkward dance and tried to see himself in its black button eyes.

"Is it for Susie?"

Richard went from one set of lifeless eyes to another.

# Some Leave Some Go

I want to go out." Richard slid his tray onto the table and sat down one seat over from Vic.

"Today didn't count?"

"I mean: *out*. What you did. Where I won't be bothered by anything."

"He's not here, if that's what you mean."

"Who?"

"Bug. He ain't here. Left a while ago with a whitecoat. Don't ask:

who knows. Maybe he needs some glasses, too. C'mon, I'm joking! Forget it."

"Forget it? *Forget* it? Are you fucking kidding me? That fuck threatens to kill me, and I'm supposed to forget it? I don't think so. And don't give me that look. The look, the *look*, like I'm a nut. Don't do it to me."

"OK, OK. *Sheesh.*" Vic's contrition. "When?"

"Tomorrow. After my doctor's appointment."

Vic plotted, "We'll go after lunch. But you know who needs to come along. Our roommates. Listen. *Listen.* It'll be easier, believe me. It's better that way. *Insurance.* Nobody *inside* knows you're *outside.* That's the way it should be. Plus the buddy system. Plus..."

"Beer?" Richard was OK with bringing Eugene, but: "You got a new roommate?"

Vic studied the clean tines of his fork. "When you went to the zoo they moved him in. Things change, you know. The Green Lantern..." He used the fork to pick his teeth, gnawing at the end of the tips. "There."

Richard followed Vic's stare across the cafeteria to the end of the food line where, clutching a tray to his chest to smell the food on the plate, Philip stood, and Richard, unbelieving, retraced his stare back to Vic, who for the first time seemed confused and defeated by his circumstances.

"He's not so bad. Really. C'mon. I can't leave him in here all day when I'm out. It won't work. Bucky's a snake and Psycho's a nut. They're both lousy liars. We need to keep them on a short leash. Psycho can buy the beer."

"*I* can buy the beer."

"Not that shitty three-two stuff they let 18-year-olds drink. I mean *beer*. And I'll take care of Bucky. *I'll take care of him.* C'mon. We need to stick together on this." It was almost begging. "C'mon. If all four of us go, nobody's inside we don't trust. Plus we got it over them. That's how it should be. Nobody inside knows we're outside. And we got it over them."

Vic was right. He supposed. But: What's *he* got over *you*?

"C'mon."

What's he know?

Vic twitched the eye hair patch away.

It hard-rained that night, the night before they were to go out. Richard listened to it in the dark of his bed, the torrents slapping against the plastic window, and thought of Noah, the real Noah, hearing the moaning and the wailing outside, the scraping and the screaming to be let in. Let in to what? More madness? The madness of a floating zoo. Had they even known what was happening, what they had brought upon themselves? And what happened to the ants? Where, how, did those dots of life passenger?

He got out of bed. He knew he shouldn't, wasn't supposed to, but he did anyway. He got out of bed and went to the window, for what he did not know. He wanted to see.

"What are you doing?" Eugene whispered.

"Nothing," Richard said. Pulled the heavy curtain aside, saw a flat black square filtering murky elements of the outside world, rain sheeting. Years ago in gentle Spring childhood nights he would look out his bedroom window on their backyard where his father had set up his Adirondack chair, and there in the void the red-orange aura of the lone cigarette burned bright on the inhale, faded on the arm-drop, thoughtful tracers. Most times Richard watched he tried to think about what his father was thinking, but nothing ever came, and sometimes he had to hold himself back from calling out to his father, waving to him from across all that darkness and space—Here I am, Dad. Here I am.

Down the hall the moaning was starting.

"What's out there?" Eugene whispered. "What do you see?"

"Nothing," Richard said.

Screeeeeee?

Seeeeee. Seeeeee. Seeeeee.

At the fence along the edge of the cliff the four of them stood watching the gulls, the sodden grass, the lake, anything but each other because, Richard felt, if they did, it would come undone—"it" being the unnamable force drawing them all together.

With one look he had asked Philip, What did you tell Bug? Where's the gun?

And with one look he responded, What do I have to do with you?

Richard did not know any of them, and suddenly he was glad for the fence holding them all in.

Up sprayed water on enormous blocks of concrete covering the slope to fight erosion. Many had fabricated tongue-and-groove ends, but without abutting, looked like Legos in a jumbled pile. Rusted orange rebar poked or humped to daylight and bled down the concrete. In that moment he could jump, he knew it, he pictured himself jumping, he knew he could do it, but as clearly as he saw the jump he felt the pain that would follow in his face-first impact, teeth shattering against cement, and he had to say to the odd thought as if to a person, to stop it:

No. No. No.

I will continue with this day instead.

West, over the lake and Cleveland, gray-black clouds formed a low wall rising. "Storm."

"Nah," Vic said. "It'll blow over." He defied the wind, hair twirling, in his "Wally the finger" shirt.

Richard wasn't so sure. It was a spring day native to northeast Ohio: cold dry Canadian wind fast-pushing the warmth aside to make a new sticky air under a steaming sun. The wet of last night's storm was being sucked up in anticipation of a double dose later in the day.

"I have a question," Eugene said.

"I have an answer," Vic said.

"What if we get caught?"

"What if we get caught." Obviously: "Don't get caught."

Richard and Philip and Eugene regarded the hospital.

"Whatsa matter?" Vic asked them. "You don't like that answer? Did we not go over this shit already?"

"That doesn't help," Richard said. "You know?"

"I told you," Eugene said to nobody, to all of them, "I'm not going back."

"Nobody's getting caught," Vic said.

"I'm not going back in there," Eugene said. At Richard: "Where he went. That's where they do it to you."

Everyone listened.

"Do what?" Philip asked.

"There's a special room," said Eugene.

"Can we go *now?*" Vic demanded.

"There's no special room, Eugene," said Richard.

"Can't he have ssecond thoughtss?"

"No," Vic said. "No, he can't have second thoughts. Because we already decided to go. It's like Genius here deciding to do it with a gun next time *BAM*. That's *it. Done. Decided.* No second thoughts. Right, Genius?"

"Fuck you."

"What'll they do to uss if we're caught outsside?"

"Isolation," said Eugene. "They strap you down and hook you up. Ask him." He pointed to Richard. "Tell them about the screaming. I'm not going back in there. We all heard you screaming."

"Like a little girl," said Vic. "They strap you down, hook you up, like this?" Vic did his convulsing imitation of ECT. "They do that to you? Clear your head out? No. I didn't think so. You wouldn't even remember."

Eugene looked ready to bolt.

Richard had had it. "You know what?" he said to Vic.

Vic smarted a look, No, what? And rested his hand across his pocket.

Richard smiled. He was getting tired of that used-up threat. "Is that what they did to you?"

Who told you that? Vic looked.

"We heard you sscreaming."

"I'm not going back in," said Eugene.

"I was seeing things," said Richard. At Eugene: Not like you. "They strapped me down. Gave me a shot to calm me down." He didn't know why he was telling them all this. To gain respect from Vic? to settle Eugene?

"I'm not coming back," Eugene said and dashed and ducked for the gap in the fences.

"He'ss not sseriouss?"

"No he's not serious." Richard felt responsible for him, for them all, because he thought he was the most normal of the bunch. "It's just talk."

"Crazy talk is right," said Vic, going after him. "Let's go!"

Head after ass they went, Eugene, Vic, Philip, footing their way down the cement blocks, gingerly, and Richard gave one last look into the empty yard before following, scooting down the boulders, grabbing for balance, rebar roughing orange across his palms. Sunlight in drops of water dotted the skins of the boulders. Near the shore the water misted rainbows translucent, transfiguring, and from the surf a confusion of voices crashed his name. The rocks were alive.

"Reeechaaard."

He stopped, balanced.

"Reeeeeeechaaaaaard."

There up on the cliff—neck shaking overdose protest—at the edge of the cliff: Bug.

He shaded his eyes and saw nothing but gulls, strung up on the air, photographs manipulated.

Reeechaaard, the voice in the wind and water called.

One by one they leapt to the beach and trudged along, single file, kicking up sprays of brown, coarse lake sand and pebbles, and he listened to the water rejoicing, wrestling to the shoreline, dancing foam, surf-bubbled suds tickling the limits of its sand-stained grasp. Wind whipped grit in mouth and eyes, sour smell of fish. They clumped 50 yards to the bottom of a path zigzagging the slope up into woods and above that the green tree-steepled sky. Roots of things shot out of the earth under the cliff. Here there were no boulders, only sprigs of sick green-brown weeds, crushed and rusting beer cans, cigarette butts, bits of broken glass, driftwood, and the smell of rotting fish over everything. Here the sound of the shore hushed. They were far enough away from the hospital's fenced yard so that no one would be able to recognize them. Richard felt nervous and free.

Vic wasn't hiding his laugh at Eugene. "Where'd you get *that*?"

"I found it in that rock over there." Eugene tugged at a baseball cap on his head that probably once had been a bright banana color but through weather and water had bled away to a sunless yellow.

Richard thought they should get going, get off the open beach. "So is it putt-putt or a movie?"

"I don't like putt-putt," said Eugene.

"Let'ss go to a movie then."

"How about that video arcade?" Richard offered.

"You fucking morons," said Vic. "First thing we do is get some beer and porn." Everyone looked at him. "What."

"Ssodom and Gomorrah."

"It's one o'clock in the afternoon," said Richard.

Eugene blinked rapidly. "I'm... not allowed... to drink... alcohol." He searched the others for support and explained: "The doctor said alcohol would affect my medication."

"You Psycho," said Vic, "none of us is *supposed* to drink. None of us is *supposed* to be outside that fucking fence. We're *all* on meds. We live in a *nuthouse*. Don't you get it? Don't you know *where* you are? Don't you know *who* you are?" Vic's ugliness transformed into cheerfulness: a coin flipped right side up. "So, OK, first thing we do is get the fucking beer and porn."

"Who ssayss you're in charge?"

"My idea to go out." Vic's coin teetered on its edge. "I lead."

The other three snuck glances.

"Who ssayss?"

Vic dared, "Who would you suggest?"

Philip dared back. "The oldesst sshould lead."

"That would be Eugene," said Richard.

Everyone looked at him in his stained baseball cap. "What."

"Jesus Christ."

"Sstop taking Hiss name in vain."

"What?"

"Oh fuck you, Bucky."

It was unraveling already. "I'm second oldest," said Richard. "I'll lead."

"What?" Eugene said louder. The other three paid attention to him now. "OK." He addressed the space several yards up the sloping trail, his gaze following up and up and up. He went by them and did not stop until he was on the ridge, where he shouted down, "Over here."

Richard thought he should be used to it, but every time he did it he felt the same *click click click*. Life's needle skipping.

"OK, Genius," said Vic, "he's your buddy."

"I don't know how much is bullshit and how much is him."

Philip took the path between them, cantillating, "The madman undersstandss where the path leadss—how the ssun burnss at night— where the rainbow'ss foot ressstss upon the earth."

Richard said to no one, "I'm a magnet for the insane."

The trees along the crested ridge formed a thin line that in parts lifted up and over the cliff, reaching for the very heart of the lake.

Richard stepped carefully, keeping a few feet from the edge; the straight drop to the beach was 50 feet, and some small trees grew unnaturally, clinging desperately to life on the ridge. He stopped to take in the enormous view, all of its beauty and hurt. Gray-blue water filled his vision up to the level light divider, innumerable bright-pointed ticks of water-light undulating horizon to horizon to horizon, bits of turning flame set in colored cathedral panes of saints and apostles. To the west clouds of burnt marshmallow bricks were stacking quickly one upon another. Bumps of buildings signified Cleveland. To his right, nothing but coastline and trees. A cool wind tinged his face, and he shut his eyes and listened to the leaves, the waves, the gulls, the sounds of life and lives all around him and in him, and he imagined if he jumped, if he did do it, it would be to leap, to fly, glorious, out up over the lake.

"You're not high enough."

Open.

"You're not high enough," Vic repeated, coming up from behind, "if you jump, to kill yourself. You'll end up like the wheelchair kid."

"You mean 'David'? His name's 'David'. People have names, asshole. I wasn't thinking of that, anyway. I was thinking what a beautiful view it is."

Together they peered over the drop.

Vic slapped him on the back of the neck and held on tight, gripping. Richard shouldered him off but Vic held on, and Richard grabbed a fistful of Vic's t-shirt at his neck to have something to hold on to, there at the edge.

"You don't have the balls to even think about what I tried, do you?" Richard felt a little contempt for those who could not or would not think themselves to that rotten edge of their own nothingness. How could you know the value of your life if you'd not weighed it in your heart?

They jostled, judging, standing on opposite ends of the Earth.

Vic let go first. "C'mon then. You can lookit that shit anytime."

They ambled out of the line of trees into the backyard of a house undergoing construction: an add-on sunroom being framed in. The work site was silent, supplies and equipment covered with blue plastic tarps, puddling water floating dead bugs and leaves.

"Let's check this out." Vic went for the framed doorway, and Richard followed.

When his father had built the huge shed in their backyard, everyone was there to help, his grandfather, his brothers, his mother bringing plates of sandwiches and a pitcher of iced tea. Alan had his plastic hammer, pounding pretend nails everywhere, watching his father and pointing and asking, "What dat? Doin' Daddy?" His father barked for them to keep out of the way. Richard wanted to help, grabbed loose ends of beams when he could. He had to hunt down his mother to take care of a splinter.

Everyone stopped when Alan screamed, stuck up on a rafter; he'd climbed the ladder and now was too afraid to climb back down. His mother left him and was below Alan, yelling up at him to hang on.

His father laughed, told him to stop crying, don't move, I'll be right there. How he glided up the ladder. The way he held Alan, like the girl in that newspaper photograph. Only none of this was frozen, and Richard wanted to be rescued, too.

The sound of smashing glass brought him back. Vic was winding up for another throw; there was a hole in one of the room's new windows.

"What the fuck are you doing?"

"What's it look like I'm doing?"

"It looks like you're being an asshole. You destroy stuff for fun?"

"Like I care." But he didn't throw it.

"That's fucked up, you know that? These people worked and planned and paid for this, and now you come in here to mess it all up for them? What is wrong with you?"

"Fuck you."

"Fuck you right back. You know what your problem is? You're an idiot." Richard went out the framed doorway half-expecting the rock to come sailing out through the window at his head, but what he heard was Vic coming out after him.

They walked between houses on a residential street parallel to the lake running with a row of cottages. Eugene and Philip strolled down the lake-side sidewalk toward the hospital.

"Where're they going?"

"It's alright," said Vic. "The road curves around to the main drag, and the 7-Eleven is right there. C'mon."

They jogged to join their roommates, marching along, enjoying the scenery. The small homes, most of them cottages or bungalows, sat close together, the type of house that decades ago served as summer getaways for city dwellers. Along the street a green canopy formed from new-leaved trees with hundreds of skeletal limbs and knuckled stalks, tens of thousands of fingers tapping at the unseeable sky. Sun strobed through branches. As the street curved right then left Richard recognized that this was the handful of homes backing up to the fenced yard of the hospital; the side of the hospital showed between houses. The front yards were empty except for one person on their side of the street, closest to the hospital, the old man, raking a flower bed. He was distracted from his work; Richard raised a hand.

The old man did a slow and curious double-take.

"What the fuck?" Vic said.

"Faster," said Richard.

"Are you stupid?"

"Why?" said Eugene.

"Jesus fucking Christ."

"Faster," said Richard.

"Sstop taking the Lord'ss—"

"Come on, Bucky." Richard started into a jog and kept at it until he was nearing the end of the curve at the boulevard. There he slowed and did a few long steps backwards. The old man's front yard was empty.

The others came up huffing.

"What wass it?"

"Nothing," Richard said. "I thought I saw someone I knew." He could not believe how stupid he'd been.

"You dumb shit," Vic said. "I oughta kick your ass right here and now."

Richard ignored him.

"Did he ssee you?"

"What the hell were you thinking?" Vic didn't want an answer. "What the fuck did we just go over?"

"What?" Eugene said.

Vic snapped, "Shut the fuck up, Psycho."

The main road was a city highway: Two lanes in both directions, a turning lane in the middle, spotted with manhole covers and re-repaved potholes, hemmed in with fearfully low and crumbled curbs. The posted speed limit was 45 but cars blurred by in strong gusts. Their path was a dry mud trail worn through sun-burnt weeds.

"Where'ss the sstore?"

"Up there." Vic motioned down the road.

They set out again in single file: Vic, Philip, Eugene, Richard. How good it was to be out, the sun, the wind, the joy. Richard thought about how normal they must look: four friends walking. Pretending

that it was just a day out,

a normal day out,

going for a walk.

That everything would be alright,

they wouldn't get caught,

he wouldn't be strapped down ever again.

Bursts of car wind blew over.

A thought inserted itself: how easy it would be to throw himself into the street; there would be no time for the driver to stop or swerve; in an instant it would be done, tires racing over his chest and arms, or legs twisting in the underside of some stranger's car. He vacillated between joy and a quick death, between skipping along the path and throwing himself in front of the oncoming traffic, wondering how his mind could so whimsically turn to thoughts that seemed to be beyond his control, but it was a comfort to him to think of death like this, like some hard nugget of truth that lived separate from himself, when Eugene said, "A dead raccoon." He was pointing to the stiff body in the dirt curbside, silent snarl, intestines open, flies feeding. The thought of him ending up like that, doing that to himself, was sickening.

Vic picked up a stick.

"What are you doing?" Richard didn't want him to touch it.

"Watch," Vic said and knelt.

"Leave it alone," Richard told him. It seemed wrong to disturb it. He felt sorry for it and wondered if it was a mother raccoon or a father raccoon, or even a boy or girl raccoon that would never get to see its mom or dad or brothers again, and he was nearly crying for it. *"Leave it alone!"*

Vic stopped, pre-poke.

"It's dead," said Eugene.

"I can see that, *Psycho*, I was just gonna have some *fun* with it." A wave of his hand shooed the flies.

Richard said, "That's sick, man. Let's go."

Vic gave the slightest nod and tossed the stick into the street and stood up.

The others followed.

Richard shuddered in the breezes brought by each passing car and every new death, grateful for the end of the path at a sidewalk where they could walk abreast, the buddies in pairs. Not very long could he stand no talk. "What do we do after we get the beer?"

"Try to get laid?" Vic said over the traffic. "There's a high school down the street."

"I can't," Richard answered, "I haven't had a hard-on since I got here."

"Goddamn ice cream. I told you!"

Philip *tsked*.

"Ice cream tastes good," said Eugene.

The sidewalk ended at the corner of an asphalt parking lot of the 7-Eleven. Vic halted. "Alright."

Richard reached for his wallet.

"Inside?" Vic prodded. "You're not gonna buy it. He is." Thumb at Eugene. "Let's go, beer boy."

Richard felt a little foolish and a little pissed at Vic for all of this. They trudged to the store and went inside.

"Space Invaders!" The video arcade machine sat beside the door. Richard loved playing this one. Outside, in normal life, he used to go out of his way—at the mall, at bars—to play whenever he could. He approached the cashier, a tall skinny woman whose face was blocked by the overhead cigarette dispenser.

"Quarters, please?" From his wallet Richard pulled a dollar bill, and then one more, laid them flat on the countertop crowded with display boxes for candies and doughnuts and beef jerky and matches and a squat sunglass carousel, complete with tilted mirrors, and a hot dog machine with deeply bronzed, sweating links revolving drowsily on silver rollers.

The woman tinkled the coins into Richard's palm. "Hair ya go, hon."

"Thank you." His veins rushed energy.

Vic's mouth strained. "We're gonna play video games?"

"Yeah," Richard said, "*I'm* gonna play video games." He pocketed four quarters, stacked three where the metal ridge overlapped the glass game housing, palmed the last one. "Don't be so dramatic. You can watch or leave. I don't care." He did care, but Vic was getting in the way of his fun. "Want to watch, Eugene?"

Eugene nearly danced with excitement.

Philip observed. "Pagan distraction."

Richard fed a quarter to the slot, the game lit to life, his blood tingled, and it all came back to him, like riding a bicycle. But he was game-clumsy. It ended too soon. He dropped another quarter.

"You're playing *again*?"

Richard elbowed Vic out of his field of view. "You're invading my space, man." He giggled at his own joke.

The second game went better, the third best. He was alone by then, checking the store between game levels. Philip was by the magazine rack boring through a *Playboy* and Vic was modeling sunglasses at the counter and Eugene was hugging a beer pack by the cold case wall and his mother was the next customer walking into the store and

he was strapped to a bed and the straps were chewing his skin to a scream that exited his lungs a perfect rainbow prisming stuck flat to the wall in a finger painting that jumped to life but before he could see what the grooved colors did it scrolled closed in a consummation of flames in a deep well cut overhead by penciling birds.

"Honestly, sometimes I don't know *what* is in your head." She saw right through him on the way to the counter rummaging through her purse. Vic, sunglassed, pivoted, Richard to his mother, mother to Richard; Eugene walked up to the countertop with the beer, and Richard shook his head and flapped his hand furiously: Go back! Go back!

The comprehension in Eugene's face came from being silently yelled at.

Still digging, Richard's mother ordered Eugene, "Oh you go ahead... I can't find... that darn..."

He clunked the case of beer onto the counter and suddenly recognized the woman as a ghost from a meeting past and was about to say hello to it.

o god

"I'll need some ID with that, hon."

Richard stepped backwards down the aisle until the scene disappeared from view and he bumped into Philip.

"Hey!"

"Sorry."

"Where'ss the beer?"

"Eugene." Richard shuffled around Philip and backed up to the wall of refrigerated glass doors.

"What'ss wrong?"

He could not tell. He heard talking, the cash register ringing, then… more talking, and then… his mother was walking out the door.

His mother was walking out the door.

He could breathe. He breathed. Approached the front of the store, peered between posters on glass at his mother getting into her car and pulling out and driving away onto the main road, away from the hospital. Vic hadn't moved and Eugene hugged the bagged 12-pack.

Well? he said without saying.

"I bought the sunglasses."

"I got the beer. Your mom bought cigarettes."

"We have to go back."

"No we don't." Vic was fingernailing the price tag glued to the nose bridge.

"That was my mom."

"Mom's gone." Vic led them to the door and outside. "She left the other way."

"I want a hot dog," said Eugene.

"Did she see you? Did she know who you were?"

In the sunshine the sunglasses became black mirrors. "Relax, Genius. It's not always about you. It's too early to visit. She wasn't here for that. The hospital is *thataway*," Vic thumbed, "and she went *thataway*," pointed opposite.

"Eugene, did she see you? Did she recognize you?"

"I want a hot dog."

"Goddammit, Eugene, those hot dogs have been basting in their own sweat for a week. You don't want one of those. Did she see you?"

Philip walked out of the store with a magazine bag.

"Hey, Bucky, what you got?"

Philip scowled.

"That what I think it is?"

"Eugene?"

"I want a hot dog."

*"Did she recognize you?"*

"Bucky got the porn. Way to goooo, Bucky."

Eugene hugged the sack and cringed, not from Richard's questions but from what approached: three high school girls, two average-looking ones bookending a pretty one, who bounced and cooed "Hiiiii" at Eugene. Her two friends wore tight rock concert t-shirts and hip-huggers, and they had the power to wedge their circle open.

"Shouldn't you be at the game?" the pretty one asked Eugene. "I mean, it's almost starting." Before any of them could speak she sparkled at the sack he cradled and did a teasing whine, "Ohhhh, could you guys buy us some beer? We have money." She used her sex as currency, did a coy struggle inserting two fingers down her rear pocket, unsheathing a tightly folded flat damp ten.

All the boys hung on her moves.

Lucky bill, Richard thought.

The girl wrinkled her nose when she read Vic's shirt; and Vic saw opportunity.

"Sure." Vic snatched the bill and tromped off and said over his shoulder, "C'mon, Genius."

Right. He needed him—for what? At the door Richard checked: the three girls and Philip and Eugene eyed the trees and sky and ground with some concern. "This is pretty stupid, you know that?"

Vic pulled him into the store. "You wanna die a virgin? C'mon, Captain America. You saw how she looked at me. You can have either one of the others."

"They're out there with Eugene and Philip."

"What can happen in three minutes? Psycho and Bucky'll warm them up for us normal guys. You worry too much, that's your problem. C'mon, we got the beer, now we go buy the beer, because Psycho bought the same beer two minutes ago. You hungry? Me neither. Yeah. Remember us? We're with the guy who bought the case. Right.

He walked out, forgot we wanted two. My buddy here is old enough, anyway. Not for the real stuff, heh. Show her. Now pay the lady. See how easy it is? Can you get that? We're done before we start and out the door."

Alone in the parking lot waited Eugene and Philip.

Vic charged. "What the *fuck*? *Where's* the girls?"

"I'm the pitcher," Eugene said.

"*What?*"

"Pitchers are important."

Vic raised his hand in a traffic cop pose. "Shut up, Psycho. Let's hear it, Bucky."

"She said, 'You look like the pitcher.'"

"Stop it, Eugene. You're not the pitcher."

"Where's the girls?"

"She said, 'You look like the pitcher.'"

"And I said, '*SHUT THE FUCK UP!*'"

The sunglass-reflected world trembled.

"They ssaid they had to leave, go to the game before it sstarted."

"That's what they said," Eugene seconded.

Richard didn't believe them.

Vic twitched his eye hair patch off his sunglasses. "They ssaid they had to leave? Go to the game, before it sstarted?"

"That'ss what they ssaid."

"That'ss what they ssaid." Vic parroted. "That'ssss—what they—ssssaid."

Philip mirrored the stare defiantly.

Vic spat out. "What are you, a homo?"

This was getting stupid. "Are you done? Can we go now?"

"You only had to keep them here for one fucking minute. What did you do? What did you say? You tell them 'bout the old snip-snap?" Vic scissored his fingers around the base of a finger of his other hand, and Philip's jaw ground, making breathing bones. "And you," Vic started in on Eugene, "you start talking to your dog again?"

Eugene blinked, confused, reached into his pants pocket.

No!

"I'm the pitcher."

Vic exhaled wearily, went to Eugene, and Richard quick-stepped between them. Vic was shorter than him, and Richard thought he could take him, no sucker punches, if he had to.

"You his guardian angel now?"

"Fuck you. He can't help how he is. Leave him alone." Like Mike said, he thought, and somewhere inside Vic's head he must be thinking, remembering how he had gone "completely nuts on Bug," and from this Richard drew a certain strength, implacability.

His reflection in Vic's lenses bobbed.

"Fuck me?" Vic asked. He stepped back so he could thrust his arm full-length into Richard's face and flip him the finger, did the Wally. "Fuck *you*." Then Vic started to step around.

Richard tensed.

"Just getting a beer," said Vic and continued, rattled his hand into the bag, ripped out a bottle, twisted the cap, chugged.

"That'ss not legal."

Done, Vic answered Philip with a long, loud, ugly burp, licked his lips over the remains. "Arrest me." He shoved the empty into the bag. "That's one for me. Who else?"

"Maybe later," Richard said.

"I sstopped drinking."

"I'm the pitcher."

"Shut the fuck up, Psycho."

Richard intervened, "Did they say where they were going?"

"They ssaid they had to go to the game at the high sschool. Lakeview." Philip nodded down the boulevard.

"Alright then." Vic brightened. "Not too far. Not too far for pussy."

"Vanity of vanitiess."

"I'm on the Rangers," Eugene nodded around their circle. "I'm the pitcher."

"Shut the fuck up."

"You're not on the Rangers, Eugene."

"She said I look like the pitcher."

"You're not the pitcher, Eugene."

"Let's go, beer boys." Vic was already moving out and tossed to his buddy: "Don't forget the porn."

Philip scowled.

Richard adjusted the girls' bag of beer under his arm. "I can't believe my mom was just here."

"It'ss a ssmall world."

Eugene checked around the world. "It is pretty small, what you can see, when you think about it." He checked around some more. Started humming.

"What the fuck are you doing?" Vic said to Eugene.

"It's a small world," Richard grinned at Vic. "Isn't it?"

Eugene kept measuring the world up and down and around.

"What the fuck are you doing?" Vic asked Richard.

Richard started humming, and Philip joined.

"Fuck you all," Vic said.

Eugene joined, loudest.

"Fuck you all," Vic said and moved out.

They went down the street, again in single file, Vic, Philip, Eugene, Richard, with only the boulevard traffic as background, humming and singing, Vic telling them to shut the fuck up at every refrain.

It felt good to be out, walking free, thinking free. Living inside the hospital had clouded his normal way of being.

Which was what?

Wearing the wrong glasses, thinking about killing myself every day, how to do it, when to do it, every morning waking up thinking: is this day worth living through to the end? Is this the day I'll do it?

It all felt foreign to him now.

Was he misremembering his own life?

"A sock, in the middle of the road." Eugene pointed.

Richard confirmed, "A sock, in the middle of the road." A dirty, mangled, dried up lump of an athletic sock. For fun he hiked up both pant legs and checked. "I'm good."

Eugene imitated his buddy. No socks. His eyes drifted.

no

Over the curb he went.

Horns blared car swerved.

"EUGENE!"

Almost there.

He never saw the car.

Horn and brakes and driver crescendoed: "ASSHOLE!"

A break in traffic. Eugene strolled out of the road with the ratty clump.

Vic came screaming, "*What the fuck is wrong with you?*"

"Shut up, Vic."

"A sock in the middle of the road," said Eugene.

"*I know what it is, Psycho. It's a fucking sock in the middle of the fucking road. Do you know what you just did?*"

"What is wrong with you? Just settle down."

"He almost got run over. *With the beer!*"

Eugene pocketed the sock.

Vic stepped to Eugene, and Richard cleared his throat. "Can we go?"

"I need another beer," Vic said but his tone meant, I'm not going to hit him, yet. He rattled one out, twisted the cap, stood, downing it. "Two." Jammed the empty into the bag.

"Can we go?"

"Yes, we can go."

"Can we go *now?*"

"Yes, we can go *now.*" Vic was working his hand into his knife pocket. "What is your fucking problem?"

"What is *my* fucking problem? You dickhead. Don't even threaten me with that shit unless you intend to use it. That's right. We'll see who ends up in Isolation and who ends up in a hospital. My *problem* is: this whole situation is *unnaturally* stressing me out."

"Well you need to relax, then, Genius. Have a beer. You know what your real problem is?"

"No, Vic. Tell me. Tell me in all your infinite wisdom what my real fucking problem is."

"Your problem is you think too much."

The high school sat on flat acreage down a side street lined with small homes on neat lawns cooled by towering oaks. They shortcut over the brown-green expanse, four abreast, beelining for the fields behind the school. Gray clouds slid overhead, a pre-storm stillness dampening and dulling the air.

"Gonna storm," said Richard.

"Maybe we sshould go back."

"Maybe we should go forward. C'mon, the game's started." Beyond the parking lot spread the ball field with players in positions. "And we got the pitcher right here. We gotta bring the pitcher."

Eugene looked *aw-shucks*.

"You are such a dick," Richard said.

Vic pulled out two beers, twisted the caps, one for himself, one for Eugene, and they toasted.

"Thiss issn't a good idea."

"Really?" What makes you think that? We're four guys—Psycho, Bucky, Vic, and Dick—going to a ball game. Four guys out for fun. On their day out of the mental hospital.

"Three!"

Vic's bottle arced end-over-end across the stretching lawn, spewing its undrunk contents, and Eugene's followed.

"Four!"

Vic playfully smacked Eugene on the side of his head and laughed,

"You Psycho, count your *own* fucking beers, not somebody *else's* fucking beers!"

"One!" Eugene shouted.

"It's not a good idea, Bucky."

Philip plodded ahead.

Vic started wrestling with Eugene, standing up. The sack of beer rattled in alarm.

Richard yelled at Philip's back, "You're leaving?" It got nothing. He'd have to do it himself. He jogged to the wrestlers with the girls' beer bottles jostling, trying to make light: "Hey hey hey. C'mon. What're you guys doing?"

Vic tore loose. "Just having some fun, that's all. Right, Psycho? Pitcher? Goddamn, look what you did to my sunglasses." He tossed the broken pieces aside: two black sockets spun in opposite directions. "You know what *fun* is?"

Eugene stood there, not inhabiting his body, or, if he were, battling for control with five other creatures inside him. "Fun!" The black eyes twittered.

"Let's go to the game," Richard said. It would be safer there, with the crowd to pressure everyone into normal—he checked himself—*good* behavior. He started out under the clouds that he knew would beat them to the game and with the black lenses watching from the wide green earth behind him.


Wind twirled mini-tornadoes around the second baseman. The yellow-capped team was the visitors; a school bus parked at the end of the lot. So the visiting team side would be best, Richard thought, with Eugene's cap. He led them through the crowd of parents and students and up the bleachers.

"Iss that rain? Did you jusst feel a raindrop?"

"Maybe," Vic said, settling in, adjusting their beer sack between his feet, "ssomebody'ss sspitting on you."

Philip looked ready to punch him.

"Maybe we should leave," said Richard.

"Maybe we should watch the game," said Vic, grabbing Eugene by the arm and pulling him down to sit.

Eugene fidgeted. "I just touched gum."

"What?"

"Under the seat. I just touched gum."

"Whosse sside are we on?"

"Then don't touch it, Eugene." Richard patted his knee.

"We're the visitors, Bucky. Yellow caps. Like our pitcher. Get with the fucking program."

They got with the fucking program. They watched the game. The home team was at bat, bottom of the third, no score, and Eugene sat forward, twitching at every pitch and thump of the catcher's mitt. When a bat cracked foul a line drive everyone ducked, but Eugene shot up a hand to catch it. Spectators gawked and one old man asked, "Why ain't you in the game, boy?" Richard grabbed Eugene by the arm to lower his showing prize.

"Psycho's making new friends."

Now Richard felt like punching him. "Watch the game."

They watched the game, and the storm, gray-black clouds forming loaves with marbled veins brilliant white. Here and there people exited, shuddering the aluminum bleachers on every footfall. Women flapped into summer sweaters. Umbrellas mushroomed. The wind expired.

"I think we should leave," said Richard.

"I want a hot dog," said Eugene.

"We can't go yet." Vic waved up the leader of the girls from the 7-Eleven parking lot.

"I want a hot dog."

The girl pranced up the bleachers and dropped herself on the bench below Vic. "How's it going, guy?" Her nose crinkled at Eugene. "Is that a sock in his pocket or is he just happy to see me?" Vic's eyes popped. "Anyway, shouldn't he be with his *team*?"

Vic eyeballed Richard: Take Psycho to get a fucking hot dog.

Richard eyeballed back: O fucking K.

The concession stand was around the corner. Parents and children and high school girls and boys crowded the way. Richard led Eugene to the stand, ordered the food, and, hands full with two silver-foiled dogs and two soft drinks, motioned Eugene ahead of him through the crowd.

Above, thunder boomed.

Eugene spasmed. "Will they call the game?"

"Only if it starts lightning, or really starts coming down."

That signaled the sky. Thunder cracked electric claws at the tree tops lining the edge past the outfield fence. People pricked. A single authoritative shout lifted from the diamond. Players scattered: a school of startled fish.

The crowd heaved in every direction; people shoved between them, calling to each other. The drink lids squeezed off, sloshing shaved ice and Coke over his fingers. "Eugene." He had to dump everything before it ended up all over him. "Eugene!" Several yellow caps bobbed a few bodies in front of him. He did a quick sidestep to a garbage can to dump everything, then waded into the push and shove.


Vic and Philip were waiting in the parking lot.

"Well?" Vic had the sack of beer at his feet.

Richard scanned the crowd in the parking lot once more, about to suggest they go back to the bleachers, when Eugene appeared. Of course. Richard grinned for his buddy. "There."

"Where?"

Richard waved dumbly to Eugene flapping his hand furiously from his seat in the back of the visiting team's school bus pulling away onto the street.

"*He'ss leaving?*"

The bus gear-ground down the street past the neat trees and homes, and nearly out of sight a head poked out a rear window, Eugene, signaling with his yellow cap, his banner of freedom. Richard had to grin, happy for his mad roommate.

"What are you waving at him for?" Vic pissed out. "Are you a nut?"

"We can't let thiss happen. We can't let him go."

"No fucking shit, Bucky. No fucking *shit!* He's *your* roommate." A finger slashed. "*You* were supposed to be watching him. What the fuck were you *doing* with him? *All you had to do was get a fucking hot dog.*"

"Oh, shut up," Richard said. "That's what I was doing. I'm not his keeper."

"Well he needed a keeper, dumbass. What did we talk about before we left?"

"We can't let thiss happen. We can't let him go."

"*Now* what're we gonna do?"

Richard hadn't thought about that.

"We have to sstop him."

"You think you can go back there *without* him? That—*maniac* takes meds every goddamn morning, noon, and night. You want Isolation for a *week* this time?" He raged at Philip. "*Shut the fuck up! He's not coming back! Just shut the fuck up!*"

A few people nearby looked over.

"Vic. C'mon." Richard didn't appreciate the nut comment or the attention of the people and wanted to jab back. "Are they still adjusting your medication? Are you *taking* your medication?"

Vic stopped. Restarted, "Now," calmly—

Now I know.

—"we are completely *FUCKED.*" He stamped his feet in a wide circle, kicking at stones in the parking lot and swearing.

A father or two scowled; mothers scurried their young.

"Vic, *c'mon.*" He'd never seen anyone so hysterical; it was beginning to frighten him. Flecks of spit landed on his arm and cheek, and he rubbed them off. As Vic rattled on the flecks landed quicker, fuller.

"Is that what I think it is?" Vic froze, unbelieving, huffing.

Richard smiled at the sky. He had not been in a storm for weeks, forgotten how kind was the start of near-summer rain on skin. Tender capsules of warm skywater tingled open on his face. Plops. He remembered dancing in the rain when he was a child, dancing and running with his arms out like wings, and his mother yelling at him from the door what's wrong with you do you want everyone to see?

"What the fuck are you doing?"

He had forgotten that wet smell of new rain.

Philip cupped a palm. "We sshould go."

Richard sensed the reality settling upon them with the quickening rain. He moved first, grabbed the beer sack, and led them in a trot, silent, back the way they had come across the field in front of the high school. At the boulevard fat drops of rain were falling. At the 7-Eleven the water came smoothly, coolly, goosebumping his flesh. Street lights were turning on because of the darkness of the storm. As they ran from light to light they formed and shed handlinking shadows, slippery liquid things, bizarre multiple casts of bodies. At the mouth of the tunnel of trees the sky let loose. The rain and mist on his glasses distorted everything. A warm worm smell steamed up in white curlicues from the spoiled lawns, and red bits of string wiggled in puddles on the sidewalk. They stopped on the ridge, heaving for air, hands on knees, hair and clothes matted. Their view was an unending gray screen of shifting water. The path twisting down to the beach frothed brown foam.

Richard asked in gasps, "What, do we do, with the beer?"

"Fuck it," said Vic, righting himself. Tore a bottle from the sack. "Four."

"Give me one." Richard held out his hand. Might as well. If they got caught, they got caught. Might as well get caught *after* a beer. Bottles tinkled over the downpour, a cold one slapped home. He guzzled it, let it dribble out and mix with the rain. Philip watched, apart and aware. Their empties sailed toward the surf, plunked.

"What about the resst?"

Richard grabbed the bag, did a Vic. "Fuck it."

"Wait!" Vic pulled a bottle free. "One for the road."

Over the cliff the bag went tumbling, sliding to a stop.

Time waited.

Richard heaved himself over, whooping and slipping and sloshing through the muddy path, tearing at the sheets of water in the air for balance. On the beach the rain mixed with the angry waves and washed them in a cold wind. He led them, struggling up the boulders. What had been a fun descent earlier in the dry day was now a treacherous climb, and he regretted chugging the beer, forced to think twice for every handhold and footstep, adjusting his glasses and having to hold on with one hand and pull himself up with the other. There were no intrusive thoughts of letting go. He wanted to live, now. Brown water rivered from the gap between the broken fences, and through this they squeezed and crawled, emerging on the hospital grounds.

Their clothes were a wet skin. Richard's glasses dripped, haloing lights and flickering images. They tramped to the side doors of the building through beaded, swirling curtains of water. The comforting thought of the warmth and dryness inside was stopped by Philip voicing a sudden realization: "We can't go in there like thiss."

Richard tried the obvious. Locked.

"That's fucking great."

Philip tried, too, rattled the handle, saluted his hand to peer inside.

Vic yanked him. "Get away from the window, dumbass."

"Don't be a dick," said Richard. "We're in this together."

"Now you're sticking up for him? Jesus Christ, you are one of a kind, you know that? You take the fucking cake alright. I think Lou was right about you."

What?

Vic screwed the cap off his last beer. "You heard me."

Fuck you, Richard looked. You don't know shit.

The rain poured over them, they had no cover.

Vic chugged once, and long. "Five." Then the bottle was arcing, spurting beer into the storm. "We are in some pretty shit now."

"Why?" Philip whined. "Let'ss jusst go in the front. Let'ss jusst go in and—"

"And what?" Vic trembled, waiting for either of them. "And *what*?" It was unanswerable.

"We can't sstay out here all night."

"We can't go in *there*," Richard said.

"We sshould go in and tell them. Jusst tell them."

"Tell them *what*, Bucky? Tell them *what*? That all four of us *left* today? Decided to go for a walk? That we lost a *fucking* schizophrenic out here? No way, man. *No way. You* don't know what it's like. *You* don't know what they'll do to us. *You* haven't been hooked up."

"It'ss the right thing to do."

*"It's the fucking stupid thing to do!"*

"Let'ss wait for it to sstop raining, then we'll go in."

"Are you a retard? Did you lose your mind when you cut your fingers off? Cuz that's what I think happened."

"Shut up, Vic, just shut up, alright, *you're* the one who sounds like the retard right now. *You're* the one who sounds like the psycho."

Vic shot up his left hand, fingers splayed. With the index and middle fingers of his right hand Vic made a scissors and "clipped" off his left index finger. "Ow." Clipped his ring finger. "Ow." His pinkie. "Ow." The middle finger remained, erect and raging. "Fuck you, Four Eyes. Fuck you. You been standing there doing *nothing*, cuz you got *nothing* to lose cuz you're a goddamn crybaby on a goddamn vacation from real life, you know that? It's like you made all this shit up. At least you got a home to go back to. You got a family to go back to. You think you're so goddamn *smart*, fucking Genius, think of something, *get us out of this!*"

Richard told Vic fuck you, too, and added a term he immediately regretted and made Philip snigger.

Vic postured deafness. "What did you say? What did that bitch tell you?"

318

"Guyss, don't fight. We have to think, get insside. Don't you ssee how the devil—"

"Shut up!" Vic thundered. "*You're* the devil! *You're* the goddamn devil!"

"Sstop taking the Lord'ss na—"

Vic's hand cut the word in half at Philip's throat. "Shut up already, just shut the fuck up or I swear to fucking God I will show you the devil." His arm cocked, fist balled.

Philip's cheek turned, a plea to Richard.

They made a bleak tableau, curtained within the pouring rain, and in the back of a school bus Richard pictured Eugene sitting, smiling, and somewhere a single bubble broke the still surface of a cold pond over a boy's stiff blue body, his father watching with him, warning, now do you see?

Vic's fistball knuckled home in Philip's face, a dull crunching slippery sound, and before it landed again Richard lunged and tackled Vic and all three flailed to the sopping ground. He wasn't going nuts, he was landing solid punches. Vic kicked and rolled away and scrambled up, dug out of his pocket the knife and snapped open the blade.

"Sstop!"

"You want some, Four Eyes?"

They circled, the blade trying to steady to the center, Vic a little unsure from the beer.

The rain showered down loud so that he had to shout, "What're you gonna do, Vic?" The blade swiped the air back and forth. Like a cornered child. "You want this?"

Knife forward Vic came slogging through the rain and dark, and Richard sidestepped and shoved him away so hard he stumbled to his knees. Down on him he followed and stomped the hand holding the knife. Vic howled up and Richard grabbed him in a headlock and put his weight on his clamped arm.

"*Is this what you want?*" Vic broncobucked and Richard went for the ride. "*Stop it.*" He twisted down hard on his neck. "*Stop it!*" Vic was winding down and so was the rain. "*Listen.* Are you gonna *listen*? I know how to get us in. I know how to do it." Vic went limp and Richard relaxed.

Philip was rubbing his cheek. "How?"

"We need to make them come outside, so they're like us, soaking wet, so everyone looks the same."

No response.

Richard tightened his headlock. "Alright?"

Vic nodded.

"I'm going to let go and you're not going to do anything, *right?*"

Vic nodded.

Simultaneously Richard let him go and jumped away.

Vic got to his feet, wouldn't look at either of them, swiped the blade clean on his pants, closed it, put it away. Philip waited for anything more and better.

"One of us has to sneak inside and pull a fire alarm. They'll all have to come out." Richard watched the rightness of his plan materialize across their faces.

But Vic said, "There's no fire alarms in there. It's a nuthouse." To Philip: "Have you seen any fire alarms in there?"

"They do in the kitchen," said Richard. "Every kitchen has a fire alarm."

More of the new look with respect and fear.

Until Vic said, "How? How do you know how to do that?"

"My dad's a fireman."

They stood in the rainfall looking at each other.

"Your dad'ss a fireman?"

"Your dad's a fireman."

"Where can you ssneak in?"

"The kitchen door. It's the one door that's usually open, right? You told me before, you saw it yourself. Eugene, too. Nurses don't go back there, and it'll have an alarm close to the outside door."

"OK."

"Your dad's a fireman."

"Shut up, Vic, and listen. Shut up and listen, alright? Do I have to tell you in slow-motion? You two wait here. I'll sneak around to the kitchen door and pull the alarm. Everyone'll have to come out. Hang back a little, let them get wet. Hide until they look like us. We'll meet up with them, act like everything's normal." His last idiotic word left them searching one another with dispirited eyes.

Sneaking and stooping, Richard made his way along the side of the building unseen by those inside. As he crawled below a lit window he was tempted. To be outside, looking in.

He took his glasses off and wiped water from his eyes.

When I pull the alarm, someone will come.

It's never a joke, his father used to say. Kids think it's funny, but it's not. Some guy's putting his life on the line every time that alarm sounds, trying to get there as fast as he can. People can get hurt, die, trying to save themselves, trying to save others. It's never a joke.

Richard wasn't thinking of laughing, climbing the wood-slat fence.

The firemen would rush, to rescue, to save. Where would his father be? With them, or home? There was no telling. But someone would come. Someone always comes for an alarm.

The open outside kitchen door bled light into the liquid green-gray yard. This side of the building was windowless, so he edged to the door. Peered.

An industrial kitchen, red tiled, stainless steeled, smelling of burnt grease and bleach. Next to the door where he thought it should be and within easy reach was the red and white pull-down alarm: IN CASE OF EMERGENCY.

Like that awful moment the surface of the black pond broke around the lonely bubble.

It was a terrible commotion.

Short blasts trumpeted, patients cried and howled, and the rain... the rain... it returned to him. Joey doesn't like the rain.

He ran back to the side doors, but no one was there. Those fuckers! After what he'd done for them!

The side doors burst open and into the rain poured bedlam, spooked animals herded by frantic shepherdesses. The fat girl danced in one spot. Joey howled at the end of a nurse's arm-leash. Housewives hugged themselves for warmth. Richard milled. No one paid any attention to him. He was free to go. He went to the parking lot to watch the arrival of the fire trucks.

Among the patients David flailed in his wheelchair trying to keep his cast dry.

"Keep it covered," a nurse squawked, "keep it covered."

Richard wanted to run up to him and apologize.

He heard someone call his name above the tumult in the parking lot and distant sound of sirens. Vic and Philip approached, buddied in crime.

Nurses clucked, "Stay together, stay together," ricocheting from huddled group to huddled group. Names were shouted for the missing, and the missing called out of the storm. One by one the lost were found. But one. And the wordless pact among the three of them drew them to face one another.

A nurse called once more.

Vic made the first connection. "I think I saw him."

"Where?"

"Over there." He pointed to the side yard. "By the fence."

She hesitated, perhaps because it was Vic.

"I think I saw him, too." The words opened Richard's mouth. "By the cliff."

"I ssaw him, too."

The nurse was judging for herself. "What do you have there, Philip?"

The magazine bag Philip carried from the store was a soaking lump. "Nothing."

"Show me nothing."

Guilt dripped from Philip as he slunk to her.

"I'll kill that shithead if he says anything."

Sure, Vic.

Secretless, they drifted apart, and out of the gloom loomed Bug, a rain-blurred matted and greasy image on his lenses. "Hey, Four Eyes. Tomorrow, in the side yard, before the dance." He was gone as quickly as he'd appeared.

Sirens and lights swirling through the rain signaled the approaching fire trucks and emergency vehicles. A red-blue-silver whirligig fixed in the grill of the first vehicle and slowly dying made it seem like there should be some fun place to go, to be. The heroes were here. A fist twisted in Richard's gut. He knew their routine, their order, had seen it a hundred times, expected his father... *there*, there he was, knew him by his walk, striding toward the front doors of the hospital.

Does he know? Could he know?

His father carried an ax: the blade shone wet and reflected all the brilliant colors.

In his dreams that night he could not undream the screaming.

# Sky the color of blue cherries

The cafeteria was alive from the night's events. He caught wisps of conversation rising from tables.

"—all that screaming—"

"How could you—"

"—stabbed—"

"How could you *do* that to yourself?"

"—took his roommate next door."

"—fighting—"

"—stabbed *himself?*"

"—in his eye—"

"—both—"

"—in his *eye?*—"

"—hospital—"

Richard.

He flinched.

Who said that?

The table of high school kids became aware of his presence.

"They're still having the dance."

"Everyone's been dying for that."

He felt their desire for him to move along to his table to sit alone against the wall.

And now?

What did those two nuts do?

They'd left him.

He was alone.

They'll find out. They'll come for you. Strap you down. Shock your head. Like Noah. Like Vic said.

That's crazy.

You're crazy.

You have to get out now, while you can.



He remained alone. Waiting for them to come for him. Waiting for Eugene or Vic or Philip or Bug. But no one came for him. He went outside to wait some more.

The sun had burned back the clouds, leaving a deep tight sky, a blue so bright it was ready to explode with what it was, a sky the color of blue cherries. There was not a hint of fish in the air; the sun had dried everything up, the blue had absorbed it; only a clean pure water breeze blew. He thought of Vic and Philip and Eugene and where each might be—in the real hospital next door, out on the road on the way to a secret place—and how, of all things, he did not want to be alone. Not alone. He figured whatever anyone had said about their outing, if they had said anything, it didn't include his name. Silently he thanked them for that. The gravel path ended at the sidewalk, the edge of the visitorless parking lot. Oil slicks rainbowed under the sunshine where cars parked in their white-lined slots on the blacktop. Gulls called for him to see.

When he turned to go inside there was Bug at the window.



Susie said she would come.

Mom with Dad, too. She called before lunch and asked if they could visit together, come to the dance after dinner. He said a yeah, imagined a hundred scenarios of meeting the man from the photograph. Then gave himself up to speculation and brooding. And avoiding Bug. A touch of the same feeling he had had while stacking and unstacking the pills on the bathroom countertop soaked into his heart and gurgled in the marrow of his bones. So he moved from room to room, darting, flitting, a smaller fish fleeing from a bigger fish. In time, before the dance, he discovered himself back in his room, wrestling with words locked in his solid heart; he got out Eugene's black magic marker.



He could not in his mind construct their conversation from home to here.

Through the front window-wall he watched his parents clamber out of their car and surrendered to the thought: What am I of but you. And they were of a time past that showed in their faces and clothes: she in a plain summer dress from his own childhood, he in a white dress shirt and black slacks and shoes. Thin jackets. Frowning. Beaten children of The Great Depression hardened and moved through time to a now where they were uncomfortable in it and of ill use as guides to anyone and themselves. Rarely would he ask them their thoughts on a matter because their advice was obsolete. He pitied them and loved them and loathed them. How he would survive in his room in their house as they cannibalized each other daily he did not know. His blood thrummed that he could never change, he would be trapped, until death set him free. He went to them like this, sifting through the wreckage in his sorry heart.

Everyone was embarrassed. Father and son mumbled greetings and glances. She hugged fiercely. "How are you doing?"

"OK."

"I love you."

He did not know what she meant.

"I love you, too," he said.

He did not know what he meant.

It did not matter.

Everyone uses their own dictionary.

"What's that on your hand?" she asked.

not for you

"Did you write something?"

"It's nothing." He closed his fist; did not want to reveal the truth. "Let's walk in the yard."

His father was astonished. "They let you walk around out here?"

Her eyes darted.

Their moods funneled through him. "Yeah, Dad, they let us walk around out here."

His mother gave up. "Why don't you go on by yourselves, I'll check us both in." The extra-meaning caught them. "We need visitor tags," she said and hurried off, abandoning them, she their choreographer, and, alone, father and son stared after her for clues.

Richard led the way to the side yard, afraid to speak first.

His father carried the weight. "You got a nice view here." They headed for the cliff, his father sightseeing.

Richard waved at the old man.

"Huh," his father said. "Kinda looks like grandpa." His father waved, with his grimace-for-a-smile, and the old man returned both. "Never know who's watching out for you."

Richard looked at his father but his father kept walking for the cliff.

"Nice view. Almost makes you think you can see the other side." At the fence he stopped and talked over the water. "You know, years ago, I drove over there. Because I could, I guess, just to see it from the other side, I don't know," he kind-of laughed, "get another look at things, it was after you were born. I found a real nice park over there, a beautiful park, walked the whole afternoon, sometimes look across the water, try to see the other side, think about your mother with you and your brother, think about what they were doing without me, if they could be without me." His father's gaze narrowed with such sorrow and penetration to some truth of a matter between them that it seemed to Richard his father was focused on not the physical horizon line miles out over the unending water but a distant and unforgiving demarcation in his past nearly lost to time and memory he had all of a sudden recalled how and why he had determined to cross and connect, irrevocably. "I knew she couldn't do it alone." He let out a breath, would not stop trying to figure the horizon. "Sometimes I drive to the beach, down by grandpa's house, and just sit and look out over all this water. Feels like you can see to the end of yourself."

This was their second pond, with another body rising from the sediment, and Richard wanted to hold his father's hand.

"I came back because I wanted to be here." That wonder-filled face from the black and white photograph. "I never told anyone that." His eyes shifted to the side doors. "Not even your mother. And I didn't tell her about last night. Or this." From inside his jacket he produced folded notebook sheets, Dear Mom and Dad, By the time you read this.

Richard took the pages, part of himself awakened, pocketed them, wondered about being his father's child.

Out of the side doors his mother scurried, dog paddling through the air, waving two clip-on VISITOR tags and jacket flapping, yelling, "We need to wear these!"

His father said to Richard so that his wife could not hear, "You know how much she loves you?"

Expertly she handed a tag to her husband and clipped hers over her tired slope of breast. "Well put it on."

His father was viewing the tag suspiciously.

His mother frowned.

Richard played their arbiter. "You have to put it on. So they can tell who the patients are." His mother frowned at that, too, and his father gave him a quick-wink.

"Your father hasn't been to your room. Can we go to your room?" She was all at once so bright and so dim for him, he felt, what she had unwittingly created, that he could not help but pity her and want to protect her from what he was, and he wondered if this could be their definition of love.

"Here it is." All three stepped in, his father a visitor in a museum, tapping the edge of his ID tag against the door.

"Well how about this." She discovered the clay box next to the delicate dancer. "Did you make this?"

"Yes."

"Well isn't that something?" she said. "Isn't that something," she asked her husband. "You made this all by yourself?" she asked Richard.

Yes.

"Isn't that something?" she asked her husband.

"It's something," he oathed.

"What's inside?" Her fingers approached the lid.

don't

Up it went.

Ohhh, her expression emptied as if she had just laid eyes on the body.

"What is it?" asked his father.

"Us." Richard picked it out and showed him. Marveled at his father remembering; everything you know alone you know together.

Before either could respond she was away. "And what's this? A penguin?" She tweaked the penguin's nose. "Where did you get this? Did you get this from someone?"

Richard blushed.

Ohhh, she discovered.

His father said, "Well."


Music filled the hallway near the gym; he was relieved his parents were hearing it. The dance had begun. White and blue bunting encircled the tables. On the gym floor Joey swayed with a nurse. Someone had snapped a conical party hat to his head, and the tip was knifing at her throat. Richard went to an unoccupied table near the doors; he knew neither of them enjoyed parties; this could be their neat escape.

"Does anyone want some punch? I'll get some punch." His mother fussed. "I'll get some punch; you two make yourselves comfortable." Leaving her last word hanging ineffectually, she was off to the table of food and drinks, a few covered dishes the nurses brought in from home, bags of potato chips torn open, and jugs of fruit punches. A nurse and two high school girls served the hungry and thirsty, blocking all the posters but leaving exposed the nerves and vessels and Pathway and Concepts.

There was Susie. Next to his mother. At first he didn't recognize her because she wore a dress and had her hair waved up sideways and pinned on top. He was staring at the dress, a summery, flowery thing exposing her shoulders.

The air was heavy and warm and unbreathable with mad desires eviscerating him—run to her, *from* her—laugh, shout, dance, cry— any sexual thing he could imagine doing with her would be ruinous.

Over the loud music his father asked him if he was saving it.

*What?*

"Your note. Saving it for someone special?" His father grinned the way a father should grin to a son.

Yes. He closed and opened his fist. He was saving it for someone special.

"You going to dance with your mother?"

He searched his father's eyes for any recognition.

"She'd like that."

Richard never imagined his father thought of what his mother would or would not like. "I guess, if she wants to, I don't know," I don't know how.

A shout went up on the dance floor from the middle of a widening circle of nurses and patients where David was spinning, spinning, spinning and laughing.

Joey was sitting now with an older woman Richard had never seen before. She was fork-feeding him potato salad, talking to him, and he was smiling, waiting to be fed. The woman could only be his mother, and he was her son.

When his mother returned stretching fingers around three large plastic cups, hurrying, he noticed how she had put on a little extra makeup and had done her hair a little more carefully, how she seemed to be trying, always trying, never tiring of trying, and he thought, taking in the dancers and Susie, girls are the same everywhere, they like to be special and noticed and appreciated, and a warm wave surged through him, not unlike the drugs they shot him up with, but this was real; and Richard knew how it would happen before it happened; nothing could stop it from the foundations of the quick earth.

She was huffing. It's the cigarettes, he thought. She smokes too much. He reached to help.

Joey howled.

She jumped with the cups exploding red cold claws at his shirt and pants.

"Oh no!" his mother wailed. "Oh no! What a dummy I am! What a dummy. Let me help." She was at him with a bunch of napkins off the table.

"It's OK, Mom."

Her hands were shaking, blotting his shirt with napkins. "I ruin everything!"

"It's OK, Mom. I'll go change. I'll go change."

"You should change, Richie, you should go change. Do you have clean clothes?"

"I'll be right back." He almost ran past Susie.

"Richie." She breathed the name as beautifully as her dress smoothed circles round her thighs. She smelled not of bubble gum but of the flowers in Spring outside his bedroom window.

"I have to change. I'll be right back." He made his escape without waving. Not yet. He wanted to surprise her with his gift, ask her to dance.

Space and time from the gym to his room stretched and dissolved, like that clay-pig-falling moment, so that when he arrived in his room his first thought-prick was: I'm seeing things again:

Shards of clay box shattered dust on the floor with dancer body parts.

Shreds of rainbow painting tossed around the room.

Chunks of dictionary.

Pillow innards.

The penguin, flipperless, stuffing bleeding from limb holes.

Father and son torn apart.

Fearfully, fearfully.

What was looking to devour him.

Bug stepped out of the bathroom. "You don't listen so good, do you, Four Eyes. That why you inside? Not a good listener?" The gun was very real and, pointing at him, sapped all he had. "I tell you get offa me, you don't get offa me. I tell you meet me in the yard before the dance so we can settle this."

Flickered gun sunlight. His words were about killing and

Richard was saying you don't understand, you don't understand like I do.

"Take your time."

Time. Redeem the time?

"Had a little accident at the dance? Gonna change?"

Change.

Yes.

Everyone's waiting. Everyone will see.

"I don't mind. I seen plenty a skin before." The black circle of the barrel was an empty eye unblinking. "Fresh skin."

He was not afraid to drown.

"Strip." The cold "o" of the barrel pressed the flesh of his temple, forced him out onto the ice.

The bullet

He felt his body undressing itself, undressing, undressing. He was in his naked room and he was not ashamed because there was no abyss.

"What's this?" The barrel penned open his palm. A chuckle from hate. "You pussy." The "o" brushed his eyelash. "Open your mouth." Clicked past his teeth. "You like it."

He was tasting death, and death tasted like gun metal.

"Richard," said his father's voice out of the hallway, then he blotted the angel.

The barrel clicked out.

He was naked before his father.

The three of them were trapped inside an expanding silence.

Richard popped the bubble, "It's not loaded."

Bug sneered.

"Son, listen—"

Both boys reacted.

"Reggie."

The sound of his true name turned him.

They shuffled in a rush a flurry of crisscrossing arms and the distinct cracking of ice, *POP, POP,* the give of weight underfoot. His father's body sank, eyes twittering startled birds, red dots patterned his white shirt-page. "I

Pond-side, witnessing, Richard was listening. Hadn't he been listening, all his life, didn't he have ears to hear?

The gun soft-plopped on the bed, a shadow passed over the angel. remember."

Richard knelt.

Soft recognitions pooled.

My father is a goldfish.

"*RICHIE*

It was an unfamiliar voice in an unfamiliar tongue, calling him from his tomb.

Where did my little Richie go?

His father's red fingers handcuffed his wrist, a tiny crimson-coated bubble collapsed in the corner of his lips.

Don't leave, Dad.

Down the hallway a high sickening shrill—"*RICHIE*"—agonizing, delivering him all over again.

They held hands. They were holding hands.

Don't leave.

Up, down, they were passing one another in icy black water, the grip relaxed, gifting a red bracelet, blood finger-painting new vessels through his private heart.

His angel was calling: Rise up.

What new picture could be seen?

Rise up like a lion.

What new heaven could he reap?

Bloody and naked and newly skinned, Richard picked up the gun. It felt how he forever knew it would feel, sure and true, but it was not for him. On his way he swept his fingers along the hem of the ascending messenger pointing.

Before, once, he always felt out, outside, peering in, but now was coming around, circling back to the beginning, in with what was alive, vital, floating, connected, inside with all the screaming and flailing and pain and love and blissful bloody mess of every new birth and knew he could find his way, claw his way, to circle back, circle back, to a beginning, to his beginning, where he could feel everything, where he could be, where he could believe himself to be something in

CPSIA information can be obtained at www.ICGtesting.com
Printed in the USA
BVOW03s1016160414

350836BV00004B/134/P